PORT CITY SHAKE DOWN

by Gerry Boyle

Down East

ISBN: 978-0-89272-795-7

5   4   3   2   1

BOOKS·MAGAZINE·ONLINE
www.downeast.com

Library of Congress Cataloging-in-Publication Data

Boyle, Gerry, 1956-
Port City shakedown / by Gerry Boyle.
    p. cm.
ISBN 978-0-89272-795-7 (trade hardcover : alk. paper)
    1. Interns (Civil service)--Fiction. 2. Police--Oregon--Fiction. 3.
Portland (Or.)--Fiction. 4. Psychological fiction. I. Title.
PS3552.O925P67 2009
813'.54--dc22
                    2009007580

For Vic, my constant,
from start to finish.

I am grateful for the generous assistance of
sailors Dan McCarthy and Ave Vinick, who read the manuscript,
paying close attention to all things nautical. Special thanks
to my other readers (you know who you are) for their consideration
of Brandon and Mia. You will meet again.

"When beholding the tranquil beauty and brilliancy of the ocean's skin, one forgets the tiger heart that pants beneath it; and would not willingly remember, that this velvet paw but conceals a remorseless fang."

—Herman Melville, *Moby Dick*

CHAPTER 1

It was a little after five on a cold afternoon in May. Drizzle speckled the windshield, the smell of low-tide mudflats coming into the cruiser, mixing with the odor of Griffin's stale hazelnut coffee.

This was on a side street off of Congress, the harbor side. Griffin was at the wheel, Brandon Blake riding shotgun, a misnomer since he didn't have any gun at all, just a Kevlar vest and an I.D. that said, "Portland P.D." In smaller letters, "Intern."

Griffin had said he'd cover Brandon's back, which Brandon wondered about, whether that implied Brandon would go in first. Not that it mattered, not yet. It had been three days and they hadn't done anything dangerous: rousted a couple of old drunks who would keel over in a strong wind, took reports on a bunch of burglaries with the burglars long gone, Griffin spending most of the time in between talking about his kids.

Brandon tried to be polite, Griffin a nice guy and probably a good dad, but going on and on, Brandon finding it hard to relate—not having kids, not having a father—only half listening like he was now.

Then Griffin pulled over, the cruiser sliding to a stop. Griffin jumped out. He reached back for his baton, slipped it from its holder on the cage and held it in front of him, one hand on the grip, the other eight inches up.

The ready position.

Blake jumped out, too, stood by the hood, and watched. A scruffy guy on a bike coasting by, turning to see what the cops were doing, the older one with his baton out, ready to swing.

"Tied up two-two, bottom of the sixth, two out, man on third," Griffin was saying. "Three and one, hitter's count. Infield in. Jeremy's hitting like four hundred, already ripped a hard foul, vicious line drive just wide of third. So what does he do?"

He paused.

"This is a kid, remember. Little League,"

7

"I don't know," Brandon said.

The motor whuffed softly like a sleeping dog, the guy on the bike still circling.

Griffin punched the air with the nightstick.

"He lays down a bunt, first base line. Pitcher goes for it, first baseman breaks. Second baseman comes over to cover, but he's late. Jeremy beats it out."

Griffin beamed, all white teeth and thatchy brown hair—the boy inside the cop. "Run scores. We—"

Something on the radio stopped him. Brandon turned and listened, Griffin already heaving himself into the seat, no smile now. Brandon scrambled back, the passenger door still open as the tires screeched.

"What is it?" Brandon said.

"Fight."

"Where?"

"Funeral," Griffin said, swinging across traffic onto Congress, lights and siren forcing cars to the side of the road.

"Whose?" Brandon said.

"Inmate, county jail."

Griffin hit the klaxon horn, squeezed between a bus and oncoming traffic.

"The inmate's dead?"

"Somebody in his family."

"So they fight at the funeral?" Brandon said.

"Hey," Griffin said, "we all grieve in different ways."

CHAPTER 2

A funeral chapel in a strip mall. Low, vinyl-sided place looked like it used to be a restaurant. Two cruisers out front, Portland black and whites, at the side door a green and white van from the county jail.

"I'm off," Griffin barked into the mic and swung out of the car, slipping his baton into his belt. Griffin didn't say not to, so Brandon followed.

They heard muffled shouting as two stolid funeral parlor guys in dark suits swung open the double doors.

Griffin strode by, hand on his pepper spray. There were inner doors, too, and he yanked one open and moved in, Brandon behind him.

A casket at the center of the room, pink lining and an old lady in a light blue dress, like an egg in an Easter basket, the only one not shouting or screaming. To the left, two deputies working their way to the door. There was a guy between them. Handcuffed, small, and skinny, wearing a suit, the jacket two sizes too big, like the clothes in the after picture in those diet ads where people lose fifty pounds. One of the deputies, gray-haired and stout, was fending off two other guys—collared shirts, no jackets— who were trying to get at the skinny guy, the inmate? The deputy sprayed the guys, got them and a woman behind them, who put her hands to her face and shrieked.

Chairs scraped. A vase of flowers wobbled, then fell and broke.

Griffin waded into the crowd to the right, flinging people aside and shouting, "Police. On the floor."

Brandon went in on Griffin's left. "Police," he shouted, leaving off the intern part, feeling like he was watching himself in a movie. He moved between some kids who were standing on chairs to see. Approached the outer ring of spectators, a woman screaming, "You hated her, you two-faced piece of shit."

Brandon shouted again. "Police, back off," and a big guy actually did, leaving an opening. Brandon slipped through, found himself standing over a tangle of women on the floor: an older one, red-headed, big and wide and thick-legged, and a younger one with short black hair. They were pounding on another woman, her blonde hair all askew. It was a writhing knot of limbs, tattoos flashing, arms pumping, legs splayed, the woman on the bottom missing a high-heel shoe, her black stockings torn. The sound of fists hitting flesh and bone, a growling coming from the young woman on top as she flailed away, jaw clenched.

Blood sprayed. The woman on the bottom looked dazed, wasn't defending herself.

"Police," Brandon shouted again, and the older woman turned. He stepped in, started to pull her back, her upper arm big and soft, like tofu.

"Get your fucking hands off me," she said, and somebody hit Brandon in the back, then the side of the head. He held onto the red-haired woman, lifted and pushed her aside. Reached for the flailing woman, felt someone kick him in the leg, grab his arm.

"Come on, now. Stop it. Calm down," Brandon shouted as the flailing woman landed a right, the blonde woman real bloody now, her mouth and nose painted with dark red streaks, like lipstick run amok. Someone landed on Brandon's back, the red-haired woman, heavy and soft, breasts pressing against him, the smell of sweat and cigarettes and perfume, nails digging into his neck like talons. He had her partner by the shoulders, but let go to pull the hand off, clawing at his chin now, the blonde woman coughing, the women all gasping, "You bitch."

Brandon tried to lift himself, couldn't with the weight of the big woman, felt her nails digging into him, clawing at his mouth, slashing at his eyes, scratching just below his eyebrows. He let go of everyone, braced himself, and threw an elbow up and back, hit the red-haired woman in the face and the hand fell away. Brandon turned and saw the big woman sitting on her butt, blood streaming from her nose, dripping from her chin onto her white sweater.

She cupped her hand under the flow and bellowed.

The blonde woman with the bloody mouth started to crawl toward her stray shoe. The woman who had been punching her staggered to her feet. Brandon slipped through the women to the side of the room, stepped aside as deputies dragged the skinny guy in the big suit toward the door. Griffin was behind them with another guy, older and bigger, his shirt torn to show a swaying gut, an unidentifiable blue tattoo on his hairy shoulder. He was cuffed behind his back, pepper-sprayed eyes red and swollen, shouting blindly, "You all suck."

Brandon pressed through the mourners, two groups shouting at each other. A kid threw a hymnal. Someone threw it back, pages fluttering. Brandon ducked, looked to see where the book had come from, turned, and was face to face with the skinny guy, still held by his handcuffed wrists, like a dog on a short leash.

Narrow face, upper lip stuck out over bad teeth. A goatee and straight greasy hair. Dark, close-set eyes that flicked across the room. Then back at Brandon. He returned the stare as they stood there, stuck by a bottleneck at the door.

"Who the fuck are you?" the inmate asked.

For a moment Brandon didn't answer, just held the guy's gaze, not backing down. "You from the jail?" he said.

"My grandmother, it's her funeral. You don't got a name?"

"Blake."

"You know why I wanna know?"

Brandon shook his head.

"That was my ma you beat the shit out of."

"Shut up," the deputy said, and he gave the inmate a hard shove from behind. The inmate lurched and recovered. From deeper into the room, more shouting, another skirmish flaring up.

"Where you from?" the inmate said. "The goddamn neighborhood watch?"

Brandon stared, didn't answer. The inmate smiled, a cold carnivorous grin. The crowd moved, the deputy stumbled, and the inmate fell into Brandon, hung on with his chin digging into Brandon's shoulder blade. His mouth was close to Brandon's ear.

"Eye for an eye, dude," the guy said through clenched teeth. "Times fuckin' ten."

CHAPTER 3

They were riding back along Commercial Street, on the inner harbor, the long way back to the P.D. Letting the Sheriff's office handle the arrests, the big hairy-bellied guy taking the hit for the whole clan.

"Rest of 'em can crawl back in their holes," Griffin said.

Brandon looked out at a tanker, offloaded, hull riding high, readying to leave port, diesel smoke billowing from its stack. He pictured the same stretch of river a hundred years ago, schooners floating up on the tide, pilots rowing out to meet them.

One of the hazards of reading history books, you were always picturing things that were long gone.

"You did alright back there," Griffin said.

"Thanks," Brandon said, picturing the inmate, his black eyes shining. "This Fuller guy—"

"Scumbag," Griffin said.

"Think he's all talk?"

"Hard to say. Mostly it's been nonviolent stuff: theft, stolen goods, fraud. Charged him once with arson, but it got dropped. Some guy over in Westbrook ratted him out for selling pot, so Fuller threw a Molotov cocktail through his window. Or somebody did. Awful hard crime to prove, arson. Fire went out anyway. Isn't as easy as it looks in the movies."

They had gone under the ramp of the bridge that spanned the harbor: Portland on one side, South Portland on the other. The downtown sidled up to the water on the Portland side; oil tanks and marinas across the water. The islands of Casco Bay showed dimly through the mist.

It was a well-used harbor, fishing giving way to condos like everywhere else. They drove past the container terminal, the ferry terminal, too, the ferry gone to Nova Scotia, parking lot mostly empty.

Brandon pointed across the harbor.

"I'm right over there," he said.

Griffin pulled over and they sat, the radio chirping softly, like a baby bird in a nest.

"Where?" Griffin said.

"There."

Brandon pointed out over the harbor, white mooring buoys showing against the blue water, the surface rippled like sand on a beach. Brandon loved to watch the way the wind played the water, never the same way twice.

"See all those boats? I have a slip over there."

"You live on a freakin' boat?"

"Yeah."

Griffin looked at him again, more closely.

"What is it? A yacht?"

"An old Chris-Craft. A cabin cruiser, you'd call it."

"Why?"

"Why what?"

"Why don't you live in a house?"

"Kind of a long story," Brandon said.

Griffin stared across the harbor at the tangled nest of masts and moorings. "Winter, too?"

"Sure," Brandon said. "You frame it in with plastic. Heat it with propane."

"Don't think I could do that," Griffin said. "Claustrophobic, you know?"

"It's not for everybody."

They were quiet as they looked out, Griffin thinking he wouldn't last one night stuck in the bottom of a cabin cruiser in some little bed, the ceiling two feet from his head. "You never played ball, did you?" he said.

Brandon shook his head.

"I could tell," Griffin said.

"Nothing against it. Just never had the chance."

"That 'cause you always lived on a boat? No yard or anything? Couldn't you play at school?"

"Just never got into it, I guess," he said.

"Your parents live on the boat, too?"

"For a while I lived in an apartment with my mother. But she died when I was little."

"Sorry. Your dad?"

"AWOL," Brandon said, flashing a smile. "Never reported for duty."

"Can't understand people like that," Griffin said. "Every minute I can, I spend it with my boys."

Brandon shrugged. Griffin reached across to the glove box, got out a small pair of binoculars, Nikons. He got out of the car and walked across the scrub and looked out at the water. Brandon followed. The tanker was spewing more diesel smoke against the gray sky now, waiting for the tide. The plume drifted away on the damp southeast wind.

"So this boat of yours," Griffin said, holding up the binoculars. "It's on a dock?"

Brandon nodded.

"See the big dark-hulled sailboat, the one with the Jolly Roger. Look just to the right."

"Oh, yeah. Wood on the top."

"Right."

"You don't have it anchored out in the middle?"

"I get a slip free because I work there."

"And go to college?"

"One class at a time."

Griffin didn't say anything for a moment, just gazed out at the harbor.

"This boat, Blake," he said.

"Yeah."

"Can you get to it from the land?"

"Walk down some stairs and out onto the docks."

Another pause and Griffin said, "No security?"

"A fence. The gate's locked, but the owners are always leaving it open."

Griffin turned away from the water, started to walk back to the car. Stopped and looked back to Brandon.

"Sometimes they surprise you," he said. "Guy's been stealing stereos out of cars and all of a sudden he pops somebody. Breaks into a house, the wife's home. Had a guy a few years back did that. Ties the lady to a chair, ends up strangling her with the cord to an iron. Can't leave a witness. From punk to murderer, just like that. And sometimes they like it."

"The rush?" Brandon said.

"The power," Griffin said. "Pretty amazing thing to take somebody's life."

They stood looking at the boats, all lined up.

"If I was you sleeping on that boat," Griffin said, "I'd have a gun. And more than one way out."

"There's a forward hatch, but be tough to get out in a hurry. But I do have a gun."

Griffin glanced at him. "Loaded?'

"Should it be?"

Griffin shrugged. "Hard to tell these days, who's gonna try to kill you and who's just a regular asshole."

CHAPTER 4

Brandon punched himself in with the security code, felt like a wimp for liking the sound of the chain-link gate snapping shut behind him. He crossed the yard, waved to a couple of owners, hurrying so they didn't have a chance to press him into service. Yet.

He unlocked the office, stepped in. The place was dark, the answering machine flashing frantically on the desk, a morning's worth of calls. Branson closed the door, snapped on the lights, walked over and hit the button, grabbed a pad and pen.

The usual real estate people trying to reach Sam, the owner of Windward Point Marina, one saying it was "imperative" that they have a conversation. "Good luck," Brandon said. Sam was in an assisted living center outside Fort Myers, hadn't had a conversation since his stroke. Maybe if the guy wrote him a letter.

A woman with a sultry voice, saying she was looking for a place for her 28-foot Sea Ray. Brandon thought the name was familiar, the husband calling two weeks before.

The owner of the 36-foot Bertram in slip A-12, saying the freshwater hose leaked all night, he couldn't sleep. A guy from Cape Elizabeth, asking if there was a mooring available.

Get in line, Brandon said to himself.

A call reporting the ice machine was acting up—Johnny in the *Absolut*, in C-9, who would know. Dave Browne— with an E— asking if his sailboat, an Ericson 35, still was scheduled to launch the next morning. It was, last boat scheduled to go in on the lift.

A woman wanting to talk to Sam about business opportunities. A guy asking if his Sundowner 22 was still in storage (it was), and sorry about not paying the bill last year or two. It was three.

There was a knock on the door.

Brandon looked up, still scribbling names and numbers.

"Hey, Brandon."

Doc Lynch, white-haired and whiskey-cheeked, came in, waited as the last caller said his number, and the machine beeped.

"No nibbles on a charter?"

"It's on the Web, Doc," Brandon said. "On the board. But there are a lot of boats out there."

"Bargain for three thousand a week," Doc said.

"Not a bargain, Doc, unless somebody's looking for a bareboat and your boat stands out. *Ocean Swell* is a nice boat, but there are a lot of boats out there."

"Well, pitch it hard, Brandon. I'll make it worth your while."

"She's number one on my list."

"I mean, 46-feet. Six-foot-eight headroom in the main cabin and salon. Sleeps seven, for real, not a bullshit seven. You got that on there?"

"Not a bullshit seven. Got it."

"And the pressurized hot and cold."

"Yup."

"Handles easy," Doc said. "Meticulously maintained. Spotless through-out. New radar, state-of-the-art GPS, autopilot."

"Gotcha," Brandon said.

"Full shore power, remember. Plug-in heater. Cabins heat up good."

"You don't have to sell me, Doc. She's a very nice boat."

"Might as well have somebody enjoy her before the so-called wife gets hold of her."

"How's the divorce coming?" Brandon said.

"They're bleeding me, Brandon. Hanging me by my feet like a stuck pig. I need this charter."

"I'll talk it up, Doc," he said.

"Don't ever get married, Brandon."

"Not likely."

"If I only knew then what I know now."

Brandon remembered the nurse, from a certain angle looked like Christina Aguelera. The last straw for Mrs. Doc.

"Hey, but if she wants to play rough, I can play that game. Her lawyer, smarmy son of a bitch, hope he doesn't think I'm gonna roll over. I don't get mad, Brandon, but I sure as hell get even. It's the Irish in me. We know how to hold a grudge, let me tell you."

Doc's eyes narrowed, glistened. The look of revenge. Second time that day.

The afternoon went by in a blur. Ice machine (a broken hose), a tender with an outboard that wouldn't start (screw fell out of the carburetor), the guy with the unpaid storage bill backing up to his boat with a pickup, starting to write a check, Brandon sending him off for cash.

A complaint about loud partying on *Absolut,* Johnny promising to keep it down, the season off to its usual start. Clearing stuff out of the way of the *Ericson*, getting ready for the morning launch. A salesman looking for "the boss," disappointed when Brandon said he was it.

And finally, after six, up the wooden steps that led over the stern of *Bay Witch*, Brandon's Cavalier cruiser. He turned back. Looked out at the yard, the owners coming and going, the gate now propped wide open with a dock cart.

Security had included Doc Lynch's yappy poodle, but the poodle had gone with the wife.

Brandon climbed aboard, the boat rocking almost imperceptibly as he stepped into the cockpit. He went to the cabin door, opened it, stepped down and in. It was close and hot and he reached up to turn on the fan, rigged to suck air up through the bow hatch. He glanced at the cabinet, the door closed, an old Marlin rifle leaning inside.

The gun had belonged to his grandfather, who he'd never known. Brandon had simply taken it from this grandmother's attic with a box of old shells. He was thirteen, and he rode his bike out of town, the gun in its canvas bag tied to the cross bar, turning off when the woods seemed deep enough.

Like most things, shooting a gun was something Brandon had learned on his own.

Turning to the galley, he bent to take a beer from the refrigerator. Picked out a bottle of Geary's ale, grabbed a book and flashlight off the berth, went back topsides, and walked up to bow. He sat in the canvas chair on the foredeck in the deepening dusk and took a long swallow, looking out across the shimmering water, now green against the sunset.

Brandon opened the book to the marked page: Crime Scene Investigation: Chapter 4. There was a list, and Brandon's eyes ran over it. *"Establish the perimeters of the crime scene and document this location by crime scene photographs and sketches, including written documentation. . . . Reconstruct aspects of the crime in formulating the search. . . . Ascertain the legal basis for the search prior to any seizure of evidence. . . ."*

He flipped the page. The flashlight beam showed a picture of a man, the eyes covered with a black strip. *Asphyxia due to drowning*, the caption said, noting the foam coming out of the man's mouth. Brandon flipped more pages. A woman on a bathroom floor, blood pooled under her head, eyes still staring, stabbed by her husband. A chapter heading on the top of the page: *The Psychopathic Personality Stalker.*

Brandon closed the book. Stood and slipped down the ladder, and into the cabin. He opened the cabinet, took out the faded green canvas gun case. Slipping the rifle out, he ran his hand over the wooden stock. Reached and opened a locker over the settee bench and rummaged. Found a box of .22 shells. Sitting on the bench, he slid the rod from the magazine tube under the barrel. Dropped in 18 shells, counting them out one by one. Slid the rod back in.

He looked at the cabinet, glanced back to the bow. Walked over and laid the gun carefully down on the narrow shelf beside his berth.

The barrel was pointed toward the cabin door.

CHAPTER 5

Word had gotten around that Criminology 203 was a gut, which was why, as Brandon looked around the classroom, he saw one guy sleeping, his head on his arm, mouth open, a girl with her phone on her lap tapping out a text, another guy with one earphone in, the iPod in his pocket.

Brandon sat in the front, by the window. Next to him was the girl from Minnesota who wanted to be a writer. Mia, "after Mia Farrow." When she'd said that during introductions the first day, nobody in class had known who Mia Farrow was except for Brandon, raised by a grandmother who drank wine and snored in front of old movies on TV. Professor Shurstein knew because he was old.

Mia was already out of Colby, a graduate student. She was slight and blonde, attractive if not pretty, narrow face and prominent nose with a little bump. She and Brandon were the serious students, and after the first class she's moved next to him, stayed there ever since. The other students were glad to have them to provide cover.

The chapter du jour was "Crime and Punishment" and Shurstein was talking about the number of inmates in American prisons and how it kept going up and up. Suddenly he paused, ran his hand through gray Groucho Marx hair, and said, "Why?"

The class looked up and froze, like rabbits hearing a rustle in the brush.

"Why are there so many people behind bars?" the professor said. "Where do they all come from? Why can't they obey the rules?"

There was silence, students sitting stock still like they were camouflaged and any movement might give them away.

"Drugs," Mia said. "And laws that address the symptom but not the root cause of the problem."

"Which is?"

"Hopelessness." The other students looking at her, a gelled-hair guy rolling his eyes. "Their lives are dead ends."

"So, assuming that criminals are made and not born, and I think we can agree about that, the crack addict who mugs you on the street was not always a drug addict and a criminal. He wasn't born bad. How do we intervene? How do we break the cycle?"

"You can't," Brandon said. "We're all the product of our experiences. Millions of people are already out there. Full of flaws, reproducing. You lock them up. You keep sticking your finger in the dike. Some learn from their mistakes. Mostly you deter enough people to keep society working."

"You're saying 'corrections' is a misnomer, Mr. Blake?" the professor said.

"Not all of them," Brandon said. "But I ran into a guy yesterday. He's in and out of jail. Robbery, burglary, assault. He's inside right now. His family are mostly outlaws of one sort or another. He's never gonna play by the rules. He just can't. Isn't in his DNA."

"He could reform himself," Mia said. "Find religion or something. You read all the time about murderers, they find Jesus in prison, or Islam. Turns their whole lives around."

"Religious faith can be a powerful thing," the professor said.

Brandon smiled.

"I don't think so," he said. "Not this time."

"How do you know?" Mia said. "How can you just write somebody off like that?"

"You weren't there," Brandon said. "You didn't look into his eyes."

As the clock on the wall ticked to 10:50, the students jumped up like the building was on fire. Shurstein shouted an assignment into the din of scraping chairs and retreated to his desk. As the crowd thinned, he motioned Brandon over. Mia stood by the door, waiting.

"Mr. Blake."

Brandon nodded.

"How many courses are you enrolled in?"

"Just this one," Brandon said. "I take one at a time."

"Why not more? You're a very capable student. Why not full-time?"

Brandon shrugged.

"I work."

The professor took a step closer.

"Wait a minute. Are you the one—"

Shurstein glanced at Mia, back at Brandon.

"—the one who pays cash," he said.

Brandon hesitated.

"Something wrong with that?" he said.

"No, not at all. And it's none of my business, but if it's financial, there's assistance, you know."

"I don't need any help," Brandon said.

Shurstein gave it another shot.

"Loans, grants. That's what they're for."

"Thanks, but I pay as I go."

Shurstein looked at him like he was a museum specimen, a rare species.

"I take it you're on your own," the professor said.

Brandon shrugged, books on his hip.

"I guess that explains why you're more motivated than most."

"I don't know. You'd have to ask them about their motivation."

"What do you do? For work?"

"Work in a boatyard," Brandon said.

"And if you don't mind me asking, how long does it take to come up with the money for a course."

"I worked for six months for this class. Saving on the side."

"Worth it?"

"Yeah, except you coddle the deadbeats too much," Brandon said. "They don't do the work, I'd toss 'em."

"You're a little tougher than me, I guess," the professor said. "Like with your unsalvageable criminal. Acquaintance of yours?"

"Briefly. He's in jail."

"Maybe he's being rehabilitated as we speak," Shurstein said.

Brandon looked at him, smiled.

"What?" the professor said.

"You put these people in jail so they can't hurt anybody. Like a mean dog behind a fence."

Shurstein shook his head, peered through his big glasses.

"Awfully hard for somebody your age."

"Nothing to do with hardness," Brandon said. "I just don't kid myself," and he turned and walked away.

CHAPTER 6

Mia and Brandon were on the sidewalk, other students all around them. Guys in football shirts, baseball hats on backwards. Girls in jeans, tank tops, tattoos showing at bare waists like bugs crawling out of their pants.

Brandon tried not to stare—at Mia. Blonde hair, reddish in the sunlight. The nose with the bump, but a pretty sort of bump. Pale blue eyes that would mesmerize him if he let them.

"Where'd you see this guy?" Mia said.

"A funeral," Brandon said. "They had a funeral and a fight broke out."

"A fight at a funeral?" she said.

"I guess the family has some issues," Brandon said.

"Why do you get the good stuff and I'm stuck in a lab watching somebody get DNA out of piece of gum?"

"Sometimes you get lucky," Brandon said.

"So tell me," Mia said.

"Tell you what?"

"Come on, Brandon. Tell me what happened."

He did, as they stood on the sidewalk, the crowd of students dwindling to nothing, cars pulling away. Soon it was just the two of them, Brandon describing the old lady in the casket, the women fighting on the floor. Mia was smiling, rapt.

And then Brandon got to the part about Joel Fuller, the chin on his shoulder, an eye for an eye.

"Times ten?" Mia said. "What's that mean?"

"That he does to you ten times what you did to him."

"Scary."

"I don't know about scary. Just sort of crazy. This look in his eye, like his mind doesn't work the way a normal person's does."

"God, I wish I had been there," Mia said, her blue eyes glowing. Brandon smiled at her, wondering how many girls would want to see a brawl close-up.

"Why?" he said.

"It's real life," Mia said. "I mean, my life is boring. I have a nice mom and dad. I grew up in a big house. I went to a good college. The typical American family."

"Maybe not so typical."

"My dad's a lawyer and my mom's in human resources and my brother's in med school. Dartmouth. Gonna be a cosmetic surgeon, get rich. My dad, he says it's time for me to forget this writer stuff and get a job, but he doesn't, like, disown me about it."

"Pays for your school?"

"Which is great, but I don't know. Nothing big happens. I need to see lives that have drama and conflict and, I don't know, big moments, events that change people."

Brandon paused, said, "Careful what you wish for."

They walked up the street, stopped by a new red Saab. Mia opened the door, tossed her bag on the passenger seat and turned back to him.

"Actually, I did have one change in my life," she said.

"What's that?" Brandon said.

"You know that boyfriend I had?" Brandon nodded.

"I don't any more," she said, and she reached out and tapped his hand. "Want to get coffee or something?"

"Have to get back," Brandon said. "The owners get cranky if there's nobody on duty for too long."

"I'll come visit."

"Sure."

"I can finally see this boat of yours," Mia said.

"I'm around."

He looked at her, the eyes, the softness of her neck. A dangerous girl, the kind you fall in love with, the kind it hurts to lose.

Or not. Who was he kidding? A few coffees at Starbucks. She gets the stories she needs, writes them into her novel. Flashes the eyes, full of promises, then gone. Back to Minnesota. Her lawyer dad, the big house in, where was it she said? White Bear Lake?

Brandon would be left with the girls from the Old Port, like the last one, who, standing by the bar, had said over the din, "Boats are really, like, awesome. They're, like, great places to, like, party."

Mia waved as she pulled away. Brandon started up the street to his truck, parked under a maple with pale late-spring leaves, translucent against the gray sky.

Tossing his book on the duct-taped seat, he got into the truck, pumped the gas. The old Ford started with a puff of blue smoke, like a magic trick. Brandon checked the mirrors, looked behind him. Pulled out and, as he started down the street toward Back Cove, he checked again.

An eye for an eye, times ten.

CHAPTER 7

Portland District Court was full, a dozen inmates from the jail in the dock. Defendants were in the rows of seats, families in the courtroom, little kids and wives and girlfriends coming to support Daddy as he stood before the judge, an attractive fortyish woman just appointed to the bench.

She flipped through stacks of files, looked a bit confused. A lawyer rose from the seats, tall and rumpled, running a hand through his hair. He came through the gate, plunked a battered briefcase on the defense table, motioned to the row of inmates. The bailiff looked to the prosecutor, a harried young woman, hair tied back, and said, "Ready?"

Joel Fuller got up from his seat. He walked to the defense table as the traffic-case people watched, wondering if his orange suit meant he was a murderer or something.

"Joel W. Fuller," the judge said.

"Mister Fuller is here, your honor," the rumpled lawyer said.

"This is a petition for release?" the judge said.

"Yes, your honor," Fuller's lawyer said. "Mister Fuller has completed four-fifths of a five-month sentence. He is eligible for release."

The judge tossed folders aside, finally opened one, flipped through a stack of documents.

"I see you're a regular, Mr. Fuller. And last time was for—"

"Criminal threatening, your honor," the prosecutor said, finding it just in time. "The defendant threatened to burn someone's house down if they didn't pay him for a four-wheeler."

"Which was stolen," the judge said, still looking at the papers.

"The defendant wasn't aware of that," the defense attorney said. "And he had no intention of burning anyone's house. It was just talk. Hyperbole, your honor, if you will. Street talk. That whole case was a series of misunderstandings."

"It's been a whole lot of misunderstandings," the judge said.

"There are extenuating circumstances," the defense attorney said. "Now my client just wants to go home and start over. He has obligations he needs to assume. There's been a death in the family."

"Your honor," the prosecutor said, "Mister Fuller was released just yesterday to attend his grandmother's funeral. A brawl broke out."

"I fail to see how Mister Fuller can be held responsible for that," the defense lawyer said. "He was in shackles, deputies on both sides of him. It isn't his fault—"

If his family is hopelessly dysfunctional, the judge thought.

"The original sentence was—" she said.

"Five years in jail, all but six months suspended," the prosecutor said.

"He's done almost four months," the judge said.

The prosecutor waved a pen. "And we feel that if you get a furlough for a family emergency and it turns into a brawl that takes a half-dozen officers to break up, then that's not a reason to send you home early."

"Are you worried about the defendant's safety, counselor?" the judge said.

"No, your honor. Mister Fuller is more than able to take care of himself. His record, your honor—assault, criminal mischief, criminal threatening, threatening with a firearm, theft, negotiating a worthless instrument—"

"Those cases have been adjudicated, your honor," the defense lawyer said. "We're here to talk about this case."

"But your honor, this case is just the latest in—"

"He paid for those. We're here to—"

"Okay. Just stop it," the judge said. "Both of you."

She looked at Fuller, sitting at the table, hands folded in front of him like a schoolboy eager to clap the erasers.

"Mister Fuller," the judge said.

He stood, put his hands behind him.

"Your honor," he said. "Ma'am."

"Why should I not keep you in for the full duration of your sentence?"

"Well, your honor," Fuller said. "I can see why you might not think I deserve any sort of special consideration. But I have been in counseling in the correctional center, and I've been talking with the minister, Reverend Bill? I mean, your honor, I know that record doesn't look too good, but I kind of got off on the wrong foot. My father was abusive, then my stepfather. As the counselor explained to me, I've been conditioned to lash out when confronted by adversity."

"You weren't lashing out at this memorial service?"

"Your honor, I walked into the middle of something I wasn't aware of. I been away, your honor. If I'd known there was this trouble brewing, I promise you I would not have asked to attend that service."

"Who died?"

"Gramma Daley," Fuller said. "She was a dear, dear old lady. Gramma

Dailey was very good to me, at a time when I really needed someone solid in my life. The only thing I'm glad of is she didn't live to see that disgraceful exhibition."

"Which you weren't part of?"

"Except for ducking, your honor."

There were chuckles from the audience and the judge pounded her gavel. She looked down at the documents strewn on the blotter in front of her. Sighed.

"Some people might say you're a lost cause, Mister Fuller," she said.

"My client knows that, your honor," the rumpled lawyer said. "But he's very much committed to his counseling. It's like he's seeing himself for the first time, without the haze of alcohol and—"

"Okay," the judge said. "But you screw up, Mr. Fuller, you're coming back to serve the whole five years, you understand?"

Fuller nodded, looked somber.

"He does, your honor," the lawyer said.

The prosecutor leaned forward on her hands. "With all due respect, your honor, I don't think—"

"That's it," the judge said. "The petition for release is granted. Process him asap and send him home."

"Thank you, your honor," Fuller said, smiling gently. "I won't disappoint you."

The judge was gathering up the papers, stuffing them back in Joel Fuller's folder. He was led away from the defense table, back to the row of inmates. He sat back in his chair.

The inmate next to him muttered, "What a crock of shit." He snorted, smothered a laugh. The bailiff looked over.

Fuller put his hand over his mouth and whispered, barely moving his lips. "You make one more fucking sound and I'll find where you live. While you and your lame-ass family is sleeping, I will burn your goddamn house down."

The inmate went silent. Fuller looked over at the judge and smiled.

"I swear to God," he said, like a ventriloquist, his smile firmly in place.

CHAPTER 8

Brandon sat in a folding chair on the after deck, watching the Portland skyline emerge, red lights blinking atop the bank towers, lights glittering on the harbor.

The ferry to Nova Scotia was back, the terminal floodlights illuminating the cars lined up for loading. An oil barge slid out of the harbor, pushed by a rumbling tugboat. Cabin lights bobbed on boats at their moorings, like torches carried by some unruly mob. When the breeze shifted, cool and damp from the northeast, Brandon heard voices from the boats across the water. From the main section of the marina, a big cruiser owned by a guy who worked in Portland at Merrill-Lynch, he heard music. Bob Marley.

A half-hour gone by, he tried again.

Brandon clicked the flashlight on. The book fell open to a chapter titled, "Estimating Time of Death." Brandon flipped the pages, the flashlight beam illuminating photographs of dead bodies, images from nightmares: A skull with long black hair, the body in a bathtub. A hand clutching a gun. A woman recovered from a lake, her arms outstretched, saying "Save me," but rigor mortis had set in.

Brandon closed the book. Looked out at the boatyard and listened. There was a clink, a chain rattle. The gate opening out by the road. He looked at his watch. Nine forty-five.

He tensed. Waited. Peered into the deepening darkness, then heard footsteps. A noise like someone had stumbled, then a pale figure coming out of the shadows and gliding down the ramp to the dock like a ghost.

Brandon eased out of the chair, opened the door to the companionway, the path to the cabinet with the gun.

Waited. The figure kept coming, across the yard, down the ramp, moving his way on the float.

"Hey," Mia said, emerging from the darkness.

"Hey yourself," Brandon said.

"I was driving around. Procrastinating. Anything but reading about seizure of evidence." She was on the steps now, and said, "Do I have to ask permission to come aboard?"

"I'll get my captain's hat," Brandon said.

Mia climbed over the rail, stood in front of him awkwardly, slim and blonde, small but with that electric presence, a twitching of energy. She saw the book on the chair.

"Making me feel guilty."

Brandon shrugged, smiled. "Just getting to it, really. Hey, take the chair."

"You only have one?"

Brandon looked around the cockpit. "Yeah, I guess."

"So you don't entertain regularly?"

She said it not as a judgment, but as a question. It was the first thing he'd noticed about her. She always had another question.

"Not exactly Donald Trump's yacht," he said. "But it's home."

"Cool. But where do you go in the winter?"

"Right here. You wrap the whole thing up, plastic on this wooden frame."

"Like a cocoon," Mia said.

They both stood. Mia looked around. Brandon looked at her, then away.

"Kind of retro, huh?"

"Yeah, well, it's old. Early sixties. They built pretty boats back then. Want a beer?"

Mia grinned, her eyes pale, shining even in the darkness.

"Sure."

Brandon went down into the cabin, came back with two bottles of Geary's ale. Mia had moved to the side of the boat, was peering around the cabin toward the bow. He opened the beers with the opener on his Leatherman, handed her one.

They touched bottles.

Sipped.

"Does it have a name?"

"She's called *Bay Witch*."

"It's a girl boat?"

"They all are. Tradition."

"Is it *Bay Witch* like Bay Watch? Pamela Anderson and all that?"

"No, the person who named it—" He paused, then recovered, smiled. "—she just thought it was a good name, I guess."

"So it was a woman who named it?"

"Yeah."

Another pause, this one longer, and Mia noted it, filed it away.

"If you want to know, it's a Chris-Craft Cavalier, thirty-five foot. Chevy powered, single screw, a small V-8. If you care about that stuff."

"Kind of like a floating camper," Mia said. "We had one when I was really little. My dad towed it all over the country with this big Suburban. All the places he said we had to see. He had a list. Yellowstone and the Grand Canyon."

"I'd like to see that," Brandon said. "Read a book about the first guy to go through on a boat. Powell."

"It's amazing," Mia said. "Makes you feel really, really small. Kind of like the ocean."

She drank again and Brandon watched, thought she was almost beautiful in the dusky light. Short blonde hair glinting, that glitter in her eyes. Silver earrings that swung like the things hypnotists waved in front of you.

He looked away and Mia walked over to the helm and touched the wheel. Jiggled it back and forth and looked toward the stern, to see if something might move.

"You're from around here, right?" she said.

"Two miles, by boat."

She touched the throttle, the wheel again.

"So did you bring your boat here and then get the job?"

"The boat was here. It was in the family."

"Really. Was it your grandfather's or something?"

"Or something," Brandon said. "Now it's mine."

"That's so neat."

"If you worked on it you might not think so. It's old and it's wood—a lot of maintenance."

"Like what?"

Always questions.

"Topsides, needs varnishing, painting, polishing. Last year, me and Sam, he's the old guy who owns the marina. He's in Florida, had a stroke, but he knows boats. We hauled it and redid the bottom. Actually, I did it, he told me what to do. Replaced some planks, painted it, did some refastening."

"Huh."

She had turned back toward him. She took a couple of steps and bent to look down the hatchway to the cabin. "That's where you sleep?"

"Right."

"Can I see?"

Brandon hesitated, the cabin his private world.

"You can say no," Mia said.

"It's fine, let me turn on the light."

He led the way and she followed. She stumbled on the way down the steps, put her hand on his back. The touch electric.

Brandon turned the lamp on by the vee berth, and stood in the center of the cabin, his head nearly touching the ceiling Mia surveyed the berth the built-in shelves filled with books, an acoustic guitar in a beat-up case, the lid open.

"You play?"

"Some. Not very well."

She ran her hand over the neat writing desk that folded down from the paneling, eyed the plaid curtains over the windows.

"Oh, those are so cute," she said. "Did your mom make them for you or something?"

Brandon tried not to darken, saw her eyes catch something. She was always watching.

"No. I made them myself."

"You're kidding me. You sew?"

"You learn to do a lot of things yourself on a boat like this. Otherwise you go broke paying people."

She turned. Opened and closed the cabinets. Ran her hands over the gleaming galley counter, the spices and condiments in their rack.

"No TV?"

"No."

"Internet?"

"Wireless, from two boats down."

"Really."

Mia's eyes kept sweeping the cabin, her mouth frozen in a half-smile. She noted the beat-up laptop. An old iPod.

She picked it up.

"May I?"

Brandon shrugged.

"My brother says looking at somebody's iPod is like going through their desk. I just think it's interesting seeing what people listen to."

She spun the wheel.

"Huh. Old rap. Public Enemy? Rage Against the Machine? Angry music, Brandon. I thought you'd be more mellow."

Brandon smiled. Mia put the iPod down on the little table.

"God, you're neat. Can you come over to my apartment?"

"You have to be neat on a boat, it's such a small space."

"What do you cook?"

"Stew. Curry. Pasta."

"Really. And all these books? What are they? All history?"

"A lot of 'em. "

"No novels?"

"I like things that have really happened. Things that are real."

"Not my made-up stories, huh?" She picked up a book, flipped the pages. It was a history of Portland.

"You know the city burned twice?" Brandon said. "The British shelled it during the Revolution. Then Americans burned it again during the Civil War. Fourth of July. Party got out of hand."

"Huh," Mia said. "So you sit down here and read. It's so cozy. The little refrigerator, the stove. Do you go out on voyages?"

It was an odd way of putting it, and Brandon smiled.

"Once in a while," he said.

She turned her back to him, and Brandon let his eyes run over her, head to toe, quickly, a stolen glance.

"My ex-boyfriend, he was into boats, too," she said. "He teaches sailing back home, crews on big sailboats. They race on the Great Lakes and stuff. And we have a ski boat on the lake at home. Do you water ski?"

Brandon shook his head, felt his mood sour, a black cloud, made it pass. Mia started for the hatchway, said, "Can I walk up on the top part?"

He would have said yes, but when he caught up she was already up on the sidedeck, easing along, one hand on the rail. Brandon followed. On the foredeck, she looked down through the cracked hatch, light spilling up, illuminating her face. She turned away, looked out at the Portland skyline, the lights of the harbor, the sheen on the water glistening like a black mirage.

"Beautiful. You have friends around here, Brandon?"

"I did. Two went away to school. One's in prison. Oxycontin."

"Huh," Mia said. "That's not very many."

"I don't like to need people too much," Brandon said, looking at the water.

"Why?"

"You don't really want to know."

She smiled.

"Sure, I do."

"If you don't need people, you can't be disappointed by them."

"You've been disappointed?"

Brandon shrugged. "No big deal. People just make a lot of promises they can't keep. Say things and then they don't deliver. Not a problem, unless you believe them in the first place."

They stood a couple of feet apart, the boat moving almost imperceptibly under their weight. Lights glided by in the darkness and the subject changed.

"It's like the boat's breathing," Mia said. She sipped her beer, stepped to the rail, and looked over. Came back.

"Your parents, what do they think of you living on a boat?" she said.

"They don't," Brandon said.

"They don't care?" Mia said.

Brandon hesitated. Drank more beer and lowered the bottle, looked out at the glittering lights of the skyline.

"No," he said. "I never had a father. My mom, she died."

Mia frowned, put her hand on top of his.

"I'm sorry. I didn't know."

No," he said. "It's a logical question."

Brandon looked at her, the tenderness in her eyes. Mia turned and moved to the bow, standing in the darkness now, just out of reach of the soft yellow light streaming up through the hatch. The cool May night was falling, the smell of salt and sea rising from the low-tide mud.

"So," Mia said, facing him, suddenly awkward. "You're all alone here?"

"Yeah."

"Nobody else? I mean, you're not seeing someone?"

She grinned. "Sorry if I'm direct. It just saves a lot of time, you know?"

Brandon smiled, shook his head. "Not for quite a while. She found somebody a little more, I don't know, normal."

"I think you're way better than normal."

"Likewise." Brandon grinned. "I'm just kind of a loner, I guess."

"Me, too. When you're alone is the only time you can really think about things. It's what bugged me about school. All these people, all the time. Where'd you go to high school?"

He took a deep breath.

"I didn't."

"What do you mean? You didn't finish?"

"Never went. Home schooled. Sort of."

"Really."

Brandon paused, part of him not wanting to tell it, part of him wanting very much for her to know.

"Okay, this is the way it went. "Nessa, that's my grandmother, she was gonna raise me just right. After my mom died. Not let me fall in with the wrong crowd. Except for one thing."

He sipped the beer, deliberately. Two beers a day, his way of showing it couldn't conquer him the way it did Nessa.

"She drank most of the day, was passed out after lunch. So I pretty much was on my own. You have to do these reports for the state, saying what you've learned. I even did those myself. Made up most of it."

"Huh," Mia said, fascinated, trying not to let it show.

"Weird. I know. I can see that now. For two whole years I didn't read anything except World War II books. One year I studied polar expeditions. You know, the guys up there dragging sledges over the ice? Ask me about Perry and Shackleton. Go ahead. I did the Amazon explorers, too. Blue Nile and all that."

He shook his head, gave a half laugh. Mia touched his hand. He smiled.

"As long as there were books, Nessa figured I was learning something."

"So what were your days like? I mean, your routine?"

"There wasn't one. I read, prowled around the bay. On the rocks, rowing in this old leaky dinghy. Came back in time to make dinner, get it into her. Went around the house picking up the wine glasses, put a cork in the bottle, if it wasn't empty."

"She didn't see that that was wrong?"

"Full of plans until the first glass, usually by ten-thirty. Lots of promises. We were gonna go to Europe, see Normandy. That was during my World War II phase. Disney World 'cause she got it in her head every kid had to go to Disney World."

"Never happened?"

"None of it. She meant well."

He smiled.

"She's alive?" Mia said.

"Oh, yeah. I'll see her tomorrow. I make sure she's okay, but most of the time I'm around here."

Brandon paused. "Wondering how to bail out of this?" he said.

"No way."

"Not exactly what you expected."

"I knew you were different from guys I know. You're serious, like you have some sort of secret."

She reached out and put her hand on his arm, let it run down to his hand. He took her hand and clasped it, small and soft and a perfect fit. They drew each other closer, Mia thinking that his eyes were like tunnels, deep and dark and leading somewhere, to a place very faraway. That was the difference between him and the others. They were defined, had a beginning from which she could see clear through the middle and all the way to the end. In an instant.

With Brandon—watching him for weeks in class, talking, now standing here—she felt she was close to something important, mysterious, maybe even wonderful.

Brandon was thinking that she was cut from no mold he had ever seen, beautiful and inquisitive, like she was on some sort of mission.

"Sometimes I row out at night, just sit there, look at the lights."

"Really," Mia said. "I'd love to do that."

"Sometime we will," Brandon said, but she was looking at him, her gaze unavoidable.

"What's wrong with now?" Mia said. "Or is that one of those promises that don't come true?"

CHAPTER 9

The jail van dropped Joel Fuller on Congress Street at Longfellow Square. He flipped the van off as it pulled away. Not as good as a rock through the back window, but better than nothing.

Fuller headed downtown, plastic bag under his arm holding toothbrush, deodorant, underwear, and socks. He saw five chicks he would have given it to in a minute, one of them a little old, probably forty, but who cared after four months inside? People on the sidewalk looked up at him, swerved to the curb. Guys on a bench watched him pass, seeing the bag, knowing what that meant.

"What are you fucking looking at?" Fuller said.

"Want to buy some reefer?" one of the guys said.

Fuller couldn't buy reefer, couldn't even buy a shot. He had two bucks and change, enough for a draft, Old Milwaukee. Two blocks down, he took a right, headed toward the harbor, and stopped at a bar called Jolly's, the only place the rich shits hadn't ruined.

It was full, ten o'clock. Crew just off a fishing boat, their night just beginning. Five bikers, flabby old guys thinking leather vests from harley. com made them tough. Fuller sat at the bar, asked for an Old Mil, then, after it came, stared at it for a minute. Watched the bubbles rising to the surface. Took a deep breath and then the first sip. He felt a wave of mellow euphoria sweep through him. Fought off the urge to drain the beer in one gulp, knowing the bartender wouldn't let him run a tab.

He looked around. One of the bikers was playing AC/DC on the jukebox, "Hell's Bells," over and over. Fuller figured that oughta get somebody pissed off, hoped it was the fishermen so he could watch them kick some fat biker ass. Guys off the boats, man. Some tough mother fuckers.

Fuller finished the beer in three gulps, skinny little rip-off glass. Got up to take a leak and snagged a five-dollar bill and a couple of quarters, somebody's change on a table at the back. "Score," he muttered to himself, slipped the bill in his pocket, went to the bathroom. Came out and went to the pay phone, all dusty now that everybody had cell phones.

He dialed.

Kelvin's wife Crystal answered, a kid screeching in the background, television blaring.

"Get Kelvin," Fuller said.

A pause and then Crystal said, "He ain't here."

"The hell he ain't. Go get him."

"Just stay away from us, Joel," Crystal said. "We're getting our shit together. We don't need your—"

"Get him, you stupid cow. Don't make me come over there and drag him out."

The phone slammed down, Crystal stomping off, Fuller picturing the trailer rocking, Crystal's big boobs bouncing. Kelvin had really screwed up the day he married that crack whore.

A clatter.

"Hey. Where are you?" Kelvin said.

"I'm out."

"Fucking A. That went by fast."

"Maybe for you," Fuller said. "Meet me at Jolly's."

"Ah, shit, Joel. I can't. I mean, I got the kid, Crystal's supposed to go to her sister's, I just—"

"Kelvin. Listen to me. Jolly's in an hour."

"I don't know. I mean, the car ain't registered—"

"And bring some dinero. I'm broke."

He looked at his watch. Sipped his third beer. Stared at the TV behind the bar, some show about a family of assholes, all yelling at each other. "Hey," Fuller murmured. "It's Kelvin and Crystal."

At 11:03, an hour on the dot, Kelvin walked in. He took the stool beside Fuller, held out his hand, and they bumped fists.

"Welcome back, dude," Kelvin said.

"Yeah, right."

Fuller signaled the bartender, draining his glass at the same time. Kelvin dug in his jeans and tossed a 10-dollar bill onto the bar. They sat, not talking, waiting for the bartender to come. He set down two beers and Fuller held his up in front of him. Kelvin reached over and clinked his glass on Fuller's.

They drank. Wiped their mouths with their hands.

"So, how was the food?" Kelvin said.

Fuller looked at him, wondering how Kelvin came up with this stuff, always asking questions like that, which was why he was living in a beat-to-shit trailer with the most annoying chick on the friggin' planet.

"Delicious," Fuller said. "What do you think?"

He paused, added, "I got a job."

"What? Work release?"

"Not that kind of job."

Kelvin looked puzzled, but only for a second.

"Oh," he said, noncommittal and wary.

"Let's go. We'll talk in the car."

"Dude, I still got half a beer," Kelvin said.

"We can buy some for the road."

Fuller was off his stool, bag under his arm. He crossed the barroom, gave the fishermen a wide berth, but threw the fat bikers a cold stare. Kelvin caught up on the sidewalk, stopped at a rusting Chevy Caprice.

"You still driving this piece of shit?" Fuller said.

"Shouldn't be. Took the plate off this wreck that got towed in down the road," Kelvin said.

"Why don't you register it? Good way to get picked up, plates don't match."

"Kinda short. Kid got sick, Crystal goes to the chiropractor, pays cash."

"You are whipped," Fuller said, yanking the door open. They stopped at 7-Eleven and Kelvin grudgingly went in and bought a 30 of Bud and two packs of Marlboros, Joel's getting-out-of-jail present, the second in nine months. Fifty yards down the road they both opened beers, lit cigarettes. Cans tucked between their legs, they drove up the hill to Congress, took a right.

"Rich assholes taking over up here, too," Fuller said, as they passed restaurants, an antique shop, a guy carrying an L.L. Bean canvas tote, cream with a red monogram. "You know what would happen to that douche bag in jail?"

Kelvin didn't answer because he was checking the rearview mirror for cops before he took a swallow of beer. Maybe he was a wuss, but so what, he thought. He drank. At the end of Congress he took a left, swung down into the parking lot that overlooked the bay, all black with twinkling lights. He pulled up beside a Subaru with kayak racks and shut off the motor. Fuller finished his beer, tossed the empty into the back seat, and reached for another. He got one for Kelvin, too.

Fuller sat back, pleasantly buzzed.

"So this job," he said.

"Oh, yeah," Kelvin said, disappointed that Fuller had remembered.

"We gotta get this asshole. He punched out Sylvia."

"Your mother?"

"We were at my grandmother's funeral."

"She died?"

"No. They had it fucking early so she could watch. Of course she died."

"Oh. That's too bad," Kelvin said.

"She was an old bag. Got me out of jail for half a day."

"Why'd this guy punch Sylvia?"

"Who the fuck knows? Everybody started fighting, this kid is some kinda cop wannabe. Wades into it, picks out Sylvia. Busts her nose."

"Surprised she didn't break his arm back. Who is he?"

"Brandon something. Brandon Blake. I had a guy ask around. This guard, he'll do anything for blow."

"You got some coke?"

"No, not yet. Gave him a rain check. Sucker."

Kelvin looked disappointed, stared off at the bay, the lights on the bean plant across the cove. Fuller sucked down half the new beer, rested the can between his legs. A woman in running shorts came jogging up to the Subaru, taking care not to look at the two scruffy guys in the old junker.

"Nice ass, honey," Fuller murmured, as the woman slammed her door, locked it. "You're nuts running around here at night, fucking perverts loose all over the place."

"So how you gonna get this guy?" Kelvin said.

"I'm on probation forever. I gotta be careful, stay out from now on. I ain't gonna do no five years. So you gotta do it."

"Like I need another assault charge?" Kelvin said.

"You owe me," Fuller said.

"For what?"

"Who took the hit for the coke you left in the glove box? Who took the hit for the tools—nice of you to tell me they was all stolen. Who didn't say shit? Who sat there in jail for four months while you were out having a good time, even if it was with Crystal."

Kelvin was quiet.

Fuller finished the beer, crumpled the can and flipped it into the back seat. Lit a cigarette with the lighter in the dash.

"The guy goes to college, riding with the cops is part of some goddamn class."

"Like you're gonna learn shit doing that," Kelvin said.

"The cokehead at the jail, he ran him for me. Address is someplace in South Portland. Even found out the class meets Tuesday and Thursdays, over off Forest Avenue."

"So we put on trenchcoats and walk into the room and blast everybody?"

"Kel, I'm not kidding around. This guy busted my mother's nose."

"You don't even like your mother."

"That's immaterial," Fuller said, liking the sound of the word, now that he wasn't hearing it from the defendant's table. "It's the principle."

Kelvin took a deep breath, not liking this at all. Joel out for what, two hours? Already dragging him into something. But then Joel had kept his mouth shut about the cocaine.

"What do you wanna do? Bust his nose back?"

"Fuck that," Fuller said. "This is like the Israelis."

"The what?"

"Watched a lot of TV in there. History Channel, dude. I like those Israeli guys. They got a rule. You kill one of them, they come back and kill ten of you. You fuck with them, they make you pay bigtime."

"Israelis. That's Jewish people, right?" Kelvin said.

"I don't want you to kill him," Fuller said, not listening. He gazed out at the water, the red winking lights on the channel buoys.

"For taking the hit for three grams of coke and a ripped-off table saw?" Kelvin said. "I wasn't planning on it."

"We'll bust his knees. Come up behind him, take a bat to the bastard. You do it at night, you wear a mask. Two swings and out. Do it myself but the probation—"

"No blood," Kelvin said. "Fucking DNA."

"No blood from a knee," Fuller said, relaxing now that Kelvin had agreed. "Just a big bundle of bones and cartilage."

"He big?" Kelvin said.

"Nah, average. Hey, he's some dipshit college boy. Don't worry."

"Busted Sylvia's nose—that takes some balls," Kelvin said.

Fuller took a long drag on his cigarette.

"Only if you know her," he said.

CHAPTER 10

"I guess it's kind of like swimming in the ocean in Maine," Brandon said. "The hardest part is getting in."

"So just dive," Mia said.

They were sitting in the skiff at the edge of the cove, red and green running lights clamped to the bow, glowing like candles.

The wind had shifted to the northwest, clouds clearing out. Stars were painted overhead, pinpoints on the blue-black canvas. Across the harbor, headlights streamed. A tug slid under the bridge, trailed by a distant rumble. Brandon pulled on an oar, turned the bow in the direction of the wake that was moving toward them.

"Your parents," Mia said, from the stern seat.

"Okay. Well, the story is, well, this is going to sound strange, telling you out here, but my mother, she was lost at sea. Sailing from Maine to the Caribbean, the boat disappeared. Lost with all hands, as they say."

Her face fell. "I'm sorry."

"It's okay. I was four. I mean, it's the way I grew up."

"Huh. So where was your dad?"

Brandon hesitated, almost never told this part. But something about her, the way she listened. "My mom got pregnant when she was nineteen, the guy wasn't from here, just working on a dragger. He took off. So she never put his name on the birth certificate, wouldn't tell anybody who he was. Said he didn't deserve it."

Mia's eyes were liquid in the reflections off the water.

"So it was just the two of you?"

"Three, if you count my grandmother. Nikki, my mom, she was funny. She really rebelled, I guess. Her dad, my grandfather, was this bigshot doctor, at least for Portland, Maine. And she didn't even go to college. Worked in bars, had me. A huge disappointment, I'm sure. But on the other hand, she and my grandmother were really close. Almost like friends. Maybe 'cause it was just the two of them after my grandfather died."

"How'd he die?"

"Smoked and drank and ate a lot of meat. Worked all the time until he had a heart attack. Nikki was eight. Their only kid."

The tug's wake moved across the harbor like a water snake. The dinghy rocked and Brandon pulled the oars to steady it. Mia waited, then said, "So your mom went on this sailing trip and left you home?"

Brandon smiled. Held his empty beer bottle. "You have to understand. That was Nikki. I mean, I don't even call her mom. She was kinda wild. Good person but just, I don't know, restless."

"Like in what way?" Mia said.

A deep breath, the hard parts to admit.

"Like she'd rather go out to the bars than stay home, rather hang out with her friends than be home with her baby. Always ready for something new. Very easily bored. Probably A.D.D., but nobody ever said that."

He paused. "It was like she had me but she was missing some piece of maternal instinct or something. Like you know how some animals in zoos, they have to take the baby away because the mother doesn't pay attention to them?"

"Who took you away?"

"My grandmother. She kind of took over."

"Huh. So then Nikki, she went on this voyage?"

That word again. Brandon smiled.

"Right. Supposed to go to the Caribbean, didn't make it."

"They never found it?" Mia said.

"The boat? No. Disappeared off of Charleston."

"A big storm?" Mia said.

"No, not really. It just disappeared. Left the harbor one night and was never seen again."

"Huh."

"Happens. Sailboats get hit by freighters, even a big trawler. Everybody's below. No chance to get to a radio. Bang, you're just gone."

She pictured that— a crash, screaming, water rushing in, darkness. She shuddered, the black water looking ominous now. "What was the name?" Mia said.

"Of what?" he said.

"The boat."

Curious like a little kid, Brandon thought.

"*Black Magic,*" Brandon said. "It had a black hull. Maybe that's why it was hard to see at night."

Another pause, the sound of the chop slapping against the skiff.

"How many died?" she said.

"Four. Three guys and my mom."

"Who were they?"

"Just people she met. They weren't from here. Came through on their way south from Canada, but I don't think they were from there, either. One of them had lived in California. My grandmother didn't even know their real names. They went by nicknames. Ketch and Lucky and Timbo."

"Your mom just jumped on a boat that pulled into the harbor?"

Brandon winced inwardly, the image of his mother hopping onto a boat like she jumped into a bed, his own hook-up of a conception.

"No, they were here for a few weeks. Motor problems. They ordered parts, hung out."

The boat rocked gently like a porch swing. There was a puff of cool breeze.

"Her friends went off to college or whatever. She worked the bars in Portland. Bought an old boat herself, which was kind of crazy. My grandmother could never tell her what to do, I guess. Even when she was little. So these guys came into port and they got to be friends and off she went."

Mia pictured exotic sailors from a big sailboat charming the locals.

"Like pirates," she said. "I can see the appeal."

She wondered what her lawyer dad would think of Brandon, a part-time student, drives a beat-up truck, lives on an old boat.

Like writing, just another of Mia's phases.

"Did she leave on these trips very often?" she said.

A long pause. The boat slid on another wake, this one from nowhere, out of the darkness.

"Nessa says Nikki was an optimist. There was always a guy she hoped would be the one. One time she went to Belgium with this sculptor, except he didn't really sculpt anything. I remember he smoked these dark brown cigarettes. Another time she rode to Utah on the back of some guy's motorcycle. We had a picture, them in front of these big stacks of rocks. It was a Moto Guzzi. He had a pony tail."

"So every—"

"Every few months she'd take off for a week or two. I'd stay with my grandmother. I think my grandmother, she just kept hoping the guy would be the one, too."

"Not knowing," she said. "That must've been hard on your grandmother."

"Still is," Brandon said. "She started drinking hard back then, hasn't stopped."

They were quiet for a minute, Brandon thinking of Nessa and her drunken rants, Mia thinking about this young woman who chased her dream to the bottom of the sea and left a little boy behind. He flicked an oar in the water, turned the dinghy so she could see the lights of the Portland skyline.

"Pretty," she said.

"Yes," he said.

"So all of that didn't keep you away from boats, the water?"

"No," Brandon said.

He hesitated, then kept going. "It's weird, but in a way I guess I feel closer to her here. When she was going—I still remember this—she got down on her knees, said, 'Listen, Mister B.' She called me that. 'This is a dream for me, sailing away to a beautiful place. And you have to chase your dreams or they never come true.'"

Mia watched him, waited, knew he wasn't done.

"It's my way of kind of staying with her, I guess. And—"

He paused. "The ocean doesn't make any promises. It doesn't owe you anything. I know that sounds weird."

"No," Mia said. "It doesn't." She looked at him, said, "This was her boat, wasn't it?"

Brandon nodded, thought to himself that she had him figured. The boat rocked, as if in agreement.

"So I want to write great novels," Mia said. "What dream are you chasing?"

He thought for a moment, about how to answer, why he felt that with Mia he could reveal anything. "I want to be a detective," Brandon said.

"Create order from the disorder?" Mia said. "Punish people who break the rules?"

He looked at her, startled at how much she knew about him. "Yeah," he said.

Mia was still looking away, the spray of lights against the sky. She said, "Can I say something?"

"Last time a girl asked me that she said I was way too spooky," Brandon said. "She said she never really knew what I was thinking."

"I feel like I do know," Mia said. "When I don't, I want to know."

"You understand," Brandon said. He flicked the oar, the boat turned. Mia leaned forward, toward him.

"It's the weirdest thing, Brandon. I mean, I don't know you that well. We've had coffee what? Five times?"

"Six," Brandon said.

"It's like I feel like I really know you. I feel—"

She hesitated. Reached out and covered his hand, still on the oar.

"I feel like I'm falling in love with you. Maybe already have. And it's not like I want to. It's like I can't help it. It's just—"

"Meant to be," Brandon said.

He spun the boat toward shore and started to row.

In the vee berth in the bow, they made love tenderly, neither wanting to tip whatever delicate balance they had achieved. He was strong, muscled, and lean, but at the same time gentle, his touch like some big animal's caress. She was perfect, he thought, one graceful curve and slope leading to another, her skin softer than anything he'd ever felt, yet her kisses determined and intense.

They rolled over and over in the berth, at one point feeling the boat rocking gently beneath them.

"Was that from us?" Mia said, breathless.

Brandon knew it was a wake, probably from a passing oil barge, but he only said, "Yes."

And she laughed, like it was some sort of triumph, to have rocked the boat.

When the boat was still and they were, too, they huddled under the blankets and comforter as the chill night fell. Brandon apologized that he didn't have wine and Mia said she'd ask for more tea but that would mean getting up.

He got up, naked, and went across the cabin to the stove and put the kettle on. When he came back, they settled into each other, like boats coming to a stop. Brandon kissed her forehead and she said, "It *was* meant to be, wasn't it?"

"Yes," he said, still a little stunned, overwhelmed.

"You alright?"

"Yeah."

"Because this is supposed to make us happy."

"I know."

"Bring us closer," Mia said, "but now you're far away"

Brandon leaned to her.

"No. I'm not. It's just—"

"Just what?"

"Just that, I don't know, all of a sudden I'm breaking all my rules."

"Like don't ever love anyone?"

Brandon looked away, realizing he'd never recited them out loud.

"Don't need anyone. Don't let yourself need anybody. Never ask for help."

He took a deep breath.

"Don't love anyone. Don't let yourself be loved."

She kissed his cheek, hovered there, her breath warm and soft. "Have you broken those, too?"

Brandon didn't answer.

CHAPTER 11

Brandon pulled the truck through the gate, parked by the garages. He went in through the back door, into the kitchen, and called: "Nessa. You ready?"

"I'm coming," she called. He heard the click of switches as she turned off the lamps, a drunk's frugality, why spend money on electricity when you could spend it on wine. The shuffle of her shoes on the hardwood floor.

"You don't have to do this," she said, coming into the kitchen, sweater on, hair brushed. "I can just stay home."

"You've got to get out," Brandon said. "It's good for you."

He held the door for her and they went out to the truck. He held her by the arm as he helped her climb in, smelled the cologne, then the whiff of alcohol. It was the smell he had been so ashamed of as a kid, sitting beside her in the old Volvo wagon as she wove her way to the grocery store.

Always another few bottles in the bag.

The same Volvo wagon was still in the garage, coated with dust. The store delivered the wine now, mailed Nessa a monthly bill. It was the one she paid first.

Nessa looked out, said again, "It's a pretty house, don't you think?"

It was, a big shingled cottage on the bay, a little shabby. A reverse mortgage kept Nessa going as she drank up the equity; the bank knew it could always count on waterfront.

He backed up and drove out of the gate and headed for the city. Through the back streets, up to the bridge, over the harbor, the marina to their right.

"I don't see how you can live on that boat," Nessa said, for the thousandth time.

"I like it there," Brandon said.

"Damp and cramped and dark," Nessa said, and then they were off the bridge, driving through the city. They moved down Congress, Nessa turned toward the sidewalk, watching the people: business types, the pierced-up art-school kids, Thai, Cambodian, Somali immigrants.

"You'd think they'd freeze in the winter," Nessa said. "Their blood is thinner than ours, you know."

A Portland P.D. cruiser passed and Brandon watched it, glancing up at the rearview mirror as it receded. Nessa, sharp-eyed and critical, noticed.

"Is that really what you want to do? Ride around all day in a police car, sweeping up after these people?"

"Maybe," Brandon said. "It'd be interesting, the problems you'd have to fix, bad guys you'd arrest."

"Leave it to the roughnecks," Nessa said. "Used to be the police were all Irish, big and tough and you know how they love to drink and fight, the Irish. You should be a teacher. Doesn't pay much, but you've always liked history."

Brandon sighed inwardly, turned off at Monument Square, headed down toward the harbor. Nessa would talk about the Old Port, how it used to be a dump, then about how the harbor used to be full of fishing boats. When her husband was alive, starting out in Portland, one of his patients had been a fisherman and a foul-mouthed old cuss he was, too. Brandon turned onto one of the narrow cobblestoned streets, got ready to listen to her take on the new chi-chi restaurants.

"Oh, my God," Nessa said.

He braked, turned to her. Her face was ashen, her mouth open.

"You alright?" he said.

"Oh God," she said again. She jerked around in her seat, the shoulder belt stretched tight. Put her hand to her chest and twisted the other way. A heart attack, Brandon thought.

"Stop," Nessa gasped.

He braked, pulled over. Leaned toward her.

"What's the matter?"

Nessa twisted in her seat, peering back.

"It was him," she said.

"Who?" Brandon said, looking at her, then back down the street.

"It was Lucky," Nessa said. "Lucky from the boat."

CHAPTER 12

"Where?" Brandon said.

"Back there," Nessa said, straining to see. "With a woman. He was walking."

"Are you sure? It's been a long time since that picture—"

"Yes, it was him."

Brandon opened the truck door, said. "What was he wearing?"

"A dark shirt, blue maybe, and light slacks. And the woman. Tall and dark hair and pretty. Fancy looking. Black slacks and high heels and a red sweater except it was on her shoulders."

Brandon rolled out of the truck, started back down the sidewalk at a fast walk. He pictured the guy in the old photograph: wiry and small, no taller than Nikki. Impish sort of smile.

He broke into a trot, slowed for the first alley, a brick courtyard, a gallery on the corner. Brandon glanced into the gallery window, people there but no woman with the red sweater. He came back out onto the street, continued on, threading his way between people coming out of bars, couples arm in arm, business types with jackets slung over their shoulders.

No sweater.

Brandon went down the block to the corner, peered into every storefront. There was a wine bar on the second floor above a bakery and he went up the stairs two at a time, burst in. People looked up from their tables and couches. No Lucky.

Back on the street, Brandon walked up the block on the opposite side, the truck ahead of him, Nessa still in the passenger seat. He walked by her, up the block in case they'd circled back, just making a loop.

Nothing.

Brandon went back to the truck, found Nessa huddled in her seat, her seat belt still on. He got in, shut the door.

"I didn't see them," he said.

Nessa stared straight ahead, a gray-haired waif.

"It was really him, from the picture?"

"It had to be. I mean, it was the same smile, like he was still cute, left-over from being a little boy. That's what I remember about him."

They both were quiet for a moment.

"And the woman," Brandon said.

"Taller than him. Looked like she had money. They both did."

"But he's dead, Nessa."

"This means that—"

"Nessa, don't. Don't do this."

"If he's alive, she could be."

Brandon looked over, saw tears running down her pale cheeks. She bit her lip, swallowed.

"Brandon, what if she was hurt? What if she doesn't remember? What if she was put in jail in some godforsaken place, those filthy little countries, and they wouldn't let her call."

"Nessa, it's been seventeen years."

"You see it on TV."

"Nessa."

"It's possible, Brandon. It's possible."

He looked at her, her eyes shining, not just from the tears. He heard her voice filling with hope, felt it seep into him like a virus. He fought it off.

"Nessa, she's gone."

"We don't know. We all thought this one was dead and now he's walking around, alive as can be."

Nessa turned to him, her gray-streaked hair askew, moist lines traced on her.

"In all these years, I've never said, 'There he is.' Have I?"

Brandon looked away, up the street, across at the passing people, no red sweater, no shortish guy.

"Then we'll find him," he said.

He started the truck and pulled out, drove slowly down the street. He and Nessa scanned the sidewalks, slowed for every guy in khakis, every tall woman in heels. At the end of the block they turned, swung around to do the next street. Restaurants here, a pub, a shop that sold kites, a café that was closed. Knots of guys around the pubs, cars slowing, looking for parking.

A guy in khakis and a dark shirt, inside the entrance to a restaurant. Brandon stopped the truck, left it running, ran inside, past the hostess, who said, "Sir? Can I help—"

The guy was about to sit at a table with a woman, short blonde hair. Brandon walked by them, turned back. A beard. Glasses. Not Lucky.

Back outside, a Jaguar behind the truck, gray-haired man behind the wheel, scowling. Brandon climbed behind the wheel, eased off slowly, Nessa beside him, his partner on patrol.

"Not here," Nessa said.

At the end of the block they turned again. Cruised a third street, this one rougher, younger crowd, more guys in baseball caps. "They wouldn't come here," Nessa said. "She was too dressed up."

"Maybe they'd be up the hill more," Brandon said.

He turned, circled back, the truck motor rumbling. Nessa, normally complaining by now that she was tired, wanted to go home, was erect in her seat, eyes narrowed, vigilant. Again they did the street where she'd seen them, Brandon getting out to check another restaurant, telling the maitre d' he was looking for friends.

Nothing.

Circled and did another block, this one more shops, Brandon peering through the plate-glass storefronts. No red sweater. One guy with a blue shirt and light pants, but way too big. The next block up was giving way to offices, most closed. A few people walking, but not them.

They started again, both quiet as they scanned the streets, not noticing the old car that followed them from a distance, turning left, right, pulling over when they stopped.

CHAPTER 13

Nessa held the photo in one hand, tapped it with a bony finger, cigarette ash falling onto her lap.

"Maybe I'm wrong," she said.

Brandon waited.

"I mean, he was much older, but it looked like him," she said, peering at the picture. "I remember when they were leaving. I was down there on the dock and you were giving her a hug goodbye and this one, Lucky, he came over and shook your hand."

"Just him?"

"The other guys were on the boat. Coiling up ropes and things like that."

"What did he say?"

"He said your mom would bring you a present. I remember thinking, Don't say that 'cause what if she doesn't? Nikki, we were lucky to get a postcard."

"He was the nice one?"

"The talker. Called me Mrs. Blake."

Brandon watched her, her eyes on the photo, letting out a sudden sigh of weariness. "You should sleep," he said.

"Yes. This has been quite a day." She said it like it was a good thing, the night after a wedding, a graduation.

"I'll talk to you tomorrow."

"We'll look some more?"

"Sure," Brandon said. "But you know, Nessa—"

"What?"

"People resemble each other."

"I know that."

"It was from the truck. You didn't get a good—"

"But I did."

"Still, Nessa—"

"Four faces I've memorized, Brandon. Your mother and these three."

She looked again at the picture, then stubbed her cigarette out on the saucer on the table, lifted herself from the chair.

"You go, dear. I'm tired."

She offered her cheek and he kissed it, and she turned, started for the bedroom. Brandon paused, watched her as she tottered toward the door. He said, "Nessa."

"What?"

Brandon was about to say that this wasn't one of her soap operas where somebody comes back after twenty years with amnesia. But instead he walked to her, took the photo from her hand, and studied it. Lucky's chipmunk cheeks. The way his eyes narrowed when he smiled. The turned-up nose, the leprechaun look.

"I'll need this picture," Brandon said. "And the clippings."

Nessa hesitated, then said, "The closet in the living room. On the top shelf, in my metal box. I put them where I couldn't get to them."

She turned, took an unsteady step, then turned back.

"Brandon."

"Yeah?"

"You know she loved you. In her own way she loved you very much."

Brandon pushed things aside. A cardboard carton of Christmas decorations. A vase with a block of foam in it. The metal box was back there and he took it down, noted that the top was wiped clean of dust. Nessa put it where it wasn't easily reached, but that didn't stop her.

He put the box down on the coffee table, opened it. There were Social Security papers, a registration for a car his grandfather had sold twenty years before, a folded life insurance policy. Brandon opened it; it paid $10,000, enough for the burial. Tucked underneath it all was a manila folder. Printed on the tab were the words, "Nikki's things."

He took it out, sat down in his grandmother's chair, opened the folder. Tiny snapshots fell out on his lap. School portraits.

His mother in third grade, unruly curly hair tied back, a mischievous glint in her eye, a smile like she was about to laugh. Another photo, junior high, the woman beginning to emerge. Cheekbones higher, hair billowing loose, a bemused expression like she'd already seen through the charade. A snapshot from high school: Nikki at the beach with her friends. Guys flexing their muscles, Nikki with her hand over her mouth in mock amazement. Nikki in a bikini, lean and tanned, the guys jostling for her attention.

Nikki and Brandon, a tiny baby. She was holding him awkwardly, a girl who had never played with dolls. She had always been like that, never quite sure what to do with him or how. Three years old, he'd sensed the relief she felt when she was free of him.

And then she was gone.

But if she'd lived, he thought, if she knew him now, it would be different. They'd be friends, tell each other funny stories. Nessa didn't talk a lot about Nikki, but she did say Brandon's mom had been a joker, smiled her way through school, grinned her way into restaurant and bar jobs, always ended up with a bunch of friends, every week off doing something, usually leaving Brandon at home.

More photos. Nikki and Brandon, at two, with some guy who had Brandon on his shoulders. Brandon had no idea who it was. Brandon and Nikki and Nessa in front of a Christmas tree, Brandon kneeling by a new red dump truck, a yellow backhoe. They were gone now, lost in one of their moves from apartment to apartment, old boyfriend to new boyfriend. All of it lost. Nikki, too.

Under the pictures, the clippings: the *Portland Press Herald*, the *Charleston Post*, a yellowed chronicle of diminishing hopes. Sailboat overdue, sailed south from Portland .... Caribbean-bound boat missing ... Portland Woman Among Those Feared Lost at Sea ... Sailboat Sighted Was Not *Black Magic* ... Fears Realized as Life Vest Found ... Coast Guard Calls Off Search for *Black Magic* Survivors.

Brandon read them all: October 8, 1989, the alarm sent out when Nikki didn't call; October 9, *Black Magic* reported last seen resupplying in Charleston, September 23, October 12, the Coast Guard searching thousands of square miles; October 17, just five miles off of the South Carolina coast, a fishing boat picking up a cushion, and the life jacket with *Black Magic* written on it in marker; October 30, Nessa holding out hope, having read about sailors who survived for weeks and months in a lifeboat. *Black Magic* was equipped with a life raft.

And through all of the stories, this: authorities had only identified two of the crew; Marshall Dean III, 29, of Santa Cruz, California, the owner of the boat, and Nikki Blake, 23, of Portland, Maine. The *Press Herald* added this:

Blake is the daughter of Mrs. Vanessa Blake of Portland and the late Dr. Luther Blake, a local physician who died in 1981. Vanessa Blake said her daughter had gone along for what was to have been for her a one-way trip to the Caribbean. At that point, Blake was to have flown back alone to Maine. Vanessa Blake said she had met the men on the crew only twice and did not know the boat's ultimate destination.

"Of course she was coming back," Mrs. Blake said of her daughter. "She has her little boy here. A job. She was just taking a break."

The boat reportedly arrived in Portland from Canada, after stopping at Halifax, Nova Scotia. U.S. Customs officials say they have no record that Black

Magic *put in at a port of entry as it crossed into the U.S., as required by law. It seemed unlikely that the sailors would have been unaware of that procedure, sources said.*

"They seemed to have sailed all over," said Maura Walters, who worked with Blake at the Seafarer, an Old Port bar. "Australia, Africa, the Azores— I'm not even sure where that is—they'd been everywhere."

Portland residents who met the sailors said locals only knew the newcomers by their nicknames: Ketch (identified as Dean), Timbo and Lucky.

But how lucky could he have been?

CHAPTER 14

Brandon laid the clippings back in the folder, put the rest of the stuff back in the box, and slid the box back onto the shelf. He listened at Nessa's door, heard her snoring softly. He walked to the kitchen and out the back door, locking it behind him. It was like a door had been cracked open that he thought was nailed shut.

Someone had come back from the dead, bringing all their baggage. And his.

The folder under his arm, walking down the dark driveway, Brandon made a mental note to try to find Maura Walters. The Wayfarer was long closed, but maybe she was around. Maybe she had been sort of close to Lucky, maybe he'd call her. If not, she still might know who he would look up in town.

Brandon dug for his keys, was almost to the truck. Reached for the door handle, felt something move behind him.

He turned, saw a man, a mask, a black bat, the guy sprinting toward him. Brandon put one hand on the edge of the pickup bed, started to vault over, felt the bat graze his foot, hit the truck bed. He was across the truck in a step, the guy coming around the back, moving fast. Brandon was off the truck, in mid-air for what seemed like forever, hit the pavement as the guy came around. Brandon skidded on sand, did a split, rolled as the guy came at him.

Trying to get away.

A blow to the hip, a jolt of pain. On his feet, one side numb, a stumble, a swish as the bat almost missed, clipped his shirt at the shoulder. The guy was on him and Brandon turned, rushed at him, got inside the swing, grabbed the bat arm with both hands. Thought of screaming, but nothing came out, just grunts, the guy cursing between clenched teeth.

Brandon took the forearm, both of them spinning now, the guy kneeing at Brandon's groin, wrapping the other arm around his neck. He squeezed and Brandon could feel the arm getting under his chin. He took a hand off the guy's bat arm, pushed the arm away from his neck.

Dropped his chin and sunk his teeth into the guy's arm.

A bellow, the guy writhing to get loose. The bat flailing, hitting Brandon's head, his neck, his shoulders. Glancing blows and Brandon kept pushing into the guy, remembered a self-defense brochure he'd seen at the S.O. For women. Stomp the tops of the assailant's feet. He did, pounding at them like he was stamping out a fire, the guy's work boots absorbing the blows. Brandon kicked back at the guy's shins, started to spin, the guy still on his neck but the grip loosening, the arm stretching out like they were figure skaters locked in a pirouette.

Brandon got both hands on the bat, jerked it, hit the guy in the back of the head with the handle. Heard the guy's breath burst out. Banged him again, and the guy shook loose, raised the bat.

And then a car, lights showing through the cedars. The guy swung, missed, ran.

"Hey," Brandon shouted, started after him, felt a jolt of pain in his hip and slowed, limping. The guy went right, through the deserted streets. Brandon was out in the road, running slowly. The guy was gone, rounding a corner, the sound of his footsteps fading.

Brandon stopped. He heard a car motor rev in the distance, knew he should have pulled the mask.

He told the South Portland cop this and the cop, a woman with a stern face and short-cropped hair, looked at him and frowned. "You're right. 'Cause this isn't much to go on. A big guy with a ski mask, work boots, a baseball bat, except he won't have the mask or the bat, or maybe the boots. That leaves us looking for a big guy."

"He had leather gloves on. Did I say that?"

"They'll be gone, too. Didn't say anything? Demand money? Try to get your wallet?"

"No. I wrestled with him for maybe thirty seconds. Hit him twice on the back of the head, but not very hard. And I bit him."

The cop brightened.

"Good for you. Break the skin?"

"Yeah. I kind of freaked out."

"Sure. That's okay. Most people would."

"I mean, I've never been just attacked like that. Just a couple of days ago was the first time I really—"

"Where was it?" the cop interrupted.

"Where was what?"

"The bite?"

"Oh. Lower right arm. Above the wrist."

She spoke into her shoulder mic, said the assault had occurred fifteen minutes prior, told the dispatcher the subject should show a bite wound to the right arm, possible injury to the back of his head.

Another patrol unit called in, said they'd take the Portland bridge. Brandon waited, then said he was taking a law enforcement class at the college.

She looked at him, whoop-tee-do.

"I was sort of threatened," Brandon said. He told her about the funeral parlor, Joel Fuller and his mom.

"You think it was this Fuller guy?"

"Way too big."

"Could have brought a friend. Called in a favor."

Brandon rubbed his hip, already feeling better.

"So if this was something to do with this fight on your ride-along, doesn't sound like they got even," the cop said.

Brandon shook his head.

"Yet," the woman cop said.

The folder was in the truck bed, the photos and papers scattered. Brandon collected them, brushing off dirt. He walked back into the house. Nessa was standing in the kitchen, red bathrobe on, hair flattened on one side, eyes wide.

"It's okay," Brandon said.

"What? What happened?"

"Somebody tried to jump me."

"Oh, my God," she said. "You mean, like mugged you?"

"Sort of. We wrestled around and he ran away."

"You're limping. Are you okay?"

"Fine. Just a little bump."

"What did they want? To rob you?"

"It never got that far."

"Druggies," Nessa said. "They're everywhere now. It's on the news."

"Police are looking for him."

"So he won't come back?"

"I don't think so."

If it was Fuller, he'd been following along, watching the house. In the code of retribution, maybe grandmothers and mothers were of equal value.

"I'll sleep on the couch, Nessa. Go back to bed."

It was a fitful night, dreams of someone chopping at his boat with an axe, Brandon stuffing rags in the holes to keep the water from pouring in. He awoke at 6:30, pulled on his jeans, made his way barefoot to the kitchen. Nessa was sitting at the table, holding a mug of tea.

"You're up early," Brandon said.

Nessa sipped, said, "I'm up late."

"You were up all night?"

"I was thinking."

"About Lucky?"

"About your mother. I've been wondering what she'd look like, trying to picture her. There was a show on TV, this computer thing where they can make you look old. They had a little boy and he'd been kidnapped when he was four and now he would be fifteen. And the computer did this thing and there he was." She sipped again, her face haggard and old. "So I was thinking I could send them a picture of Nikki and they could change it to what she looks like now. And we could maybe put it on television, on those shows about people who are missing."

Brandon sat down.

"Nessa," he said. "Nikki isn't missing. She's gone."

"We don't know," she snapped. "We just know she didn't come home."

"Oh, please, Nessa. Just because this guy supposedly shows up. It could have been somebody who just looked like him. It's been a long, long—"

"It was him. Like a ghost. Maybe there's a mother somewhere thinking *he's* gone forever, and here he is walking down the street in Portland, Maine."

"If his mother hasn't seen him in seventeen years, then he might as well be gone," Brandon said, "staying away all that time."

The thought of Nikki out there, abandoning him.

"No," Nessa said. "That's not true. I still need to see her. I need to talk to her. I need to hear her voice and see her. With what? Gray in her hair? Lines in her face?"

Her jaw clenched, her face went taut, her lips pressed like she was trying not to cry. She lifted her mug and it shook with her hand. She put it back down, closed her eyes.

"I just need to know if she's alive," she said. "I just need to know that."

Her eyes opened.

"Don't you, Brandon? Don't you need to know?"

He hesitated, a near lifetime of bitterness and resentment swirling to the surface. And then he choked it down.

"Of course," he said.

CHAPTER 15

A fresh morning, the mist burning off the harbor early, the water calm, the wakes of outgoing boats long and sweeping like tails on exotic birds. Brandon drove across the bridge, the attack of the night before made even more surreal by the day, beautiful, full of promise.

Maybe it was just some nut, thought he'd knock him down with the bat, grab his wallet. As Nessa said, there were druggies everywhere now.

Pretty to think so. He took out his cell and called.

He was rolling up to the marina when she answered.

"Hey," Brandon said.

"Hey yourself," Mia said. "Up early."

"Did I wake you?"

"No, I just got back from a run."

"Nice day for it," Brandon said.

"Beautiful."

"Most days like this, I'd go for a row."

"But not today?"

"I've got something I need to do. And I was just wondering. I could use some help and I thought maybe—"

"What kind of help?" Mia said.

"Asking questions."

"Questions about what?" Mia said.

"Finding a guy," Brandon said.

"What guy is that?"

"I'll tell you. There's a diner. Milk Street, off Middle."

"When?"

"A half-hour?"

"Okay, what should I wear?"

"For clothes?"

"Yeah," Mia said. "Who are we asking these questions of? If it's some fancy lawyer, I dress one way. If it's some lobsterman—"

"Look nice," Brandon said. "You know, maybe a little—"

"A little what?"

"Pretty."

"A little pretty? Thanks a lot."

And then he was out of the truck, on the way to the boat. He didn't notice the white van slowing out on the street. On its side was illegible lettering sprayed over, dull gray filler around the rusting rear fenders. It coasted to a stop on the shoulder.

"Well, look at that," Fuller said, peering out through mirrored aviators under the visor of a black baseball cap, both shoplifted at the dollar store in the strip mall down the road. "Our boy belongs to the freakin' yacht club."

"So we knock him around and send him swimming," Kelvin said, rubbing his arm, red welts showed in the crescent of a bite mark.

"You think small. This guy hangs out here, we don't give him a beat down. We milk him like a goddamn cow."

They had parked on the edge of the lot, the back of the van facing the marina, mirrors adjusted so they could see the boats. Ten minutes passed since Fuller had spoken, the thing about the cow. Kelvin had been puzzled at first, then figured that it had to do with squeezing money out of the guy, not any sort of bodily fluids.

"How you gonna do that?" Kelvin said. "Guy didn't exactly roll over."

"It's all about pressure points," Fuller said, used to the way Kelvin thought, the weird timing.

"The old lady?" Kelvin said.

"You're not half as dumb as you look."

"You gonna threaten to burn her house down?" Kelvin said. "That worked real good that one time."

"Don't know," Fuller said. "I feel like this one is just unfolding, like maybe we better sit back and watch."

"You can watch. I'm going home."

Fuller took a long drag on his cigarette, flicked it out on the sidewalk.

"Speaking of home, I need a place to stay. Camper still out there in the back woods?"

Kelvin nodded hesitantly, knowing what Crystal would say if Joel came back.

"Okay with you? Or you gotta get permission from the boss?"

"No, it's fine," Kelvin said. "But I ain't been down there since you left. Probably mice and—"

"You know what they called me in third grade?" Fuller said, something stirred up by the gleaming boats, the silvery masts, and tinkling rigging, the unfathomable amount of money it all cost.

Kelvin took a drag on his cigarette, shook his head.

"Cootie. You know why?"

"Nope."

"'Cause I had lice. Bitch nurse, picking through my head like a god-damn baboon, tells the teacher right in front of everybody. Whispers in this loud voice. They all laugh, run to the other side of the room."

"Fuck them," Kelvin said.

"I get home and I tell Ma and she tells the old man to get off his ass, fix the furnace, there's no hot water so nobody wants to take a bath. 'Now the kid's got bugs.' "

He lit another cigarette, the smoke reflecting in the glasses.

"So he drags me by the arm out into the garage, pours gasoline on a rag, and scrubs my head with it."

"Nobody light a match," Kelvin said.

"I'm screaming and yelling, practically passing out 'cause of the fucking fumes. Old man's got his hand clamped on my forehead, squeezing so hard I felt like he was gonna bust my skull. I'm squirming and finally he takes the rag hand and hauls off and smacks me in the face."

"Huh."

"So now I'm bleeding *and* he's scrubbing gas into my head, calling me a worthless little bastard, filthy little shit."

"Wasn't your fault."

"I'll never amount to anything, he doesn't know why he even had me, I'm just there to make his life miserable, just like my mother."

He paused. Took a swallow of beer and reached for another cigarette. Smiled coldly.

"Drags me back in and turns on the shower, ice fucking cold, shoves me under, still in my clothes, my sneakers on. My only sneakers. My mother's screaming, 'Get him outta here, you'll stink up the whole house.' The old man scrubbing my head with soap, my nose still bleeding like a faucet so the water is getting these pink drips in it. I remember that."

"Huh," Kelvin said.

"Next morning I gotta go to school, my sneakers still fucking squishin', my head still stinking like gas, everybody laughing, saying, 'Cooties, Coo-ties.' The teacher makes me sit by myself by the open window."

He paused.

"Recess that day I busted a fourth-grader's nose. Buddy comes to help him and I knock out his front tooth."

Fuller sucked on his cigarette, nodded toward the yacht harbor.

"Guy here is gonna make us some serious cash," he said. "And soon as he does, I'm gonna get some people off my ass. I'm gonna buy a new truck, something fresh, none of this rusted-out crap. Drive out to the cemetery in my new ride, the leather and the CD and the eight-speaker fucking stereo, and have a few drinks."

He smiled contentedly.

And then I'm gonna take a nice long piss on the old man's grave."

Fuller held his hand out to Kelvin, half of a high five.

"You in or what?" he said.

"Me? I don't know. I mean, what's it gonna involve?"

"Yes or no. That's what it involves."

Kelvin thought of Crystal, screaming at him about letting Destinee sleep too long, not letting her sleep long enough, not getting the kid's butt clean when he changed the diaper. Let her change the goddamn diaper. What did he look like?

"How much we talking?"

"You saw the house. You see all these goddamn sailboats. These kinda people got money to burn," Fuller said.

Kelvin looked out at the boats, cabin cruisers with blacked-out windows and sailboats with masts high as telephone poles. See what Crystal said when he came home with a pocket full of hundred-dollar bills, said, "Go ahead. Pay off the goddamn Visa. Stop your goddamn whining."

"Whatever it takes," Kelvin said.

Fuller reached over, they bumped knuckles. Sat back and smoked.

"You know what's funny?" Fuller said.

Kelvin sure as hell didn't.

"If my grandmother hadn't kicked off, and Sylvia hadn't decided to smack her sister-in-law, and the pussy jail deputy hadn't called for back-up, we never woulda been sitting here."

He took a drag on his cigarette, watched the mirror. "Goddamn interesting how things work out," Fuller said, murmuring to himself now. "This guy ain't never gonna know what hit him."

CHAPTER 16

It wasn't really a diner, more like a café decorated to look like one, hip people sitting at the booth in the window, walking up and down on the cobblestone street outside. Brandon waited, sitting in the truck. People passed, mostly young, mostly good looking, Brandon scanning them for Lucky, looking up at the mirror just in time to see the Saab pass behind him. He turned, watched as Mia drove halfway up the block, pulled into a space and parked. He saw her emerge from the line of cars, head down the brick sidewalk.

A denim skirt and tangerine sweater. Heeled sandals and sunglasses. A pretty little package, Brandon thought. Who could say no to her?

"Hey," she said. "The man of mystery."

"Hey," he said. "You look very nice."

"All dressed up. Need a place to go."

He opened the door to the diner and they went in, guys looking up at Mia, the waitress hurrying by, saying, "Sit anywhere."

They did, at the back in the corner, away from the other diners. They sat, ordered coffee from the speeding waitress, Mia looking right at him as they waited. He took her hand.

"You remember?"

He smiled. "Every single moment."

The waitress came back, put two mugs down, cream and sugar in metal containers.

"I guess I needed to talk, Mia," Brandon said.

"I'm listening."

He looked at her, the pale blue eyes so intense they seemed to glow.

"It's a long story."

"I like your long stories," she said.

Mia smiled, squeezed his hand. And he began, starting with the guy at Nessa's house.

"The prisoner from the funeral," Mia said.

"This guy was much bigger," Brandon said.

"His big brother. Are you okay?"

"A little sore, but fine."

"Do you think he'll come back?"

"Be pressing his luck."

"Wouldn't be the first time. That's why he was in jail."

"Probably right."

"But what else? The rest of the story."

The waitress came back, holding a notepad. She asked what they wanted, called them "folks." Brandon ordered eggs, home fries, toast. Mia ordered a muffin. The waitress poured more coffee and wheeled away.

Brandon sipped and began. The ride with Nessa, Nessa seeing Lucky's ghost. Up and down the streets, looking for Lucky and the woman.

"My God," Mia said. "Could it really be—"

"Him? I doubt it, but if you'd seen Nessa's face. It was total shock. Instantaneous."

"So what do we do?"

"Find him, if it's really him," Brandon said. "Find him before it's too late, he moves on."

"Why wouldn't he get in touch. Back then, I mean."

"I don't know."

Mia held the coffee mug with both hands.

"And why show up now? Here?"

She finally sipped.

"What's the statute of limitations?" Mia said.

"On not reporting that you're not dead? I don't know that it's a crime. Hindering an investigation?"

"What if you faked your death. For insurance," Mia said.

"Or to get cops off your trail," Brandon said.

"Or to get out of child support or a pile of debt or somebody who wanted to beat you up with a baseball bat."

"Or maybe," Brandon said, "he was just lucky."

It was Mia's idea, she'd seen it in a movie about a guy with amnesia. They copied the old picture at Kinko's, fanned out across that part of the city. Restaurants, the ones that were open, kitchen workers unloading produce. Shops, from antiques and handmade blouses to kites and specialty condoms.

Two hours of walking, talking, smiling at clerks. Mia was asked on two dates. A woman in a bakery gave Brandon a free scone. At a café, the woman behind the counter said, "Brandon Blake, where you been?"

"Around," Brandon said.

The woman, mid-twenties, dark-haired and dark-eyed, looked hard at Mia and said to Brandon, "Give me a call, Brand. I owe you a drink."

Outside, Brandon said, "She doesn't read and she's afraid of the water."

Tiring of the whole thing, they stopped in a wine shop on Middle Street, two birds with one stone. The woman behind the counter was pale with white-blonde hair and blood-red lipstick. She peered at the photo.

"Why do you want to know?" she said, without looking up.

Brandon's heart skipped.

"He's a friend of my family's from way, way back," Brandon said. "I heard he was in town and I haven't seen him in a long time. A friend of ours saw him in the Old Port last night, but by the time she stopped and went back, he was gone."

She looked at Brandon, eyes narrowing. Then at Mia.

"You need a better story," the woman said.

"It's true," Brandon said.

The woman looked at him. Gave her head a little shake.

Brandon grinned. Waited. Seconds passed. The woman looked at the picture more, holding it up. Her nails were painted blood red.

"Gray in his hair now. Other than that, sort of the same."

The heart again. Brandon smiled.

"So he was here?"

She handed Brandon the paper. "With a woman. Very, I don't know, striking. Foreign, I think. He knew his wine. Bought a bottle of Cabernet from South Africa. Nothing flashy, but very good. Some people just look for a pretty label."

"Just the one bottle?"

"Yes. He said they were walking."

"Did they say where they were going?"

"No. Went out the door, to the right."

"Did he leave a credit card slip or anything?"

"Paid cash. Told me to keep the change. The Cabernet was forty bucks, he gave me fifty."

"Did he say he'd come back?"

"No."

"Did the woman say much?"

"Looked at labels, waited for him. She had some shopping bags. Clothes or something. Said she was tired. She had an accent."

"Like what?"

"Russian or something, maybe? German? I don't know."

"She was tired?"

"He said, 'We'll walk back down.'"

"Down the hill to the harbor?"

"I don't know."

"And this was yesterday?" Brandon said.

"Oh, no," the woman said. "I was off yesterday. This was today. Like, fifteen minutes ago. If you go now, maybe you can catch him."

CHAPTER 17

"**She was tired?**" **Mia said,** as they started down the brick sidewalk.

"Right," he said. "And they had the wine and some bags. They'd go back to—"

"Their hotel," Mia said.

They looked up. Across Commercial Street, on the water. The Harbor-front Hyatt.

"They've got money, right?" Mia said.

It was hushed inside the lobby. Behind the counter, clerks bent over computer screens, discreetly tapping on keyboards. Brandon felt the crumpled photocopy in his pocket, knew the old-friend story wouldn't work here.

"She was right about the story," he said.

"We need one," Mia said.

"You're the writer," Brandon said.

Mia thought for a moment. Another.

"Stay here," she said.

Mia hurried back up the hill, around the corner, and down the block to the shop. The woman asked if they'd found their friends. Not yet, Mia said. She grabbed a bottle of Windy Hills California Merlot, a steal at $9.99.

Mia told the story.

"So go for it," Brandon said.

"You can."

"You're used to these places," he said, staring at the doorman, the smoked-glass entrance.

"You talk to wealthy people all the time," Mia said

"Only about boats," Brandon said.

They crossed the street, circled a black Town Car unloading luggage. Brandon veered off and Mia went inside, running a hand over her skirt, adjusting her sweater. Stepped up to the clerk, a thirty-ish woman with hair pulled back so tight it kept her from smiling. Her name plate said, "Gretchen R."

"Hi," Mia said.

"Can I help you?" the clerk said, her face a polite mask.

"I'm from Les Bouteilles, on Exchange Street."

No comment, the mask in place.

"It's a wine shop."

The woman nodded.

"And we just had customers, they left maybe a half-hour ago. They were headed back here and they left this bottle on the counter."

Mia held up the bag, the logo of grapes on a vine.

"You have their names?"

"No, but I can describe them."

"I'm afraid that—"

"Oh, okay. I just thought it was worth a shot. It's just that this is a very nice wine."

Mia leaned closer.

"Very, very nice."

"Oh."

The woman looked at the bag more closely.

"And I thought I'd save them searching for it, coming back up the hill."

"I know but—"

"And I have to tell you. My mother stayed here a couple of weeks ago. From the West Coast? Small woman? Dark hair? From Palo Alto?"

"We get—"

"Well, she just raved. The room. The view. The dining room. The service. She said she's stayed all over the world and this was one of the nicest hotels. I think she was going to e-mail the president of your company."

The woman's face melted slightly.

"We take customer service very seriously. In fact, we just got the Gold Shield Award. That's company wide, recognition that—"

"Well, you deserve it. My mom can be very picky, and she had nothing but good things to say. That's why I didn't want this couple to have to, you know, come all the way back down, up the street."

The woman looked down at the computer screen.

"He's about forty. On the short side. Very nice smile. Sort of boyish. She's taller, dark hair, very attractive. From eastern Europe or something. Maybe Russia or—"

"Oh, you mean—"

The woman caught herself. Tapped at the computer with a rouge-painted nail.

"So they are here?"

"Yes, but how 'bout I send it up."

"Oh, great," Mia said. "Thank you so much."

"No," the woman said. "Thank *you*."

She looked to her right, caught the eye of a bellman. Mia handed her the bag. The bellman, a young blonde guy, smiled at Mia. The woman handed him the bottle.

"Ten-seventeen," she said. "They forgot it at the shop."

He gave the bottle a pat.

"Careful," the woman said. "It's a very, very nice wine."

Mia smiled. The woman did, too. She was picturing another e-mail to the president, special service on her watch. She called the guy back, handed him her card.

"Put this inside," she said.

Mia thanked her, turned away. Walked quickly to the door, circled through. Brandon was outside, had been watching.

"Worked?"

"I missed my calling," Mia said. "I should have been a liar."

The doors opened. They stepped out. Ten-seventeen was to the left. They walked slowly down the hall, room-service dishes left on the floor outside doors like offerings. They listened. A television on in one room. No sound from the next two. Brandon went first.

Stopped.

"Listen," he whispered.

A door closing, a closet. A radio, except it wasn't playing music. Brandon heard the squawk of a boat captain, the robotic voice of the weather report. And then a woman's voice, saying, "I wouldn't drink this piss."

Russian, or close to it.

"Leave it for the maids," a man said.

"And I've really had enough of this place. How long are you going to screw around?"

Russian?

The guy answered, his voice more faint. "Chill. This isn't something you set up in an hour. I'm seeing someone at eleven."

The woman saying, "We did not come here to sit in a hotel room."

Then quiet.

"You knock," Brandon whispered. "Ask for him. If they don't open, go down and wait for me across the street."

He moved fifteen feet down the corridor, stepped into an alcove. From the pocket of his denim shirt, he took the photo—the real one, not the copy. He looked at it again, took a deep breath. Mia stepped up and knocked.

The room went silent. Then there was the almost imperceptible sound of someone moving across the carpet to the door. Mia smiled, as she sensed someone peeking through the peephole.

"Hello," she said. "I'm from the wine shop. I need to talk to Lucky."

Silence again. Then faint footsteps. No response.

Mia knocked again.

"Is Lucky there?" she said. "I think I made a mistake. Someone left a bottle of wine here?"

More movement behind the door, a soft shuffle. The door rocked slightly as someone leaned against it, probably Lucky looking through the peephole. Mia looked concerned.

"Are you there? Hello?"

They waited. There was murmuring behind the door.

"There's no one here by that name," the woman said, the accent clear now. "Sorry."

Mia turned away, went to the elevator. She waited, the bell dinged, doors opened, and she stepped in. The doors closed and Brandon listened. The corridor was quiet, the faint sound of televisions playing. Brandon stood in the alcove, waited.

Ten minutes. Twenty. A half-hour. A chambermaid came out of the elevator with a linen cart, but went the other way.

Forty minutes.

A rattle. A click. The door opening. It creaked faintly, then closed. Brandon heard the sound of footsteps coming toward him. He stepped out.

And there he was.

Grayer, like the wine clerk had said. But the same guy, the same round-cheeked boyish face. He looked at Brandon and nodded.

"Lucky," Brandon said, stepping in front of him as he started to pass.

"I beg your pardon?" the guy said.

He moved left. Brandon cut him off. He held up the photo.

"I'm Brandon Blake," he said, as Lucky peered at the picture, "Nikki was my mom."

Lucky stared at the photo, something registering in his eyes, a decision being made.

He smiled. Held out his hand and clasped Brandon's, first with the one hand, then with both, his palms callused, his grip strong.

"Nikki's son," he said, staring at Brandon, examining him. "Of course you are. You've got her eyes."

"We need to talk," Brandon said.

"Yes," Lucky said. "We certainly do."

And he squeezed Brandon on the forearm like he was a long lost friend, leaned closer, and gave him a hug.

How much you figure?" Kelvin said.

"That place?" Fuller said. "Three-hundred a night. More if you want to see the friggin' water."

"Jesus."

"Dude in jail stayed in a place like that after he scored some cash. Charged some old lady like fifteen grand to trim her trees. Got half in advance. Blew three grand in a week, hookers and booze and drugs. Got eleven months, but said it was worth every minute."

"Like to get that little blonde babe in one of those rooms. Case of Heineken, big soft bed, porn on the flat screen," Kelvin said. "How's this college guy rate, anyway?"

"Don't know," Fuller said, craning to watch through the mirror. "Dude's full of surprises. All good, too. He doesn't have the cash, sure as hell his buddies here will."

"Cash for what?" Kelvin said.

"You'll see."

Fuller kept his gaze on the mirror, said, "They're going back in."

"Huh," Kelvin said, playing Snake on his cell phone.

"You know what we need? We need another vehicle. Something different that he hasn't seen."

"To jump the guy again?"

"Kelv," Fuller said. "You are four steps behind."

CHAPTER 18

Lucky said his friend was cold, was taking a bath. But what if they had coffee. Met downstairs in an hour?

Brandon said that would be good, and went down the elevator. He crossed the lobby. Outside, he looked for Mia, spotted her in the doorway of a shop that sold fancy pots and pans. Mia saw him and left the shop entrance, walked to the corner and turned, out of sight of the hotel.

She turned. Brandon nodded.

"It's him," he said.

Mia hugged him, said, "Oh, my God. What did he say?"

"We're having coffee in an hour. Meet downstairs. That's what he said, anyway."

"What about the woman?"

"I think she's coming, too."

"Then why did she say he wasn't there?"

"I don't know."

A pause, then Brandon said, "You take the lobby, I'll take the side door."

"Okay. What about the garage?"

"It's valet parking. They bring them to you."

"So you don't trust him," Mia said.

"He seemed glad to see me, said I had my mother's eyes."

"Do you?" Mia said.

"Yes."

"So that much is true."

"He's one for one," Brandon said.

They waited, but saw no sign of Lucky making a run for it, of the woman slipping out the back. In an hour, Brandon and Mia met up in the lobby. A minute later, the elevator opened and Lucky and the friend stepped out.

Lucky waved, came across the lobby, the woman a step behind. They both were in black, the woman in the same slacks but with a black filmy top over a black camisole. Lucky in black jeans, a black cotton sweater over a black T-shirt. Mia said they looked like film producers, actors on the way to an interview. Brandon thought they looked like some of the boat owners he knew, a certain relaxed confidence.

Lucky turned, took the woman's arm, and brought her alongside him.

"Brandon, this is my fiancée, Irina."

"This is Mia," Brandon said. "My friend."

Hands touched. They exchanged hellos. Irina said Mia was a pretty name.

"And where are you from?" Mia said. "You don't sound like a Mainer."

"My first time here," Irina said. "It's a lovely city. I'm from Warsaw, originally. But then I met this guy."

She gave Lucky a squeeze. He smiled. She was striking. Mia was thinking that Irina's shoes were very expensive, her makeup was perfect, the ring on her left hand a big blue sapphire with diamonds.

"Let's go up," Lucky said. "There's a decent restaurant up top. Lovely view of the bay."

They stepped into the elevator, the four of them and a couple with a little boy, about five. The little boy was turned back toward Lucky and Irina, the couple in black. He was staring up.

"You look like ninjas," he said. "Do you beat people up?"

The parents shushed him, but Lucky said, "That's okay."

He bent down and said, "We are ninjas. But we're on vacation. Unless we see some bad guys."

The boy looked at him, wide-eyed. The dad picked him up. The elevator stopped and the door opened and closed.

"Lucky," Irina said, with a false scold. "You shouldn't."

They emerged on the twenty-second floor, crossed to the restaurant. The hostess brought them through the near-empty room to a table by the window, facing southeast. They stood for a minute gazing out at the view of Casco Bay, the islands showing on a blue-green sea, the surface of the bay all ripples and swirls, like wind-shaped desert sands.

"I'd pay just to come up here and stare," Lucky said.

"All laid out there, isn't it," Brandon said.

"Beautiful," Irina said. "Look at all these islands."

Brandon pointed. "Peaks, just to the left is Great Diamond. Behind that you can see Long and Cliff. Past Cliff is Jewell, but you can't really see it."

"You a sailor?" Lucky said.

"More a general boater," Brandon said.

"Brandon lives on a boat across the harbor," Mia said.

"Really," Lucky said. "Power or sail?"

"Power," Brandon said. "An old Chris-Craft. Wood."

"A purist," Lucky said.

"Boats, don't let them get going," Irina said to Mia. "Let's sit. I need my coffee."

They went to the table, still with a fifty-mile view. A waiter came and they ordered: espresso for Lucky, coffee for everyone else.

"A bad habit I developed in Rome," Lucky said.

"That and cigarettes," Irina said. "Everyone in Europe smokes. After living here, I go back, I can't stand it."

"So, Lucky," Brandon said, "was Rome before or after Maine?"

The table went quiet.

Well, Mia thought. He gets right down to it. Brandon watched Lucky, his expression turning somber.

"Yes, well, it was after. I think I owe you an explanation."

"Yeah," Brandon said. "I think you do."

A long pause, Irina's smile frozen in place.

"First of all," Lucky began, "I liked your mother very much."

He looked up from the table, met Brandon's gaze. "Nikki was a good person. So full of life, loved the ocean, the sun. Lived every day to the fullest. She was a good friend. I mean, we thought the world of her."

The coffee came, the espresso. They all sipped, eyes still on Lucky, holding his cup in two hands.

"It was her great adventure," he continued. "We'd crossed from Ireland, left from a place called Castletown Berre, this little fishing port way out in West Cork. Came across to Newfoundland, a little weather but no big problems. Spent a few days in St. Johns. Across and along the coast, down to Maine. Then we lost our engine. Threw a rod coming out of Northeast Harbor—better there than a thousand miles out in the Atlantic— so we came into Portland under sail, but *Black Magic* handled so well, a Hinckley Bermuda Forty. You know the boat?"

"Only by reputation," Brandon said.

"They got it all just right, like Hinckley usually does. Lovely, responsive boat. And stable, too. Perfectly balanced. Ketch inherited her from his uncle in California, sailed her all over the world."

"So from Northeast Harbor to Portland?"

"We called ahead for a mooring, got one out in front of DiMillo's Restaurant. So we arrive under sail, like I said, Ketch brings her into the harbor, wind out of the east. It was about eight, all of the people out there eating. Ketch took her through the harbor, rounded up, we dropped sail. The boat stopped like a golf ball falling into the cup. I reached the mooring with a boat hook. Just like that."

Another sip. Lucky gazed out at the view. Brandon caught Mia watching Irina. She was listening like she'd never heard this story before.

"Ketch, he was a pure sailor," Lucky said. "A natural."

"But that didn't help him," Brandon said.

"Nothing can, at a certain point. As you know, right? The ocean is a big, powerful thing. We're just little ants out there, living on a little skill and a lot of luck."

"So how did you meet Brandon's mom?" Mia said.

"Well," Lucky said, with a sympathetic look at Brandon. "Nikki was working in this bar on Commercial Street. The Wayfarer. A boat place, sailors and fishermen, mostly locals. We kind of camped out there while the motor was being rebuilt. In a day it was like we'd known Nikki all our lives."

Brandon remembered that about his mother, how she collected friends. The clerk at the hardware store, the ladies who knew Nessa, neighbors. A big smile, an openness. He could feel it now, though he couldn't explain.

"So we hung out, stayed at her place a couple of nights in the beginning, she had this roof deck. Sleeping bags spread out. Then we sublet this apartment on the wharf. Got into the partying, you know. We were young and the city was hopping and there was music and talk. Lots of talk."

The waiter came back, asked if they wanted pastry. Without looking at him, Irina said, "Yes, please bring the cart."

"So was there one of you who my mother was closest to?" Brandon said.

"You mean romantically? Well, I'd say she and Ketch really hit it off. He was a big, strong, handsome guy. A little older than us. He'd sailed all over the world. Lived for a couple of years in Cape Town, on the boat in the harbor. Malaysia, Indonesia. He was like something out of a movie, you know?"

"How did he support himself?" Mia said. "Boats like that cost a lot of money to keep up, don't they?"

"Oh, yeah. But we'd work when we put in somewhere. Cleaning fish, washing dishes."

"This guy Ketch washed dishes?" Brandon said.

"No, that was me and Timbo. Ketch, you know the same uncle who left him *Black Magic*? He left him a nice fat trust fund. He was always calling his bank in California, having them wire money."

"So he never had a job?" Irina said.

"He used to say his job was to keep the boat shipshape and live up to his uncle's expectations. Ketch said he was never going to grow up, not that way."

Brandon could picture his bartending mom falling for this tanned adventurer. He reached into his pocket and took out the photograph. Handed it over to Lucky.

"My God," he said, studying the photo. "There we all are."

And then Lucky's eyes began to moisten and he wiped at them with his fingers.

"I'm sorry. It's just that … that they were all good friends. And Brandon, I'm very sorry about your mom. How old were you? Four?"

Brandon nodded.

"Like that little boy in the elevator. Such a shame. Such a damned shame."

Irina reached over and patted Brandon's arm, the sapphire glinting in the morning sun. Brandon noticed that her arms and hands were strong looking, slightly out of place with her outfit.

"So where were you going from Portland?" Mia asked.

"Well, as Timbo used to say, it was time we commenced a wanderin'. So off we went. It was September, we thought we'd make our way south along the coast. Hurricane season and all. You don't want to get caught too far offshore.

"So our nominal destination was Key West, then maybe on to Aguadilla, on the west coast of Puerto Rico. Ketch had sailing friends who were gonna winter there and we thought we'd check it out."

Lucky paused. Looked up from the table to Brandon.

"But really, we didn't know. Nikki was going to go along for a couple of weeks, fly back from wherever we were at that point. I remember Ketch telling her, 'Don't fly back. We'll just fly Brandon down. No better place for a kid than a boat.'"

"And what did she say to that?" Brandon said.

"She said something like, 'I can't just leave my mother all alone.'" There was a long, uncomfortable pause. It was Mia who said, "So you got down to South Carolina?"

"Yeah, we made our way. Stopped in Provincetown. New York City, motored right up the Hudson. Your mother had never seen New York from the water. I remember her sitting on the foredeck, just looking up, amazed."

"It is a beautiful spectacle, New York at night," Irina said. "I remember the first time I saw it. It was like a whole city of sparkling castles."

"And then where?" Brandon said.

"A week to Charleston. Put in there to resupply for the rest of the trip. Only stayed three days."

He paused. Finished his espresso. There was no need to ask the question.

"When they left, I stayed behind. I met a woman in a bar. I thought I was in love. Not sure that was the case. Maybe I just wanted to do what Ketch had done, you know? Find the girl of my dreams."

"Is that what my mother was to him?" Brandon said.

"I think so," Lucky said. "I remember we were sailing between Cape

Cod and New York and we were both on watch, Nikki and Timbo sleeping. Ketch said, 'You never know when two souls will join.' He talked like that sometimes. Sounds weird, but it wasn't, coming from him. I think he was talking about your mom."

Another pause. Lucky looked out the window at the bay, spoke without turning back.

"So I leave the woman, big tearful goodbye. Get down to the dock, but Ketch has sailed. Always late, I guess Ketch decided to teach me a lesson. I walk out to the highway, start hitching down Route 17 for Beaufort 'cause Ketch said he was gonna put in there for a night, check out the history. Ketch loved the historical places."

"I like history," Brandon said.

"Hey, you would've hit it off with him. I mean I was pissed at him that day, but really a great guy. Interesting, always thinking. You'd be looking out at the ocean, cruising way offshore, and Ketch would say, 'You know how Galileo figured it out?'"

Irina looked impatient, like she didn't like where the story was going.

"Figured what out?" she said.

"That the earth revolved around the sun," Lucky said.

"How did he?" Mia said.

"I don't remember, but Ketch knew all about it. I think he loved sailing, loved being on the ocean, but mostly I think it gave him time to think."

"What did he talk to my mom about?" Brandon said. "I don't remember anyone saying she was much for history or that sort of thing."

"Oh, they'd kid back and forth. She made him laugh, kind of took him off his high horse 'cause he could be pretty serious sometimes. She'd imitate him, stand there by the wheel and stare off into the distance and say, 'Do you know why they call that bird a twit? Did you know the Figeroans could sail three thousand miles on a boat made of poison-ivy leaves?' We'd just crack up. Ketch would try not to, but he couldn't help it."

Brandon smiled. That sounded like the Nikki he knew. Nessa said it was impossible to stay mad at her when she was little, she was so funny.

Lucky took a deep breath.

"I figured I'd be there at the dock when they put in, jump on just like I missed the bus. So I hung out, but they didn't show up the next day. I stayed in this dive hotel, went down to the docks every day. Nothing the next day, either. Only about forty miles from Charleston to Beaufort."

Part of Brandon didn't want to hear it, this account of his mother's death. But he had to hear it, had to hear this, the closest thing to a witness.

"I wait. Another day goes by. That night I call the Coast Guard, report *Black Magic* as overdue. I'm thinking they must've changed their minds, blew on through. But then a fisherman reports picking up a life jacket off Kiawah Island. Then a chunk of the dinghy washes up, flotation attached to it. What I think happened is they went four, five miles offshore that first night, swung southwest, got hit by a freighter or a tanker. 'Cause there was no mayday, no nothing. That happens, you get hit at night."

Lucky paused. Looked at Brandon.

"There's no time."

The table was silent, the view of the bay paled in that moment.

"So what did you do?" Brandon said.

"I was in some bar when it came on the news. So I just started walking. Got a ride to the highway, hitched up to Columbia. South Carolina, I mean. Didn't matter where anybody was going, I just went there, too. Caught the I-20 and went west. Wanted to be as far from that ocean as I could get."

"Where'd you end up?" Mia said.

"Oh, jeez. Santa Fe, for a while. Then a little town called Jerome in the mountains in northern Arizona. Just hid out. Stayed drunk and stoned most of the time, completely numb. I mean, these were my best friends in the world. Your mom, too, in a way."

Lucky took a deep breath, let it out as a sigh. "I'm sorry, Brandon. I'm very, very sorry for your loss."

"Thanks," Brandon said.

"She was a great person, I can attest to that. Sweet and full of energy, like I said. And she was happy on that trip. Just effervescent."

Irina looked at Brandon, smiled.

"But now you're back," Brandon said.

"Love affair with the sea, I guess," Lucky said, giving a little snort. "Got in the investment business with these guys from Sedona. Didn't set foot on a boat for ten years. Then I met a woman—not Irina, sorry honey—and she talked me into getting out on the water again. We did a couple of bareboat charters in the Caribbean, out of St. Thomas. That ended, the relationship, I mean, but it got me back on the water. Now it's Irina's turn to get a taste of it. That's why we're here."

"You chartered a boat?" Mia said.

"Not yet. Just started looking."

"What are you looking to do?" Brandon said.

"Just mosey up the coast. Nice and easy, stay inshore where we can grab a mooring. A nice easy sail. Get some sun. Lobster and white wine at the end of the day."

"What size boat?"

"Bigger than two people need," Lucky said. "I want something forty, maybe a little bigger. Hey, who knows if we'll be talking by the time we get back. Might need some room."

He grinned at Irina. Tapped her arm.

"Just kidding, babe."

"I know of a boat that's available," Brandon said.

"You do?" Irina said.

"I work in a marina."

He pointed across the harbor to South Portland, masts showing like trees in a flooded forest.

"One of our owners has a 46-foot Condor he wants to charter out."

"Really," Lucky said.

"How long you want it?"

"A week to start. We have a good time, take it again, maybe."

"It's three thousand a week," Brandon said.

"Sounds reasonable," Lucky said. "Good boat?"

"Immaculate. Comfortable. Easy to handle. Come over, check it out."

"So this sailboat," Irina said. "Can we see it?"

"Sure," Brandon said. "Royal Point. Across the harbor."

He turned and pointed.

"We'll come," Irina said. "Maybe tomorrow."

"This is great," Lucky said. "It's sad and it's difficult, but I think maybe it was meant to be. I mean, what are the chances after all these years? That we would meet. I really think some things are predestined, don't you?"

Irina smiled first.

CHAPTER 19

Kelvin watched as Brandon and Mia left the hotel, crossed Commercial and headed up Milk Street to their car. As they moved up the block, Brandon took Mia's hand.

"College boy gonna get it on," Kelvin said, and he turned back to the window, peered into the lobby.

"Yeah, they were with this short dude and this wicked hot babe," he said into his phone. "Something out of a freakin' James Bond movie. . . . You see 'em now? I didn't know he was screwing her. . . . Uh-huh. . . . Money? I guess. High class, all mirrors and shit. . . . No, I'm looking for 'em now. . . . Must be staying here. Maybe their yacht's in fucking drydock or something. . . . They was here a second ago. Hang on."

Kelvin went through the revolving doors, walked through the lobby toward the elevators. The concierge watched from behind his lectern, ready to move if Kelvin got in an elevator, but Kelvin just turned around slowly like he was looking for someone, then started back for the doors the way he had come.

From behind a tall plant, Lucky and Irina watched.

"He was watching them," she said.

"What the hell would he want?" Lucky said.

"I don't know, but I get nervous when I have men in bad clothes following me," Irina said. "It's my upbringing. In Riga they watch the bank machines now. Lookouts call back to say who's coming with a wallet full of cash. Knock them off."

"That's what happens when you don't have police," Lucky said.

"It's Latvia," she said. "The robbers *are* the police."

"That's why your whole goddamn country wants to come here, Irina. Most of our cops aren't criminals."

"Yeah, right," she said softly, still watching the big man as he crossed the sidewalk to the street. "And the streets are paved with gold."

They headed along the waterfront toward the bridge, Mia sitting in the middle of the truck seat, pretty legs crossed, her hand on Brandon's shoulder.

"What do you think of him?" Brandon said.

"Nice enough, I guess. He seems like he was fond of your mom."

"What do you think of him running away?"

"I don't know," Mia said. "What would he have been able to say if he'd stayed? They were gone. Lucky talking about them wasn't going to bring them back."

"I know. I can see wanting to avoid the whole thing. The questions. The reporters."

"The families," Mia said. "I can see not wanting to have to be with all those families."

They were quiet. To their left were the jumbled wharves where big fishing boats put in: stocky draggers, tugs that moved the tankers and barges in and out. Mia looked over, saw the yachts in the basin on the far side of the harbor.

"All his friends killed," Brandon said. "I can see why he'd go as far from the water as he could get."

They were circling up onto the bridge, and Brandon looked out onto the bay. He pictured their boat leaving, people watching from the dock as it grew smaller and finally disappeared into the haze.

"Survivor's guilt," Brandon said. "Soldiers have it. People who survive plane crashes. But I thought he was alright. Trying hard, but it was awkward, the way we found them."

"I don't quite get her," Mia said. "They don't seem to go together."

"She seemed like she should be running something. A big business."

"Those were eight-hundred-dollar shoes."

"Won't be wearing those on the boat," Brandon said.

"She just doesn't seem like the boat type. Maybe lying around in a bikini on the deck in the Bahamas."

"Won't be doing that on this trip."

"It's cold," Mia said, "and there's nothing but woods and rocks and no casinos or dancing or shopping."

"Maybe they'll just anchor and—"

Brandon caught himself, but it was too late. Mia smiled.

"Go down in the cabin and screw?" she said.

"Well, yeah."

"You know what?" Mia said. "I didn't feel any of that, either. That chemistry."

"She was very good looking," Brandon said.

"It was all for show. She didn't feel anything for him."

"You could tell that?"

"Women can sense that sort of thing," Mia said. "It was like they worked together, this is a business trip."

"She took his hand once at the table."

"Not like she meant it."

She let her hand fall from his shoulder as they came off the bridge. It rested on his thigh and he took his hand off the steering wheel and took hers. She squeezed.

"Do you mean it?" Brandon said.

"Yeah," Mia said. "I do."

They circled through the car dealers and strip malls, out onto the coast road. The houses thinned and soon they were winding along, woods on the left, an occasional driveway threading through the trees. Brandon slowed the truck, turned in between two granite posts, rusty chain hanging from one. The driveway was gravel and Brandon went left and right around the deeper ruts, and then the trees gave way to a clearing with a stone cottage tucked off to the left. The house faced an overgrown field, a band of brush separating it from the shoreline, beyond which was the bay.

Mia took it in. The field that perhaps once had been lawn. The grass mown close to the house, the gardens a mix of perennials and wildflowers. The garage door was open and an old red Volvo was parked inside, one taillight broken.

Brandon parked behind the Volvo. He led the way into the garage, past a line of wine bottles, liter-size jugs that had held grocery-store Chardonnay. Brandon paused at the inside door, said, "There's something you should know about my grandmother."

Mia put her hand on his arm and said, "It's okay."

He opened the door and went inside and Mia followed. They were in the kitchen, dark wood and avocado refrigerator and stove, glass jars that held coffee, sugar and flour. Mia smelled cigarettes, saw another wine bottle on the counter, dirty glasses in the sink, a loaf of dark bread, the bag half open. Brandon picked it up, twisted the bag closed, and put the bread in the cupboard. He whisked the glasses into the dishwasher, wet a cloth and ran it over the counter and the butcher-block table.

I get it now, Mia thought. The child of an alcoholic.

From another room, Mia heard the radio. It was opera, the Sunday afternoon broadcast from the Met. Brandon called, "Nessa. We've got company."

There was a clunk from deeper in the house, a thud, someone getting up. Mia heard a door close, and Brandon took her by the arm and led her down a hallway. It opened to a living room with big windows facing the ocean. There was a leather couch with the imprint of a body, like someone had been vaporized. On the side table was a wine glass, half full, and a cigarette burning in a glass ashtray.

"Nessa?" Brandon said.

There was a rustle behind them and Nessa appeared. She was slight and still faintly pretty, wearing black stirrup pants and a red sweater, gray hair tucked behind a black headband, black driving moccasins. Mia could tell that she'd just put on makeup, her lips reddened like her cheeks, less grandmother than faded movie star.

Nessa smiled, stepped unsteadily toward Mia, and held out her hand.

"This is Mia," Brandon said. "She's a good friend of mine."

"Mia, dear, I'm Vanessa Blake," Nessa said.

Her voice had a deep smoker's rasp, her eyes dark like Brandon's, but unfocused. Mia smelled the sweet odor of wine, a whiff of perfume. It was almost eleven o'clock.

"So good to meet you, Mrs. Blake," she said, holding the small, cold hand. "You have a lovely home. What a beautiful view."

"Nessa, please. And yes, the ocean certainly is unavoidable here," Nessa said, giving it a passing glance. "Have you had lunch?"

"Thanks, but we're all set," Brandon said. "We just had coffee in town."

"Oh, you kids and your Starbucks," Nessa said. "Let me just make some sandwiches, nothing fancy. You'll have to forgive me, Mia. I haven't had a chance to do groceries, I've been so busy with—"

Brandon put a hand on her shoulder.

"Nessa," he said. "We just saw Lucky."

Her mouth fell open and Mia could see the line of salmon pink lip where the lipstick hadn't covered. Nessa took a step back, then another, and Brandon eased her down onto the couch.

"Lucky," she said softly. "Are you sure? Like you said, it could have been someone else, it's been so many years."

"Nessa," Brandon said, leaning over her. "We had coffee. We talked to him."

Nessa didn't look at either of them, just stared somewhere in between.

"My God," she said. "He is alive."

"He said he was never on the boat, Nessa," Brandon said, sitting on the edge of the couch beside her. "He said he was late and they left without him. He tried to catch up, but they never made it to the next port."

"But," Nessa said, her voice weak, the rasp nearly gone. "Where has he been? All these years. Where did he go?"

"Out west," Brandon said. "Santa Fe and Arizona. He said he had to get away from the ocean."

She looked at Brandon, leaned over for the wine glass on the table. She hurried it to her mouth and look a long swallow, then clutched the glass in both hands. Mia sat down on the edge of a chair.

"Why is he back?" Nessa said.

There was an edge of panic in her voice.

"He's with a woman. He's showing her the Maine coast. They want to charter a boat."

"They're staying?" Nessa said. "But I thought you said he had to get away from the ocean."

"I guess he got over that," Mia said. "He's been sailing in the Caribbean."

"What does he do now?" Nessa said. "Does he have a job?"

"He said he made money in investments," Brandon said. "He seems pretty well off."

"His friend is from Poland," Mia said.

"I think he really liked Nikki," Brandon said. "He said she was so happy on the trip. He said she was—what was the word?"

"Effervescent," Mia said.

"Mia's a writer," Brandon said.

"What does he want?" Nessa said.

"He said he'd like to come see you."

"No," Nessa spat.

She shook her head.

"I don't want to see him."

"Okay," Brandon said. "I just thought, because he seemed to like her so much, that maybe you'd—"

"No, it's all over. You're right. It was a long time ago and she's gone and seeing him, it's just . . . it's just too much."

Another gulp of wine, the glass empty now, Nessa searching for the bottle, spotting it on the floor at the end of the couch. She leaned for it, started to fall, and Brandon caught her automatically, pulled her back up.

"Why didn't he call? Why all this time?" Nessa said, half to herself. "Oh, it just brings it all back, and we're over it, we've locked it away, you know? Locked it away in a box."

She looked at Mia.

"That's what they say to do, dear. Do your grieving, then lock it away. Don't keep getting it out and looking at it."

She reached for the wine again, caught the bottle this time, brought it up and filled her glass, a half-inch from the brim.

"You sure I can't get you anything? A glass of wine? A cup of—"

"No, thank you," Mia said.

"I don't usually have wine before lunch," Nessa said, "but this is very upsetting."

Another quick sip. Brandon looked at her, this sad little woman, not over it at all. And he wondered, for the millionth time, why she couldn't heal, why she couldn't accept that she'd lost her daughter in an accident at sea.

"So I'm glad you talked to him," Nessa said. "If it helps you, that's fine.

But I just can't. So he can take his goddamn boat and sail away, just like they did before. You know—"

She paused. Another swallow, the rim of the glass pink from her lipstick, like blood had been spilled.

"I went down to the dock and said goodbye. I did. And everything was fine. They were putting things on the boat. And Nikki was so happy, such a big smile. Oh, she had a beautiful smile. Just melted you. And do you remember? How she took you around the boat? You remember that, don't you, Brandon?"

"Sure, Nessa," Brandon said, also for the millionth time. "I do."

"She showed you the cabins and let you hold the big wheel thing. You must remember that."

"Sure."

"She hugged us and she was going to be back soon, just a couple of weeks. It was no problem, it was a happy time. And they all seemed so fun, those fellows."

Nessa paused, the film playing on in her head. And then some imagined scene overcame her and she started to cry, heaving breaths from deep in her chest, wringing tears that ran down her cheeks like something squeezed from a sponge. She moaned, said, "Oh, God. Oh, God. Oh, my beautiful baby. Oh, my God."

Brandon took her by her shoulder and said, "It's okay. It's okay." Mia got out of her chair and crouched in front of Nessa, put a hand on her knee, and rubbed. Nessa was sobbing, saying, "Oh, I'm sorry, I'm so sorry."

Mia said, "It's okay, Mrs. Blake. It's good to cry."

"After my husband died, Nikki was all I had. And when he was alive, he was never here, never home, always working. Used to say to him, 'Don't you even *want* to be here? Don't you *want* to be with me?'"

Mia was thinking, oh, what was it like to grow up with this.

She said, "Oh, Mrs. Blake, I know. My dad, he's in court, he's flying to meetings, taking depositions. Never home. And then my mom, when he does come home, one time she said to me, 'He's like a stranger.'"

Nessa focused, looking at Mia.

"Oh, you sweet dear. So you understand. I know you do, She was everything and then I couldn't lose her, too. So I—"

She paused, catching herself, turning to Brandon. "So you'll tell him? You'll tell him I can't see him?"

"Sure, Nessa," Brandon said. "I'll tell him."

She took another drink of wine, and this time looked between them, beyond them, like she was staring into a portal into the past.

"He was gone," Nessa said. "He can't just come back."

CHAPTER 20

Kelvin and Crystal at dinner, Crystal badgering him about money, saying they couldn't wait for the settlement because what if it didn't come? Kelvin saying if he got a job the company would find out and that would be the end of it, after all he'd been through.

She said it didn't look to her like he'd been through much, and if he wasn't working he could maybe come home and babysit Destinee instead of hanging out with that asshole Joel Fuller. And maybe she could get the hell out of the house sometime, and not just to go to work at the store, go to her mother's to pick up the baby, come home and do laundry, make supper, pick up all the goddamn crap he left behind him everywhere he went.

"I can't take this," Kelvin said, and he got up from the couch, where they were eating and watching TV, pitched his burrito in the sink, took the last two cans of Bud out of the refrigerator, and slammed his way out.

"So go," Crystal shouted, the baby starting to cry, standing up with her fists clenched on the side of her playpen like she was in jail, screaming at the guards.

"We don't need you. You're worthless. Worthless piece of shit!"

Kelvin squealed the tires on the edge of the road, opened the beer as the car accelerated, swallowed a third of it, flipped open his phone, muttering "goddamn bitch," as he punched in the number.

Fuller answered, a crunching sound in the background.

"Where are you?" Kelvin said.

"The old lady's house," Fuller said. "Doing some recon."

"I'm coming into town."

"Take the hotel."

"They still there?"

"Good chance. Went down to the harbor this afternoon, looked at some boats. Went back at four, I figure they hopped in the sack, about now they'll be getting hungry. Or at least thirsty."

"If they come out, what you want me to do?"

"Just sit on 'em, go where they go. I got a feel on this one. I mean, it takes one to know one, and everything about them says they're working something."

"Watching me watch the college kid and the babe?"

"And me watching them, reading their minds. Who is this guy? What's he want? He gonna try to rip us off?"

"What if they see me?"

"That's okay. We'll let 'em sweat a little, see how they react. There's a pot a gold here somewhere, I'm telling you."

"I ain't going home," Kelvin said.

"Stay with me in the camper."

"Yeah, but we'll have to park and walk. Crystal's loaded for fucking bear."

"Something new and different. I'll call you in an hour."

Kelvin rolled down Congress, put the Caprice in a pay lot, took the tag off another car and stuck it under his wiper. He walked down the hill, with the couples coming out of happy hours, lurching against each other, laughing about nothing. Opposite the hotel, he found a doorway, leaned and watched the revolving doors. He was watching this one couple, the guy in little flip flops, a pink shirt, tan shorts, the girl with him an ass to kill for. Wondering what the hell she saw in that dipshit, Kelvin spat, shook his head—and saw Blake's buddies leaving the hotel.

They started up the block, the woman in high heels, the guy holding her arm on the brick sidewalk. Kelvin waited for them to draw ahead, then started down the block after them. They paused at the corner, glanced back, and walked on.

A right at the corner, Kelvin behind them. Down to Commercial, where they paused, looked around, crossed over, trotting to beat the traffic. They turned down one of the wharves, fancy restaurants down there with the fishing stuff, bars where rich kids went. At a place called Scrimshaw they paused, turned. The woman seemed mad about something, the guy giving it right back to her before they walked in.

"Hey, if you don't want her, I'll take her," Kelvin said to himself, walked up to the door, and stepped in.

It was dark, bigger than it looked from the outside, tables to one side, bar at the other, tanks full of bright-colored fish, and a deck out the back. There were people knotted here and there, waitresses in jeans and little black tank tops moving through the crowd with trays of beers, glasses of wine. Kelvin slipped between them, found a seat at the bar next to where the waitresses picked up the drinks.

He ordered a Bud, slapped a twenty on the bar as it came. The bartender, a guy who looked like some fashion model, was watching soccer on the

TV. Figured, Kelvin thought. He turned and scooped up the bill. The beer was half gone before the guy brought back the change.

"Thirsty, huh?" the kid said.

You try living with her, Kelvin thought, and looked around. It took him a minute, but he spotted them, sitting at a table against the wall near where a door opened onto a deck. The deck looked out on the water, masts sticking up from boats below. The woman still looked unhappy, frowned as she sipped a glass of wine. The guy looked away from her, poured some fancy pussy beer into a glass.

So everybody's in the same boat, Kelvin thought. Rich guy with his supermodel ain't getting any, either.

He finished the Bud, nodded to the bartender for another. It came and Kelvin held the cool bottle in his hand, the beer inside him already calming him down. He'd just looked away for a minute, checking out a table full of women who looked like secretaries or something, when the guy walked by him and out the door.

Kelvin turned. She still was there, staring into her glass. He could see a long leg in black pants, a high heel hooked around the rung of the stool. He looked back at the door.

Nothing.

He looked back at her, watched the door for five minutes, then another five. The woman finished her wine, tipping the glass back, and got up from the table, started across the room toward him. He figured she was going to follow numbnuts there, slug it out at the hotel.

As she passed him, she stopped. Turned. Stepped up to the bar next to him and said softly, "You look familiar."

Kelvin turned and looked over at her, taking her in, trying to think what the hell to say to that. "Yeah?" he said.

"We've met somewhere."

She looked at him closely, like there might be clues on his face. Kelvin smiled, amazed that this was happening, thinking only way back in his mind that this might be a problem, that he might look familiar because he'd been following her around.

"I know you from someplace," she said. "Buy me a Stolli on the rocks with a twist and come sit."

She walked back to the table by the wall, Kelvin looking after her, heart racing. He looked around like there might be a camera on him, some kind of joke. But nobody was paying him any attention, or her. He motioned to the fashion model, said Stolli on the rocks with a twist.

"Lime or lemon?" the guy said.

Kelvin guessed. "Lemon," he said. "Two of 'em. Doubles."

The guy turned, hooked the bottle off the shelf. Kelvin looked over to see if she still was there, like she was a winning lottery ticket that he had to cash in quick. He dug in his pocket for another twenty, paid for the two drinks, in brimming cold glasses. Grabbing his change, he started walking over. Told himself not to seem too ready to jump her bones.

But man oh, man, he thought. She's gorgeous.

Five inches taller than Crystal, half as wide. He put one drink down on the table in front of her and she looked up and smiled, dark deer eyes looking up at him. He pulled the chair out and sat.

"What is with you Americans?" she said, smiling at him, her luscious mouth. "Budweiser and watery wine. Sometimes you need a real drink, don't you think?"

She held out her glass and they clinked and she said, "Salud."

"Here's to ya," Kelvin said. He sipped the vodka, felt it kick him all the way down, fought off the urge to cough. She sipped, never lost the smile.

"So what's your name?" she said.

"Kelvin," he said. "What's yours?"

"Angelika," she said. "With a K."

"You're not from around here," Kelvin said.

"No, I'm from Poland."

"Huh," Kelvin said, not sure what to add, not having thought of Poland in a long time, maybe not ever. He strained to come up with something, finally he said, "They make sausages there, don't they?"

The smile flickered.

"Oh, yes. Great sausage like you've never tasted. We like to eat in Poland. Eat and drink and talk. Those are the only three things to do in Poland. Well, there's one more." She winked.

Whoa, Kelvin thought. He smiled back, looked across the room, took a big swallow of Stolli. No kick this time, just a warm glow. He looked back at her.

"What do people do in the winter here, Kevin?"

"It's Kelvin. I don't now. Ride snowmobiles. Ice fish a little."

"Don't you get cold?"

"You find ways to stay warm," he said, holding up his glass.

She turned, looked out at the crowd. He stole a glance at her, the full lips and high cheekbones, the hard sleekness above her breasts, the cleavage showing above some black lacy shirt underneath a jean jacket. He'd seen women like this, but only on television.

"Where'd your friend go?" he said.

"My friend," she said. She gave a little snort. "That's one way of putting it."

"Your husband?"

"God, no. He's my boyfriend—or he was."

"Had a little argument?" Kelvin said, trying to keep the elation out of his voice.

"Argument, yes. Little, no. He wants to control me, he wants to be the boss of me, but I can't live like that. I am an independent woman. I throw off his leash."

This leash thing conjured up an image Kelvin had to fight off if he was to navigate this conversation.

"Well, maybe things will get better when you both cool down," he said, trying to sound concerned.

"You're right. It's hot in here," she said. "Let's go outside."

She got up without waiting for an answer, took her bag and her drink, slipped through the crowd, and went out the door to the deck. Kelvin followed, turned right, waited for his eyes to adjust to the dark. She was standing against the rail, one foot up, beautiful butt to him, looking down at the boats. He walked over, took his place beside her, and looked down, too.

She held her glass out again, touched his, took a swallow of vodka.

"In my country, everyone drinks vodka. Some people drink it all the time."

"I couldn't get anything done if I drank vodka all day."

"What do you do?"

"I work construction. I build things."

"Like big fancy American houses?"

"No, more like additions, garages."

"Really," she said, like a garage was more of a feat than a bank tower. "I can't hammer a nail."

"Well, you don't have to. You just hire somebody like me."

Kelvin smiled, confident now. He could do this.

"Hey," she said. "You want to smoke a little ganja?"

He felt like pinching himself, make sure he hadn't died and gone to heaven.

"Wouldn't say no," Kelvin said. "But in this country, they frown on smoking dope in public."

"Then we'll go for a walk," she said.

She walked to a gate that led off the deck to the side of the building. He followed, and they walked side by side down an alley, onto the street fifty feet from the bar entrance. She went left, down the wharf. He walked alongside her, hyperaware of her legs, the tap of her shoes, the angle of her jaw. She was like a racehorse walking up to the gate, sleek and strong.

"You come over here right from Poland?" Kelvin said.

"No, went to New York first. I met my friend there."

"He Polish, too?"

"Oh, no," she said, as they stepped off the sidewalk, around stacked fish crates, moving deeper into the darkened end of the wharf. "He's American. We got hooked up through an agency."

"No shit," Kelvin said. "You're one of those mail-order brides?"

He'd seen it on the Internet. Meet beautiful Russian women, sign up here. All of 'em looked like swimsuit models, until you got past the home page, saw lots of Crystals, except they actually tried to look soft and nice. He knew how long that would last.

Her smiled thinned. "I prefer to think of it as online dating," she said.

"Well, whatever you call it, he lucked out," Kelvin said. "Big time."

"Thank you. He doesn't think so," she said. "He thinks I'm difficult. He thought because I came from Poland and I wanted to meet an American man, I would do everything he said."

"Screw that," Kelvin said, coming to her defense. "You're not a servant."

"Right," she said. "Hey, I should've hooked up with you."

It was dark now, the little light emanating from a spotlight on the next wharf, the lights out on the harbor. She stepped off the roadway, led the way alongside a dock and behind a shed.

"Easy," Kelvin said. "You could fall."

She stepped around a fishing net mounded on the wooden slats of the wharf. Stopped beyond it, where the walkway ended at the water. Leaning against the shack, she dug in her purse, came up with the joint and a lighter. She flicked the flame alive, blew out the flame on the lighted end. Handed it to him.

Kelvin looked at her, put the joint to his mouth, and inhaled deeply. Suppressed the urge to cough, then slowly exhaled.

"Jesus," he said. "Where'd that come from?"

"Afghanistan," she said. "Go ahead. You hold it for a minute."

He did, smoked it halfway down. When he handed it back, she watched him, took a tiny puff, blew the smoke out. Handed it back. Kelvin thought of Fuller, how he sure made the wrong choice of assignment, crawling around in the bushes outside the old lady's house while Kelvin partied with James Bond's girlfriend.

The marijuana was powerful, packed a rush that went right to his head, like it was more than pot, maybe dust or meth or something. They stood for a few minutes, Kelvin smoking, handing the joint to her so she could hand it back. She said something about the beautiful lights, Kelvin not seeing what was beautiful about them but agreeing so as not to spoil the mood. He wondered if she'd get a hotel room for them, in the morning tell that New York butthead to kiss off. He looked at the shape of her buttocks, the line of her breasts. Couldn't wait to touch her, wanted to know what it would feel like to hold a woman like that.

More about the lights, then she was talking about being homesick for Poland, her sisters. Kelvin put his hand on her shoulder, consoling her, hoping to slide his hand downward. The dope was starting to work and her voice was humming in his ears, the lights starting to sparkle like fireworks.

And then she said, "I know where I know you from."

Kelvin waited, not knowing the answer to that one.

"The hotel. You were watching them."

"What?" he said, shifting gears, slamming on the brakes, the roaring buzz all of a sudden not such a good thing.

"You were watching the guy and the girl. And then after they left, you came in and you were looking for us."

"Not me," Kelvin said. "What hotel?"

"Why were you watching them?"

She turned to him, put her hands on his shoulders, and drew herself close. He could smell her perfume, the vodka. Her lips were parted, so close he could taste them. She smiled.

"Is there something I should know about them? You can tell me, Kelvin." She ran her hand over his neck. "Help me out here. I'm new to this country. I need a friend, someone I can trust."

Kelvin felt like an unlikely candidate for that job, but the way she looked at him, pressing up against him now, her chest jutting into his, he had to say, "If I tell you, will you keep it between us?"

She touched a long, beautiful finger to her juicy lips.

"Okay, it's like this. We're not really watching you. And it's not really me," he said. "I'm just kind of helping out. This buddy of mine, he just got out of jail? That guy, the one with the blonde girl? He punched my buddy's mother. The guy was with the cops."

He felt her stiffen.

"I thought he was in university."

"He is. Went with a cop on a freakin' field trip or something. They go to this funeral and my buddy's there from jail, it's his grandmother who's dead. Then there's a fight."

"At this funeral?"

"Different people in the family, they don't get along so good. So they get wrestling around and this guy comes with the cops to break it up and just smacks Joel's mom in the mouth."

"The poor woman," she said.

"Oh, she can handle herself. She's one tough bitch. But she got whacked really good. So my buddy, Joel is his name, he decides to find the guy, even things up."

"Uh-huh," she said, her voice husky.

"But then we find out this college boy is into yachts and shit and Joel, he's always looking for an angle, he decides maybe we can work something, get even some other way. It's only fair."

"Of course it is. So what was this Joel in jail for?"

"Ah, Joel's always in some sort of scrape, always got something going, too. Buying, selling, dealing. Joel says he's in the leverage business. He gets stuff on people." He held up the stub of the joint. "Joel's like a coyote, you know what I'm saying? He's always got his eyes open, nose down, sniffing for an opportunity."

"An entrepreneur," she said.

"Yeah. I mean, you should see these boats over there where this Blake guy lives. You gotta have bucks to run with those dogs, you know what I mean? So we're just scoping the kid out, looking for the opening. His girlfriend's along for the ride, I guess. So then they meet up with you guys and my buddy Joel, he's watching, he's asking himself, 'Who are these people? Where do they fit?' He's one smart son of a bitch, always thinking."

"I'm sure," she said.

He was really buzzing now, his voice a million miles away, coming out of somebody else's mouth.

"So you're staying in that hotel, that's big bucks, too. We're just getting a lay of the land. Between us, Joel's more interested in the grandmother, you know? She lives in this fucking big house on the ocean, place is kinda beat, but that's when you find wads of cash under the mattress, some old lady living with a hundred friggin' cats. I mean, it's an opportunity. We wanted to know what you were up to here, where you came from, just because we don't know how that fits into the total picture. It's nothing personal."

Suddenly he pulled her close, tried to kiss her. She moved left and he missed her lips, got a brush of cheek and a little ear. Damn, she smelled good.

She pushed him away, but she smiled. "Oh, you are frisky, aren't you? So what did you little detectives find out?"

Kelvin smiled, tried to kiss her again, got a little lip this time, soft and succulent. He tried to focus.

"We know you rented a car, it has Georgia plates. We know you pay cash for everything, which Joel thought was interesting. We didn't know you just got here from Poland. Joel thought maybe you was drug dealers or something, 'cause of the cash thing."

She gave a little giggle.

"I know," he said. "He comes up with some wild shit sometimes. I think he's got too much time on his hands, sitting in a jail cell, you know? He's like that, though. Wants to know everything, once he sets his teeth into something, he's like a fucking pitbull, he don't let go."

Kelvin reached for her and this time she didn't resist. He pulled her closer, smelled her perfume, ran a hand across her cheek. "You know you're gorgeous," he said.

"Oh, you're a sweetheart," she said.

Her left hand was on his shoulder, and he leaned in, tilted his head to kiss her lips. Felt her fumble for something in her bag, had a vision of a condom coming out.

Felt something sharp pressed against his neck.

He froze.

"You know what that is, Kelvin?" she said, her voice a purr, the point pressing harder.

"No," he said, not moving.

"It's an ice pick except much, much sharper. It's pressed against your jugular vein. You know what happens if I stick it in?"

Kelvin didn't answer, the two of them in each other's arms.

"All of your blood pumps out until there's none left. You know what you are then?"

"Dead?" Kelvin said.

"Smart boy. And I hope this Joel chap is smart, too."

"Oh, he is."

"Good, because my friend, the guy you've been watching me with? He's a businessman. Very successful. And he likes his privacy. He's got a huge thing about that. He would be very unhappy if I told him you were watching us. Or our friends."

"Uh-huh."

"And you know what else?"

She pressed the point harder and Kelvin felt something warm like blood.

"He's got a foul temper. I mean, he makes me look like Mother Teresa."

"Gotcha."

"He just wants to be left alone, enjoy his holiday."

"Right," Kelvin said.

"So you tell Joel. What's his last name?"

The point pressed, definitely drawing blood now.

"Fuller."

"You're not making that up?"

"No," Kelvin said quickly, starting to shake his head, then stopping as the pick jabbed deeper.

"Well, tell Joel Fuller to find some other mark," she said. "You're way out of your league. Where I come from guys like you are stepped on like bugs."

"Right," Kelvin said.

"And you know what, Kelvin? If I didn't like you, I'd tell my friend. And that's what I'll do if I ever see you again."

And she dropped both hands and shoved him backward. One, two, three steps and over the edge, a long, tumbling, windmilling fall down into the black, cold water. As he surfaced and thrashed, coughing up sea water, Kelvin heard her heels tapping on the boards of the dock.

CHAPTER 21

They were in the car, driving through the dark in West Falmouth, the heat on full. Kelvin sat with his boots off, socks pressed to the heater vent, feeling like he was wrapped in soggy bread.

"I ain't gonna fit in your clothes," he said.

"They're sweats," Fuller said. "They'll stretch."

"I'd like to get my hands on that bitch right now, she wouldn't know what hit her."

Fuller smiled, leaned back in the driver's seat. "Tell me again," he said. "What she said."

Kelvin did, starting with when Angelika saying he looked familiar, ending with the plunge.

Fuller grinned, tossed his head back, and chuckled.

"I'm glad you're enjoying this," Kelvin said.

"Dude, I was right. I was so fucking right. An ice pick. A sharpened ice pick, stuck in your neck. Dude, she's a freakin' pro. She's a goddamn professional criminal."

"So are you," Kelvin said, feeling the bloody welt on his neck. "Big shit."

"Oh, but these people ain't doing paving scams on old ladies."

"Those worked pretty good."

"Man, you don't see it, do you? These guys are big time. Mister Smooth there spends more money in a week then you and me see in a year. And if that's just setting up the deal, then what the hell you think the payout is on the other end?"

"Pretty big," Kelvin said.

"Mega," Fuller said.

The car slowed on the dark country road. The lights picked out a running shoe nailed to a tree, the reflective part shining. Fuller braked, pulled off onto a track, just two tire ruts leading into the tall grass. He drove in fifty feet and stopped, and they got out. Kelvin sat on the seat to pull on his sodden boots.

"Maybe they steal these fancy boats," he said.

"No, too hard to unload. And the people who want 'em don't need to buy stolen ones because they're rich already or they wouldn't be wanting one to begin with."

"Maybe not."

Kelvin got his boots on, didn't lace them. Feet squishing, he followed through the brush, walked down a path deeper into the woods.

"No, they're here for something," Fuller said, "and they don't want us poking our noses in. I'll tell ya, he finds out she stuck you, shoved you in the fucking water, he's gonna be pissed. He's gonna say, 'Don't you get it? You just told them what they wanted to know.'"

"She did?" Kelvin said.

"She told us that whatever it is, it's worth sticking you to protect."

"I coulda fucking drowned."

"Right. And you know what that means."

"Payback's a bitch," Kelvin said.

"No," Fuller said. "It tells us we just stepped in the shit. Megabucks, dude. Big time."

He turned and held up his fist. They touched knuckles.

"Are we good," Fuller said, "or what?"

Ten o'clock, clear skies, a cool dry wind out of the northwest at fifteen to 20 knots. They were on the dock, greetings done, sizing each other up. Lucky was in jeans and pale gray Nikes, a black Patagonia vest. Irina was dressed in khakis and trainers, a turtleneck and a handknit sweater. Doc Lynch, wearing a bright yellow jacket with the name of a medical conference embroidered on the breast, pointed to *Ocean Swell*, riding on a mooring in the midst of the marina fleet.

"My baby," he said. "My soon-to-be ex said, 'Sometimes I feel like that boat's more important than me.' I said, 'What do you mean, sometimes?'"

Lucky grinned. "Spoken like a sailor, man," he said. "I can tell you the name of every boat I've spent any time with, but the women—just kidding!" He looked at Irina and she shook her head in mock dismay.

Brandon started the Whaler, the marina launch. Mia took a place beside him at the helm and the other three stepped aboard, took hold of a rail. Lucky gave them a shove from the float and they motored off, threading through the boats.

Mia watched Irina, standing by Lucky, both of them leaning on the bow rail. It was cold, the wind cutting, but they stayed apart, six inches of daylight between them.

Brandon brought the launch alongside *Ocean Swell*, held the throttle as Doc stepped aboard. He held out his hand to Irina and she climbed over the lifeline and jumped heavily into the cockpit. Lucky stepped across easily, and Mia followed, held the Whaler as Brandon shut the motor off, moved to the bow, took a line, and stepped aboard. As the Whaler drifted, he tied it to the sailboat's stern.

Lucky looked up into the big boat's rigging.

"Harken roller furler?" he said.

"Can go all season, never touch a sail," Doc said.

"Ever sailed her single-handed?" Lucky said.

"Sure," Doc said. "My wife, every time we went out it was single-handed. Seriously, she's very predictable. The boat, I mean. Not my wife. Autopilot is new. Not the fastest in light wind, but a very easy sailer. And getting in and out under power, very manageable. Don't know where you're going, but there's some tricky little entrances on the Maine coast."

Lucky touched the polished brass.

"Trickiest entrance I remember was just north of Mombassa, in Kenya," he said. "Don't even try go into the harbor there. Bitch to anchor and the locals have very sticky fingers. Couple of Aussies we were cruising with showed us this little harbor twenty miles north, Mtwapa Creek. You gotta make the run in through a break in a reef at the peak of an incoming high tide. Then hit this hard dog-leg channel just right."

"Really," Doc said. "What were you doing over there?"

"Delivery crew," Lucky said. "Young and footloose. Took a boat from the Red Sea all the way down the east coast of Africa to Cape Town. Now there's a gorgeous spot."

They smiled, moved to get underway. Charmed, Doc hustled, the two of them working like they'd sailed together for years. Doc took the helm, powered up to take the slack off the mooring. Brandon worked the Whaler up the side of the sailboat, ready to tie it on. Lucky unhooked, handed the mooring line to Brandon. He cleated it onto the Whaler and Doc steered them clear. Under a cold spring sky, they eased out of the moorings, toward the big bridge.

They swung back, pointed the bow toward the harbor mouth. Lucky moved to the starboard side, looked to Doc and he nodded. Lucky cranked the winch and the mainsail unfurled, snapping in the wind and pulling the boom out. The boat heeled, Doc shut off the motor, and in that first moment of quiet, ears adjusting to the sound of the wind ruffling the sail, the near-silent rush of the water sliding over the hull, the slap of the chop, the gurgle of the wake, they smiled.

Irina said to Mia, "Let's see below."

They went down, leaving the three men on deck. Brandon stood aside, watched Doc and Lucky as they peered up at the sail. They were posturing for each other, a game Brandon could never play. Maybe not growing up with a dad, a brother, another guy.

They ran a long tack that cleared the point, then came about, the big boat doing a neat pirouette, Lucky watching as the sail filled again. Portland was on the port side, receding as *Ocean Swell* skimmed toward open water. Early in the season, there were a few lobster boats working, a ferry headed for the islands, a big cruiser coming in.

"Time for the jib?" Lucky said, and he moved forward, unfurled the sail, adjusted the sheets. Doc called, "Lucky, come take the helm."

He did, the two men peering upward at the sails like old buddies. The boat was doing seven knots, and Lucky said, "She's got more in her than this." Doc cranked and Lucky adjusted course and the boat heeled, the starboard gunwale dipping to the water. Lucky whooped.

"Now we're sailing," he said.

They ran out to Peaks Island, easing off as Doc showed Lucky the electronics: radar, state-of-the-art GPS with chart plotter. The boat slept seven, had a two-burner stove, head with a shower and pressurized hot and cold water, the linens all supplied. Irina and Mia came up and Doc met Irina's gaze. She nodded to him, said, "It's perfect."

"A lot of boat for the two of you," Doc said.

"You can never have too much boat," Lucky said, a hint of sadness that Brandon caught. If *Black Magic* had been sixty feet would they have survived?

They brought the boat around south of Peaks, began beating back into the harbor. The wind had picked up and the boat was heeled, Brandon, Mia, and Irina pressed against the windward side of the cockpit, Irina hanging on tight. Doc and Lucky sailed wordlessly, the boat snapping about, settling into each new tack like a swimmer following a turn.

"Do you want to take the helm?" Doc said to Irina.

She smiled and shook her head. "My job is usually dinner and drinks," she said.

Soon-to-be-divorced Doc melted at her accent. "Hey, if we didn't already all have plans, I'd say the whole bunch of us should take a week and go for a cruise," Doc said.

Irina gave him a quick smile and looked out at the city skyline.

They came up to the mooring under sail—Lucky at the helm, Doc dropping the sails as the boat turned into the wind. They eased *Ocean Swell* alongside the Whaler like a limo driver parking at a curb. Brandon uncleated the pennant, and Mia reached a line from the launch and held on. Brandon made the mooring line fast, moved back to the cockpit.

"Well, my friend," Doc was telling Lucky. "I guess you passed the test with flying colors. Love to have a few drinks sometime, hear more about your travels. I've never sailed her south of Block Island."

"We'll do that, Doc, my friend" Lucky said. "And she's a beautiful boat."

"Yes, it's really lovely," Irina said.

"Yeah, we'll treat her right. Just gunkhole our way up the coast," Lucky said. "Putter along. Irina's never seen Camden or Bar Harbor."

"But I don't know if I want you making the boat tip way over like that," Irina said, smiling coquettishly.

"Don't worry, darling," Lucky said. "Just the boys getting a little carried away."

As Brandon eased the Whaler back to the stern, and Mia climbed aboard, Doc and Lucky were finalizing the deal. Brandon had seen this done before, usually with a check. Lucky took a thick wallet from his vest pocket and unzipped it.

"You don't mind cash?"

Doc shook his head, thinking this was money his wife would never see, eyes fixed on Lucky's hands as he began peeling bills off of a roll.

"There's the three thousand for the week, and here's five for the deposit," he said.

He zipped the wallet shut, moved toward the launch. When they were all in, Brandon headed for the dock, Mia beside him on the helm seat, Irina and Lucky in the bow. Mia was watching them closely as Brandon wended a route between the moored boats. They eased up to the marina dock, and it was Mia who moved around, stepped off, and held the boat steady so the others could get off.

They did, Irina wavering as she found her balance on dry land. Doc and Lucky shook hands again, Doc slapping Lucky on the back in a sort of man-hug.

"You'll have a good time," Doc said. "And you get caught in fog, you got the radar. And just let that GPS show you the way. Hell, that thing'll navigate for you."

"I've always gone by compass and watch and a little feel," Lucky said. "You know what's worse than fog? Snow. Did a late season crossing from France once, forty-six-foot Cambria. Real nice boat, headed to Newport. We're coming down the coast of Newfoundland. You couldn't see six feet."

"Snow," Doc said. "Now there's one I haven't tried, eh Brandon? We do have to have some drinks when you get back."

Another back slap and Doc walked to an inflatable, stepped in, and started the outboard, headed back out to button *Ocean Swell* up for the night. Lucky and Irina walked with Brandon and Mia up to the office, paused, and Lucky said, "So you live aboard? Where's your boat?"

"Beyond that point," Brandon said. "It's a small cruiser."

"Well, let's see it," Lucky said, giving him a tap on the shoulder, and turned. They trooped off down the boardwalk, Lucky pointing out a Tashiba cutter, saying he sailed one like it from Ireland to Portugal, riding the winds south. Irina was looking straight ahead, Lucky talking about the boats, saying *Ocean Swell* was a very nice boat, not a great one.

"I know," Brandon said. "She's got kind of a homely stern."

"Could have been me, new to her, but feels a little like you're dragging something when the boat comes about," Lucky said.

"Was *Black Magic* a great boat?" Brandon said.

Lucky paused, said, "Yeah. Great design—a Hinckley Bermuda Forty. Classic. But that particular boat had heart and character, too."

"Some boats just have it," Brandon said.

"Exactly right. And she did. Everything in balance."

"Ketch knew that?"

"Oh, yeah."

"Was he a good sailor?" Brandon said.

"A natural. I learned a lot from him."

"But he couldn't save them."

Lucky hesitated.

"It's the ocean," he said softly. "It's like life. Sometimes you're up against forces beyond your control."

They walked in silence for a couple of minutes, and then they were at *Bay Witch,* and Irina said, "What a cute boat. It's so cozy."

"A Chris-Craft," Brandon said. "It's old."

"It's really nice inside," Mia said.

Lucky turned to Brandon and said, "*Bay Witch.* This was Nikki's boat."

Brandon hesitated, said, "You've been on board?"

"Once. Except the boat was across the way in Portland. You weren't there."

"Were you all partying?" Brandon said.

"Probably."

"Then I was with Nessa. My grandmother."

"I remember Nessa," Lucky said. "How is she?"

Brandon hesitated. "Okay," he said.

"She was a sweetheart," Lucky said. "Tell her I'll come by when we get back."

Brandon was about to say Nessa wasn't well, she didn't have company much, but Lucky had taken Brandon's hand. He gave it a quick, firm shake, said thanks for connecting them with Doc and the boat. He bussed Mia on the cheek, said it was so nice to make new friends. Irina said, "Bye now, guys," and they turned and headed off down the walk.

Brandon and Mia stood watching, his arm linked through hers, just the two of them now.

"What do you think?" Brandon said.

"He's a real charmer," Mia said. "But they definitely aren't sleeping together."

"And she doesn't like boats," he said.

"She'd rather go to Saks," Mia said.

"He's a good sailor, but it's still a big boat to handle by yourself," Brandon said. "Especially if you don't have to."

"Maybe he does have to," she said.

"Get back on the horse, you mean?"

"His friends all drowned," Mia said. "That's got to be hard."

"I don't know," Brandon said. "When we were out there and he had the rail in the water, all that sail up—it didn't seem hard at all."

CHAPTER 22

It was a little Pearson centerboard sloop called *Sea Pony*, the old couple who owned it just back from their winter place in Georgia and in no hurry to get out on the bay in the cold of early June. On the job list on the board in the office, the little sloop had been queued up behind the boats of squeaky-wheel owners who started calling before the snow melted. But the priority boats were in the water. *Sea Pony*'s time had come.

Brandon had left Mia curled up in a chair on the foredeck of *Bay Witch*, turned to the sun. She was writing in a notebook, and covered the page with her hand when Brandon got close.

"What?" he said.

"It's like a painting," she said. "The artist doesn't let anybody see it until it's done."

He leaned down and kissed her forehead. She smiled, kept her hands on the page. Between her fingers and on the edges, Brandon saw a few words: something about sea and sky, something about a liar. He turned and made his way back to the stern and went to work.

He was thinking about her writing as he stood in the back of the yard beside *Sea Pony*, a grinder in his hands, respirator mask over his nose and mouth. She divided her time between reality and fiction, a couple of times telling him about people, their upbringing, going on for a while before Brandon figured out it was part of a story.

He smiled thinking about it, this odd contradiction. Mia studied real things to death, why people did what they did, what the sky looked like, and then turned it into something completely made up.

Tucked between a big lobster yacht and an Alden ketch, he was sanding off loose bottom paint, stuff laced with chemicals that killed barnacles and the other things that liked to fasten on a floating boat like it was an island. Brandon had ear protectors on, iPod buds under those. Tupac.

A tap from behind. Brandon lowered the grinder, reached for his mask—and froze.

The guy smiled. Held up his hand, gave a little wave. There was another guy beside him, much bigger, hands tucked inside the pockets of a gray sweatshirt. Brandon pulled his ear protectors off.

"Hey, Brandon," the small guy said. He smiled like they were old friends.

Brandon nodded.

"You remember me?"

"Sure. Fuller."

"I'm out now."

"They let you go or you escape?"

"I just had a couple of days left. That's why I didn't go crazy on you at the funeral."

"Is that right?"

"Yeah. I unload on you, I'm in for another six months."

"Good thinking," Brandon said.

"Thanks," Fuller said. "They teach us that inside. Had a program, it took all one morning: 'Considering the consequences of your actions.'"

"Well, I guess it worked," Brandon said.

Brandon put the heavy grinder down on the ground, kicked the air hose away from his feet. The movement caused the other guy to flinch, the hands coming part way out of the pockets. The hands went back in. Brandon crossed his arms on his chest.

"You look familiar," he said to the big guy.

"He's a friend of mine."

"Keeping you company?"

"Something like that," Fuller said. "We work together sometimes."

"Oh, yeah? Doing what?"

Fuller shrugged.

"This 'n that."

"You working now or are you on a break?" Brandon said.

"I'm working," Fuller said. "He's on the bench, waiting to see if he'll be needed."

"Well, I've got to get this bottom painted, so you got something to say, go ahead and say it. Unless you want to help."

"My ma," Fuller said. "She—"

"It was an accident. I was just trying to get her to stop choking me."

"That's not what she said. She said the plainclothes cop looked right at her, said, 'How you like this, bitch?'"

Brandon shook his head, smiled. "Never happened."

"You're not calling my mother a liar are you?"

An ominous edge to his voice. The big guy watching the two of them like it was a tennis match, his eyes tick-tocking back and forth.

"Not calling her anything. I just know what happened. I just wanted to shake her off me. She was gouging at my face."

"It's her face all busted up," Fuller said.

"So get a lawyer," Brandon said. "Sue the city."

"I ain't got time for that. I figure I'll just get the money from you."

"I'm not paying you ten cents."

"I was thinking more like ten thousand," Fuller said.

"You can think ten million, if you want. Thinking it isn't gonna make it come true."

"College boy, hanging out at the yacht club. You can get the money from mommy and daddy."

"Ten bucks an hour to scrape and paint. And it's a boatyard, not a yacht club."

Fuller smiled. "Don't know much about boats. When I was growing up, we didn't have money for fucking toys."

Brandon didn't answer. It threw the big guy off his rhythm and he looked from Fuller to Brandon and back to Fuller again.

"Didn't have a house on the ocean. Didn't sit out on the porch and sip my little glass of wine and watch the boats go by."

Brandon stared, now knowing what this was about.

Fuller looked away. "Must be lonely, these old ladies living all by themselves in these big houses. Noises at night. House creaking and animals scuffling around outside the window. Or at least you think they're animals. Hard to know unless you get up and go out and check."

"What are you trying to say? 'Cause I'm busy."

"Just saying it must be hard for old people living alone. My ma, she lives with my sister and her whiney-ass brats. She ain't ever alone."

"Is that right?"

"When you're all by yourself, what are you gonna do? Call the cops, but what if the phones ain't working? Then what?"

Brandon didn't answer.

"There's accidents. Old people is always falling. My grandmother, you met her at the funeral. She fell, busted her hip, took her four hours to crawl from the bathroom to the phone. Two weeks later she dies of friggin' pneumonia. It's all interconnected, you know what I'm saying?"

Brandon stared, said nothing.

"Fires. Burglars. Fucking drugs are everywhere now. Junkies look for old people, figure they got a house full of meds. I know this one guy, breaks into this house, cleans out this old bastard's medicine chest. Ends up selling the shit for like five grand."

"Jackpot," the big guy said.

"He speaks," Brandon said.

The big guy scowled, like he was unsure whether he was being made fun of. Brandon bent and picked up the grinder, the air hose hissing.

"Same thing goes for these people who live on boats," Fuller said. "Creep me out, stuck down in there."

"You don't have to worry about that, do you," Brandon said.

"Well, maybe if you don't worry about yourself, you should worry about that girl you're with, little thing out here all alone. You gotta look out for—"

Brandon moved a step closer, grinder in front of him.

"You go near her, I'll kill you. You go near my grandmother, I'll kill you." He glanced at the big guy. "I'll kill you, too."

"Whoa," Fuller said, holding up his hands. "We're just chatting and you're getting all wound up. We came here to talk about compensation for injuries?"

"You talked, now go."

"But to sum up," Fuller said, borrowing another one from his lawyer. "We got an offer on the table."

"No deal," Brandon said.

"Well, you think about it. You think about everything I said. You ain't got the cash on hand, you might consider a personal loan. That guy with the sweet Rusky babe, maybe. He's fucking loaded. Ten grand to him is nothing."

"Get the hell out of here."

"Dude, you got a bad attitude. Easy on the caffeine, dude."

Kelvin laughed. Fuller looked at him, grinned. "Try to have a conversation, the guy flips out."

Kelvin shook his head.

"Stay away from everybody I know," Brandon said.

Fuller took two steps back, said, "You can have this place. I wouldn't want to live here. I mean, sleeping on a boat? Know what I'd always be worrying about? If it sinks and you're asleep. And what if there's a fire? Tanks fulla gas and shit, all these fumes. Thing would go up—" He held up his right hand and snapped his fingers. "—like that."

CHAPTER 23

The notebook was spilled onto the deck at Mia's feet. Her head was back, her mouth was open, her delicate throat bared to the sun and the cool harbor breeze. A lock of hair had spilled over her forehead.

Brandon bent to wake her, let his hand hover over her shoulder. He paused, looked at her, then turned and looked back toward the shoreline. Where were they watching from? Would they know every time he left her alone? Would they wait until no one was aboard, sneak on with a gas can and—

"What?" Mia said, jerking awake. Fright in her eyes, then a groggy smile as she relaxed, pulled herself up. "You scared me, baby," she said. "I know it's silly but I was having this dream. I was—"

"It's not silly," Brandon said. "I don't think you should stay here."

Her smile fell away.

"What?"

"I had visitors," Brandon said, and he lowered himself and squatted next to her chair. He told her who had come and what they had said.

"So now that they know where I live," he said.

"Where are *you* going?" Mia said.

"I think I'm going to Nessa's."

"Oh."

"You'd be better off at your apartment."

"I'd worry. How 'bout you come stay with me."

"That doesn't solve anything. They'd just follow us there."

"I can stay with Nessa, then. That way you don't have to just sit there and wait. We'll take turns."

Brandon considered that. Looked out on a tug moving upriver under the bridge, its wake rising behind it like a serpent. All of it, the normal things, seemed slightly unreal now. Reality was Fuller, his cold grin, the eyes that never smiled.

103

"They won't try anything, not yet," Brandon said. "They hurt somebody, they've played their hand. If it doesn't work, they've got nothing left to use for leverage. Their strength now is the threat card, the bluff that they'll play it."

"Right. So we don't cave," Mia said. "And we don't run."

Brandon looked at her, the sun giving her skin a pearl-like iridescence like she was glowing from deep within. Where did this beautiful woman get this toughness? "Why are you talking about 'we'? It's not your fight."

Mia reached out and took his hand. "Sure it is. It became my fight the first time you kissed me."

"If I'd known that, I wouldn't have," Brandon said.

"We don't have any choice, Brandon," Mia said, like she was privy to some dark secret. "You don't. I don't. You know why, don't you?"

Brandon thought he knew the answer, took a moment to let the unfamiliar words form. They were frightening, even shocking words, words he'd avoided for most of his life, until Mia came along. And uttering them would change everything. The stakes would be exponentially higher. Now he could hear them, in his voice. *I love you.*

Those words stuck in his throat. "I think I do," he said.

There was a long pause and then the wake from the tug reached the outermost float, rocked it gently, like a child being pushed on a swing. A gull swooped low over the boat, banked, and circled back, double-checking that there wasn't something edible to be had. It swooped low a second time, then shot off again, Brandon thinking that it looked like it was carrying an urgent message.

"So what did you say to them?" Mia said.

"I told them if they came near you I'd kill them," Brandon said. "I said if they went near Nessa I'd kill them."

"With the rifle in the cabinet?"

"Yes."

"What is it?"

"It's just a twenty-two. An old lever-action Marlin Model 39. It was my grandfather's."

"Show me how to shoot it," Mia said.

CHAPTER 24

"So it was all implied," Griffin said, "except for the part about the ten thousand."

"Right," Brandon said.

"No witnesses."

"Except for his big buddy. You're sure it's this Kelvin guy?"

"Ninety-nine percent. Unless Joel has made a new friend of that description since he got out."

"They seemed like they'd known each other a long time," Brandon said. "A lot of unspoken stuff going on."

They were in the cruiser, an hour into the day shift, slowing for each house on Blackstrap Road in West Falmouth, just north of Portland, Griffin calling Falmouth P.D., saying he was looking for a witness in an assault investigation, the voice on the radio saying, "Ten-four." Griffin had written the description of the place—blue and white mobile home, wishing-well out front, a white van shoved into the brush to the right of the driveway—on a piece of paper. Brandon was holding it, watching as each house came into view.

And then the trailer, set back under a canopy of pines.

The white van.

Griffin pulled in, drove the cruiser as close to the front door as he could.

They got out and walked to the door. A big dog barked inside as Griffin knocked. The barking turned into a frantic snarling and a baby started crying. A woman's voice said, "Shut the hell up."

Neither of them did, but the barking grew muffled, like the dog had been shut in another room. The door opened.

It was a big busty woman, barrel shaped, with blonde hair and bangs with a band of dark roots. There was a wide-eyed baby in her arms, both baby and mom staring at the cop with suspicion.

"Morning, ma'am," Griffin said. "Officer Griffin. This is my colleague from the Portland Police Department, Brandon Blake. We're looking for Kelvin. You Crystal?"

"Yeah, and he ain't here."

"But Kelvin does live here?"

"I kicked his ass out."

"When?"

"Three days ago. Ain't heard a word since."

A pause, Griffin's way of letting her know he thought she was lying.

"You know where Kelvin might be staying?"

"No idea and I don't care."

"Has Joel Fuller been here?"

Crystal gave a short I-told-you-so sigh, tried to catch, it but couldn't.

"So you know Joel," Griffin said.

"I thought he was in jail," Crystal said. The baby, a little girl, looked at her, reached out and grabbed her face. She pushed its hand away.

"He's been out three days," Griffin said. "Kelvin's been seen with him."

"Ain't been here, if he has. I won't let Joel Fuller in my house."

"Why's that?"

The baby on her hip, she reached into the back pocket of her jeans and fished out a pack of cigarettes. True Menthol. She shook one loose, fished it out with her mouth, tossed the pack into the room behind her. Dug a lighter from a front pocket and lighted the cigarette. Took a long drag and blew the smoke out, away from the baby.

Griffin and Brandon waited, Brandon thinking Crystal had mastered the art of the dramatic pause.

"Why? 'Cause he's a piece of shit, that's why."

"Oh, yeah?" Brandon said. "What's he done to you?"

Crystal looked at him, wondered what a colleague was. No uniform, too young to have made detective. Or maybe they'd started using these young guys undercover. This one was kinda cute. She stood up straighter to accentuate her chest. The baby reached out and grabbed her right breast.

"I got nothing to say about Joel Fuller except he's nothing but trouble. Kelvin wants to go down the toilet with that piece of crap, go right ahead. But they both better stay outta my life."

She took another drag on the cigarette, forgot to turn her head, and blew smoke around the baby. It grimaced.

"Well, ma'am, if you do see Kelvin," Griffin said, "tell him I'm looking for him. Here's my card."

He handed it to her. She glanced at the card, shoved it in the front pocket of her jeans. Jiggled the baby up and down like she was full of something that had to be shaken.

"Give him this message, too," Griffin said. "Tell him I want to talk to him before he makes a serious mistake."

"Ain't seen him. Ain't planning on it," Crystal said. "You think I want my daughter growing up having cops knocking on the door asking about her daddy? Screw that."

Another cloud of smoke. The baby screeched. Crystal flicked the cigarette out onto the packed ground in front of the door.

"Word to the wise, Crystal," Griffin said. "These guys are hiding here and we bust them, that could be endangering the welfare of a child. You want Child Protective knocking this door down? I'm telling you right now, that's what'll happen, we find you've been lying for these guys."

Crystal scowled, slammed the door. The dog barked. Brandon and Griffin walked back to the cruiser, climbed in, and sat staring at the trailer for a minute.

"That got her attention," Griffin said.

"Would that happen?" Brandon said.

"No," Griffin said. "But it plants the seed. She can choose him or she can choose the baby. At least that's what she'll think."

"So now we wait for the phone to ring?"

"Let her stew," Griffin said. "I give her a day."

Baby still on her hip, Crystal waited in the living room, back from the window. She watched as the two cops talked, finally backed the cruiser out, and drove off in the direction of Portland. She went to the phone, dialed.

"Hey," she said. "I need you to watch Destinee for a little while. Now. But drive by once, check and see if there's a cop car down the road."

She hung up, went to the bedroom, and put the baby down on the bed. Destinee rolled over and scooted for the edge. Crystal grabbed her and held on, leaned down to put on Nikes. The baby squirmed as Crystal got the shoes on, picked Destinee up and went back to the window and smoked and waited.

Finally an old blue pickup pulled in and her mother, a stout gray-haired woman, got out, marched to the door, walked in without knocking.

"How's my pumpkin?" she said, taking the baby from Crystal's arms.

"Anybody out there?" Crystal said.

"Not that I could see," her mother said. "What, you got the police watching the house? What's Kelvin into now?"

"I don't know and I don't care," Crystal said. "Give me twenty minutes," and she walked through the kitchen, out the back door of the trailer, and into the woods.

CHAPTER 25

The path was overgrown, ruts from a four-wheeler, a ruff of asters and burdock grown up in the center. Crystal walked quickly, arms swinging, chest thrust out like a shield. She kept to one side of the path until that side turned to mud, and then she hopped over to the other side and kept going.

She slapped a blackfly, brushed choke cherry aside. Chipping sparrows flushed ahead of her, just tweetie birds to her, something Kelvin used to shoot with his shotgun when he was into the coffee brandy. She thought of the time he got completely hammered at their first family cookout here, went and got the shotgun, and lined up pots of her mother's flowers on the back lawn, blew them to smithereens.

When she asked him why he did such a crazy thing, he said, "Because nobody wanted me to."

Should have known then the whole thing was doomed. Better late than never, though. And she was damned if she was going to let Kelvin get busted for some stupid shit, not if he expected to use her money for some goddamn loser lawyer, hold his hand when he was found guilty.

She strode along, her Nikes spattered with mud, muttering to herself. "Let asshole Joel foot the bill, if he thinks he's so goddamn smart. Yeah, right. If he's so smart, why's he in jail half the time—"

The path curved, merged with a wider path, an overgrown logging road. She turned, continued deeper into the woods, big trees now, mostly spruce and pine, an undergrowth of grass and bushes. A hundred yards farther, in a cul de sac cut out of the woods was a small pickup camper. It was painted brown and green camo and it stood on metal stilts, one off kilter so the camper slanted to one side.

Crystal went around the back to the door, banged it with her fist, the aluminum rattling.

"Kelvin. You get the hell out here. We're gonna talk."

She squinted. Waited. Tried the door, but it was locked.

"Kelvin," she shouted. "You here?"

She turned away from the door, looked into the woods. Just like Kelvin to be out there right now, watching her. The thought made her seethe with rage.

"Listen to me, you son of a bitch. You think I'm gonna lie for you and that goddamn Fuller and lose my baby, you got another think coming."

She paused. Listened. Heard birds, no Kelvin. She was sure he was out there. She could feel it.

"I got cops here, looking for the two of you. And you know what? I'm gonna go right back up there and call them and say, 'You want to know about drugs? I'll tell you about drugs. You want to know about stolen guns? I'll tell you about stolen guns. You want to know about a guy faking he hurt his back? You want to know about who ripped off that guy from Mass. with all the oxy? You hear me? They're not taking my baby, you son of a—"

"Bitch," Fuller said.

He stepped out of the camper, pressed the muzzle of a gun to the back of Crystal's neck.

"Don't you touch me, you piece of shit," Crystal said.

"I ain't touching you. I'm just listening to all you know. You're a regular wicko-pedia, you know that? Drugs and guns and your old man's poor aching back."

He pressed the gun harder and Crystal half stumbled, took two steps.

"Yeah, well, they ain't taking the baby. I don't care."

He moved behind her, pushed her away from the door, toward the woods.

"You stupid cow. You think they want your fucking screaming brat? They're just playing with your head."

"They ain't taking her," Crystal said. "You tell Kelvin to get his ass home."

"I got a better idea," Fuller said. "Why don't you tell him yourself?"

"He's here? I knew it. Kelvin! Get out here."

"He's down here hiding. I'll take you to where he is."

He took her by the arm, lowered the gun to his side. She moved with him, uneasily.

"What cops were they?"

"Just cops."

He squeezed her arm hard.

"Okay. Older one, soldier type, real hard ass you could tell, even though he started out trying to be nice."

"State police?"

"Portland P.D."

"Just the one guy?"

"No, a younger one. No uniform or anything."

"College boy?"

"Yeah, looked like he mighta gone to college. I don't know."

"Uh-huh. What'd you tell 'em?"

"I said I didn't know where the hell Kelvin was. I said I wouldn't allow you in my house."

They were moving down a path, the one worn by the two guys going into the woods to take a leak.

"Who's with your kid?"

"My mother."

"What'd you tell her?"

"I'd be back in twenty minutes."

"Well, how 'bout if you never come back," Fuller said, and he yanked her around, put the barrel of the gun between her eyes.

"Cut it out," Crystal said. "You crazy?"

"Maybe that kid'll never see you again," Fuller said.

"What are you—"

"Maybe I'll go up there and pop both of 'em, after I do you. Get all three generations, do the world a favor."

"No," Crystal whispered. "Stop it."

"I think I oughta end this line of bitches right here."

"No, Joel. Stop it."

"Kneel down."

Crystal started to cry, the tears streaking her cheeks black with mascara.

"No, don't," she said. "Please."

Fuller pressed her shoulder down, pushed her to her knees.

"Oh, no. Oh, no," Crystal said, her breath short, coming in sobs.

"Gonna rat me out? Bad plan, you know why? 'Cause I always get even. They give me ten years, first thing I do when I get out is find you and your kid."

"I won't say anything, Joel. I won't say a word. I was just mad 'cause Kelvin, he isn't working and we got no money and now these cops are coming and it's all messed up."

She kept talking, as though he wouldn't shoot if she were in the middle of a sentence.

"And all I want to really do is take the baby and move to Florida. I got a friend, she moved down to Ft. Lauderdale and she said there's waitressing jobs all over the place. Childcare, that's not a problem, 'cause I could work a breakfast-lunch kinda place and she works nights so she could take care of Destinee while I was working and then when I got home it would be time for—"

"Shut up," Fuller said.

She did, the only sound the rustle of the woods and her soft, rhythmic sobs.

He pressed her head into the grass, put the gun to the back of her head.

"Oh, my god," said. "Oh, my baby. Please don't hurt my baby. You can kill me, but don't hurt my baby. Oh, please."

Fuller thumbed off the safety. Crystal felt the movement and closed her eyes. She wanted to say a prayer but she couldn't think of one. She let out a low, sad moan and in the moment that it ended, as her breath ran out, he leaned down, yanked her hair, and whispered into her ear, "If you ever talk about me to anyone again, if you tell anybody about this, I'll load the gun. And I'll kill the baby first."

He shoved her and she fell forward, her face in the cold grass. As he walked back up the path, Crystal began to cry, a muffled, defeated whimper.

And Fuller smiled.

CHAPTER 26

The northwest wind blew cold again the next day, the sky clear, puffs of high clouds sailing by like blown snow from some cold place in Canada. Lucky and Irina arrived at the marina at nine sharp, backed the Land Cruiser in, and popped the back open. Lucky took out four cartons of groceries, a smaller carton holding four bottles of wine. Irina slid two big L.L. Bean duffels from the back seat.

Brandon propped the gate open, pushed a dock cart to the car. "You ready?" he said.

Irina, face made up like she was going to a formal dinner, bundled in a new North Face shell, said, "I guess so."

"She's raring," Lucky said. "Keeps blowing like this, we'll be in Boothbay Harbor for cocktails."

"Shouldn't be a problem," Brandon said. "Not supposed to shift to the north until sometime tonight. You'll be beating into it the rest of the way."

"No hurry," Lucky said, hefting a carton onto the cart. "No need to be any particular place, nobody waiting for us. That's when you get in trouble, you get caught pushing to make some schedule—"

Brandon thought of Ketch keeping *Black Magic* on the move. Lucky, noticing Brandon darken, put a hand on his shoulder and said, "Hey, I'm sorry. I shouldn't have said that."

"It's okay," Brandon said. "It's always okay to say what's true. And it is true. The ocean doesn't care about your schedule."

Irina smiled at him and Brandon continued loading.

They put the cartons and duffels in the Whaler, towed the inflatable behind them out to *Ocean Swell*. Brandon lifted the stuff over the stern to Lucky, then came aboard. He gave Lucky the standard charter briefing: the boat was fueled, water tank topped off. The waste tanks were empty, batteries charged, electronics all checked. There were charts for the entire coast of Maine, and towels and linens were on board. Doc had left them a complimentary bottle of Krug, and Irina popped up from the cabin holding it, saying, "Thank him for us. That was so sweet."

Brandon helped stow the boxes in the galley, the bags in the stateroom forward. He noted that Lucky and Irina bought expensive food, everything from a downtown gourmet shop. Under the groceries was a new chartbook for the eastern seaboard, a couple of pages with dog-eared corners. Brandon looked back toward the hatchway, flipped the book open.

The marked charts were for the Canadian Maritimes, the waters east of New Brunswick, out to Nova Scotia. It looked like Lucky was hoping Irina's shakedown cruise would be a success and someday they'd go way Down East.

All about the weather, Brandon thought, as he tucked the book back. It rains for four days, she'll stick to the Caribbean. There's a storm, she'll never set foot on a boat again.

He came up on deck, walked with Lucky to check hardware, the rigging. Back in the stern, he shook Lucky's hand and said, "Good cruising." Irina leaned close and they touched cheeks. Her skin, toned and spa-tanned, wasn't soft like Mia's. Brandon got into the Whaler, started the engine, and drifted off. He stayed, circling against the wind as the anchor came up and *Ocean Swell* motored slowly off like a big swan.

Lucky waved from the wheel. Irina, sitting in the cockpit near him— her hood up, pulled tight against the wind—waved, too. The boat moved out of the marina and out into the channel. Brandon watched until they cleared the buoy at the harbor entrance, still under power. He buzzed the Whaler out into the harbor and, as *Ocean Swell* bore northeast, in a last glimpse he saw the mainsail go up.

Two hours later, Lucky sighted the buoy marking Seguin Ledge, some twelve miles east of Portland. From there he could set a course to the northeast for Boothbay Harbor, up Sheepscot Bay. He could stay outside, make for Matinicus, a lobstering island 23 miles out, or stay south of the island, run down east to Mt. Desert Rock.

He'd memorized the bearings, the buoys. An eye on the compass, he adjusted, setting a course for the long run down east. Irina switched on the GPS, watched as their bearing came up on the screen. She punched in another set of coordinates, watched as the course direction came up. Eighty-four degrees, nearly due east. Lucky peered up at the sails, said to Irina, "The jib's luffing."

She glanced upwards, saw the sail snapping, moved quickly up and along the deck. Grabbed a winch handle from its holder, and cranked until the sail was taut. She came back to the cockpit, looked out at the white caps tumbling off a following sea.

"She's not a bad boat," Lucky said. "Making seven knots."

"Won't be doing that on the way back," she said.

"This wind keeps up, we'll be good, at least for the trip out."

"How long?"

"Tomorrow, before noon," he said.

"When do you want me to take the helm?"

"Thirteen-hundred hours," Lucky said. "After you make me a nice lunch. A little smoked turkey, some Irish cheese. A bottle of English ale. Hustle now."

"In your dreams," Irina snapped.

"Yes, you always are," Lucky said, but she was down the companionway and gone.

She was annoyed, once again. Lucky grinned.

CHAPTER 27

The bay in close was rippled, but calm in the lee of the land. Nessa was on the sun porch, still warm from the morning. She sat in a rocker, dressed in black stirrup pants and a red sweater, a glass of Chardonnay in her hand. She tried not to put down her glass of wine, didn't like the feeling of panic when she couldn't find it. Like a chain smoker with multiple cigarettes, she sometimes ended up with more than one glass going: today, with this girl here, having to talk, there was one upstairs in the bedroom, where she'd been changing the sheets. Another in the kitchen, where she'd been listening to the radio news. She'd taken the bottle with her to the sun porch.

"The shadows come so early on this side of the house," Nessa said. "Brandon used to say it was nighttime in the living room, but daytime in the den."

"A nice place to grow up," Mia said, sipping tea in the second rocker. "Right here on the water."

"Lonely, especially in the winter," Nessa said. "If you live in the city, you have neighbors. I have the bay and the ferries. Always the ferries. Sometimes I feel like I'm Robinson bloody Crusoe out here."

"Why don't you move?"

"It's home. It's my life, where it all took place." She took a sip of wine. Swallowed. Another. "I can look around and see them, you know? I can hear them talking."

"You mean Nikki? Your husband?"

"You must think I'm a crazy old coot," Nessa said, "but you'll find out someday. The best days of your life don't come at the end."

"You have Brandon."

"Do I?" Nessa said. "Sometimes I feel like I've lost him. Moving out to live on that old boat. Wanting to do this police stuff, which for the life of me I don't understand. My husband would be so disappointed, that his only grandson wanted to be a common cop."

She drank. Crossed her legs and jiggled her shoe.

"Your husband didn't like the police?" Mia said.

"He was a doctor, a general surgeon. Very well respected. Everybody knew Dr. Blake. I think he would have wanted more for his grandson than going around handing out parking tickets."

"I don't think that's all Brandon sees in police work."

"What does he see? People who fight at funerals? My God."

"That was strange."

"And now see where it's gotten him. A prisoner in my own home because of some thug."

"Brandon and Officer Griffin will take care of it," Mia said.

Nessa didn't answer. They looked out at the water, a raft of ducks rounding the next point, paddling into the cove; in the distance the white specks of two sailboats boats far out on the bay. Mia watched them for a few minutes, then turned to write in the pad on her lap. Nessa finished her wine, then could put the glass down.

"What are you writing?"

"Things I want to remember."

"If I sat down with a pad like that, it would be all the things that come to me in the middle of the night, the things I want to forget."

Mia hesitated as Nessa lifted the nearly empty glass to her lips, swallowed the last drops. As Nessa lowered the glass, Mia plunged.

"Like what, Mrs. Blake?" she said.

Nessa got up from the chair, stood unsteadily for a moment, took her glass and went to the sideboard and poured more wine. Came back and sat down heavily, the chair rocking backwards and Nessa concentrating on the wine glass, now full, keeping it from spilling.

She sipped, put the glass on the table beside her, but kept her fingers on the stem, looked out at the bay. The sailboats, once close together, were now far apart. Closer to shore, the ducks were diving where the seaweed rose and fell with the swell. "Those weren't the most happy times," Nessa said. "Even before we lost Nikki."

"Oh?" Mia said.

"My husband, he worked a hundred hours a week, drove himself to exhaustion."

"I know," Mia said, wondering if Nessa remembered saying this before. Mia repeated, "My dad's a lawyer. He was always gone. If he had a big case we wouldn't see him for weeks. I almost never saw him growing up. I still don't."

"All about the career," Nessa said. "Push and push. I said, 'You're going to have a heart attack, you keep this up.' And sure enough. Walking to the car at the hospital. Boom. Like he'd been struck by lightning."

"I'm sorry."

Nessa took a swallow of wine.

"It was a hell of a shock. You'd think I wouldn't have been surprised, considering I was the one who predicted it."

"But when it happens, I'm sure—"

"Your life just shatters," Nessa said. "You try to picture what it's going to be next, but you just can't. The pictures are all wrong, no matter how you rearrange them."

Mia waited.

"So it was just Nikki and me, here all alone. We were both so sad, it's what we had in common. And then things just went along. Nikki decided not to go to college, which would have just killed her father. She got in with that Portland crowd, they were awfully fast. I hadn't worked since Nikki was born."

"So what did you do?"

"Sold some land we had, house lots we'd bought along the shore. Be worth a fortune today, stupid me. But they kept me going, and then—"

Nessa's fingers worked the stem of the glass. She looked like she was going to cry. She was going to talk about losing her daughter, Mia realized. After seventeen years, she still couldn't talk about—

"It was a strange time," Nessa said, her voice starting to slur. "I was younger, the people she was with were older than her. I was with little Brandon a lot. All I wanted was for her to have a life."

Mia could make no sense of it. She smiled, waited. Nessa drank, the shadows lengthened over the shoreline, the ducks moved north, almost out of sight.

"She wanted to buy the restaurant down in the Old Port, she and this other girl were starting to spruce it all up. But that takes money and—"

Nessa took a deep breath, shook her head at the recollection of something. "Of course, it all went wrong. If they'd waited for him. If they'd stayed another day. If she hadn't gone, if I hadn't—"

Finally she started to cry, a woozy sort of weeping. Mia got up from her chair and went to her, put her hand on her shoulder. "It's okay," she said. "It's not your fault."

"But it is," Nessa said. "If I—"

And the phone rang. Mia said, "It's probably Brandon," and left the room, following the ringing. She found a phone in the living room, on a table by the window. She looked out as she picked it up.

"Hello," Mia said. The window faced a narrow band of lawn bordered by dense cedars.

"Hello," Mia said again.

She looked out at the trees, trunks dark in the shadows like a crowd of people massed for something. "Hello," she said again. Listened. Heard someone breathing and then they hung up.

CHAPTER 28

It was gray-blue light, the first stirrings of dawn. Diesels chugged somewhere across the harbor. Gulls warbled from roofs of the sheds, a tern chattered overhead. The wind flicked chop against the hulls, a soft slapping, a hundred different rhythms, one for each of the boats.

Brandon had been aboard *Bay Witch* since just before four, and now he sat in a chair on the top deck, turned so he could see both the harbor and the shore. He was bundled in two blankets and an extra pair of socks.

The lights of the Portland skyline were fading, a few headlights moving. No boat traffic showed, and above him the stars were dimmed by a wash of barely visible clouds.

Brandon sipped coffee from a mug, thought about the day. Back to Nessa's. Class at nine. Meet with Griffin after that. Back to the marina to work. How much easier it would be if Nessa would come sit on the boat, even for a couple of hours.

And then he heard a rattle from the yard. The jingling of someone on the chain-link fence. Then another jingle, a thud. Someone had climbed over, dropped down.

Brandon eased out of his chair, moved around the deck, down into the cockpit. Slipped into the cabin, and then back up and off the boat, a flashlight stuck in his back pocket, the rifle in hand.

Silently, he moved down the dock, up the ramp, and into the yard. The sheds were shrouded in the shadows, the gate illuminated by the bare bulb of a single streetlight. He paused at the top of the dock ramp and listened.

Another fence rattle, from the direction of the big gates, the east shed. Then a faint brushing noise—someone moving through the vines that covered the fence behind the building.

A whisper, someone saying, "Be quiet."

Brandon moved to his left, to the corner of the big north shed, crouched by a tangled stack of boat stands. Took out the light. When two figures materialized from the shadows of the brush, he waited. Heard feet scuffing on the gravel, then the soft-shoe footsteps as they started across the yard.

Two of them, moving single file. They were headed across the yard, toward the ramp. Frozen in the darkness, Brandon waited for them to pass, raised himself up, and fell in behind them. As the closest guy sensed him and turned, Brandon flicked on the light.

"Hold it," Brandon said. "Security."

They bolted, feet thudding on the gravel, headed for the west side of the yard, Brandon behind them, the beam of the light sweeping in front of him.

They passed the ramp, sprinted into the big storage yard, the guy in front headed for the stored boats. The closest guy was slower and Brandon gained on him, called out, "Security, freeze."

The figure swerved left, into the open bay door of one of the rusted sheds.

Brandon followed. Stopped.

Listened.

The shed was dark. Still. He played the light.

White mooring buoys. Coils of rusty chain. A wooden day sailer on stands. A broken golf cart, one wheel off, listing to one side. A dinghy draped with a green tarp.

He took a step in. Heard rustling near the ceiling. A barn swallow, disturbed by the light, fluttered on a beam. The light flicked up, back down. Raked the clutter.

Behind the dinghy, Brandon saw a shoe. Black. Sole up. Someone on his knees.

Brandon moved quickly to his left, away from the boat. Stopped. Turned the light off and stood in the half light, then spun and rushed back.

The guy was lunging to his feet when Brandon caught him from behind, shoved him hard, sent him sprawling onto the concrete floor. His feet were scrabbling when Brandon put a foot on his back and said, "I have a gun."

The guy froze.

It wasn't Fuller.

Wasn't Kelvin.

It was a kid, his cheek against the floor. Brandon told him to turn over slowly and he did, wide-eyed and pale above his black T-shirt. Brandon listened for the other kid, heard trucks rattling on the bridge, nothing closer.

"I.D.," Brandon said, trying to sound like Griffin.

"I don't have any," the kid said, but half-heartedly.

"Then I'll let the cops figure it out," Brandon said.

"No," the kid said. "My back pocket."

"Take it out."

The gun was pointed at Brandon's feet, but the kid eyed it as he eased a wallet out of his jeans. Brandon took it, flipped it open with one hand. The kid's name was Jason D. Roberts. He was a sophomore at South Portland High.

"What are you after here?" Brandon said.

"I don't know," the kid said. "Whatever."

"Who's your friend?"

The kid didn't answer.

"You can tell me or the cops."

"No. Jonathan. Jonathan Gault."

"Same age?"

The kid nodded, head raised up from the concrete, hair dark streaks against his white forehead.

"Live around here?"

"One block over. We were just walking around. Jason started climbing the fence and I just kinda followed him."

"What'd you think you'd do? Steal motors? Break into boats?"

"No, we were just gonna look around, I guess."

"Cops won't believe that. They'll charge you with attempted burglary."

"Don't call the cops. We'll just leave. Jonathan's probably home by now."

"Your parents home?"

"Yeah. But don't call 'em, please."

"They know you're out?"

He shook his head.

"You always wander around in the middle of the night?"

"Sometimes."

Brandon looked at the school I.D. again, then back at the kid on the ground.

"Then maybe you can help me. And we'll forget this whole thing."

"You see anybody hanging around on the street out there at night, you call me. I'll give you my cell number. I'm looking for two guys, one big and stocky, wide face and a mullet. The other small and weasely, looks like a ferret."

The kid was listening.

"So we just have to make sure these guys aren't trying to get in here at night?"

"Right."

"What if they come here and we see 'em and call you? Is there a reward?"

"Virtue is its own reward."

"What's that mean?"

"Don't always have your hand out. Somebody famous said it. "

"Who?"

"I don't know," Brandon said. "Google it."

"So do we get any money?" the kid said.

In a string of fleeting images, Brandon saw *Bay Witch*, the deserted boatyard, rusted sheds. He saw Mia, asleep in the cramped cabin, her eyes closed, mouth barely open, her breath like the softest whisper. He pictured Fuller, his bitter smile, heard again the simmering anger in his voice.

"Twenty bucks," Brandon said.

"Each?" the kid said from the floor.

Brazen little bastard, Brandon thought, but then he heard Fuller say how easily the old wooden boat would burn.

"Sure," Brandon said.

CHAPTER 29

Shurstein was sitting on the front edge of his desk, pants hiked up, a swatch of white hairy leg showing above his socks and Topsiders. The class was nearly over and he was talking about fingerprints, the three types. He asked if anyone could name and define them.

The class stared back at him like suspects.

"Oh, come on," Shurstein said.

"Three types," Mia said, sitting by Brandon near the door. "Plastic. That's when you put your finger on something soft, like soap or something. It leaves a negative impression."

"That's one," Shurstein said.

"Visible prints," a girl in the back said. "Like when you have blood on your fingers and you touch something."

"Right," the professor said. "I hate it when I do that. Especially after I've killed someone." He grinned, letting them know that was a joke. They looked at him like they were weirded out. Brandon smiled, knowing the guy meant well. Shurstein fastened on a sympathetic face on him, said, "And the third type, Mr. Blake."

"Latent," Brandon said. "Sweat or the oil on your skin leaves an impression. Usually on glass or something smooth like that. These are the prints they get by dusting or using chemicals."

"Exactly. Nothing shows to the naked eye, but the secretions, if they mix with dust or dirt, leave a distinct impression," Shurstein said. "It's really amazing the trail we leave everywhere we go, on everything we touch."

A guy near the door asked why anybody cared about fingerprints when we had DNA. Shurstein said DNA was found in traces of saliva, semen, blood, hair, bits of skin.

A fingerprint can come from any contact.

"And what's another advantage?" he asked.

"Cheaper," Mia said. "DNA analysis is expensive and takes time."

"Anything else?"

The girl in the back waggled her red-painted fingernails. "There's more fingerprints on file than DNA samples, especially for older cases," she said.

"Very good," Shurstein said, smiling now, feeling like the class had been a good one. He slid off the desk, moved around to pick up a stack of handouts. Brandon stared, but unseeingly. He was thinking about Nessa, at home on the point with the doors locked. Would Fuller think about prints? Would he wear latex gloves? Would he leave a cigarette butt behind, impregnated with saliva? Did his buddy have prints on file? Had Crystal called Griffin back?

"Okay," Shurstein was saying, moving across the front of the class to hand out the papers. "Tire tracks and footprints. Question: Are all Nikes the same? Anybody? Mr. Blake?"

Brandon was thinking about Crystal, whether he should go see her alone. She'd looked at him like she was interested, maybe would talk to him easier than to Griffin, because Brandon was less of a cop.

"Brandon," Mia whispered.

He looked over at her, then up at Shurstein, staring from the front of the classroom.

"You okay there, Mr. Blake?" the professor said. "Looked like you'd left us for a minute."

"Shoes wear differently," Mia said. "Depends on the weight of the person, how they're built, how they walk. A shoe can actually be like a fingerprint."

"Exactly," Shurstein said. "So the thing to remember is, we leave traces of ourselves everywhere we go. You know the old saying, 'Disappeared without a trace'—it doesn't happen very often."

Pleased by the flourish, the professor wheeled around, headed back to his desk. Mia looked at Brandon, caught the shadow that flickered across his face. He turned to her and mustered the barest of smiles.

"Sure it does," he said.

CHAPTER 30

Dusk at sea, a hundred and fifty miles east of Portland. Irina was at the helm, lifeline clipped on, the boat headed northwest. The sun was setting, the endless sea shimmering like a billowing sequined cloth. The wind still moderate, four- to six-foot seas. At the tip of each wave, spray showed like someone waving a white flag.

Irina saw the speck of a vessel to the west. Lucky, coming up from below, said, "No problems." Irina nodded, pointed to the ship off their port side. Lucky took binoculars from the storage bin under the compass post, peered into the sun, hand over his eyes.

"Ferry out of Bar Harbor," he said, "headed for Yarmouth. They'll cross south of us, but to make sure, let's swing north twenty degrees."

Glancing at the compass, Irina turned the wheel. Lucky moved to the winches on the starboard side, cranked, and came back to the helm. The radio crackled, nothing audible. From below came the sound of music.

"You put on Mozart?" Irina said.

"Yes, it's calming," Lucky said.

"Weather has cooperated," she said.

"Shifts to the southeast tomorrow morning," Lucky said. "Could be wet coming down the coast."

"Just so it blows," Irina said.

"Right. But we're still ahead of schedule."

She reached to tap the teak on the gunwale behind her.

They stopped talking, stood side by side. The boat rose and fell, spray coming off the bow as it plunged into the swells. There was a gust and the boat heeled, Lucky looking to the hatchway as Irina adjusted course, easing off. She looked to the screen of the GPS, the boat a flashing dot on the tracker. They were sixty miles south-southeast of Grand Manan Island. Lucky looked up to the sails again, said, "Why don't you go below, see about food. I'll take it for a couple of hours, anyway."

Irina nodded, unclipped, and moved from the wheel as he took hold. She opened the cabin door and the music was louder, blending with the whistle-rattle of the wind in the rigging, then muffled as she closed the door behind her. Lucky watched the sails, the ferry to the west, the sun drifting down, a white ball behind a thin veil of clouds.

To the south he saw two fishing boats moving in tandem, fishing together. He watched them, thought they looked like trucks crossing a plain. He was thinking of this, the ocean as a desert, the waves like ripples in the sand, when he heard a faint clatter.

He listened. Turned left and right, and then to the stern. Saw the helicopter coming in low from the southeast.

"Shit," Lucky said, and called out, "Irina."

After a moment, the cabin door opened and she popped up, heard the helicopter, and frowned.

"Canadian Coast Guard," Lucky said. "Look happy to see them."

They turned and waved as the orange chopper roared over. It went a couple of miles north, then banked left and started to circle back. As it passed on their port side, they could see the pilot, then a crewman peering down at them with binoculars from the window in the bay door. As the helicopter slowed and hovered off their stern, the radio squawked.

"*Osprey*, *Osprey*, this is Coast Guard, go to channel 9, sir."

Lucky waved, grinned, picked up the microphone, shouted over the din of the chopper.

"Hello, Coast Guard, this is *Osprey*, over."

"Lonely out here, skipper. What's your destination?"

"Grand Manan, sir."

"Home port?"

"Yarmouth, Nova Scotia, sir. Just like it says."

"Who's on board, skipper?"

"Just the two of us. Me, Martin Mahoney, my wife Caitlin."

Irina felt the binoculars on her and gave a shy wave.

"Canadian citizens?"

"Aye, aye," Lucky said. "Nova Scotians from birth, sir."

"Comfortable out here, skipper?"

"Not a problem. Wind shifting southeast tomorrow, we'll probably stay in Grand Manan for a few days, wait for a better direction, blow us back home."

"Low-pressure system coming through. Keep a close eye."

"Ten-four," Lucky said, and then with the mic off, added, "Keep smiling, Caitlin."

She did, gave another wave, and the chopper dipped and whoofed by them, the pilot giving a salute as they passed. Lucky and Irina watched it grow smaller, an orange speck flying low over the waves.

"You think they'll come back?" Irina said.

"No. My guess is he's headed for St. John for the night. But to be safe, as soon as it's dark, we'll swing southwest. Get well into U.S. waters before dawn."

Irina stepped to the stern rail, where the Canadian flag was snapping in the breeze. She leaned over. The white plastic sheet was still in place, the words "Osprey," and "Yarmouth, N.S." dipping in and out of the water as the boat rose and fell.

"You've got to scrape every bit of that epoxy off before we get back," she said. "The registration numbers, too."

"Nothing a little acetone can't handle, Mrs. Mahoney," Lucky said, bristling at the nagging. "Everything under control."

Irina turned and went down into the cabin, Mozart billowing out as the door opened. Lucky stood at the helm, holding the wheel with both hands, feeling the big boat careen over the green foaming swells like a living thing, a sleek and giant porpoise, riding on the wind.

But the wind was cold, the salt spray like ice water on his face. He clipped on.

"Maybe Greece in September," he said aloud to himself. "Or Morocco. Maybe the ice princess would melt."

CHAPTER 31

Nessa was having white wine for lunch, a salad on the side. She was in her chair on the porch, the *Times* beside her, only the headlines read. She heard the door rattle, but didn't flinch. Just lifted her glass and sipped, said to herself very softly, "Go ahead and kill me. Who gives a good goddamn?"

But it was Brandon who came through the door, and Mia, too.

"The door wasn't locked, Nessa," Brandon said.

"I must have left it open when I put the trash out," she said.

"You can't do that. And where's your cell phone?"

"I can't keep track of the damned thing. Dragging all this junk around."

"Nessa, this is serious."

"I'm serious, Brandon," Nessa said. "And I'll tell you, too, Mia. I'm not going to live like a prisoner in my own home."

"It's just until we find him," Brandon said.

"Some hooligan who couldn't find his way here with a road map," Nessa said.

"Sure he can," Brandon said. "And I'm sure he has. I'm sure he's sat right outside the gates and watched this place."

"Barbarians outside the city walls," Nessa said. "This town is going to hell. I've been predicting it for years."

She drank. Brandon looked down at the plate of lettuce and tomato.

"Is that your whole lunch?"

"I had a big breakfast."

"What was it?"

Nessa hesitated.

"You need to eat better than that, Mrs. Blake," Mia said.

"Call me Nessa, dear."

"How 'bout some bread with that," Mia said. "We stopped at the bakery." She turned and left for the kitchen. Nessa drank again, a long swallow.

"What are you doing to yourself?" Brandon said. "It's not even noon. You can't do this, not now."

"It doesn't matter."

"What? That you're gonna be asleep in the chair if they walk in?"

He looked at her, the defeat in her eyes. "What is it?"

"Some criminal is stalking me," Nessa said. "What am I supposed to do? Have a party?"

"Have your wits about you. Not be passed out at noontime."

"What does it matter?"

"What do you mean? Of course it matters," Brandon said.

"You go be with your girl, dear. She's lovely, by the way."

"What is it, Nessa?"

Brandon crouched by the chair. Nessa drank, looked grimly out at the bay, the criss-crossing ferries moving like busy yellow bees.

"What's what?" she said.

"You've been sliding for a week."

"What do you expect? I'm worried about you, these hoodlums you've gotten involved with."

"It's not Fuller. It didn't start with him. It started with Lucky. Is it that it's bringing it all up again? Nikki?"

"It's very hard, seeing him," Nessa said, her voice low and sad.

Mia walked back in, holding a plate with a sliced roll and a pat of butter. She stopped short of Nessa, stood and held the plate.

"I understand that," Brandon said, "but he liked Nikki, didn't he? And I didn't even really know her, Nessa. For me, it's just been a chance to hear things firsthand, what she was like, what it was like when she was around. I don't know—"

"They weren't good times, Brandon," Nessa said, somber and serious, staring at the window but not seeing. "Things were out of control. Nikki, neither of us were taking care of ourselves. Or taking care of you. It was—"

She paused and they waited. "—a bad thing."

"What? That she died?" Brandon said.

"No," Nessa said. "Before that. Losing Nikki, that was the end. It wasn't the beginning."

She suddenly looked at Brandon, reached out and took his hand. "Please forgive me," Nessa said, and she started to cry.

"It was an accident," Brandon said, clasping her hand in both of his. "It was a boat that was lost. There was nothing you could do."

"Just say you forgive me," she said, tears running down her cheeks. "Please."

Brandon hesitated, then said, "I forgive you."

She turned away, raised the glass to her lips like a chalice, and drank. Put the glass down on her thin thigh and held it tight.

"I don't deserve it," she muttered, and continued to cry.

CHAPTER 32

Mia stayed at the house, kissed Brandon goodbye at the door, pepper spray and cell phone in her hand, Nessa asleep in her chair in the room overlooking the bay.

"I'll keep checking on her," Mia said.

"Something's eating her up inside," Brandon said.

"Hasn't it always been? I mean, the way she drinks."

"No, it's like something was dormant and it just woke up. When Lucky came."

"Memories," Mia said.

"Or nightmares," Brandon said.

He leaned to her and they kissed, her lips soft. He hugged her once, said, "Three hours," and walked to the truck. Pausing at the truck door, he opened it, reached behind the seat. Took out the Marlin and walked back to the house. Mia opened the door, looked at the gun.

"If you're not comfortable with—"

Mia reached for the rifle, cradled it in her arms. "Is it loaded?" she said.

"Yes."

"Show me the safety."

Brandon did, loosening the thumbscrew, tightening it again.

"How many bullets?"

"Eighteen, including the one in the chamber," Brandon said. "Call the police first. This is just a last—"

But Mia turned away, walked back into the house.

Brandon walked to the truck, started it, and looked back at the door. Drove down the drive, stopped the truck, left it running as he went back and hooked the rusty chain across the stone gates.

Griffin was talking baseball, Little League not Red Sox. "It's like I told Jeremy, you reach a level where natural ability alone isn't gonna do it for you. I said to him, everybody's got talent in the all-stars. It's dedication that gets you to the next level. So I throw him a bucket of balls. Curves, change-ups, fastballs, taking something off, of course. You gotta recognize those pitches coming and that takes practice, practice, practice. And then you know what we do?"

"What?" Brandon said.

"We pick up the balls and we do it again."

They were just off the highway in Falmouth, headed west on a two-lane road through woods and fields. Griffin finished with Jeremy, who was eleven, moved on to Michael, who was eight. Brandon wondered what it would have been like to have this guy for a dad, instead of Nessa. Sometimes it seemed the only thing Nessa had taught him was how to handle a corkscrew.

"With Mike, it's fielding. I hit him a hundred ground balls last night. He fielded sixty-one cleanly. That's up from forty-two a week ago."

"Good for him," Brandon said.

"I told Mikey it takes patience and perseverance. It's like police work. Rushing around like a madman doesn't solve crimes, catch bad guys. You gotta be unrelenting. Bad guy is the hare, you gotta be the tortoise. He runs, stops for a breath, and looks back, you're still behind him, still coming on. He takes off, stops to rest, you're still there. Now he starts to panic because he knows you're not giving up. And when he panics, he makes mistakes. And you're right there to snap on the cuffs."

He slowed the cruiser, waited for an oncoming truck pulled into Crystal's dooryard.

"I ran Kelvin. He's got an eighty-six Caprice, registration expired. A Ranger pickup, expired even longer."

Brandon pointed to the nose of a black truck, peeking out of brush and tall grass to the side and rear of the house.

"Truck's there."

"So chances are he's driving the Chevy, probably slapped some stolen plates on it. We'll run that by the mother of the year."

A Monday afternoon, a white Mitsubishi parked out front, a baby seat in the back. Crystal was home, the television blaring so they could hear it on the front steps. Griffin knocked and the dog began to bay, the baby started screaming. Crystal shouted at one or both of them, "Knock it off."

The door heaved open and Crystal looked out, the baby in her arms. The baby had an orange stain on her pink shirt. Carrots, Brandon thought. Crystal was wearing jeans and a black tank top and there was a whitish stain on the shirt just below her left breast. Over her right breast was a tattoo of a rose.

Crystal didn't open the storm door and they looked at each other through the glass, like visitors meeting an inmate.

"Hey, Crystal," Griffin said. "Don't mean to bother you, but wondering if you've seen Kelvin."

She shook her head.

"Nope."

"Talked to him?"

Another shake.

"And you have no idea where he might be?"

"Not a clue," Crystal said.

Brandon looked at the baby. Her mouth was circled by a red stain. Punch.

"How 'bout Joel?" Griffin said.

Crystal's face froze, hardened. Her jaw clenched. She shook her head again, deliberately.

"He's been here, hasn't he?" Brandon said.

"No," Crystal said quickly. "Ain't seen him. Ain't seen neither of 'em."

"Does he know we've been here?" Griffin said.

Crystal shrugged. The baby reached up and stuck a small finger in her nose. She pulled the hand away without taking her gaze off the cops.

"Don't know how he would. I ain't told him."

"He'd know just from talking to you," Brandon said. "He can read people's voices. He can tell if you're lying."

"You find him, you know him so good," Crystal said.

"Is Kelvin driving the Caprice?" Griffin said.

"Couldn't tell ya."

"What happens to you, Joel thinks you ratted him out?" Brandon said.

She turned, the baby looking at him, too. "I ain't rattin' out nobody."

"Didn't say you were. Just asked what would happen if he thought so."

"He ain't gonna think that 'cause it ain't true."

"People get the wrong idea," Griffin said. "If we keep coming around."

"Wouldn't you sleep a lot easier if Joel was in prison the next five years?" Griffin said.

Crystal didn't answer, her face a closed mask. The baby kicked, clawed at her mother's breasts with her small, fat hands, leaving faint pink streaks on Crystal's skin.

"We violate him, he's gone," Griffin said. "You won't have to worry. You won't have to worry about your baby there, either."

Crystal pulled the child closer, took a step back. Griffin slipped a card from his pocket, stuck it in the frame of the storm door.

"You call me, Crystal," he said. "You call and we don't have to keep coming around."

The door closed. The lock clicked. Brandon and Griffin walked to the cruiser and climbed in. They sat in the yard for ten minutes, the motor running, police radio on loud, windows down. Brandon said he thought

Fuller was a sociopath and Griffin agreed, then recounted other sociopaths he'd known and locked up. Every couple of minutes the blinds moved in the front window. Cars passing on the road slowed, the locals checking out the cops. Finally Griffin put the car in gear, said, "Enough squeezing for today."

CHAPTER 33

It was four-thirty, and in twenty-five minutes they were back in the city, Congress Street, out by the bus station. There were a couple of bars on the block, a no-star hotel. They took a right at the bus station, drove a couple of hundred yards, and turned in at a lot surrounded by chain-link fence topped with barbed wire.

Inside the fence were two dump trucks, a bulldozer on a flatbed, asphalt mixers on wheels, buckets and boards and junk. They parked in front of a small building, beside a tall, black pickup truck that said, "Ibezia Paving" on the side. They were getting out of the cruiser when a man—short, stocky, bald, with a black goatee—came out of the door of the building, turned, and locked it. Looked up at the two of them and said, "Yeah?"

"Officer Griffin. This is my colleague, Brandon Blake. We're looking for Kelvin Crosby."

"Crosby? He been gone for weeks."

"Quit?

"Got hurt."

The guy held up two fingers on each hand and waggled them. "Hurt," he said again.

"He's out with an injury?" Griffin said.

"Out. Whether it's an injury is up to worker's comp to decide."

"So you haven't heard from him?"

"Heard from his lawyer, some lowlife ambulance chaser."

"So he's suing you?" Brandon said.

"He's bluffing. But what these guys don't realize is, I don't settle. You say you got hurt on the job with me, you better have bones sticking out of your skin or I'll see you in freakin' court."

He moved toward the truck.

"Learned my lesson early on that one. Settled with this one clown, says he's got a ruptured disc. Find out he's moonlighting with one of those tree services, you know? Climbing trees with a chainsaw."

"What's Kelvin's injury supposed to be?" Brandon said.

"Some back bullshit, excuse my French."

So Kelvin had gambled on a settlement and there was no payoff in sight, Brandon thought. Until Fuller came along.

"You know where he might be?"

The guy shrugged, put a hand on the door, and then stopped. "He going to jail?'

Griffin's turn to shrug. "Depends."

The guy thought, figured this was cheaper than his lawyer.

"Crew used to ride Crosby a little. Big guy, strong, but not the sharpest tool in the shed, you know what I'm saying?"

They nodded.

"Guess his wife rode him hard, too. Kelvin musta said something to them about getting kicked out of the house 'cause they had this way of ragging him. They'd say, 'Kelvin's sleeping in the camper. Whatsa matter, Kelvin? Sleeping in the camper?' That kinda thing."

"So there's a camper somewhere?"

"I pictured the guy walking out the door in his boxers, you know? The old lady tossing his pillow out after him, like in the cartoons."

"Gotcha," Griffin said.

"Well, if she was thinking she was gonna get rich off me, she was wrong," the guy said, opening the pickup door and swinging into the seat. "I work hard for my money."

"I'm sure," Griffin said.

The guy started the motor, smiled, and said, "If you talk to him, give him a message for me. 'Over my dead body.'"

Brandon thought of Fuller, said to himself, "Be careful what you wish for."

They drove back to the sheriff's office, quiet for a few minutes. Griffin swung off under the bridge, took the roundabout route along the waterfront. Brandon looked out the window at the warehouses, the offices, the fishing boats on the wharves.

"There wasn't a camper on the back of that black truck, was there?" he said.

"Ranger's too small," Griffin said. "Could have hauled it off, I suppose."

"I don't think anything moves much around there," Brandon said. "Finds a place and stays there until it rots."

Griffin nodded. They had moved up into the hip section of waterfront—pubs and architects' offices. Suddenly Griffin turned right down one of the wharves, easing down the narrow street, people coming and going from the fishing supply companies, a warehouse that shipped lobster, a fishermen's bar.

They drove past signs that said no trespassing, one of the perks of being a cop, pulled up at the end of the pier. The radio mast of a fishing boat poked up from the boat tied alongside the pier below.

"I don't know if I'd like it, living on a boat," Griffin said. "There's no yard. Where would you play ball?"

"Easier without kids," Brandon said. "But families do it. Just need a bigger boat."

"How big's yours?"

"Thirty-five feet. It used to belong to my mother. She—"

"I know," Griffin said. "I'm sorry."

"How?" Brandon said, surprised, suddenly wary.

"Checked you out before I took you on. Didn't want to ride around with a knucklehead."

They stood for a moment, not talking. A lobster boat appeared to their left, a kid in big boots standing on the stern. It swung into the gap between the wharves and out of sight.

"It is what it is," Brandon said.

"No dad, huh?"

Brandon shook his head. Griffin was gazing out on the water, but listening.

"Who raised you?"

"My grandmother. 'Til I didn't need her."

"How old was that?"

"Maybe ten."

"You're a different sort, you know that? Like you came out of a time warp."

"My own, I guess."

"Got many friends? Your own age, I mean."

"No. Not many."

"Don't need anybody?"

"Not usually," Brandon said. "When I do, I ask."

"Lonely sort of life," Griffin said.

"I'm fine."

Griffin let it die. Waited, watched the boats and water. Smelled the smell of the water, diesel, fish.

"I was walking a beat back then," he said, "just starting out. Things were pretty crazy down here. Hard drinking. A lot of drugs. Cocaine coming out of the woodwork. We broke up two, three fights a night, and I mean real fights, not two guys shoving each other, praying for somebody to hold 'em back."

"You remember when the boat went down? *Black Magic*?"

"Vaguely."

"Who knew the docks back then?" Brandon asked. "I mean, in terms of cops?"

Griffin considered it. The gulls swooped, engines chugged, Brandon heard none of it.

"When was this exactly?" Griffin said.

"Seventeen years ago."

"There was Jimmy Fallon, good detective, but he retired, down in Sarasota now. I heard he's kinda losing it. And there was a lady detective. Kathleen Rogan. Don't call her Kathy. She'd take your head off. Smart cop, kind of the elite. Did a lot of drug stuff. Worked some murders."

"Where's she?"

"Left the force after some guy jumped her. Scumbag was into very young girls, when he wasn't teaching school. Rogan's closing in on him. Guy tries to blow up her car. It blows up, but she doesn't die."

"She still around?"

"Yeah, does some P.I. work for lawyers, I guess. Big settlement, doesn't have to work. I just saw her at the mall back in the winter. I almost didn't recognize her."

"No?"

"Word was she had some brain damage."

"Jeesh."

"Lost an eye, had all this plastic surgery, but still doesn't look right. Like the two sides of her face don't quite match."

"How 'bout her memory?" Brandon said, as the lobster boat backed out below them, loaded with bait, the kid still perched on the stern. The gulls flocked around him like big white flies.

"She remembered me," Griffin said. "And I was just some rookie. Why?"

"I don't know," Brandon said, as they turned back to the cruiser. "I've always wondered about the guys on the boat with my mom. Not just their names. I mean who they really were."

"But she won't know them unless they were bad guys," Griffin said.

"I don't know that they weren't."

"Then talk to Kathleen," Griffin said. "That'll be the test."

CHAPTER 34

Lucky had the course charted, running down the coast twenty miles offshore, beating into the southeast wind. Now he stood at the wheel in the dark, a half-squint, a half-smile, his expression a blend of contentment and concentration. Under power, sails furled, he was threading his way through Casco Bay, the flashing beacons atop the Cousins Island towers showing the way. Behind Littlejohn Island he put the spotlight on, picked up the buoy, set a course of 249 degrees, and watched the miles tick off in tenths.

At exactly 2.8 miles, he swung the big boat east, listening now, peering into a fog that came in patches like snow squalls. After a mile he heard waves on the port side, put the light on again. Irina came up from below, looked at him, then peered out into the blackness. Not another boat in sight. She heard the waves, not crashing but falling steadily like someone was playing cymbals in a slow cadence. Lucky had his eye on the compass, adjusted course to the southeast for the wind. He hit the spotlight again, waited, and thought he saw something, a red buoy waggling from the darkness like a scolding finger.

The Sturdivant Ledges.

"Jesus, are those rocks?" Irina said.

"No problem," Lucky said, as the buoy swept past to starboard. "As good as home."

He spun the wheel, the boat veered to the northeast. Lucky motored between the markers, saw the last pair pass, then the point of Sturdivant Island, white foam from breaking waves. He slowed nearly to idle, looked to the shore, began counting the lights.

The big houses were lit up, floodlights on docks, porches, illuminating the long, sloping lawns. And then there was a stretch of darkness, pure blackness, like the entrance to a cave. It was here that Lucky turned the boat ashore.

He watched the depthfinder, saw the bottom start to come up: 33 feet,

24, 10, 8. Lucky slipped the boat out of gear, scurried up the deck, and released the anchor. It fell with a muffled sploosh, dragged, and set. The boat swung around, bow pointing south.

Back in the cockpit, Lucky killed the lights. He turned and unhooked the painter for the inflatable, drifting to stern. He pulled it close, unfastened the oars, left the little Honda motor up and out of the water.

He hadn't slept more than eight hours in three days. But his eyes were bright and unblinking under his baseball cap as he looked at Irina, smiled, and said, "Ready."

Without a word, she turned and went below.

CHAPTER 35

Nessa was asleep in big wing chair in the living room, snoring softly. Mia was in the kitchen on the phone to her mother in Minneapolis, calling while Brandon was checking the boat, making sure it was set for the night. It was ten-fifteen. He'd been gone ten minutes. He'd said he'd be back in a half hour.

"Your father's been working a lot," Mia's mother said.

"Something new and different," Mia said.

"A trial in Seattle."

"If it wasn't that, he'd have some other reason to stay away," Mia said.

"Mia that's—"

"True is what it is. Dad's allergic to home. I used to think he was allergic to me."

"That's enough."

"Just because—"

"I have some good news," Mia's mother said. "You know that client your dad had? The one with the brother in the big advertising agency?"

Mia didn't answer.

"He told your father to tell you to call him. About a writing job. In New York."

"Mom, I don't know anything about advertising."

"It's writing. And you'd get paid very well. How many writers get paid?"

"It's not writing. I mean, it is, but it's not what I want to do. You know that."

"Why not just try it? Maybe you'd love it, being in Manhattan, all the excitement, going to shows and—"

"But I like it here. And I met this guy. He's really—"

Mia let the phone fall away. Listened.

"What guy?" Mia?"

Mom. I gotta go for a sec. I'll call you right back."

She turned and looked toward the back stairs. "Mrs. Blake," she called. "Are you up?"

Mia stood slowly, silently. Crossed the kitchen, moved down the hallway. Peeked into the living room. Saw Nessa in the chair, feet tucked underneath her, her mouth open.

Asleep.

Mia walked slowly back to the kitchen, stood by the table. She looked toward the stairs, then up at the ceiling. Heard a footstep. Or maybe she'd felt it. Listened. Heard the rattle of a window.

The wind.

Above the kitchen was a bedroom. Nikki's room. Mia had started to peek, but Nessa had called for her. She'd gotten just a glimpse of high school stuff still in place. Mia had closed the door behind her.

Or had she?

She went to the closet by the back door, opened it, and took out Brandon's rifle. He'd showed her how the thumbscrew tightened the trigger mechanism, locked it in place. Showed her how to loosen it, then pull the bolt back to drop a shell into the chamber. Mia held it against her thigh, the barrel pointed at the floor. She levered the shell in.

The back stairs were narrow and steep. She took them one step at a time, pausing and listening, the gun on her hip. At the landing she listened longer, thought she heard something downstairs, somewhere behind her. A knock? A creak?

She listened again, took another step up, her head level with the second floor. She eased her way, step by step, fingered the trigger, felt the stock against her hip.

Listened.

Nothing.

Took another step and another.

The door to Nikki's room was ajar.

It was dark inside. She eased her way to the stop of the stairs, listened. Looked both ways, like a kid at the curb. Two, three steps to the door.

Paused, motionless. Pushed the door open with the barrel of the gun.

It swung and creaked. Cold air blew out.

Mia reached across and over the gun, felt for the light switch. Found it and flicked it on.

There was high school stuff. Pictures of friends in heart-shaped frames, haircuts off "Three's Company." A shriveled rose pinned to a corkboard, a skeleton of a flower. Some misshapen vases and pots.

Pottery class.

Mia pushed the door open wider.

There were French doors to the right, leading to something. The roof of a porch? Mia crossed the room, felt the breeze, the doors ajar. She turned quickly, swept the room with the gun. Nearly squeezed off a shot, but held back.

She moved on fear-stiffened legs to the doors. Called out, "Nessa?"

She spilled down the stairs, the gun in front of her. Glanced at the back door on the way by, saw that it was now ajar, too. Slipped down the hallway, hesitated at the corner of the wall, stepped around.

Nessa was in the chair, still. There was a piece of folded white paper on her chest. Mia moved toward her, saw her chest rising and falling. Reached out and took the paper with her finger and thumb.

Holding the piece of paper up in front of her, she let it fall open.

Scrawled in black marker was a message:

bill for pain and suffering is going up. 20 thousand. Cash. Sorry we missed you. I know. Its hard to be everywhere

It was signed with a streak of what appeared to be blood.

There was a noise in the kitchen and Mia whirled around, let the paper fall. As it floated to the ground, she heard footsteps coming down the hallway. She raised the gun to her shoulder, pointed it at the edge of the wall.

"Brandon?" she said.

CHAPTER 36

Dawn, the sun bleeding over the horizon. Griffin was up, in uniform, standing by the bedroom window. He watched the red ball creep upward, thought it would be a good day for baseball. He walked to the bed and stood over Denise, asleep with her back to him, the blankets pulled around her so she only showed as a ridgeline: hips, waist, shoulder, a mop of mussed dark hair.

He let his hand hover over her hip. Then he turned and went to the door. He closed it behind him and padded down the hall.

It was superstition, he knew, but cops have lots of them. Griffin never left for the job without saying goodbye to his wife, looking in on the boys. The first door on the left was Jeremy's. Griffin eased it open.

Jeremy had kicked off the covers, was asleep in his favorite Celtics shorts and a Kevin Youkilis T-shirt. On the shelf beside the bed were baseball cards in plastic cases, trophies with figures poised, a dirty Red Sox hat.

Jeremy's mouth was open. His eyes were closed, but from a certain angle Griffin could see through the space between the closed lids to the whites of his son's eyeballs. It was like a glimpse of death and it jolted Griffin. He pulled back so he could again see his son peacefully sleeping.

He stepped out and closed the door behind him.

Michael's door was ajar because he wouldn't have it shut. The younger boy was curled up in a ball at the center of the bed, like a cat would sleep.

Griffin touched the younger boy on the shoulder, knowing he wouldn't wake up, that he slept through thunderstorms, sirens outside his bedroom window. Michael didn't flinch, the rhythm of his breathing unchanged. Griffin smiled, left the room.

He was due to report at six; it was four-fifteen. He'd thought of calling Brandon, but when he'd come up with the plan the night before it had been too late. Now it was too early.

Griffin took the Interstate north, only a few trucks out at this hour. He flipped a wave to a southbound state trooper, continued on, got off the highway, and made his way to Crystal's road. He knew she and the baby would be asleep. He hoped the dog would be, too.

The houses were dark as Griffin drove, slowed as he approached the house. There was no sign of life, the white Mitsubishi parked out front. Griffin looked the place over as he coasted by, continued on around a long curve. Slowed at the place where he'd seen the path cut into the brush.

He pulled in, off the road, saw tracks where another car had pushed through the tall grass. Ahead of him in the green brush he saw red taillights, chrome, the back of an old Chevy Caprice.

Griffin smiled.

"Jackpot," he said.

He parked behind the Chevy, got out, and walked up to it. There were Budweiser cans on the floor in the back, Burger King bags on the front seat. Griffin straightened and looked beyond the car to where the opening in the brush narrowed.

There were two tracks, like someone had ridden a four-wheeler here but not this spring. Griffin started down the path and small birds flushed in front of him, yellow and black ones, rosy red ones, too. Denise would know what they were, from the book she kept on the windowsill by the backyard birdfeeder. He made a note of the birds' colors so he could ask her.

Griffin walked, thinking how pleasant it was in the woods at this hour. The leaves and grass were wet with dew, and spiders' webs were strung with droplet like tiny pearls.

The path wound around denser brush, blackberries, and, in the low spots, thickly bunched alders. He saw some old rusting drums in the woods to his right, beyond them the skeleton of an ancient car. This probably had been farmland fifty years before, now was overgrown, the farm and farmer forgotten.

He walked for a quarter mile and then saw the path branch. The grass was flattened on the right-hand fork so he took that one, moving into and out of a grove of pines. He had a sense he was flanking the house now, that it was somewhere to his right. If Kelvin had walked to the camper in his boxers, it had to be somewhere—

Ahead.

It was painted camo, standing on poles, shoved under a bank of pines. The path led to the camper, and then veered right and widened as it led in the direction of the house.

Griffin stopped. Listened and heard birds, one he knew was a blue jay, another a chickadee. He walked slowly toward the camper, watched the curtained windows. It looked like it had one room, probably a bed on each side. The door was at the back and there were windows at the middle.

He started walking again, felt something under his left boot, but couldn't stop. It was a beer can and it crushed, the crumpling noise loud and sharp.

Griffin froze. There was no sign of movement from the camper, no sound. He figured they'd been drinking and were passed out.

He counted to ten, listened. Kept walking, keeping to the path. And then he was under the trees and the grass gave way to pine needles that crunched softly under his boots.

Griffin went to the door. Unhooked the strap on his Glock. Tried the knob and it turned. He thought about it again and knocked. The door rattled.

He waited. Rattled the door again.

"Joel," Griffin said. "Portland P.D. Need to talk."

He listened, heard a thump from inside the camper, like the sound of someone rolling out of bed onto the floor. He put his hand on his gun butt. Knocked one more time.

"I'm coming already, I'm coming," came the muffled voice, high-pitched and agreeable. "Let me get my pants on."

Footsteps and then the door rattled. Griffin stepped back and it opened, and Fuller was standing in the opening. His hair was tousled and his eyes were a bleary red.

"Hey, officer," Fuller said. "Guess I slept late. All this fresh air. Ain't used to being out in the country."

He grinned, teeth stained by chew. Behind him, the camper was dark and the air that streamed from it smelled of sleep and dirty clothes.

"You alone in there, Joel?" Griffin said.

"Just my buddy Kelvin. He owns this here celebrity crib."

He turned and peered back into the dimness.

"Kelvin. Dude. We got company. An officer of the law."

Fuller turned back to Griffin and grinned. "Kelvin got into the coffee brandy last night. He's moving a little slow."

"Have Kelvin step out here, too," Griffin said, and Fuller turned away, moved deeper into the camper.

"Kelvin, man, get your ass up or I'm gonna drag you out here. Kelvin, wake up."

Griffin stepped up and the camper swayed. He waited for his eyes to adjust. He saw a big lump under blankets at the far end of the camper, up high in the part that would be over the truck's cab, had there been a truck. An arm reached out of the lump and pulled the blankets up.

"Kelvin!" Fuller shouted.

Griffin scanned the place. More Burger King trash on the floor. An empty Budweiser carton, an 18-pack. A gallon of coffee brandy on a table that came out of the wall, the plastic jug two thirds gone.

He turned to his left. Stopped.

The butt of a pistol, half covered by a dirty beige towel. Griffin took a step over, picked the towel up. It was the Ruger. Griffin picked it up, snapped the clip out. Loaded.

He turned.

"Joel," Griffin said. "You're a convicted felon. You know you can't have this firearm."

Fuller had come back, was standing beside him.

"I ain't having nothing. That's Kelvin's. It's his camper. His gun. Right, Kel?"

Kelvin didn't stir.

"Kelvin, you stupid fuck. Tell the officer this ain't my gun."

"Watch the language," Griffin said.

"Kelvin, wake up."

The mound of blankets stirred, a rumbling coming from it like something was about to erupt. Then it was still.

"Step outside with me, Joel," Griffin said.

"Hey, it ain't mine. You can't bust me for that. What you want anyway? Where's your warrant? I'm out of jail now, dude, you can't just bust in here, start searching the place."

"You gave me permission to enter," Griffin said.

"The hell I did."

"Heard it plain as day. Now step outside."

Griffin reached out, took Fuller by the shoulder. He guided him through the door, started to step down behind him when Fuller wheeled backwards and swung.

It was an elbow and it caught Griffin in the neck, knocked him sideways. He stumbled, started to bring the Ruger around. Fuller leapt at him, got an arm around Griffin's neck. Griffin shouted, "Stop, stop," hit Fuller in the side of the head with the pistol. Felt a hand at his own gun, Fuller pulling the Glock out of its holster.

"Drop it," Griffin screamed, felt the muzzle scraping up his chest. He aimed the Ruger at Fuller's head, pulled the trigger, but it didn't move, didn't fire. Griffin dropped it, reached for Fuller's arm, the one with the gun. They were spinning, Griffin trying to throw him off, when he felt the muzzle jump the top of his vest, press against his throat.

"Drop—" Griffin said, and there was a blast, sound and heat and white fire and he was falling onto his back, feeling warm wetness running down the side of his neck.

He tried to talk, but couldn't. He looked up, saw Fuller standing with the gun in his hand, his mouth gaping, eyes wide. And then, as the image faded, Fuller seemed to relax.

Griffin thought he should ask why, why the guy had shot him, but then it was like he was in a room and it was filling with smoke. He choked, tried to cough and then—.

"What the hell?" Kelvin said. "What did you do? You shot a cop?"

"He was gonna arrest me," Fuller said, still staring at the big cop, the soles of his boots, the Ruger on the ground.

Kelvin stepped down from the camper in his boxers, circled Griffin gingerly.

"Is he dead? Maybe we should, like, call an ambulance."

"He's dead. I saw him go."

"Are you out of your fucking mind? You know what they do if you shoot a cop? They hunt you down and nail your ass. Shoot you in the back. You'll be lucky you ever get to jail. 'He was gonna arrest me.' Are you fucking crazy?"

Kelvin eyes were fixed on Griffin's, staring up at the trees.

"I ain't gonna do no five years," Fuller said, his voice low, a dog's growl. "No way."

"Five years? Five years is nothin'. Five years is shit compared to what you're gonna get. You're gonna get seventy-five. A hundred. Life in prison, dude. Look at this. A goddamn cop. Must have a car here someplace. People looking for him. Shoot him with his own gun, oh my fucking word. On my property. Look at that blood, running into the ground. That's evidence. What the fuck? What the fucking fuck?"

"He gave me no choice," Fuller said, smiling now, eyes on Griffin, but his mind turned inward.

"Coulda run for it. Coulda gone to jail. Coulda shot him in the foot. Coulda—"

"No, you don't understand. I had no choice 'cause it was all planned for me. It was planned way, way back. My old man, the bastard. My whole life. It was meant to go this way. He wanted me to end up right here."

"You're nuts, Joel. You're cracking up. You killed a cop. Got nothin' to do with your old man."

Fuller looked over at Kelvin, standing there in his dirty blue T-shirt, black boxers, thick white legs, pine needles stuck to his fat feet. Fuller grinned, walked five steps, and took Kelvin's hand. He held it up, palm open. Slapped the Glock into Kelvin's palm, pressed the fingers closed.

"I didn't kill a cop, Kelvin," Fuller said, pulling the gun back. "We killed a cop."

He smiled, eyes narrowing.

"We're in this together, Kel. You got your little girl to protect, cute little thing."

He paused, let it sink in, the implication, the threat.

"I ain't got nobody, dude. Just you, you and me. We're like family, right? Old pals. What is it they say? You said it, right? When you married that bitch?"

Kelvin waited, frozen by the weird smile, the crazy look Joel got sometimes.

"'Til death do us part, man," Fuller said.

"We gotta get outta here," Kelvin said, words streaming from him. "We gotta get him outta here, find the car and move it, bring it into town and dump it someplace. And then we gotta get out, go to Florida or California, Mexico."

"No," Fuller said.

"No?"

"I ain't saying we're not going," Fuller said, walking past the body, bending to pick up the Ruger. "Just not yet."

CHAPTER 37

Mia was looking along the barrel, over the sight. Her finger was tight on the trigger. And then it lowered, swung to her side.

"It's okay," Brandon said.

"It's not," Mia said.

She handed him the gun, turned, and picked up the paper. Nessa gave a snort, then eased back into the heavy breathing of deep sleep. They walked to the kitchen, where Brandon laid the gun on the table and said, "What?"

"Someone was here. They left this. They left it on your grandmother."

Brandon looked at the note.

"On her?"

"On her chest. She was asleep."

"Did you search the house?"

"I just found it. I heard something, took the gun, and went into the other room."

Brandon looked away and listened, reached for the rifle.

"You stay with her," he said. "I'll look around."

"Let the police do it, Brandon. That's what they're here for."

"No, I'll do it. And in the morning I'll call Griffin. We'll find them, and tell them."

"Tell them what?"

"Tell them this was a very bad idea."

They went to the living room, and Mia went and sat by Nessa, pepper spray at the ready. Brandon jacked a live shell out and it fell to the floor and rolled. Nessa stirred, opened her eyes, and said, "What?"

"It's okay, Nessa," Brandon said. "I'll be right back."

He started up the stairs, the rifle held low in front of him. At the second-floor landing, he stopped and listened. Felt the cool breeze from the water side of the house, and turned to the right. He flicked the hall lights on, paused at the door to a spare bedroom.

Turned the knob.

Pushed and reached in for the light switch. The lights glared on. He eased in, crept across the room. Opened the closet door slightly, swung it the rest of the way with the rifle barrel. There was no one in the closet. No one under the bed. Nobody behind the door, Brandon realizing he should have checked that first.

He did at the next room, another guest room. Hesitated at the door to his own room, swung it open, the light glared on.

A photo of Abraham Lincoln. Toy Civil War soldiers, a model of a lobster yacht. Bookshelves on all the walls, full. History and biography, sorted by period. In that, the oddest of moments, Brandon realized it was the room of a lonely person.

He shrugged off the thought, swung the closet door open. Nothing but his clothes, his old sneakers and shoes.

He heard footsteps on the stairs, backed out of the room, and went to the hall. Mia was coming up, her head emerging like she was coming out of the water.

She turned, saw him, said, "Are you okay?"

He nodded, went to the next door, the one on the end: Nessa's.

It was the master bedroom, overlooked the lawn and the bay. Brandon touched the doorknob, felt something wet. Looked at his hand and saw a streak of blood. Looked down at the floor and saw a droplet.

He took the knob again, turned it with thumb and forefinger.

Eased the door open. Paused, reached for the light switch, put the rifle to his hip, and stepped in.

"God," he said.

"What?" Mia said behind him. "Are you okay?"

Brandon checked behind the door, under the bed, in the closet. He walked to the French doors that led to the veranda over the sunroom, found them ajar, the cold sea breeze blowing in.

He turned back as Mia stepped into the room, put her hands over her mouth, and froze. She was staring at the bloody mess on the bed, dark red drips leading from the foot to the pillows, where there was puddle of black blood below a gutted carcass, orange and white.

"I didn't know your grandmother had a cat," Mia said.

"She doesn't," Brandon said.

He searched all the rooms, the cellar and garage, too. Brandon figured it had been Joel who had come in with the note, maybe Kelvin with the cat. Dropped the note on Nessa, continued up the stairs. Probably they'd watched the house, figured out which room was Nessa's.

Left a calling card, went out the door, over the railing and down.

Nessa was sitting in the chair in the living room; Mia had made her tea in the microwave. They told her a cat had gotten in upstairs, made a mess in her room. She said she'd been out on the veranda that morning, watering the plants. There was a cat from the next house over, a big orange tom that had figured out how to get onto the veranda from the nearest maple tree.

And then Brandon squatted next to her and said, "Nessa. There's a problem."

He told her about Fuller and Kelvin, the fight at the funeral home. He told her Fuller wanted money from him, and knew where he lived, both on the boat and at Nessa's. He said he thought Fuller was all talk, but by coming to the house, leaving a note, he'd raised the stakes.

"In the morning, I'll call the cop I ride with," he said. "He's already working on it."

Nessa sipped her tea, grimaced, put the mug down.

"You can't give them money," she said. "They'll just want more and more."

"It won't get to that," Brandon said. "This cop, his name is Griffin. He'll take—"

Nessa continued as though Brandon hadn't spoken. "It isn't about money," she said. "It's about power. No amount of money will keep him satisfied. They always want more because they want to keep control of you."

It was eery, like she was speaking from experience.

"Who?" Mia said.

Nessa didn't answer, just put the mug of tea down, reached for the wine bottle, poured a new glass.

CHAPTER 38

It was a little after eight, Mia curled into Brandon in his bed, Abe Lincoln dolefully looking down at the two of them.

"You never see a picture of Lincoln smiling," Mia said.

"The Civil War will do that to you," Brandon said.

"I think some people are just basically sad. Sometimes they're not as sad, maybe even sort of happy, but sad is their default setting."

"I guess," Brandon said. "Sometimes I think sadness is a sign of wisdom."

"You're a little like that," Mia said. "But I think I make you happy."

"You do."

"Your grandmother is totally like that. I think she has two states of mind. Sad and sad and numb."

"Ever since Nikki," Brandon said.

"Most people move on. They grieve and then they put their lives back together. She had you, after all."

"I guess I wasn't enough."

"How you think she'll be today?"

"Sad and then she'll numb herself."

"She doesn't seem afraid," Mia said. "It's like—"

"She's resigned to it?"

"Yeah. Like she deserves it or something. It's strange."

"The way she's been as long as I can remember. I don't know. I'll call Griffin now. I think he was on at seven today. And I should get over to the marina, see what—"

Brandon paused. Listened, then they both heard it. Car doors shutting in the drive.

He sprang out of bed, grabbed for his jeans and T-shirt. Mia rolled out of the bed, scooped her bra and shirt off the floor. Brandon yanked his running shoes on, went out the door and down the stairs. Through windows by the front door he saw the car.

A dark blue Land Cruiser. Lucky and Irina coming up the stone walk. Irina, in jeans and heels, was carrying a bunch of fresh flowers and Lucky, in khakis and boatshoes, had a brown bakery box, the bottle of Krug from the boat. Brandon opened the door and they smiled.

"Hey, man," Lucky said. "We came to thank you. You weren't at the boat, and I said to Irina, 'I'll bet he's at Nessa's. I think I can find it again.'"

"I hope we're not too early," Irina said. "I told him, 'eight o'clock isn't a good dropping-in time.'"

"She doesn't know about Mainers," Lucky said. "Up at the crack of dawn."

"No, come in," Brandon said, stepping back from the open door. "So how was the cruise?"

"Glorious," Irina said. "I've never been so relaxed."

They stood in the kitchen, Mia putting the flowers in a vase, Brandon starting coffee, Nessa still asleep in the second guest room.

"I remember this place," Lucky said. "We sat at that table and drank beer, showed Nessa the charts."

He was somber for a moment, Irina looking at him with some sort of concern.

"So the cruise was good? The boat performed okay?" Brandon said.

"As advertised," Lucky said. "Comfortable. Easy to handle. Didn't push it too hard, just moseyed up the coast. Spent a night and a day in Bar Harbor."

"Had lunch in this lovely café," Irina said. "I had the most delicious salad. Arugula and these exquisite fresh pears."

"We spent the first night in Boothbay," Lucky said.

Irina frowned. "Tourists," she said.

"But still fun. Went out and had a drink and talked to these guys, crew for some mega-yacht that was in port. Just brought the boat up from Antigua. I've cruised all around there, so we traded stories."

"Sounds fun," Brandon said.

"Hey, I could just poke around the bay here. Explore, anchor for the night."

Lucky grinned.

"Paradise," he said.

Brandon served the coffee, put the pastries out on a plate, led the way to the sunporch, and everyone looked out at the bay.

"We have some news," Lucky said, wiping jelly from his fingers.

"We're staying for the summer," Irina said, smiling.

"She likes Maine, even if it is on the edge of the wilderness," Lucky said. "So we leased this place on the water in Falmouth. Three months."

"Been empty for a while and needs some cleaning, but it's furnished," Irina said. "I think we can make it quite comfortable."

"Sounds great," Brandon said.

"Some guy gave it back to the bank. Walked away, left everything. Wine in the cellar. Steaks in the freezer. Even a Jeep in the garage, keys in it."

"You'll have to come see," Irina said. "Bring your grandmother. We'll have dinner."

There were ships on the horizon beyond the islands, long blue shapes like a school of whales. Lucky was watching them.

"Big one's a tanker," he said. "Smaller two are fish processors, probably Russian."

As Brandon looked at the two silhouettes, he felt Lucky turn and scrutinize him.

"How 'bout you guys?" he said. "Everything okay?"

Brandon looked at Mia. They both sipped; Mia waited. Brandon said, "We've got a little problem."

There was a moment of quiet, and Lucky said, "Oh, really. Like what?"

Brandon told the story: the funeral fight, his conversations with Fuller and Kelvin, going to see Crystal with Griffin, the note and the cat.

"Okay," Lucky said. "So they're just some small-time hoods. Punks. See an opening here, think they can squeeze you for a thousand or two."

"Coming into your home. That's very creepy," Irina said.

"Yes," Mia said. "Right into Nessa's bedroom. The cat."

"My god," Irina said.

"All that blood," Lucky said. "Has to be some on them. Their shoes, the car, their clothes."

"Don't know if I can get blood analysis for something like this," Brandon said.

"You don't have to actually get it. You just tell them you have it," Lucky said. "Guy has probation hanging over him?"

"Five years," Brandon said.

"So have your man threaten to revoke him," Lucky said. "Say you found his prints in the house. Say you've got the blood samples and you know they'll match. Go after the second guy, the one with the kid, tell him he'll go away, too, unless he cooperates. His baby'll be in high school before she sees him again."

Irina looked at him and he seemed to catch himself.

"He watches a lot of 'Law and Order,'" Irina said. "I think your policeman friend probably will know best."

"Sorry," Lucky said. "Armchair detective. But I still think it's the way to go."

"Got to find them first," Brandon said.

"That should be easy," Lucky said. "At some point, they'll be right here."

"Or at your boat," Mia said.

Lucky walked to the window with his coffee, looked out at the islands and the bay.

"We got back last night," he said. "A little tricky coming in past Diamond Island Ledge. I was looking at the chart, think I know where I went wrong. On a port tack, went too far east, must've missed a marker in the dark, because all of sudden the bottom started to come up, but I knew I was past Little Diamond so—"

Lucky paused. Nessa was standing in the doorway in her robe and slippers, hair pinned back with barrettes. She smiled at Mia, saw Irina and looked startled. Lucky turned.

"Hello, Nessa."

Nessa looked at him. Her mouth opened, her wine-rouged cheeks went pale.

It's me, Lucky."

"I told you Lucky and Irina chartered a boat from the yard for a week," Brandon said. "They sailed up to Bar Harbor."

"Yes, of course you did," Nessa said, wavering on her feet.

"I'm so sorry, Nessa," Lucky said. "Sorry about your loss. Very, very sorry I wasn't here for you."

"Thank you. It was a long time ago."

"You know, for years I roamed around the world trying to get away from it. I should have called you."

"It's okay," Nessa said, her voice brittle. "I'm not sure there would have been anything to say."

"But I'd like to talk now, Nessa," Lucky said, moving toward her. She took a step back. "Not now, not today, but soon. We're going to stay the summer, you know."

Nessa looked alarmed.

"You may not like it. It's not very glamorous, not compared to—where did you come from?"

"New York City. And before that L.A., London, Sedona, Geneva, a couple of years in Brussels. I've been a bit of a vagabond, Nessa."

"You and your friends, you were like Gypsies." She paused, seemed to look inside herself. "Nikki hadn't lived like that."

"We were all looking for something new, something different," Lucky said. "We were all young and full of life, pushing the limits. You, too. You were right there with us. "

Nessa went pale again, swallowed hard. She took another step backwards, nodded at Irina, who smiled in a sympathetic way, like Nessa was a sweet but doddering old woman.

"I've got to go," Nessa said, and she did, hurrying toward the kitchen. Brandon heard her going up the back stairs.

"What was that about?" Brandon said.

Lucky stood with his coffee, watching the spot where Nessa had been.

"I hope I didn't upset her. I don't mean to. I mean, your grandmother was a ball of fire, high-energy. I swear, we didn't think of her as Nikki's mom. It was just Nessa. Nikki and Nessa, almost like they were sisters."

He went on, but Brandon excused himself, Mia saying, "They both must have been very pretty."

Brandon crossed the house and went up the back stairs. He found Nessa standing at the window in the back guest room. Brandon stood beside her and said, "I know it's hard, Nessa. Seeing him."

"You don't know, Brandon," Nessa said. "You have no idea."

CHAPTER 39

Brandon could see her from the boat as he tied the Whaler, left it rafted against the side of *Ocean Swell*. Nessa was on *Bay Witch*, on the top deck, sitting in the canvas chair, wrapped in a blanket. She didn't like the boat, hadn't set foot on it in years. When Mia had suggested they go, Nessa had said. "Fine. I just don't want to be alone."

So she sat and drank tea, looked out on the harbor while Brandon and Mia did the post-charter inspection of *Ocean Swell*. He ran an eye over the rigging, saw nothing out of place. Walking forward, he saw the sails were fully furled. Lines were coiled flat on the deck, fenders hung neatly. The salt had been washed from the rails and it looked like the deck had been washed and scrubbed.

Mia went to the cockpit, found everything gleaming. She unlocked the cabin door, eased down and into the main salon. It was immaculate, the table-tops polished, the whole place smelling of lemony soap. She checked each cabin, found the linens and blankets folded neatly and stowed in the forward cabin where Lucky and Irina must have slept.

"This wasn't a love nest," Mia said.

Brandon checked the waste tank, found it had been pumped. The water tanks had been topped off, as had the fuel. He checked the head and it glistened. Most charter returns needed a full day of clean-up; this boat could go out on charter this minute. Just hand over the key.

Doc was going to love this.

Brandon went to the chart table, slid the drawer open. The charts were in place, in order, from southwest to northeast, Kittery to Lubec. Before coming up, Mia looked around one last time; the cabin windows had been washed, inside and out. The pots and pans were clean, the sink scoured.

It was like the boat hadn't gone anywhere at all.

Brandon ran a hand over the electronics, pushed the power buttons on radar, radios, the GPS. It booted up, asked if he wanted to enter waypoints for a new trip.

He didn't.

Behind him, Mia said, "What's that do?"

"You tell it where you want to go, it tells you the course to get there," Brandon said. "Or you can let it tell you where you are, and it saves that information, tells you where you've been."

He scrolled down, pressed buttons, navigated his way to the saved waypoints.

Brandon pushed the button.

The most recent saved trip showed on the screen, a list of numbers: longitude and latitude. Brandon knew some by heart. He saw the bell at the harbor entrance, the buoy between Peaks and Cushing islands.

"So here they are, left the harbor, moved out beyond islands before swinging northeast, starting the run up to Boothbay Harbor."

Brandon leaned closer. Looked at the numbers.

"Huh?" he said.

"Huh what?"

The longitude and latitude showed the course of *Ocean Swell* had been almost due east. The GPS said it had sailed out into the bay and beyond, almost 150 miles, nearly to the western tip of Nova Scotia.

He bent and squinted at the screen.

"What?" Mia said.

West of Yarmouth, Nova Scotia, the boat had turned northwest, crossing to the southern edge of the Bay of Fundy, then due west back to Maine. The last leg was a straight shot southwest following the Maine coast.

If this was the course Lucky and Irina had followed, they'd gone to Bar Harbor via Nova Scotia.

Brandon's mind whirled through the possibilities.

Perhaps someone had been tinkering with the GPS, had set coordinates for a trip they might take but hadn't yet. With Lucky's experience, a trip like that would be a breeze. But these waypoints weren't in the reference folder. They were in the folder of the trips the boat had taken.

Someone else could have sailed this course before Lucky and Irina took the boat. But Doc's idea of an adventure was an overnight up to Camden Harbor.

"What's the matter?" Mia said.

"This says the boat went almost all the way to Nova Scotia."

"When?"

"It doesn't tell you that. But it's set to automatically save waypoints from previous trips. Doc did that because he hates fog and he tended to do the same trips over and over."

He looked at the next set of numbers. Doc running home from Camden in the rain.

The trip before that. Hard to tell, but it looked like the time Doc had taken the O.R. nurse for a weekend in Boothbay.

"Who would take this boat to Canada?" Mia said.

"Lucky could. He could take this boat to England if he wanted to."

"But they went to Bar Harbor. They talked about the restaurants."

"I know. It must be screwed up."

"Maybe Irina was fooling around."

"She doesn't have much fooling in her," Brandon said.

"Maybe she was bored," Mia said. "Whatever, they sure brought it back clean."

"I know. They should charter every boat we have here, have the owners pay them. Waste tank is pumped, fuel and water topped off. I mean, they really went above and—"

"Brandon."

The voice was distant, high-pitched and quivery like a gull's.

Nessa.

Brandon turned, saw her at the end of the dock. She was waving, calling them back. He jumped to the rail, untied the lines, and Mia climbed over and into the Whaler. Brandon swung over, stepped the helm, and Mia shoved them off. He started the motor, swung around, and saw Nessa still at the end of the dock, still waving. But there was someone with her.

A man.

They docked, Mia climbed out and tied the bow. Brandon shut off the motor, fastened the stern line, heard footsteps behind him as he crouched over the cleat. He turned and stood and the guy held out his hand. Wholesome looking, with a pistol on his right hip.

"Detective O'Farrell," he said. "I need to ask you a few questions."

Brandon nodded. "Sure."

"I understand you rode with Officer Griffin."

"Yes."

"When was the last time?"

"Yesterday."

"What were you doing?"

Brandon told him: Crystal's house, looking for Joel Fuller, his buddy Kelvin. Sitting in Crystal's driveway. He told the detective why, the short version.

"And you left there. Then what?"

Brandon went through it. The guy at the paving company, Kelvin's injury. Their talk down on the dock.

"Then he dropped me at my truck, headed home. His shift was over. I think he had baseball or something. With his kids."

"That's the last you saw him?"

"Yeah."

A sinking, sick feeling.

"Sounds like you guys got along," O'Farrell said.

"We did," Brandon said, the feeling overpowering now. "We do."

"Mr. Blake, I'm sorry to tell you this. We found Officer Griffin shot to death this morning at 5:45 at the Washington Avenue project."

Brandon reeled, a wave of nausea.

"But we don't think he was killed there. We think he was shot someplace else and then he and the car were dumped."

He moved closer, eyes narrowing.

"Tell me more about Fuller and his friend."

Brandon's mind was racing, Griffin and baseball and dragging Fuller out of the funeral and the two boys.

He focused.

"Fuller wants me to pay him money. Because I got in a fight with his mother. Broke her nose, but it was an accident. He made, I guess you could call them, veiled threats to burn my boat. Last night somebody killed a cat and put it in my grandmother's bed."

The detective took notes on a white pad with a black leather cover. "Where was this?"

"South Portland. Right up the road."

"And you think it was this Fuller?"

"He'd be high on the list."

"Where is he now? You and Griffin have any idea?"

"There's a camper," Brandon said.

"Where?"

"I don't know. Maybe around Kelvin's house someplace? Maybe not."

"We'll start looking," O'Farrell said. "I mean, could be totally unrelated, but this is a start. And I think we could use you."

"You want me to help with the search?"

"No," the detective said. "I think you'd be more help here."

Brandon looked up as gulls flew over, eyeing the two men to see if they were fishing, if there was food to be scavenged.

"Bait," he said.

"Right," O'Farrell said. "Even though they may be halfway to Florida, if they did this. If they didn't do it, we need to know that, too."

"He was a good guy," Brandon said. "He has two boys. I mean, they play baseball. Practiced with them for hours. He was just telling me about hitting one of them grounders. Over and over."

"Way it usually is," the detective said. "The shitheads live to be ninety."

They stood for a moment on the gently rocking float, and Brandon felt the weight of all of it settle onto him, like a block of stone slowly lowered onto a flatbed. And then he felt an odd sense of déjà vu. It was the stunned stillness that follows the news of an unexpected death, a protector removed, the realization that you're exposed, alone.

He could feel it now just as he had as a kid. First Nessa shrieking and crying, holding him by the shoulders. A blur of people: bartenders, waitresses, Nessa's neighbors, an old couple, their names forgotten, knocked on Nessa's door. They brought candy, like it was some weirdly reversed trick or treat.

And then the quiet. Nessa passed out in the chair in the living room. Brandon going up to bed by himself, lying there in the dark, not crying, like some four-year-olds might, just realizing that from now on, he was on his own.

But Nikki had been taken away by fate, a rogue wave, an auto-piloted freighter chugging through the night. This time, at least there was a culprit. A perp. A bad guy. A cop killer.

"Whatever it takes," he told the detective.

"We'll get the sons of bitches," O'Farrell said. "Don't you worry."

Brandon already was.

CHAPTER 40

At midnight they were still awake, lying side by side in the narrow berth, their hands clasped between them, the red light of a police radio blinking on the shelf by the bed. It had started to rain and blow, little squalls that skipped across the harbor, the patter on the deck above them hollow and faintly musical like someone flicking fingers across a drum.

"You think she'll be okay?" Mia said.

"Detectives in the house and I saw two outside."

"You know, this is a different topic, but she seemed almost afraid of Lucky."

"I know."

"Maybe the past all coming back?" Mia said.

"I don't know. She seemed to pull back from him, like a recoil."

"Do you think they didn't get along? Back then?"

"He said how much he liked her," Brandon said.

"Then what would it be?" Mia said.

"Angry that he's alive and Nikki isn't? But definitely something. She was drunk when we left. Getting drunker."

"Is that what it was like, living with her?"

"She checked out early and often," Brandon said. "Kinda funny. It was the one thing I could really count on."

"That must've been hard for a kid."

"Only for the first few years, when I still believed her when she told me something. 'You and me, we're gonna go to the circus. Brandon, how 'bout we go to a movie on Saturday? Would you like to go to a hockey game, Brandon? We'll get pizza.'"

"Didn't happen?"

"No. Meant it when she said them, but then she forgot."

"So you retreated? Into yourself, I mean."

"You have to," Brandon said. "You make it so you don't need anyone else."

The hull of the boat trembled in a gust and rain sprayed the porthole above them. Mia squeezed his hand.

"How long did that go on?"

"Still the way it is."

"Do you need me?" Mia said.

Brandon hesitated.

"Yes."

You know you can believe in me, right?"

"Yeah, I do."

"There have been other girls, though. What about them?"

"I didn't let them in," Brandon said.

"Why me?"

"You know what it's like."

"Right, it's like we're sort of alone together."

"When I'm with you, the rest of the world sort of fades out," Mia said.

Brandon turned on his side and leaned over and kissed her on the cheek. Mia turned, and they kissed.

"I think I need to be really close to you right now," Brandon said. "Is that strange? With everything that's happened?"

"No," Mia said, and they kissed again. "I feel like I need to hold you. Take you and hold you."

She slipped her tank top up and off, and they embraced, there in the cabin, the two of them setting out to become one.

And they did, making love slowly and deliberately, with a relentless, pressing fierceness. And then they kissed a last time and slept, Mia curled with her breasts against Brandon's back. He felt her relax, her breathing find an easy rhythm. He reached down with one hand to the floor of the cabin.

Touched the cold metal of the rifle barrel.

It was a thunk, like a cat landing on a roof. Brandon rolled off of the berth, reached for the gun, his boxers. He heard another step in the cockpit. A scratching at the locked cabin door.

It was early, but after dawn. In the dim light he saw Mia's eyes wide open, fixed on the door. In a crouch, he slipped his shorts on, moved through the cabin with the rifle pointed low in front of him.

Another rattle, a faint scratching. The sound of someone shifting his feet. Brandon reached for the bolt with his left hand, crooked the rifle in his right. His finger on the trigger, he reached up with his thumb and unscrewed the safety.

Slid the bolt slowly across. Turned the latch and yanked.

"Freeze," Brandon said, leveling the gun.

"Whoa," Doc said. "Don't shoot. It's me."

He was standing by the door, a piece of paper in his hand. Brandon lowered the rifle.

"Easy, Brandon, just leaving you a note. I mean, what the hell."

"Sorry, Doc," Brandon said. "There's been some stuff going on."

"Be careful with that thing. Could hurt somebody."

Brandon stepped up and out of the cabin into the cool morning. He closed the door behind him, leaned the rifle against the gunwale. Doc, in khaki shorts, a fleece vest that said "Black Dog Tavern," moved close and whispered, "I didn't want to knock. Didn't know if you had company."

"Mia's asleep," Brandon said.

He went into the cabin, pulled on jeans and a T-shirt. "Just Doc," he said to Mia, hunkered down under the quilt.

Back in the cockpit, Doc was looking out at *Ocean Swell*, riding on its mooring. He turned, held out an envelope. Brandon opened it and saw $20 bills.

"Finder's fee," Doc said. "Your friends, there. Man, that boat is clean. Cleaner than I've ever gotten it myself. They called me last night. Said they want to charter again, starting tomorrow for another week. Said they want to sail to Boston. I guess the lady's seen New York, but that's all. Come back, pick another destination."

"Good," Brandon said.

"Another six grand," Doc said. "And cash. I can tell you who isn't gonna see one goddamn penny."

Brandon smiled.

"Her lawyer'd take the shoes right off my feet, if he could. Son of a bitch. And cash. I mean, I got five thousand of Lucky's money just for the deposit. Another nine for the three weeks. All hundreds. I mean, what business is the guy in?"

"He just said investments," Brandon said.

"What, some hedge fund? That where he got his name?" Doc said. "Maybe I'll give him some of my money, if she leaves me any. But that's your finder's fee. Ten percent of the three weeks charter. That's nine hundred bucks."

"You don't have to—"

"Hey, these big charter brokers didn't do squat. You came through, buddy, you get the commission."

He turned to go, then crooked his head back.

"Sorry to bother you."

He winked. Brandon smiled.

"No bother. Hey, Doc."

Doc waited. Brandon took a step closer.

"The GPS on your boat. What's it save? Actual trips or ones you've charted out."

"Both, but one's archived, the others are saved. Trips you chart, like if I decide to go to Camden, I chart that, file it in the archive. Don't go that weekend, I got it there in the archive. Plus it saves six trips automatically. That can be a big help, let's say you're trying to get home in the fog. You just retrace your waypoints."

"You ever take the boat over to Nova Scotia?"

"Nova Scotia? What the hell would I be doing way out there? You read *The Perfect Storm*, right? Things get nasty, I want to be able to run for it. Nova Scotia, that's what, two hundred miles of open water?"

"A hundred and eighty, Portland to Halifax," Brandon said.

"Screw that," Doc said. "I'll take Camden Harbor and a glass of Glenfiddich at the end of the day."

Brandon thought for a moment. "So saved trips are the ones the boat has gone on?"

"Right. You look on there you'll see Portland to Boothbay, Portland to Camden, Portland to Bar Harbor, Portland to Monhegan, a little rustic for my taste but she liked it, who knows why. Portland to Robinhood. Now that's a nice spot, tucked away off Sheepscot Bay. Great restaurant. Took this intern from Atlanta once. Ricia—Denise had already told me to shove off."

"So where's Lucky going next?" Brandon said.

"Boston. Like I said—Irina, Lucky said she likes the big cities. I think she figures she paid her dues in Bar Harbor, Maine."

"On a forty-six-foot yacht? Not exactly roughing it."

"Whatever it was, they're good folks. Boat's spit-polished, stem to stern. You could eat off the goddamn deck."

Brandon nodded. Looked out over the marina. The wind had picked up, blowing damp and steady, and there was a wall of gray on the southern horizon.

"When do they leave?" he said.

"Tomorrow early."

"Southeast winds fifteen to twenty-five, visibility a mile or less in rain and fog," Brandon said. "Supposed to be dirty weather through Thursday."

"Lucky's sailed in worse than that," Doc said.

"I'm sure. But why drag yourself out in it if you don't have to?"

Doc shrugged. "So it gets uncomfortable, they put into Kennebunkport or Portsmouth, pick up a mooring, and sit tight. I wouldn't mind staying below with her. Man, that accent."

"She isn't gonna be thrilled," Brandon said. "Doesn't even like boats, never mind cruising in the rain and fog."

"None of my business," Doc said. "Hey, not like I don't trust the guy. Anybody that can sail around the Cape of Good Hope can sail to Boston in a little drizzle.

So what's up with Nova Scotia?"

"Showed up on your GPS," Brandon said.

"Playing with the thing, figuring it out."

"Right," Brandon said.

"I don't think Lucky knew how to use it. Said he sticks to chart and compass."

"Irina, then. Maybe just passing the time."

"I don't feel like I know much about her," Brandon said. "Lucky does all the talking."

"Hey, I'd go with her to Nova Scotia. On the ferry, in a first-class cabin. She's definitely a first-class babe. I mean, you better go to the top of the wine list, a woman like that."

"You think so?"

"Oh, yeah," Doc said. "I mean, nothing against Lucky. He's an interesting, successful guy. But I can picture her with some Italian count or some Russian mafia guy. She's got this coolness, you know? Knows what she wants and she's gonna get it."

"An odd match-up," Brandon said. "Lucky seems pretty laid back."

"And she seems like she wants to go to directly to the top. Guess they have one thing in common."

"What's that?" Brandon said.

"Money," Doc said. "Some people like having a lot of it. Some docs I've known have been like that. It's just really important to them. She's that way and so is he. I could see it when he whipped out that roll of bills. You could tell he really got off on being able to do that."

They stood on the deck, Doc leaning on the side deck, Brandon against the stern. For a moment, two, he saw the photo of the group on the deck of *Black Magic*. A little ragtag band, beards, and sun-burnished faces, Nikki lanky and tanned. And Lucky had looked, well, happy go lucky. When had the money drive kicked in? Or had it been there all along, sleeping like a dormant virus?

"Money," Doc said. "For some people it's a drug."

CHAPTER 41

Fuller and Kelvin spent most of the afternoon at Jolly's, at a table in the back corner. They were familiar enough to the regulars that they didn't stand out, not so well known that their presence would be noted.

"Maybe we could sign on with a fishing boat," Kelvin said, eating kernels from what had been a bowl of popcorn.

"What do you know about fishing?" Fuller said.

"I could learn," Kelvin said. "And if we put in at some other place, away from Maine, we could disappear."

"You wouldn't last a day. How you gonna hang onto some boat bouncing around in the middle of the friggin' ocean? Can't even pave driveways and they stand still."

"Don't rag on me. You never had no job at all."

"I'm thinking for the both of us. That's my job."

"You shoulda thought before you did it. That's when you shoulda thought."

"Just shut up," Fuller said, then he did think—that it was Kelvin's car, it was Kelvin who could testify against him. "Dude," he said. "You gotta understand I'm just kinda stressed."

He poured the last of the pitcher of Budweiser into Kelvin's glass. The beer was warm and flat because they'd been nursing it so they could stay in the bar but not get drunk. Kelvin sipped. Poured some of the flat beer into Fuller's glass. Fuller swallowed it in one gulp.

"We ain't gonna be able to work Blake like we wanted," he said.

"I guess," Kelvin said. "He sees us, he's just gotta call 911."

"So we work him another way."

"Take his boat, go south?"

"And dump him overboard?" Fuller said.

"I was thinking more like leave him on some island."

"Good luck with that, Coast Guard on your ass so fast you wouldn't

166

know what hit you. No, I'm thinking we tail him to his buddies. The rich dude and the Russian lady got more than enough cash to set us up where we're going."

"Florida?"

"No, everybody runs to Florida," Fuller said.

"You know a lot of people in this situation, huh?"

"I know how people think. Get in a jam in Maine, first thing they do is take off for friggin' Florida. Cops just sit on the Kittery bridge, wait for the car to go by."

"So where you want to go?"

"Chicago," Fuller said.

"Chicago? What the hell for?"

"No reason. That's what's good about it. Nobody could guess it ahead of time, 'cause we couldn't have guessed it either."

"I've never been to Chicago."

"You never been anywhere. We stick to places you been we'll be sitting in goddamn Old Orchard Beach."

Kelvin didn't like that, got up to pee. Fuller looked around the bar. Guys off a fishing boat, a different one from last time, were playing pool. Big blonde babe was having some heavy discussion with a flabby guy in a red sweater. Fuller figured he was her boss in some office, been bonking her and now he was trying to dump her without her going ballistic, calling his wife. Kidding himself, Fuller thought. Unless he had something on her, like she was married with a bunch of kids. Then it was a stalemate.

The blonde woman dabbed her eyes with a napkin. The guy was talking without looking at her.

Fuller looked away, trying to plan the takedown, keeping in mind that the Russian lady had poked Kelvin with an ice pick, so she probably wasn't gonna go easy. And if she carried an ice pick, the rich guy had probably been around, too. Now Blake and blondie, they weren't tough, but they were a little weird and unpredictable, living on a boat, Blake riding around with cops, the blonde always writing stuff down. A wannabe cop might wannabe a hero, too.

Kelvin came back from the john, sat down at the table. He had a speech planned, had gone over it in his head standing at the urinal. He began, "Joel, I don't think I can—"

"You don't have to go," Fuller said. "I know you got a kid, all this shit. Just help me get some dinero so I can get outta here. Then they pick you up, you say, 'I don't know where he went. What do I look like? His babysitter?' Let's go."

He was out of his chair, halfway across the room. Kelvin trailed after him, pissed that he never got to say his speech, which was about how he didn't want to mess with the ice pick lady 'cause he was afraid the only way you'd win with her, and probably the other guy, too, was to kill them and he wasn't a murderer.

But he followed Fuller down the block to where the Caprice, painted primer black in the woods that morning with a bunch of spray cans, was parked in a closed-up service station. It fit in there with the rest of the junks and Kelvin got in, waited while Fuller slipped between the cars, came back in a couple of minutes with two more license plates with valid registration stickers.

"It's like the Boy Scouts say," he said, slipping the plates under the passenger seat, next to the Ruger and Griffin's Glock. "Be prepared. Now drive up by the bridge. We need a spot where we can see."

Kelvin drove, his speech fading as he was drawn into the next phase of this craziness. He considered Chicago, had a déjà vu back to when the ice-pick babe had said she was from Poland. Thinking of Chicago he went blank again, then thought of some story in elementary school about a fire and a cow. But maybe he had that wrong. Why the hell would they have cows in the middle of a city?

They circled the block twice, finally picked the lot of an Irish bar. They parked at the far end, away from the building, backed in so they could see the road that came off the bridge.

"It's like Florida and Kittery," Fuller said. "He comes over the bridge and into the city, he's gotta come by here."

"What if he goes to the mall?" Kelvin said.

"It's percentages," Fuller said. "The girl lives in the Old Port."

"I think she's shacking up with him now."

"So they go back to her place so she can get some clothes. Or she says they should go have drinks."

"Because his buddy gets killed?"

"To console himself," Fuller said. "Drown his sorrow. Sometimes I wonder where you've been."

"Last few days, I've been with you," Kelvin said. "It's been a goddamn blast, too."

"Hey, you don't want a few thousand in cash, I'll do it myself."

"How you gonna get there? Call a taxi?"

Kelvin had him on that one, so Fuller just changed the subject, said, "A black Ford pickup or a red Saab with out-of-state plates. You look at the trucks, I'll take the red cars."

They settled in. Cars and trucks whizzed by. Kelvin wished he had a beer, a cold one. He was about to take a break, go into the Irish bar and chug a draft, when Fuller said, "There it is."

"What?"

"Her car."

It passed them, in the left lane, swung onto State Street, and started up the hill. The girl was driving; Brandon was in the passenger seat.

"Jackpot," Fuller said. "Follow them. Don't just sit there."

Kelvin started the motor, pulled out and across traffic. The red car was a block ahead and he raced after it, settling in three cars back.

"They're not going to the Old Port," Kelvin said, thinking, so much for your friggin' theories.

"I got a good feeling about this one," Fuller said as they crossed Congress Street, started down the hill, headed for Forest Avenue, the highway ramps.

"They get on the interstate, we're golden," he said.

"Why's that?" Kelvin said.

"Because we know all the places they go in the city, down by the water there, the boatyard. We haven't seen 'em go anywhere else."

"So?"

"So the players here, we know where they all live except the rich guy and the Russian lady."

"Polish."

"Same difference."

"They live at the hotel."

"Not anymore. I called. Lady at the desk said they checked out last week."

"So where are they living now?"

Fuller was watching the Saab. It slowed, the blinker came on. It swung right onto the ramp for the highway, northbound.

"We're about to find out," he said.

Kelvin turned onto the ramp, too, smelled the fresh paint on the car as he accelerated. He merged onto the highway, settled into the middle lane, four cars behind Mia.

"Five people, Joel," Kelvin said. "This is starting to get serious."

"It's been serious all along, dude," Fuller said. "You're just starting to notice."

CHAPTER 42

The detectives were very pleasant, Nessa thought. The man, O'Flaherty or some such Irish name—so police *were* still all Irish—had gone out and gotten a bottle of a very nice Riesling. He poured her a glass and then went upstairs, left her with the woman detective, who had asked Nessa to call her Jackie. Jackie had thick red hair, a long, narrow face, and looked a little grim until she sat down at the dining room table with a cup of coffee.

Jackie said Brandon seemed like a nice guy. "Tell me more about him, Mrs. Blake," she said.

Nessa said her grandson was very nice, sort of quiet, maybe even a little withdrawn. But he'd always been a bit of a loner, not unhappy, not some crazy person out in a log cabin in the woods, like you hear about. Just content with his books and his boats. A wooden rowboat when he was eight or nine. Then a beat-up dinghy with a leak and a sail.

Jackie knew Nessa had raised Brandon, but didn't know why. Nessa told her. Sipping the wine, Nessa started with the sinking, the policeman coming to the door, the look on his face that said it all. She finished the story a glass of wine later with Lucky coming back to Portland.

"Really," Jackie said. "So he wasn't dead?"

"It was just presumed," Nessa said. "Because he'd been with them."

"He never reported in?"

"Brandon told me he said, Lucky I mean, he had some sort of a breakdown and just took off."

"It must be so hard," Jackie said.

"It is," Nessa said, looking at Jackie. She had deep blue eyes that told Nessa she was a person who cared, she was not your ordinary detective. A woman understood.

"You've been through so much," Jackie said.

"It's been a long row to hoe," Nessa said, the wine bringing up that expression. "Not what I expected."

"What did you expect, Mrs. Blake?"

Nessa looked at the caring eyes, the crow's feet that crinkled up reassuringly on the detective's cheekbones.

"I thought I was going to live happily ever after," Nessa said. "Married a handsome doctor. We had Nikki, beautiful little girl. This big house on the ocean."

"It sounds so perfect," Jackie said.

"To the neighbors, yes."

Nessa took a long sip, not sure whether to get into it. But this woman was so nice, so calming.

"Lots of women thought Luther was handsome, if you know what I mean. Young nurses, they're always out to snag a doctor. But even the wife of one of his partners. Well, come to find out—I'm not sure how to say this—well, I guess you could say he thought they were pretty darn nifty, too."

Jackie looked sympathetic. "I'm sorry, Mrs. Blake."

"All the trips, the conferences, the seminars. They weren't conferences at all, unless you call two people staying at a five-star hotel with a king-size bed and champagne from room service a conference. Nikki and I, we stayed home. Waited for him. 'Daddy!' Nikki would say. And I'd say, 'How was it, honey?' Give him a hug. And he'd say he was tired, jet-lagged, go right to bed, sleep for twelve hours. All that hard 'conferencing.'"

"You poor thing," the detective said.

Nessa knew Jackie understood.

"Oh, but that was just the beginning. Luther was forty-two, he had a heart attack in the hospital parking lot. They said he was dead before he hit the ground. Nikki was in junior high. I had to go get her. I'll never forget it. She was in gym class, playing some game with a ball and a broom. They called her out and I was standing there and she saw my face and somehow she knew. Fell to the floor like she'd been shot. She loved her father."

"I'm sorry, Mrs. Blake."

Nessa poured a half glass, just one more. The bubbles settled and the surface of the wine was flat, a still, golden pond. She drank.

My, this is a nice wine, she thought. Sterling.

"That's not the sorry part. The sorry part was that he'd spent most of our savings, cashed out one of our life insurances. Spent it living like some Arab sheik bedding his harem. Had one of them in a condo."

She smiled, still bitter.

"So you had no money?"

"Oh, not no money. Just not what I thought I had. I had enough to stay in the house. And then I sold some things. Jewelry he gave me. A hideaway cottage in the White Mountains. Luther said it was an investment.

Love nest, is what it was. So that kept me in the house a few more years. Paid the back taxes. Put oil in the furnace. Kept up appearances. I sold the boat, a Chris-Craft like Brandon's, except it was bigger. I'd been on it twice. Always so cold on the ocean in Maine. I hated it. Oh, and I sold Luther's precious Porsche. And the lot we'd bought next door. Always one step ahead."

She took a quick sip, her eyes started to well.

"You okay?" Jackie said.

Nessa nodded, wiped her eyes.

"Then there was Nikki with the baby—this was later on—no father she'd admit to, working in the bars. I got little jobs here and there, tried catering because I cooked then."

Another swallow, the glass empty now.

"It didn't work out," Nessa said. "And then—" She bit her lip, swallowed. Wiped her eyes with the back of her hand. Swallowed hard again.

"And then the boat went down?" the detective said.

Nessa was trying to focus, like the detective had roused her from a dream.

"No," Nessa said. "That was later."

"What happened before that, Mrs. Blake?" Jackie asked. But Nessa looked like she had drifted off, like she had wandered through a door to another place.

"Oh, Nikki," she said, more to herself than to the detective. "Oh, Nikki. I'm so sorry."

"Sorry, Mrs. Blake?" Jackie said. "But it was an accident."

"But I put her there," Nessa said. "I put her in harm's way."

"How? How did you do that?"

But Nessa had reached for the bottle and was pouring another glass. This time she filled it to the brim. She drank and looked away and stopped talking. The detective waited, but for this time Nessa was done.

CHAPTER 43

Lucky was down on the shore, Irina said, leading the way through the foyer, into a spacious study with leather couches, a billiard table, a stone fireplace, and a view of the bay through diamond-paned Tudor windows. From there, they walked a long hallway, the walls studded with photographs of someone's family: a man in a Navy uniform, solemn and dignified; a woman in a long dress sitting on a porch swing and holding a white cat.

"The estate's selling it," Irina said. "Seems a bit strange to be in somebody's house with all their things."

"Are you considering buying it?" Mia said, wondering how many millions this place would cost. Three? Four?

"Right now, we don't know," Irina said, opening the door to the garden. "We told them we'd stay through October. We do like it here, and Lucky has really enjoyed the boating."

"Maine is a sailor's paradise," Brandon said.

"Lucky keeps telling me that," Irina said, smiling back over her shoulder as she skipped down the stairs. "I tell him, if only it would get warm. He said, 'Irina, for Maine, this is warm.'"

"In August it may warm up more," Mia said.

"Well, our last sailing, the only time I've really done it before this, it was out of St. Maarten, the Dutch side," Irina said. "The West Indies, all those beautiful little islands. So warm and the white sand, the blue water, it's so clear."

"Sounds wonderful," Mia said.

"Well, I suppose Maine may grow on me," Irina said as they crossed the overgrown flower beds, started across the sprawl of unkempt lawn. The grass was damp and they scuffed through it, where the grass was trampled. The path wound down the lawn to a seawall made of granite blocks. There was a wooden ramp going up onto the wall, and then an aluminum pier, the end of which was propped on a small float. Lucky was standing on the float, looking out at the bay, the islands, a sailboat beating into the southeast.

He turned.

"Hey, kids, glad you came," Lucky called as they started down the ramp. "Welcome to our humble abode."

"Of the moment," Irina said.

"Where is home really?" Mia said.

"She loves it here," Lucky said quickly. "It's where her heart is."

"Manhattan," Irina said. "I can't stay away from New York City too long."

"Every day she says it with a little less conviction," Lucky said, and he put his arm around her shoulder. "I'm wearing her down."

They stood on the float, breathed the salt air, watched the gulls swooping over the chop.

"What do you think, Brandon?" Lucky said. "Nice spot or what? I can picture *Ocean Swell* right here."

"Great," Brandon said. "But could you bring her in here? How much water out here at low tide?"

"Not sure," Lucky said, turning away from the bay. "Let's go up to the house and have a drink."

They were on a second-story veranda on the water side. Mia and Irina sat, fleeces buttoned tight, a bottle of Chardonnay between them. Lucky had brought two bottles of Shipyard ale from a refrigerator somewhere on the second floor, and he and Brandon sat on the short, shingled wall on the edge of the porch. Lucky held up his bottle and said, "Cheers."

Brandon drank, felt a wave of weariness wash over him. Griffin, Nessa, the cops in the house, Fuller and Kelvin out there—somewhere.

"So you still leaving tomorrow?" he said. "Supposed to be pretty messy."

"No problem. Messy weather is the South Atlantic. I remember sailing from Cape Town, boat delivery to Marseilles. Me and Ketch, two Aussies. Big yawl, sixty-footer. Left in the fall, April down there, went from thick, can't-see-your-bow fog off South Africa, big swells, then the weirdest confused chop you've ever seen, wind shifting all over the place. Man, we're crossing Valdivia Bank, go from five thousand meters to twenty-three. You want to see some wild water. Then squalls, fifty-knot gusts, totally unpredictable. I was damn glad to reach St. Helena."

"It makes my skin crawl, these stories," Irina said. "I told him, I have to be able to see land somewhere."

Lucky grinned, sipped his beer, looked out on the overcast sky, the gray-green waters.

"Relax, honey. I think we'll be okay with a little rain off Cape Elizabeth."

He paused, considered Brandon, and said, "You okay?"

"A long couple days," Brandon said.

There was a silence as the three of them waited for Brandon to explain. He mustered a smile, then began. Griffin. Fuller and Kelvin. Nessa shaken by it all.

When he paused, a long silence.

"So the police think these men killed your friend and now they're coming after you?" Irina said.

"That's one theory. It was what Griffin was working on."

"Big jump from the little stuff this guy was doing to killing a policeman," Lucky said. "My God. I mean, that's serious business."

"I doubt it was planned," Brandon said. "Maybe he tried to arrest them. They jump him, struggle for the gun."

"Brandon said he was a really nice guy," Mia said. "Had two boys."

"They play baseball," Brandon said.

Another pause, the cries of gulls faint in the distance.

"So they're waiting for them at Nessa's?" Lucky said.

"And my boat. And I'm sure they followed us out here."

Lucky and Irina looked at him. Lucky looked out at the woods that bordered the sweeping lawn.

"No kidding. Are there detectives in the bushes?"

"I don't know how they do it," Brandon said. "They asked where we were going, how long we'd be here, who we were going to see."

"They go all out when it's one of their own," Lucky said.

"Where I'm from," Irina said, "they attack the criminals and kill as many of them as they can. Dump them on the street corner so everybody can see. It's routine, this sort of—what is the word, Mia?"

"Reprisal?" Mia said.

"Yes. I knew our writer would know the word," Irina said.

"So all of this began after, what was it? You punched this guy's mother?"

"Elbowed," Brandon said. "But it's not about that. It's about money."

"Another scam, another angle to work," Lucky said.

"Then the policeman, it must have been not part of the plan," Irina said. "There's no money to be made there, you think?"

"But something went wrong," Lucky said. "A scuffle, as you say. The guy doesn't want to go back to jail. What kind of sentence?"

"Five years," Brandon said.

"Not a lifetime, but not nothing," Lucky said. "So now he's desperate. Every cop in the state gunning for him. But he's short on cash, right?"

"I wouldn't doubt it."

"So if he's smart he doesn't just steal a car, get picked up sleeping in some rest area in Ohio. If he's smart, he's right here still, looking for money to travel with, support himself until he finds the right spot to settle again."

"Your grandmother," Irina said. "Does she have money?"

"Maybe fifty dollars at a time," Brandon said.

"But she has a nice house," Mia said. "To somebody like him—"

"She's rich," Lucky said. "A cash cow."

"And if he and his friend come here—" Irina said.

She didn't have to finish the thought. Almost in unison, they all looked out over the lawn to the spruce-edged woods, dark and dense and shadowed.

"You could have a dozen Fullers watching you from there," Lucky said.

"Or detectives," Brandon said.

"Creepy," Irina said. "Let's go in."

Irina was making pannini: eggplant and tomato, cheese and olives. Lucky took Mia on a tour of the house, Lucky starting to talk about the time he sailed into Havana and visited Ernest Hemingway's place. Brandon stood in the kitchen, open-beamed ceiling and copper counters. He offered to help and Irina pointed to a grater and a block of feta cheese.

Taking a long machete-like knife from a drawer, Irina sliced eggplant and tomato. She was efficient and strong, moving with quick economical movements.

"You've worked in a restaurant?" Brandon said.

"No, but I grew up watching a good cook."

"Your mother?"

"Yes. In Poland it was an art to make something good out of very little."

"Is she still living?"

"I think—I mean, yes."

"Do you go back to visit?" Brandon asked, the grated cheese mounding on the countertop.

"Once in a great while," Irina said. "I left home when I was eighteen, didn't go back for ten years. So we aren't close. It's too bad, but couldn't be avoided."

"Did everyone else stay in Warsaw?"

"Yes, I was the prodigal daughter, except I haven't really returned. Are you still the prodigal child if you don't come back?"

"I don't know," Brandon said. "You definitely wouldn't get a Bible story."

"Someday, if I get back to Europe, I'll go to Warsaw and see them. Maybe in the spring I'll go to Paris, get away from the Maine, what do you call it? Mud season?"

"March and April," Brandon said.

"Oh, but Lucky, he'd rather sail in a hurricane than fly. Hates planes."

"He's in control of the boat," Brandon said.

Irina, slicing eggplant with the machete, smiled. "You got that right. He does not like it at all when he's not in charge."

The cheese was grated, left in a cream-colored mound. Brandon excused himself, started down the hall for the bathroom. He could heard Irina start to sauté, the hiss as the eggplant hit the oil in the pan. Brandon listened for Mia and Lucky, heard their faint voices from upstairs. He went into the bathroom and out the opposite door. Hurrying down the hall, he peeked in each door along the way.

A room with hooks for jackets.

Another room with two love seats, wing chairs.

A room with floor-to-ceiling bookshelves still full of books. Biographies of Roosevelt. Mozart. Lincoln. Novels he'd never heard of. A big maple writing desk with pens in brass cups. A leather valise on the desk, a woman's bag next to it.

Brandon listened again, heard the distant clatter of pans. He moved to the desk opened the valise. There were receipts. He glanced at the door, listened. Took the receipts out, flipped through them.

A pair of women's shoes for $1,234. Dolce & Gabbana, from Neiman Marcus at the mall in Short Hills, New Jersey. The next for a skirt, two blouses, and a sweater: $2,854 at Saks at the same mall. Bras and underpants from Victoria's Secret. $912.

Irina paid cash.

Then another receipt sticking out like a duck in a flock of chickens. Wal-Mart in Paramus. Jeans. Skirts. Tops and shoes. Underpants and bras. Something called "nightwear." The list was four inches long. $603.89. Enough stuff to outfit a college sorority for the price of one Dolce and Gabbana pump.

Did Irina send clothes home to Poland? Did she have a half-dozen sisters in various shapes and sizes?

A bang from the kitchen, Lucky's voice, distant but approaching. Brandon shoved the receipts back, flipped through the pockets and folders in the bag. Felt something stiff in a zippered pocket on the side. Slid the zipper open, fished out two folders.

Plane tickets.

British Airways.

Kennedy to Heathrow.

Departing 7:03 p.m. 7 July.

First class. One way.

Zalina N. Maricova and Willem S. DeHahn were flying to London in two weeks.

CHAPTER 44

Dinner was in the round room at the base of the turret. Lucky poured wine, a California Chardonnay from a vineyard owned by friends. He talked about the ocean, how people think that because the top of it is flat, it must be a big wide bowl. Instead, the ocean bottom is made up of canyons and ridges and mountain ranges and plains, just like the land.

"Where are you from, Lucky?" Brandon said.

"Oh, here, there, and everywhere," Lucky said, pouring more wine for Mia, answering without looking away from the glass. "My dad was in the military, moved around a lot. I guess that's why I tend to move even now. I get restless staying in one place too long."

"I guess I feel like I don't know you as well as I should," Brandon said, rolling the stem of his glass between his thumb and forefinger. "With our connection, you know?"

Mia looked at him, smiled tentatively.

"What branch of the service was your dad in?" Brandon said.

He saw Irina look to Lucky, her smile placid.

"Navy, the supply side. He made sure ships had enough Rice Krispies when they went out on a cruise. Sheets and pillowcases for everyone on the aircraft carriers. Toothpaste. I used to make up stuff to tell kids because I was embarrassed about what he really did. Changed the toothpaste and cereal to torpedoes and missiles."

"So where'd you go, following him around?" Brandon said.

"Oh, everywhere. Newport, Rhode Island. San Diego and Monterey. Subic Bay in the Philippines. Eighth grade I was in Diego Garcia, hottest place this side of hell."

"College?"

"Two years, UC Santa Barbara. Did more partying than anything else. My dad said I was wasting my time and his money. I agreed and left. Next time I saw him was at his wake."

"Traveled around?"

"Like I was blown by the wind. Thailand, Malaysia, New Guinea, New Zealand, up to London. Met a woman there, in a pub at Russell Square, slowed me down."

He patted Irina's hand.

"But not like you, dearest."

Irina smiled.

"Then it was Belgium, Amsterdam, a couple of months in Latvia. Fascinating places, these forgotten Eastern European countries. Very isolated and charming in a very backward sort of way."

Irina looked at him and smiled. Coldly, Brandon thought.

"Lands that time forgot," Lucky said. "Anyway, then to Toronto for a bit, down to D.C., met another woman, moved with her to Seattle. My mother got sick in San Diego while I was out west, I went back home and this time I got to say goodbye."

Lucky paused. Sipped. Smiled sadly.

"So in your wanderings, how did you come up with money to invest?" Brandon said.

"Good story," Lucky said, sipping his wine. "Met up with Ketch in Santa Cruz, started crewing with him, deliveries and all. Up and down the west coast. Then trans-Atlantics. Came to Maine and that's when, you know, *Black Magic* was lost."

He paused.

"Went back west and wandered a bit more, but then my mother's estate cleared probate. Back up to Seattle, met these two guys at a party who had this idea to put videos on the Internet. Sounded good to me. Kicked in a hundred grand. Five years later they went public and my investment, well, let's just say it had multiplied. I cashed in."

"Good move," Mia said.

"Dumb luck," Lucky said. "What do I know about the Internet?"

He looked at Brandon.

"I know," Lucky said. "Boring. More fun to talk about the places I've been."

"No, it's not," Brandon said, "I just want to hear about you. And Irina. What you're really about. What's important to you? I know it sounds weird, but—"

"He means knowing you as people," Mia said. "In your stories about your travels, you tend to disappear."

"That's right," Lucky said. "Sometimes I think that's why I've always kept moving. Keep from looking at myself too closely."

Irina smiled. "But why is that, Lucky?" she said. "What is it you don't want to see?"

Lucky looked at her, then at Mia and Brandon.

"Who knows? The guy who didn't live up to his father's expectations?"

He grinned. "I'm sure there's a shrink somewhere could tell me all about myself."

Brandon sipped his wine, looked to the window, the bay in the distance, a lobster boat chugging home. "You know, Lucky," he said. "You're the person who saw my mother last and I don't even know your real name."

Lucky looked at him, his mouth still smiling but his eyes hardening. And then that moment of disconnect was over, and Lucky was grinning again, his eyes, too.

"I used to make my friends in school promise not to tell," he said. "My real name is Willem." He pronounced the W as a V.

"Always hated it," Lucky said. He rose from the table and began to clear the plates.

"What time do you leave in the morning?" Mia said, filling the silence.

"Up at five, set off by seven," Irina said.

"We should go," Mia said. "We have to get back, check on Nessa."

"Be sure to give her my best," Lucky said. "Tell her I'm thinking of her. Really, make sure you do. I think a lot of Nessa. I think about her every day. Please make sure you tell her that."

Brandon and Mia left, waving from the car, then speeding out the long drive and through the stone gates.

Lucky and Irina turned from the closed door and walked to the bay room without talking. Lucky poured another glass of wine, went to the window. Behind him, Irina collected the empty glasses.

"I didn't know your father was in the Navy," she said.

"He wasn't."

"So you didn't move all around the world, live in those places?"

"As a kid? No."

"Where did that come from, then?"

"I made it up," Lucky said.

"Right there?"

"It's called improv, darling. You've been known to spin a yarn or two, my 'Polish' beauty."

"Did you travel to all those countries?"

"No. Mostly other ones."

"What was your father?"

"An accountant. Did people's taxes. Thought small. Lived small. One of those people content to let the world pass him by."

"Were you always such a liar?"

"Only after I figured out the truth was a dead end."

"He's beginning to ask a lot of questions," Irina said. "And she's always listening. And there's those idiots following them around, a zillion cops. We were supposed to be under the radar."

"Two weeks and we never see any of them again."

"I don't like the feel of it. I'm going to tell Victor."

"Tell him what? That we aren't coming? That they can turn around and go back? Unload in Nova Scotia, two hundred miles short?"

Irina didn't answer.

"We're in, baby," Lucky said. "There are no problems here. You can handle Mutt and Jeff with one hand tied behind your back."

"It was either Mutt or Jeff who shot a cop."

"Some chump, probably didn't even have a bullet in his gun. So what. And if Brandon and Mia do pry too much, I've got the trump card."

"The grandmother?"

"She knows it, too. I could tell at the house."

"If you could tell, they could tell," Irina said. "That girl, she doesn't miss any little thing. Always, she's studying us."

"She's a writer," Lucky said. "Maybe she's going to put you in her next novel."

Irina started for the kitchen, stopped, and turned back. "Is your real name really Willem?"

"Must be," Lucky said. "Says it on my passport."

"Not all of them," Irina said.

CHAPTER 45

Route 1 in Falmouth. Fuller and Kelvin in the Caprice, four cars behind Mia's Saab. There were two cops in a Jeep Cherokee three cars behind the Caprice. Fuller had the rearview mirror turned so he could see them from the passenger seat.

"Do what I say," he said.

"When?" Kelvin said.

"When I say so," Fuller said.

They drove past a shopping center, a health club, a wallpaper store. Just beyond the store, a girl, maybe 14, was waiting at a cross walk. She carried a bag, McDonald's. She stepped off the curb.

"Slow down," Fuller said.

"I see her," Kelvin said, starting to brake.

The kid waited, saw the car start to slow. She took three steps and was in the middle of the traffic lane.

"Go," Fuller said.

"She's in the—"

"Go," Fuller said again and reached over with his left foot and stomped the gas.

The car leapt forward, the girl froze and dropped the bag, soda spraying. Kelvin swerved around her and Fuller saw the cops in the Jeep stop as the girl bent to pick up the bag, the soda puddling out.

"What the hell?" Kelvin said. "I almost hit that kid."

"Right at the shopping center, all the way through," Fuller said.

Kelvin turned. They drove down the center lane, turned past the storefronts, took another right at an access road that circled behind the building. They made the circle, emerged in the far end of the lot, and circled back onto the road. Fuller saw the cops' Jeep stopped in traffic in front of the stores.

Kelvin turned right. They couldn't see the Saab.

"Left," Fuller barked, and Kelvin turned, sped down a cross road. Took another right and Fuller said, "Hit it."

The Caprice shuddered and hissed as they sped down the narrow road, estates on the left side, big new houses on the right. The road climbed a hill and at the crest Fuller said, "Got it."

"Where?" Kelvin said.

"They just turned in."

"You want me to follow them?"

"No, keep going. We gotta find a place to hide this thing, come back on foot."

"Hit the place in daylight?" Kelvin said.

"You crazy? We check it out now. Wait until it gets dark, we go in. Fast and furious. Just like the Israelis."

"You and your freakin' Israelis. What if they don't go peaceably?" Kelvin said, a word from a cowboy movie slipping in.

"It's outta my hands," Fuller said. "It's like those dominos knocking each other over."

"Since the cop."

"Since forever," Fuller said, and something new and different in his voice made Kelvin think that maybe Joel was giving it up, was going down.

"I got a kid," Kelvin said. "How 'bout I wait with the car."

They were through the gates, a drizzle falling, turning the road slick and shiny in the headlights. The woods were black as the cloudless sky and Brandon stared out, squinting, trying to see where Fuller was hiding.

Mia looked over at Brandon from behind the wheel.

"What?" she said. "What's bothering you?"

"A guy I liked a lot was shot to death."

"Something else," Mia said. "It happened in the house. Your mood."

"She bought clothes," Brandon said. "Lots of women's clothes. In New Jersey."

"Who?"

"Irina. If that's really her name. I saw the receipts. In her bag."

Mia drove, didn't ask what Brandon was doing snooping.

"Maybe she's sending stuff home to Poland, outfitting the whole family," she said. "They don't have a T.J. Maxx."

"She never talks about family. She never talks about anything."

You don't trust them," Mia said.

"They've got tickets for London in two weeks."

"A holiday?"

"One way."

"Maybe they don't know exactly when they're going to come back," she said. "They've got money. They can just buy tickets at the counter. Not like they're shopping for a deal on the Internet."

"Her name isn't Irina, not on the ticket. It's Zalina. Zalina N. Maricova. He's Willem S. DeHahn."

"Well, you didn't think his parents named him Lucky," Mia said.

"What about Zalina?"

"One of those Old World things. A nickname. Her grandmother's name. Maybe she doesn't like Zalina."

"I think they sailed almost all the way to Nova Scotia," Brandon said. "Why was the boat so completely cleaned?"

"They're neatniks."

"It wasn't neat. It was scoured."

Mia hesitated, her devil's advocate defense crumbling. "I think your grandmother's afraid of him," she said. "At first I thought it was just sadness, the bad memories. But now I don't think so."

"I know. When he was talking about Griffin getting killed, for a minute there it was like Lucky was a cop."

"Or a criminal."

"Not some ex boat bum," Brandon said.

"Hit it big on an IPO," Mia said.

"What's that?"

"Initial public offering."

"Oh."

"But none of it really proves anything," Mia said.

"Not one thing. But it all adds up."

"To what?"

"They aren't what they say they are."

"So what are they?"

"I don't know," Brandon said.

They drove across the old bridge at the entrance to Back Cove. Brandon looked out on the water, pools of it shining against the mud, a rotting pier silhouetted against the pale gray city sky.

"There's no water at that float," he said.

"What?"

"His float at the house. There's four feet of water there at low tide. Rocks all through there, out three hundred yards. That's why there's no moorings at those houses. Just small boats."

"So?"

"Lucky said he could picture *Ocean Swell* there," Brandon said. "Could never happen and he had to know that. A sailor like him."

"Why would he say it then?"

"He was totally bullshitting. For a minute he forgot who he was talking to."

"Not like him," Mia said.

"No," Brandon said. "He screwed up."

There was a church down the road from the estate entrance. It was Catholic, a statue of the Virgin Mary standing lonely vigil on the dark lawn. To the rear, an addition was going up, the slab poured, lumber in a flesh-colored stack, a trailer parked and locked.

The Caprice was pulled in behind it. Fuller was in the passenger seat, Kelvin behind the wheel. They were drinking beers, Budweiser from 16-ounce cans. Fuller had the pistol on his lap.

"Oughta toss that gun," Kelvin said. "Ballistics."

"When we're done here I'll throw it in the ocean."

"Not at the house."

"Off the bridge," Fuller said.

He held the gun up in front of him and stared at it.

"People say you need a honking three fifty-seven."

"Like Dirty Harry," Kelvin said.

"That was a magnum," Fuller said. "This Ruger. Nothing wrong with a nine. Kill you just as dead."

Kelvin froze. Took a deep silent breath. A swallow of beer.

"Know what you mean," he said softly. "But not sure I like the way you put it."

"K-Rod," Fuller said. "I need you right with me."

"When?"

"When we hit the house."

"I told you. I got a kid. I can't go around fucking holding people up."

"You jumped Blake."

"That's a whole different thing."

Fuller smiled. "I know. You're thinking like a daddy. That's nice."

He raised the gun, pressed the muzzle to the side of Kelvin's neck, just under his right ear. Kelvin was still. He could see the Virgin Mary, her arms extended. Her back was to him. He thought to himself that she wouldn't be able to testify. It made him smile.

"Dude, you stay here, you know what you are?" Fuller said.

"I'm not a murderer."

"You're a witness. You're the one person who can put me away for life."

"I wouldn't do that to a friend."

"Oh, they'd make you a deal you can't refuse."

"I'm here, ain't I? Doesn't that tell you something?"

"It tells me you could be outta here as soon as I'm out the door."

"I ain't gonna run on you, Joel."

"No, Kel," Fuller said. "You're not. 'Cause you're gonna be right beside me, son. All the way."

He lowered the gun, looked at the dime-size red circle on Kelvin's neck, an inch from the scabbed ice-pick hole. The gun was on Fuller's lap, still pointed at Kelvin, his waist. Fuller smiled, stuck the gun in the front of his jeans.

"Must be getting paranoid," he said, giving the smile that was only his mouth. "Let's go."

He rolled the window down, opened the door, got out, and closed it. Leaned back. A clean shot through the open window. Kelvin got out slowly, came around the front of the car.

"What's the plan?" he said.

"Bushwack over there. Get the lay, of the land. Wait for the lights to go out. Let 'em get to sleep, pop a door and go in. We do it right, we get 'em in bed."

"You gotta get the money."

"Not a problem."

"What if they don't want to hand it over?"

"We start with her," Fuller said. "A babe like that is almost worth dying for."

They walked behind the church, crossed a narrow road, hopped a stone wall. Some sort of animal flushed and scurried away. Neither of them flinched. Fuller slowed, let Kelvin lead the way.

CHAPTER 46

Lights were on, three rooms on the first floor, one room upstairs, the curtains there drawn. Irina was on the bed, dressed, watching television. On the show, fashion experts were telling a chubby, plain woman that her clothes didn't fit. The plain woman reminded Irina of a woman from Odessa. On the TV, the fashion people were saying her jeans did nothing for her butt, her sweater was too big, maybe if she got a push-up bra.

It was a strange world, having discussions like that, Irina thought. Her mother had never considered any of this: butt or boobs, whether a skirt made her look fat. She cooked for six kids, waited for her husband to get home from the shipyard, already drunk and ornery. Some sort of twisted miracle that they had children at all, Irina thought, not for the first time. How could there have been even that momentary joy in such a grim place?

She wasn't going to live like that. She'd been working for a year and eight months to make sure, and soon she'd be in London, turn right around and fly to the British Virgins, money in the Caymans, a little house on a hill overlooking Georgetown Harbor.

And she'd be alone.

The plain woman on the television was pretending that she didn't mind being called chubby and ugly, only a few million people watching. Who cared what—

A snap outside, like a branch breaking. Irina listened for a thrashing in the woods, a deer bounding through the brush. She heard nothing, just the television chatter, a june bug buzzing against the screen.

She rolled off the bed, grabbed a rain jacket off a hook on the door. Out in the hallway, she slipped a gun out of the jacket pocket. A Bersa .380, a gift from Victor in London. She held it against her thigh as she went to the next door, opened it, crossed the room without turning on the lights.

At the side of the window, she stood in the dark room and listened. Heard birds and frogs murmuring in the trees. More bugs buzzing. The faint rumble of the sea. A single scratching shuffle.

Irina eased toward the window and looked down. The driveway was lighted, the parking area in front of the stable and the garage. Irina watched, listened.

Saw a big man in jeans, a black T-shirt. He eased around the corner of the stable. Still in the shadows, he moved to the door that led to the tack room. He tried the latch. The door didn't open and he leaned against it, pulled the latch up.

The door squeaked as it opened. The man slipped inside, closed the door behind him. Irina was about to turn away when another figure came around the corner, smaller, thinner. He stood at the door for a moment and then it opened.

Irina saw the big man's face.

It was Kelvin. That meant the other guy was Fuller. The cop killers had come to visit, were coming in through the garage.

The room smelled of leather and hay. They crossed it gingerly, trying to be silent. Kelvin stubbed his toe on something big and heavy, gritted his teeth to keep from crying out.

Fuller was in the rear, the gun at his side. The room with the hay led to a garage with a Jeep, a boat heaped with stuff. They crossed the garage, found a door that led to the house. Fuller put his head against the door and listened.

Hearing nothing, he pointed at the knob with the gun. Kelvin reached for it, turned it slowly. The door fell open. They moved through.

Irina found Lucky in the dining room, spreading his foul weather gear, underwear, jeans, and T-shirts on the big mahogany table.

"They're here," she whispered.

He turned to her, saw the pistol in her hand. "Where?"

"Came in the garage. One minute."

Lucky nodded. "Shoot only if we have to," he said. "I don't want a mess."

He crossed to a buffet table, leaned down, and opened the bottom drawer. There were table cloths in it, white and embroidered. Lucky bent, lifted the top cloth, slid out a Mossberg shotgun, the barrel shortened to fourteen inches, the stock cut down. He stood, moved to the doorway, turned out the lights. Motioned for Irina to take the other door.

They waited, listening. Breathed slowly. Listened some more.

Minutes passed. Neither of them moved. Lucky closed his eyes to hear better. Waited. Another minute passed. And then he heard it. A footstep, almost silent, but not quite.

It was from the direction of the pantry, off the kitchen. A door led from the pantry to the garage. Lucky raised his hand. Irina nodded.

It was less a sound than a presence. Someone moving into the kitchen. A barely audible rustle. A nearly silent breathing.

Irina looked over at Lucky. Held up the ice pick. He nodded. She turned back to the door.

There was a thud as one of them bumped a corner of a table, then a shhhsshh that was louder than the thud. A shuffle as they moved across the kitchen, the grit on their shoes like sandpaper on the tile floor.

Lucky took a step to the door on his side of the room. Then another. As he glanced back he saw Irina tensing. The pick low in her left hand, the gun in the right. The left hand easing back, like a string drawn on a bow.

A figure emerged from beside the door frame. A hairy arm. A hand with a screwdriver, a black and yellow handle, the point forward and low. A shoulder. Kelvin's face, his head. He turned, saw Irina, and started to swing the screwdriver toward her.

Irina drove the ice pick into his shoulder.

Kelvin bellowed and Lucky spun out of the room, saw Fuller lunging forward, turning to the doorway, the pistol held low. Lucky said, "Freeze, police," as Kelvin fell back, his hand on the wooden handle of the pick. Fuller turned, snapped off a shot at Lucky, a black pock appearing in the wall to his left. Fuller backpedaled, crashed into a table in the next room, turned, and started to run.

Irina came out of the doorway, the pistol in two hands, stopped, and sighted on Fuller's back.

"No," Lucky said. "No blood in the house."

Fuller was through the door, pounding through the living room. They heard a rattle and bang as he went out the front door. Irina put the gun on Kelvin, still clutching the pick, breathing heavily.

"Outside," Lucky said, motioned with the shotgun.

"No," Kelvin said. "No, don't."

"I said, outside," Lucky said again.

"Kevin," Irina said. "Listen to him."

They walked through the kitchen, Kelvin going first, hunched and moaning. Out the kitchen door and into the drive. It was dark and the pavement was wet. The wind had shifted to the south and the breeze was damp and salty.

"Stop," Lucky said.

"I got a kid," Kelvin said. "Don't kill me."

"What do you want?" Lucky said.

"I don't want nothin'. He's the one wants money," Kelvin said, the pick sticking out of his T-shirt, blood running through his fingers.

"Aren't there any 7-Elevens?" Lucky said, the shotgun barrel up now.

"We gotta stay on the down low."

"You shot that cop," Lucky said. "That's really stupid."

"I didn't fucking shoot nobody," Kelvin said.

"Were you going to tie us up or something?" Irina said.

"I don't know," Kelvin said. "I don't know what the plan was."

"How much?" Lucky said.

Irina looked at him.

"How much what?"

"How much money do you need?"

"A couple thousand," Kelvin said. "So we can leave. We're going to Chicago."

"Driving?"

"Yes."

Lucky moved the shotgun to his right arm, reached back for his big wallet. He fingered out $2,000 in hundreds, took a step up, and stuck it in the back pocket of Kelvin's jeans.

"There you go," he said. "If we see either of you ever again, I absolutely promise we'll kill you. Cut off your balls and chop you up. Throw you in the ocean for the crabs to eat."

"Okay," Kelvin said.

"Now take off."

"I can't. This thing—"

"Pull it out," Lucky told Irina.

"No," Kelvin said. "It hurts."

"Okay, we shoot you right here," Lucky said.

"No. But what if it bleeds. What if I—"

"Die?" Lucky said. "You don't leave, you'll die for sure."

He jerked his head at Irina.

"Do it," he said.

Irina walked to Kelvin, slipped her gun in the waist of her slacks. Lucky put the shotgun muzzle on the back of Kelvin's head. He closed his eyes. Irina took the handle in one hand, braced Kelvin's head with the other. And pulled.

Kelvin cried out and blood oozed. He put his hands over the puncture, bloody fingers in the dike.

"Go," Lucky said, like Kelvin was an animal they were releasing into the wild. "Go."

Kelvin staggered off down the driveway, weaving slightly, breaking into a trot when they didn't shoot.

"What the hell?" Irina said.

"We kill them we have to clean it up," Lucky said. "Then we have to run and we can't go yet. This way, they take off, maybe they make it. By the time they get caught or killed, we're long gone."

"Or they get picked up down the road."

"I like our odds. I call Brandon from the boat on the way back in, he can tell us if the coast is clear. So to speak."

There was a pause in the conversation, and it was filled by the sound of the wind on the bay, waves breaking on the rocky islands just offshore.

"Or we don't go at all," Irina said.

"Not an option," Lucky said. "I'll go alone. I'll keep your share."

"You can have it."

"Victor would consider you a major liability. You know that."

Irina looked away, thinking of the fate of the last liability she'd heard of, chopped into pieces, buried in a landfill.

"What time?" she said.

"Off the mooring at five," Lucky said.

"I'll get the drop of blood in the kitchen," Irina said.

Lucky smiled, said, "I'll hose off the drive."

CHAPTER 47

Brandon ran the engine, checked the electronics, the lights, idled around to the fuel dock in the drizzle, and pumped in eighty gallons of gas, a half-week's pay. Locking the pump, he idled *Bay Witch* back out, made a wide circle around *Ocean Swell* riding on her mooring. The breeze was from the south and the sailboat's bow pointed toward shore. A south wind was better than wind out of the east, Brandon thought, if you were sailing from Portland to Halifax.

Backing into the slip, he tied up, stood in the cockpit for a moment. It was after eleven. There were lights glowing in the cabins of a few of the boats, but most of the marina was in darkness. The harbor was quiet, the ferry was out, spotlights illuminating empty piers on the Portland side of the harbor. Soft rain matted what little chop there was and the waters of the harbor were black, a mirror of the sky. Brandon stepped off the stern onto the dock, headed for his truck parked outside the gate by the south boat shed.

The yard was lit by a single lamp high on a pole. Moths fluttered weakly around the light, wings heavy in the dampness. Brandon stopped at the top of the ramp and looked over the yard.

There were open bays on the rusting sheds, dark as caves. The wind rustled the leaves in the vines that covered the fence along the road. Brandon started across the yard, staying in the shadows along the buildings. He sidestepped boat stands and dock carts, made his way to the gate. It was locked from the outside and he pulled the latch, eased it open, slipped through, and closed it behind him.

Boats were lined up in the storage yard across the road. Big cruisers, some smaller. These boats weren't launching this season. Some were for sale. Some needed work owners couldn't afford.

In the back of the yard, a couple of hundred yards from the road, tucked between an ugly cruiser and a tuna boat with its tower folded down, was the black Caprice.

Kelvin was in the front, his legs stretched across the seat, his head against the driver's window, cushioned by his rolled-up sweatshirt. Fuller was in the back, one foot on the seat but not trying to sleep.

"I know you want to run," he was saying, "but I'm right. I know I am. They didn't shoot because they can't risk bringing cops in."

"Coulda killed us and buried us in the woods there," Kelvin said.

"But that would take time," Fuller said. "Clean up the house, blood all over the walls. Gotta dig the holes, that's a bitch of a job, not like on TV. Try it sometime. Haul us out there, fill the holes back up. They don't have time for that."

"Why not? It's not like they work or anything."

"Because they got something going. And it's going down soon. Gotta be something big, for them to take this chance."

"What chance?" Kelvin said.

"Letting us go."

"What? Like we're gonna call the cops? Say we're the guys killed the cop. We tried to rip off these people and they chased us out?"

"No, but now they know that we know."

"We don't know shit," Kelvin said. "And even if we did, what are we gonna do about it? I ain't going back there. Guy with a fucking sawed-off, that bitch sticking me. This cat's used up all his lives, dude."

"It's big, I'm telling you," Fuller said. "Coke. Heroin, maybe. I saw this show in jail. These people were just smuggling money. Cash money. Big boxes, millions."

"Smuggling it where?"

"Outta the U.S. Drug dealers make all this money, gotta get it back to someplace they can put it in a bank, some fake bank in the Cayman Islands or something. These smugglers had the money in hidden compartments in trucks and shit."

"You think these rich assholes are smuggling money?"

"Would explain why they have all that cash."

"Which they still have and we don't," Kelvin said.

"I got a plan," Fuller said.

"Better than the last one? 'Cause that one sucked."

"We grab the blonde."

"How we gonna do that?"

"She's gotta be alone sometime. We take her when she gets out of her car. Or we get him out on a boat someplace, tell him one of the yachts is sinking. He goes out to check, we take the blonde, leave a note. Give 'em a day to get the money."

"You are freakin' insane," Kelvin said, his eyes closed.

"She's friends with those people. Not like they're gonna call the cops," Fuller said. "They got cash. Drive out, drop the cash, we tell 'em where little blondie is."

They were quiet for a moment. The rain pattered on the roof of the car. The windows were opaque, the light glittering through the droplets.

"How much you think those two would pay to keep her alive?" Fuller asked. And then he waited, knew it would come, knew it would be way low.

"Five thousand?" Kelvin said.

Fuller smiled and shook his head.

"Kelvin, Kelvin, Kelvin," he said.

CHAPTER 48

They slipped down the stairs at 4:30. Nessa would sleep until ten, tired after a night of wine and Scrabble with Jackie. Another cop was in the kitchen, a big football player of a guy drinking coffee in the dark. He nodded as they left by the back door, rain gear on.

The sky was dark gray, a shade lighter than night, the rain coming in windblown spatters. They took the truck, rolled out of the drive, and clicked on the lights. An SUV came out of the darkness and followed at a distance, staying with them all the way to the marina. When they pulled up to the gate, it stayed fifty yards back, lights off.

Walking to the boat, Brandon felt the steady wind out of the southeast, the edge of a big low-pressure system pushing up the east coast. There was chop on the harbor now. If Lucky and Irina set out now, they'd have two days of slop, some serious seas offshore.

It was a good test, Brandon thought, a day when nobody would go sailing for fun.

On board *Bay Witch*, Mia put water in the kettle and put it on the propane stove. She warmed her hands while Brandon stood on the berth and watched out the port window.

"If I were them, I'd stay in bed," Mia said. "Standing out in the cold rain for hours? Yuck."

"Lucky may have a different idea of bad weather," Brandon said.

"How far will we go?"

"Beyond the islands. Far enough to know whether they're swinging south."

"Is this boat up to it?"

"Sure. She's takes a sea pretty well, for her size I mean. If it gets uncomfortable, we'll think about—" Brandon paused.

"What?"

"They're here," he said.

Lucky and Irina were towing a dock cart. It was filled with duffels, cartons, what looked like plastic grocery bags. They moved down the left side dock, away from *Bay Witch,* to where the inflatable was tied up. Brandon heard the outboard start, saw Lucky head out with the first load. He offloaded on the sailboat, putted back to the dock. Irina lifted bags into the dinghy, then stepped in. The pair, hoods up, motored out between the moored boats. The outboard went silent and fifteen minutes later Brandon saw the running lights come on.

He went to the cockpit and climbed up, crouched at the helm, and watched as *Ocean Swell* cast off and swung about, motoring in a wide circle and heading out of the harbor.

Brandon waited until the sailboat passed out of sight beyond the next point, then started the engine. It coughed, then settled into a low rumble. Mia came up, climbed out onto the dock, and cast off the lines, stern first. Brandon eased out of the slip, idled out of the marina and into the channel. He left the lights off.

Ocean Swell was a mile off, still under power. Onshore, the city was quiet, only lobster boats chugging out from the wharves in a slow procession. Brandon fell in behind a 40-footer, kept it between *Bay Witch* and the big sailboat. The sternman on the lobster boat looked back at them, wondering why a small cruiser was heading out in this dirty weather.

"He thinks we're crazy," Mia said, standing by Brandon at the helm.

"Crazy is doing this in January," Brandon said.

As they left the harbor, he explained there were two logical courses if you were headed south: Hard southeast to cut between the mainland and Cushing Island, or east by southeast between Cushing and Peaks and out Whitehead Passage. The southerly course would force Lucky, if he put up sail, to beat into the wind, tacking all the way to Portland Head.

"What would you do?" Mia said.

"I'd motor east, get outside Ram Island Ledge, start sailing south."

They came out of the harbor, out of the lee of the land. A four-foot chop slapped the bow and the wind blew spray by them as the boat dipped into the waves. *Ocean Swell* was a half-mile south, bearing for the bell at the tip of Cushing Island. Brandon throttled back, kept his distance from the sailboat and two lobster boats that had taken the same course. Abreast of the island, one swung east, headed into shallower water to start pulling traps. The second continued on, shielding the cruiser from the sailboat, still bearing south by southeast along the coast.

"What if—" Mia said.

"I'm wrong?"

"Yeah. What if they're fine? What if we're thinking these things about them and the whole time—"

"There they go," Brandon said.

Ocean Swell had raised sail. Lucky had turned east at the bell and the south wind filled the sails and the boat heeled. The main was up and a minute later the jib, too.

"She's moving," Brandon said.

"When will it mean something?" Mia said, squinting into the wind and rain.

"Not yet. He could have decided to avoid some of the marked stuff off Cape Elizabeth. Go outside a mile or so, then swing south."

"Can he see us?"

"Maybe, but we won't be recognizable if we stay back. His sails are easier to see than our little hull."

"It's getting wavier."

"Just the beginning," Brandon said.

The sailboat had set a course nearly due east, driving with the southeast wind. They were two miles offshore and the chop was building, combining with swells rolling up the bay. Brandon bore south just enough to ease the rolling of the boat as it took the waves on its starboard side. *Ocean Swell* was doing eight knots, Lucky pushing the sailboat to its limit.

"He's got her rail right down," Brandon said. "If Irina doesn't like sailing, she's having no fun."

"Is he a good sailor?" Mia said.

"Very," Brandon said.

"Well," she said. "That much is true."

They followed *Ocean Swell* east, five miles, six miles. The black-green seas were building, the tops of the white caps clipped off by the wind. *Bay Witch* rose and plunged, throwing spray off the bow, the engine growling in a slow rhythm with the waves.

Mia took the wheel as Brandon, elbows braced, watched *Ocean Swell* through binoculars, saw Lucky move to furl his jib. He looked like he'd reefed the mainsail, but he still drove the boat like he was racing. *Bay Witch* was heaving over the swells, windblown spray flying across her bow. There were ledges three miles east of the outermost Casco Bay islands, and Brandon wanted to get beyond them before he had to turn north and run for shelter.

"How much farther out can we go?" Mia said, her white hands gripping the wheel.

"A while longer."

"It's getting cold."

"You can go below."

"That's okay."

"Then check the GPS. Tell me where we are."

"You don't know?" Mia said.

He took the helm. Mia peered at the screen.

"There's numbers. Forty-three and thirty-seven. Then seventy and zero-three."

"Another mile we'll be clear if we swing north," Brandon said.

"What about them?"

"We'll watch 'em on radar."

"Have you decided?"

"I decided as soon as they set course due east," Brandon said.

They stood at the helm, side by side, bumping shoulders as the boat pitched, rose, and fell. The rain grew more steady, coming in at a slant, right to left, and the radio squawked, lobstermen talking somewhere. Brandon looked over at Mia, blonde hair wet at the edge of her hood, cheeks pale in the cold. A big wave rocked them and she grabbed his arm to steady herself.

"You okay?" Brandon said, leaning to speak into her ear.

Mia nodded, but she looked frightened. Brandon fell off to the northeast to take the waves better, felt the boat settle in. *Ocean Swell* was disappearing into the gray wall, only her sails visible, like a surrender flag on some windswept field of battle. But Lucky wasn't surrendering. They were six miles offshore and the sailboat was still headed nearly due east, making eight knots with the strong south wind. Brandon bent to the radar hood, hunched, and squinted. The radar had a ten-mile range and there was only one lonely blip to the east. Lucky and Irina, sailing like hell into the teeth of the storm.

Not to Kennebunk, not to Boston, but offshore, where it was blowing hard, kicking up a serious sea. No fun. No easy cruise.

Brandon finally swung north, planning to run with a following sea, bear slightly northwest toward near Eagle Island, Commodore Perry's old haunt. They'd turn southwest inside of Cliff Island, make their way back to Portland in the lee of the archipelago scattered outside the harbor.

The wind had picked up, over twenty knots, and *Bay Witch* pitched even with the following sea, sliding down the waves, driving her bow into the troughs. Brandon bent to the radar screen, saw that Lucky was still sailing east, bearing slightly northeast but probably just a tack.

"What do you think it is?" Mia said, as if she were reading his mind.

"What?"

"That they're doing."

"Lying," Brandon said, looking up from the radar.

"But why?"

"I don't know. What do people lie for?"

"Power," Mia said. "Money. To cover something up."

They were quiet again, shoulders bumping as the boat plowed its way north, rain spattering the back of their hoods. Mia looked off to the side of the boat, watched the endless waves, the sea cold and empty like some great gray-green desert. The little boat was like a leaf blown across a lake, she thought, could disappear into the blackness without a trace. Why were they out here, she asked herself, but then she realized she knew.

She turned back to Brandon, put her hand on his on the wheel. She craned to get close, half-shouted over the rumble of the engine, the dull roar of the sea and spray and wind.

"You think this could be the answer, don't you?" Mia said.

He looked at her, then away as the boat pitched, spray exploding off the bow.

"Answer to what?"

"What happened to your mom."

The boat climbed, paused at the crest of a wave, plunged down. Water came over the bow, ran off as the boat climbed again.

"I'm getting closer," Brandon said.

Mia wanted to tell Brandon that even she could tell that people sometimes just disappeared out here, that the ocean didn't need a reason.

The boat heaved, shuddered as it hit a deep trough. Brandon was concentrating, adjusting the throttle to find just the right speed. Too fast and the boat pounded too hard; too slow and they risked broaching, turning sideways, and rolling over.

The waves were bigger now, and then one was bigger still, lifting the boat high on its crest so Mia could see the white gargling foam, the frantic sea extending into the gray. Then the boat rushed down, motor rumbling louder as the stern lifted, the bow spearing the wave. Brandon pushed the throttle as the boat climbed the next crest, readied for the crash. They held on as the bow slammed.

"The last trip," Brandon said, as they climbed the next wave.

"Ours?" Mia said, leaning over to hear him.

"No, theirs. How long did it take?"

"Four days."

"That's how long we've got," Brandon said.

"Got for what?" Mia said, but the boat pitched, a big wave sweeping it forward, turning it slightly sideways, and Brandon pushed the throttle. The cruiser climbed and Mia looked out, saw nothing but the cold ocean, no other boats, no land. She wondered if there wasn't a part of Brandon that was driven to find his mother even if it meant following her into this black abyss. Even if it meant feeling the terror Nikki had felt, the panic, the final acceptance that her life was going to end.

She thought of her father, all the things they'd never talked about, that he didn't really know her at all. She told herself she'd write him a long letter, if they got back. She looked over at Brandon, tense and unblinking, and thought how sad it would be to finally fall in love only to see it end so soon.

CHAPTER 49

The coordinates: 43, 40 north, 68, 10 west. That would put them a hundred miles west of Yarmouth, Nova Scotia, fifty miles shorter than their last trip.

It was getting busy in the shipping lanes closer to Yarmouth, they'd been told. A change of plans.

It was a little after ten p.m., seventeen hours since they'd left Portland Harbor, circling now, then heaving to, then falling off the wind again. Waiting.

Lucky had been at the helm for nearly the whole trip, Irina taking over when he had to go below to the head. While he was below he'd eaten an energy bar and washed down two amphetamines with a Red Bull. The trip out was rough; the run back would be worse. Lucky reached into his pocket. He felt his pills and was reassured.

Back in the cockpit, he took the helm. Irina stood by the rail, clipped on by her safety line, peering out at the blackness, the white streaks of the wavetops.

Lucky took the microphone, went to channel 67.

"*Baltic Star, Baltic Star,*" he said. "This is *Sea Ranger.*"

No reply, just static. The volume was turned all the way up to be heard over the wind whipping through the rigging, the slam of the hull against the sea, the spray spattering against their foul weather gear, the creak of the mast bent by the wind.

Irina scowled, wiped the salt spray from her face. Clenched her teeth. They sailed on in the dark.

Another half-hour, another three miles to the east. Lucky kept on eye on the GPS, the compass, wondered whether to keep going or heave to and wait. He called again.

There was static, then a scratchy voice saying, "Go ahead, *Sea Ranger.*"

Irina heard the accent, a little bit of home. She pointed to the north, off the port side. There was a red speck in the darkness. Lucky didn't reply, just reached for the light switch, flicked the running lights off. On. Off. On.

On the deck of the ship, a spotlight glared, then went dark.

"Like a fine Swiss watch, baby," Lucky said. "Why don't you make sure everything's ready below."

He sailed on toward a point below the ship's stern. In fifteen minutes, the ship had grown to a dark shape against the cloud-gray sky. Lucky started the motor, furled the reefed main, swung into the wind, *Ocean Swell* pitching as it sliced into the waves. He heard voices blow out of the darkness. The sound of another motor starting.

A spotlight glared on, moving toward the sailboat, the beam swinging crazily as the smaller boat pitched. Irina dropped fenders over the side, then stood by the rail and waited.

"Time to be charming, my dear," Lucky said.

"Shut up and drive the boat," Irina said. "I know how to do my job."

CHAPTER 50

A tracking dog sniffed out the place in the brush where Fuller and Kelvin had scattered the soil soaked with Griffin's blood. There were police SUVs back in the woods, a crime lab van in Crystal's dooryard, cruisers—marked and unmarked—with radios that squawked and woke the baby.

Crystal held her, afraid the cops would take her away. There was a nice one, a woman detective named Jackie who made Destinee smile, but more mean ones. There was one angry cop who started out nice but then made Crystal cry, saying, "You don't help us, you know what you'll get as an accessory to this? Fifteen years, easy. Maybe you'll get out to see your daughter graduate from high school. And you know what? She won't know you. You'll be a total stranger."

As Crystal sobbed, the woman detective patted her shoulder. The detective looked at her, hard and cold with his red cheeks, and finally said, "You think about it."

They went outside with the other cops.

Crystal went in the bedroom with the baby, took a swig of Captain Morgan from the bottle on the table. The cops had found it in the TV stand when they'd searched the house, looking for anything that might tell them where Kelvin and Fuller were holed up. Crystal sat on the bed, the baby beside her. When Crystal tried to hold her, she cried and thrashed. Crystal stood, was gathering her daughter up when her cell phone rang in the bag on the bureau.

She put Destinee back down on the floor, grabbed the phone, didn't recognize the number.

"Yeah."

"Hey."

"Where the hell are you?" Crystal hissed. "You know what you've done, you stupid son of a bitch? You know how many cops are here? Yelling at me, saying I'll never see my baby again? Huh? You stupid son of a bitch."

"I didn't do nothin'," Kelvin said, his voice low, a whisper.

"Then you get the hell in here and you turn him in."

"They'll lock me up. He'll blame me."

"Of course he will. He's a lying sack 'a shit. I told you that a thousand times. A million times. You come in first, get a deal."

"I'll turn him in from somewhere else."

"Where?"

"Wherever I can get to. That's why I need money. I gotta get outta here."

"Where's he?"

"In the bathroom. In a Wendy's."

"Call 911 right now."

"I can't."

"Kelvin."

"No. I ain't gonna go to prison."

"So the two of you are still in town?"

"I need a hundred bucks, Crystal. You gotta help me. You know I love you. I'm sorry for everything. I really am."

Crystal started to deny it, but couldn't. In his own goofy way, Kelvin did love her, she thought. But he totally sucked at being a father, had no idea where to even begin.

"How?" she said.

"Go shopping. Groceries or something. Then go to the McDonald's on St. John Street, two o'clock. Park out back. Go in, buy some food, eat in the car. Get out and toss the bag in the trash can, the one up by the trees at the back of the lot. Put the money in the bag."

"How you gonna find it? They all look the same."

"I'll find it. I'll be watching."

"They're gonna follow me."

"Let 'em. Lead 'em all over the place. Especially after McDonald's. They can't stick a cop on every place you stop."

"He know about this?"

"No. I'm gonna split on him."

"You gotta testify against him, Kelvin. It's your only chance. He'd do it to you and you know it."

A long pause.

"I don't know. I'll think about it."

"Kelvin."

"Yeah."

"You promise or no money."

"Okay."

"Your word on your mom's grave?"

Kelvin hesitated. He'd liked his mom. He'd liked his mom a lot.

"Okay."

"Say it."

"I swear on my mother's grave."

"Okay. Two o'clock."

"Thanks, Babe."

Crystal rang off. Held the phone for a few seconds, turned, and scooped Destinee up from where she was crawling across the floor. She wiped the dust off of Destinee's feet and hands, went to the front door, looked outside. The cop Jackie and the Irish-named detective were in an unmarked car, Jackie turned in the seat as she started to back the car out onto the road. Crystal went out the door, broke into a trot as she crossed the dooryard. As Jackie put the car in gear, Crystal stepped into the road, baby in her arms, and waved the car down.

Kelvin hung up the phone. He was in front of an empty Ames store on St. John Street. Wendy's was across the parking lot on the other side of the street.

"That was good," Fuller said, leaning back in his big sunglasses and Yankees hat, a gray sweatshirt that said "Maine" on the front in letters made of pine cones. His hand was under the sweatshirt, on the Ruger in the front waistband of his jeans. "The Wendy's thing. Dude, that was fucking choice."

CHAPTER 51

They idled into the marina in the rain just before eleven, a little chop kicking up in Portland Harbor but flat calm compared to offshore. Brandon backed *Bay Witch* into the slip. Mia stepped off and was bent over cleating the bow lines when Doc appeared at the top of the ramp. He waved and started down.

"Where you been?" he said, strolling up as Brandon shut off the motor. Mia was tying down the stern and Doc gave her backside an involuntary glance.

"Shakedown cruise," Brandon said. "Seeing if the radar worked, that kind of thing."

"Picked a nice morning for it. Hope you're paying your first mate here. You get outside the islands?"

"A little bit."

"Blowing pretty good?"

"Twenty-five, higher gusts, right smack out of the south," Brandon said.

"Just stopped to see if Lucky and Irina got off okay."

Doc looked toward his mooring, the white buoy straining on its chain in the wind. "Guess they did. Hope they find a nice spot to hole up. I know they were planning on dinner in Kennebunkport."

Mia looked at Brandon, smiled.

"I'm sure they'll be fine," he said. "For Lucky, this is just a little breeze."

"Yeah, but Irina, she's no blue-water sailor," Doc said. "Don't want to scare her off. Got my own selfish reasons. I'm thinking they like the boat enough, might decide to take her off my hands. One bad experience, she could say, 'No more sailing for me. Santa Fe here we come.'"

Brandon shut off the instruments, made sure to save the last route on the GPS.

"They hug the coast, they'll do okay," Doc said. "Pop in any harbor along the way. Supposed to clear tonight, wind shifting to the east then northeast. Looks like they'll be beating back home."

"No problem if you're not in a big hurry," Brandon said.

"Hey, doesn't matter to me. They can take two weeks if they want. Especially when they bring her back as clean as they do. But listen—"

Doc dug in the front pocket of his rain jacket, brought out a small plastic bag. He held it up. Inside was a piece of paper with handwriting on it.

"Didn't want to get it all wet. Thought Irina might want it back," Doc said. "Wanted to talk to her. Ask her if she has a sister, might want to come over to the States, live the American dream."

He winked. Held out the bag. Brandon stepped off the stern onto the dock and took the bag, held it up. ·

"A note?"

"Yeah, but look at it. That's not English."

Mia reached over, took the bag from Brandon, and looked at the paper.

"Cyrillic," she said. "It must be hers."

"Changed a bulb in the aft cabin," Doc said. "It was stuck up behind the light. Probably put it up there while she was scrubbing things down below. I was gonna give it to her, but then I got working, forgot about it. Figure it's a letter to her relatives or something. Quite a lot to say, all that tiny writing."

"Probably telling them all about her sailing adventure," Mia said.

"Maybe," Doc said. "But I'd give it to her directly, if I were you. My first wife, before we split, I found a note she got in little tiny handwriting like that. Let's just say it wasn't from me, and it wasn't a grocery list."

He looked at Mia.

"Just in case it's not a letter to grandma back home."

Doc turned.

"Be good, kids," he said, and started back up the dock to the ramp.

Brandon looked at Mia.

"USM," he said.

"Slavic languages," she said.

"We don't need to know all of it," Brandon said.

"Just a general sense," Mia said.

"If she's having an affair—" he said.

"It'll be our secret."

"What's one more?" Brandon said.

The offices for Slavic languages were in a wood-framed house a block over from the law school. Brandon parked the truck in a faculty slot out back and walked up the wooden ramp to the back door, opened the door and went in.

Mia, on the phone with Nessa, stayed in the truck.

There was a small room, a desk with a computer. The computer was on, somebody's e-mail box on the screen. They heard a toilet flush and water running, and a young woman came around the corner from a hallway. She was pale, thin, plain. Dark hair pulled back, glasses. A student worker.

"Hello," Brandon said, smiling.

"Hi," she said.

"I'm a student here," he said. "I'm looking for someone who reads Russian."

"Everybody here reads Russian," the young woman said, with a teasing shake of her head. "This is Slavic languages. It's kind of, like, essential."

"Oh, good," Brandon said. "I need something translated. It's short. A letter."

"There's nobody here right now," she said, leaning on her desk. "They're at a conference."

"Oh, too bad," Brandon said.

"But you could leave it and I could give it to one of the professors when they get back tomorrow," she said.

"How 'bout if I leave a copy?"

"Sure," the young woman said, vaulting from her chair. He handed her the letter: one page, written on both sides. She took it and walked to the copier. It spat out a page and she turned back and handed Brandon the original.

"Can I leave a phone number?" he said.

She liked that better, dug for a piece of paper and pen. He wrote his name and cell number and handed the paper back.

"You're Brandon?"

"Yeah."

"I'm Samantha."

"Nice to meet you, Samantha," Brandon said. She made a great show of stapling the paper to the copy of the letter.

"Anything you can do will be appreciated."

She said she'd do her best, maybe someone would come in at the end of the day. Brandon thanked her and she smiled again. He went out the door, down the ramp. In the office, the young woman, a first-year Russian Studies major, looked at the letter. She held it up, scrutinizing the tiny handwriting.

"Huh," she said, and dug in her bag, took out a phone. She flipped it open and punched in a number and said, "Hey. ... What are you doing? ... Listen, can you help me with a translation? ... No, it's not for class. ... Somebody brought in this, like, weird letter. ... Some guy who says he goes here. ... I'm not sure. I think it's like somebody writing to their family. ... Hard to say 'cause I don't really know the vocabulary, but I think it's got something to do with a boat. And I'm not sure, but I think it's somebody who's, like, really unhappy."

She paused. Frowned.

"No, that's okay. I'll do it myself. ... Hey, I was gonna tell you, the guy who brought it in? He's kinda hot. ... You snooze, you lose. Too late. Ha, ha."

Samantha smiled, put down the phone, and reached to the floor to a backpack. She unzipped a pocket, took out a book, and laid it on the desk by the letter. It was a Russian-English dictionary. She put a pencil on a word in the first line.

"Sadness?" she said. "Shame?"

She opened the dictionary. Her e-mail beeped. She ignored it.

CHAPTER 52

Brandon put on a blazer and khakis. He had dug the jacket from his closet at Nessa's. She was on the porch sipping her first glass of Chardonnay of the day. The first glass was the most special, the way the soothing mist settled over her with the first swallow. She sat in her chair and, because of the wind and rain, waited for a boat to appear in the stretch of bay.

When it didn't, Nessa watched the waves, the waters streaked by the wind, the dark clouds rolling like tumbleweed toward the horizon.

"Where's the service?" she said, when Brandon appeared in the room.

"Cape Elizabeth. The Catholic church."

She gazed out at the sea, sipped her wine.

"It's a big show, isn't it? When a policeman is killed."

"They stick together," Brandon said.

"Nikki didn't have a church funeral," Nessa said. "Told me a hundred times she didn't believe in them. She wanted her ashes scattered on the bay. Couldn't even do that."

"I know."

"The other hard thing when someone is lost at sea like that, is you don't know how long to wait. Are you giving up on them? What if they're on a raft? What if they were picked up by a freighter and they have amnesia, hit in the head with one of the masts when the ship went down?"

"Nessa."

"It's possible."

"Nessa, don't," Brandon said.

"She'd be forty-one."

"Nessa. I'm going."

"They have this computer thing now. You put somebody's picture in when they're twelve or fifteen or whatever and you hit a button and it ages them. Shows what they'd look like."

Brandon stood to the right of her chair, watched her fingers circling the stem of the wine glass.

"She's gone," he said.

"Of course she's gone," Nessa said.

She drank, her hand trembling as she raised the glass.

"Let me sit here and have my little dream. That's not so much to ask, is it?"

Another drink, the wine caressing someplace behind her eyes. And then a jab of reality, like someone had tapped her shoulder. Nessa's eyes widened.

"Where did you go so early?"

Brandon hesitated, then said, "Down to the boat."

"In the middle of the night?"

"It was morning, sort of."

"Why'd you have to go? You can share a room with her here."

"We took the boat out, Nessa."

"Today?"

"Yes."

"Why?"

"We followed Lucky and Irina in Doc's boat."

"You followed them?"

"Only for a few miles."

"Where did they go?" Nessa said, a knowing tone in her voice.

"East. Last I saw of them, they were running due east in the storm."

"Why?"

"I don't know. But they said they were sailing along the coast. They're headed straight for Nova Scotia."

"They lied?" Nessa said.

"Or changed their minds."

Nessa sat, lost in thought. A lobster boat appeared, chugging away from the harbor. Nessa watched it, but her gaze was inward.

"Nessa, when Lucky and Nikki and the rest of them were here, were they doing anything illegal?"

Nessa focused, tightened. Outside a rain squall swept across the waters, from the southeast.

"Drugs, I mean."

"Did they take drugs? I don't know. If they did, they wouldn't tell me, the mom."

"You weren't old," Brandon said. "You were forty-five. Lucky said it was Nessa and Nikki, like you were a team."

Nessa didn't answer. Stared out at the rain and sea. After a moment, she raised the glass and drank, lowered the glass to her lap, and held it there, like it was a crystal chalice.

"You and Nikki were friends, Nessa," Brandon said. "Different from a regular mother and daughter."

"Some friend," Nessa said. "With friends like me—"

"It's Lucky," Brandon said. "I don't trust him."

"You're right not to trust him," Nessa said.

"Why?"

"Because it's trusting people gets you killed. Nikki trusted me."

"You didn't get her killed, Nessa.

"Set it all in motion, Brandon," Nessa said.

Brandon waited, watched as Nessa's eyes filled and finally a tear fell down her right cheek.

"How?" he said.

She turned to him, her face drawn and flushed, the only pink in a plane of gray.

"She would have stayed home," Nessa said. "But Lucky, he wanted to go. He wanted to go terribly. He wanted her to go. He wanted me to—"

As Brandon watched, a wave seemed to sweep over her, sitting there in the chair. The rosy wine flush gave way to a pale, seasick gray.

"You were supposed to go with them?" Brandon said. "Is that what's tearing you apart? That Nikki went and you stayed here?"

Nessa looked old, pained, ill, distraught.

"No," she said. "That's not it at all." And she turned her back to the bay, stood and wobbled, steadied herself and went inside. Brandon heard the wine bottles rattling in the cupboard like bones.

CHAPTER 53

There were cops in the McDonald's lot, two plainclothes sitting at tables inside. Four were SWAT in a plumber's van, assault rifles ready. More undercover cops were eating in an old El Camino, two more chatting in an SUV. The two detectives inside—a young woman and an older guy, supposed to look like a dad and his daughter— were eating in a window seat. Across the street and around the block were three teams of two, ready to block the lot or go in pursuit if Fuller and Kelvin somehow made it out onto the street.

Crystal had Destinee in the car seat. She pulled in, tried not to look around at the other cars or up into the patch of brush above the back of the lot. Pulling Destinee out of the seat, she made the van, hoped it wouldn't be that obvious to Kelvin and Joel, but maybe they wouldn't be thinking she'd rat them out.

Her hand over the baby's face to shield her from the rain, Crystal went inside. She ordered a number four, the crispy chicken sandwich with fries and a Diet Coke, paid with the $20 bill the cops had given her.

Destinee started to fuss, as if she sensed that something was going down. Crystal got her order, pocketed the change, hefted the baby and bag, and went out to the car. She didn't look around, tried not to feel like she was on stage, though she was reminded of the time she had this tiny part in the junior-high play and was supposed to walk from one side of the stage to the other, stopping in the middle to say, "Where is he?" She'd gotten the line out, then tripped on the high heels and stumbled. Everybody laughed.

She colored at the thought, put Destinee in her seat, gave her a French fry, and got in the driver's seat and started to eat. When Destinee lost her fry and started to fuss, Crystal turned and gave her another. Six fries later, she finished the sandwich and dropped the wrapper into the bag. Reached into her purse and took out the cops' hundred bucks, slipped it into the bag.

Destinee started to cry when she saw her mother get out, and Crystal shushed her, crumpled the bag as she walked to the trash can.

She dropped the bag in, walked back to the car, and leaned back to fish a chewed fry out of Destinee's seat. The baby crammed it in her mouth. Crystal backed up, pulled forward, and drove out of the lot.

"I did it for you, honey," she told her daughter. "I did it for you."

As she drove down the street in the rain, it was Crystal who started to cry.

Fuller heard about it from a guy in jail, how you find one of these small garages where people drop their car keys through a slot when the place is closed. You grab some keys and nobody knows the car is even gone for a couple of days, until the owner calls up, says, "Is my car ready or what?" and the mechanic, he says, "What car?"

Kelvin and Fuller had found this foreign car place on Forest Avenue, all VWs and Volvos and crap. Kelvin bought a little magnet at a dollar store and they taped it to a coat hanger. With Kelvin standing behind him for cover, Fuller fished for the keys because his hands were smaller, coming up with three sets: two VW and one Volvo. They tried a blue VW, but it wouldn't start. A Volvo sedan belched white smoke. They settled on a white Jetta with Grateful Dead stickers on the back window. Fuller drove it out, met Kelvin up the block in the Caprice. Kelvin drove back toward downtown, finally pulled the Chevy into a strip mall lot and parked.

In the Jetta, Fuller driving, they drove through the city to the bridge, over to South Portland. There was a pizza place midway between the streets that led to the marina and Nessa's and they parked there, facing out. Kelvin went through the car and found some Phish CDs ("What's this wussy shit?" Fuller said.), a Visa card, and a $20 bill hidden in a magnetic key holder in the bottom of the console storage compartment.

"Score," Kelvin said, and, Red Sox hat pulled down low, sunglasses on, he went in to order pizza. It was half pepperoni and half green pepper and onion, the vegetable half for Fuller. Flicking the wipers on and off, they ate slowly, needing the reason to stay in the lot. Kelvin was starting his third piece when Fuller said, "You sure she'd sell you out?"

Chewing, Kelvin nodded. He swallowed.

"She'd tell herself it was for the baby," he said, reaching for his Mountain Dew. "I don't know what it is about that kid."

It was like a parade, Mia thought. Police everywhere, uniforms in a dozen different colors, some with round Smokey Bear hats, some wearing no hats at all, everyone somber, everyone wearing shiny black shoes.

They pulled the Saab in behind a television truck, its boom and satellite dish extended high above the street. The TV reporter had a mirror out and was touching up her makeup. Brandon straightened his tie.

"You look nice," Mia said.

"See you in an hour?" Brandon said.

"Yeah. Grab some clothes, take a shower, get the salt off of me."

"You could have taken a shower at Nessa's."

"I know. I just need a little break."

"Be careful."

"I'll be fine."

Brandon kissed her cheek, got out of the car. Mia waved, pulled away. Brandon joined the throng drifting toward the church, overheard the TV reporter reading her notes: "In a brutal slaying that shocked not only the Portland community but the entire state of Maine...."

"Somebody up there likes us," Fuller said, smiling as he slouched in the driver's seat.

"She's leaving by herself," Kelvin said.

"Like I just said. Candy from a baby, dude. Candy from a fucking baby."

They turned and followed the Saab, retracing their route from South Portland.

"Where we gonna go after?" Kelvin said.

"Don't worry," Fuller said. "I got it covered."

He smiled, feeling like everything was falling into place. Every cop in the state at the funeral, the rest of 'em sitting at McDonald's watching a trash can. The blonde chick dropping her boyfriend, heading into town all alone. He figured they could use the pepper spray on her, put a knife to her back. The credit card even had a guy's name: Timothy D. Gould. Fuller practiced saying it a couple of times in his head, using his lawyer's voice: "Hi, I'm Tim Gould. I'm hoping to get a room for one night. No, I don't have a reservation."

Then he'd give them a big shit-eating grin, take the key, have Kelvin bring the girl around. Sweet little thing, he thought, maybe they'd get a king-size bed. He smiled and tried it out loud: "I'm Tim Gould. I'm hoping to get a room."

CHAPTER 54

The family was up front: Mrs. Griffin, small, brunette, and two boys in blazers sitting on each side of their mom. The rest of the row was filled with relatives: an older man, maybe Griffin's father, a middle-aged woman who looked like Griffin, too. When they turned, Brandon could see their reddened eyes, noses rubbed raw with tissues.

The governor sat in the next row. A thin woman in a dark suit, she was flanked by other politicians, one of Maine's U.S. senators, patrician with his silver hair. The rest of the church was packed with cops, guys in uniform all sitting in rows like it was a graduation at the academy.

Brandon sat in the back. Clipped to his lapel was the I.D. card Griffin had made for him: "Brandon Blake . . . Portland P.D." The card was scuffed where it had been stepped on at the other funeral. It seemed to Brandon like months ago.

He watched, listened to the throat-clearing, a police radio inadvertently left on, but the sound of the police call somehow fitting. Someone clicked it off and then the priest came down the center aisle from the rear of the church, preceded by two altar girls, one carrying a big gold cross. Griffin's older son, Jeremy, turned to watch. The younger boy, Michael, leaned into his mother and sobbed. The organ played.

The priest, a white-haired, slow-moving old man who looked like he'd come out of retirement, told the assembled cops that they were all heroes, that the difference between them and Griffin was that God had taken him up on his offer to give his life for others. He reminded everyone that Jesus had done the same thing and that those who emulated Jesus in life would ultimately sit at the right hand of God. Brandon looked at the little boy sitting at the right hand of his mother and doubted this would be much consolation.

And then the organ played again and the family followed the coffin down the aisle. Six big cops carried the coffin. Griffin's wife broke down twenty feet from the door. As the family passed him, Brandon thought of Griffin, the proud dad recounting every ground ball, every ball and strike. He wiped away a tear of his own.

Then Brandon went out into the parking lot, stood in the drizzle with his I.D. showing, and looked for a woman with a face—how had Griffin put it?—whose two sides didn't seem to match.

He almost missed her, and when he did spot her, it wasn't the face, it was the walk.

Kathleen Rogan had a limp, a hitch left from the injuries suffered in the attack. She walked with a cane, and Brandon caught up with her as she was getting into her car, an Audi with handicap plates.

"Ms. Rogan?" he said.

She turned and he saw that Griffin was right. Her face, once handsome, was asymmetrical, the left eye drooping, the left side of the mouth turned down. She looked at him, then at his I.D.

"You're the ride-along," she said.

"Yes," Brandon said, and he held out his hand. She shook it, gave him an assessing once-over.

"Griffin liked you," she said.

"I liked Griffin."

"He was a good cop," she said. "I could tell when I first met him, that he had it, I mean. He told me he saw something in you, too."

"Nice of him to say," Brandon said.

"He was a nice guy."

"Hard for his family."

"It's a cop's life," Rogan said. "Could happen ten minutes from now, could never happen."

"Tough way to live," Brandon said.

"Let's just say, you always make sure to say goodbye. I still do it today."

"Say goodbye to your husband?"

"My partner. Her name is Marti."

"Because you never know?"

"No, but who does?" Rogan said, turning to the car. "Griffin told me about your mother. Get in the car, if you want to talk."

Brandon walked around and got in. Rogan pulled her weak leg in, reached and set the cane in the back seat. She put the key in the ignition and classical music played. She turned it off.

"Shoot," she said.

"Did you know my mother?"

"Knew who she was. Tended bar in the Old Port. Very pretty. Guys gravitated to her."

"The crew on *Black Magic*?"

"Most guys, but yeah, the *Black Magic* crew, too."

"Why were you interested in them?" Brandon asked.

Rogan thought for a moment, put her hands on the steering wheel. There was a long scar on top of her right hand, like it had been slashed.

"I've thought about this, since Griffin called."

She paused. Brandon waited.

"You have to know Portland in the eighties," she said. "A lot of drugs. Coke mostly, not heroin like today. A little bit of a Wild West attitude down in the bars. Police hadn't caught up with the drugs yet."

"Were the *Black Magic* guys into drugs?"

"Oh, I'm sure they indulged," Rogan said.

"But that wasn't what got you interested."

"No. What caught my attention was that these guys sailed in on a two-hundred-thousand-dollar boat. That's the used value. Told customs they'd come from Ireland, but who knows? The ocean is a big empty space, you know what I'm saying? Once you're out there—"

"You can go anywhere."

"They'd been all over the world. Africa, North Africa, South America, all places where drug smuggling is a way of life."

"So you thought they were running drugs on the boat?"

"Other people were moving dope that way back then. Packing a sailboat full in the Caribbean, sailing north, taking their chances. A lot of money to be made."

"But these guys, what did they do for—"

"Work? Nothing. But they had cash. Spent thousands of dollars repairing the engine, getting the boat ready. Paid for everything with hundred-dollar bills."

"So they didn't use banks," Brandon said. "Kind of hard if you're always moving."

"I calculated they spent about nine thousand dollars in a month in Portland."

"I heard Ketch inherited the boat," Brandon said. "Probably money, too."

"You want to defend them, or know more?"

"Anything you have."

"Why?"

"Because my mother died on that boat."

"I'm sorry," Rogan said. "But that was seventeen years ago. They're all gone. Why are you asking? I mean, why now?"

This time it was Brandon who hesitated. He looked out the car window, saw a TV reporter interviewing a state police detective. The cameraman turned away from the cop to get a shot of the departing hearse.

"They didn't *all* die."

Rogan turned toward him, looked at him hard, squinted with one eye.

"Sure they did. Went down with all hands, or however they say it."

"A guy named Lucky. He got left behind in North Carolina."

"He didn't tell anyone?"

"He says he just took off. Had kind of a breakdown, losing all his friends like that."

"How do you know?"

"He told me. He's here in Portland."

"Really. Smallish, wiry guy? Kind of cheerful and energetic?"

"Yeah. Real name is Willem DeHahn," Brandon said.

"Not when I was asking," Rogan said.

"It's on his passport."

"I got out the file, after Griffin called. There was no Willem on the boat. Lucky, his real name was H. Wilson Davis."

"Not anymore," Brandon said. "It's DeHahn. I saw it on a plane ticket."

"Huh," Rogan said. "What's he doing here?"

"On vacation, he says. Chartered a boat. Sailing out of Portland. Rented a big house on the ocean in Falmouth. Here with his girlfriend. She's from Poland, she says."

Rogan smiled, said, "Huh."

"They've been sailing way offshore," Brandon said, watching for her reaction.

"Really," she said. "Have a lot of money?"

"Seems to. Boat's three thousand a week. House is a mansion."

"Pay cash?" Rogan said.

"Yeah, for the boat anyway. Owner was happy because he won't have to tell his ex-wife about it."

Rogan looked out the window on her side, seemed to be thinking.

"How does he say he made all this money?" she said.

"Investments," Brandon said.

Rogan gave a snort. "I'm sure," she said.

"He's going to London in a couple of weeks."

Rogan rubbed her cheek, the sagging one.

"So what do you think?" Brandon said.

"What do I think or what can I prove?"

"Think."

"I think he was dirty then. I think he's probably dirty now. But he wasn't in charge. You're right about that guy Ketch. I think he was the brains, the strategizer. From what I could tell, he doled out the money to everybody else. I remember somebody saying the others got their allowance from him."

"Then Lucky's come a long way," Brandon said.

"Sounds like it. Must have made a big score somehow. Hard part for somebody like that is even when you're running drugs, it takes money to make money."

Rogan touched her cheek with the tips of her fingers, as though to shore it up.

"People like this," she said, "they find it almost impossible to just work for a living. They might do it for a while, but they don't have the patience. They can't stand the routine."

Brandon suddenly found himself thinking, not of Lucky, but of Fuller. Never going to settle for a normal law-abiding life. Maybe Lucky and Fuller were the same type, just a different scale.

"Anything else?" Brandon said.

"Two things," Rogan said, turning back to him. "One, look out for these people. They're con men, very persuasive. They need something from you, they'll suck you in."

"I wonder what they needed from my mother," Brandon said.

"Cover, maybe," Rogan said. "Pretty young woman on a boat. Makes it look a little less like a bunch of pirates."

"I heard they wanted my grandmother to go along, too."

"Your grandmother?"

"But she was forty-five then. Pretty."

"Even better. Nice middle-aged mom on board. Coast Guard might not search so hard."

Brandon shrugged.

"Of course, there's always something else you can bring to the party," Rogan said.

"What's that?"

"Money," she said. "If I remember correctly, your mom was sort of a wild child from a good family. Her father was—"

"A doctor," Brandon said.

"And you want to be a cop?"

"Could be."

"Then let me give you some more advice," Rogan said. "Watch yourself. There's people out there, you get in their way, they'll take you out. Especially if there's a lot of money at stake, or even serious prison time. Look what happened here, and Griffin was a good cop. I was a detective, ten years on the job, guy tries to blow me up. And you're just—"

Brandon held up his I.D. "An intern."

"Go to the academy, you want to go on the job."

She looked to the police officers getting in cruisers, the knot of family and friends.

"In the meantime, you're in this way deep, by the sounds of it," Rogan said.

Brandon shrugged. "Up to my neck."

"I was like that. Kind of a lightning rod, things just seemed to find me."

"I'm just trying to find out what happened to my mother," Brandon said. "Or why."

"Well, let me warn you, 'cause I learned the hard way. The truth, it can be a very dangerous thing."

"But did you settle for less?" Brandon asked.

"I didn't back then," Rogan said. "I do now,"

CHAPTER 55

There was a Land Rover with Connecticut plates in Mia's parking space. She sighed, backed out into the street, and set off to find a space. She turned at the end of the block, drove down Exchange. There was a bakery, spaces out back for the workers, who showed up at 4 a.m. and were gone by noon. No one would notice if it were just for an hour.

She slowed, peered down the alley. Sure enough, the three bakery spots at the end were empty. She pulled in, shut off the motor. Glanced back as a white VW drove in behind her, swung to the left. She saw the Grateful Dead stickers, dancing bears on the back window. Heard the motor running, a door open and close. She figured it was somebody running into the bakery, nobody who wanted her spot. She reached over for her bag, opened the door, and sensed someone moving to her left. Kicking her out of their spot, she thought, and started to turn to look—

The handle jerked out of her hand. For a parking space, this was too much, she thought.

But then someone was coming into the car, pushing her backwards, the shifter jammed into her back. It was a guy, big mirror sunglasses and a baseball cap, a ski mask. Teeth bared in the mouth hole. She started to shout, saw her face in the glasses. He pushed her head back, jammed something in her mouth.

A napkin, it smelled like food. She started to gag, the pain in her back, then a cold sharpness against her neck.

"Make a sound and you're dead," he said.

He lifted her legs, his hand cold against the skin below her skirt. Pushed her over the console, the knife still pressed against her throat.

"On the floor," he said, his voice cold and angry, and she knew who it was. "Don't open your eyes."

Mia slid down, curled up in a ball on the floor in front of the passenger seat. The knife moved from her throat, down her side, and came to rest with the point pressing against her bare back.

"I'll gut you like a deer," Fuller said, pulling the mask off.

The VW had backed out, was starting down the alley. Fuller put the Saab in reverse, backed out, and turned around. He put the car in gear and gave Mia's bare back a jab. She cried out.

"Shut up," Fuller said. "'Cause I'll take you down with me."

The VW had turned right on Exchange. Fuller followed down the hill toward the waterfront, driving with one hand, the knife clenched in the other. At the corner of Fore Street, a couple was in the crosswalk. Fuller stopped, smiled, waved them across. He pressed the knife harder against Mia's spine.

The couple passed and Fuller took a quick right. The white VW was at the intersection of Commercial Street, on the waterfront. It took a left and Fuller followed.

Two blocks north, he swung down one of the wharves, the VW ahead of him. It slowed before a row of garage bays, took a right. Fuller followed, taking the right, then a left. There was an open garage bay and Kelvin pulled in. Fuller drove in behind the VW, then stopped. It was a dim warehouse room, the floor wet, fish boxes stacked along the walls.

Kelvin put on his mask, walked to the passenger side of the Saab, opened the door and, putting his hand under Mia's arm, pulled her out. He led her to the VW, opened the trunk, and told her to please get in.

She shook her head. Fuller came up behind her, gave her a shove, and holding her by the thigh and arm, wrestled her into the cramped space. He pulled her hands behind her and roughly tied them with twine. Then he looped a rag over her head and yanked it tight, knotting it from behind. She shrieked, the sound muffled by the rag and the napkins. The trunk lid slammed shut.

Darkness, suffocating. Mia screamed again, a wave of panic sweeping through her. And then there was silence, until she screamed again.

CHAPTER 56

Brandon stood by the entrance to the church and waited. The hearse had been followed by the limos, then by the police motorcycles and cruisers, their blue lights flashing. Some people followed the motorcade to the cemetery, taking a left onto the main road. Some cars took a right, toward Portland. The governor, in a black Lincoln, headed back to the capitol.

There were a few stragglers, mostly people connected to the church. An old Irish-looking man came through, picking up programs left on the seats. Two women came out with vases of flowers and loaded them in the back of a Mercedes station wagon. They drove away. Brandon leaned on the stair rail and waited.

He was trying to think what might have happened. Maybe she'd stopped to get something at Wild Oats to bring back to Nessa's. Maybe Nessa had gotten talking again and Mia hadn't been able to extricate herself.

Brandon took out his phone, was about to turn on the ringer when the phone vibrated. The number was Mia's. Brandon smiled.

"Hey," he said. "Where are you?"

"She's safe and sound."

A man's voice. A jolt, a sinking feeling, before Brandon said, "Who's this?"

"Wrong question," the guy said.

Brandon thought he could hear another guy in the background, his voice muffled.

"You're supposed to say, 'How much?'"

"What is this? Put Mia on."

"She can't come to the phone right now."

"What do you mean?"

"I mean twenty grand. Cash."

"What?"

"To get her back."

"Where is she? What are you talking about? Where'd you find her phone?"

"It was in her hand," the guy said.

More muffled talk, someone telling the guy what to say.

"Put her on. I want to talk to her."

Voices, a clatter, scratching sounds. Then a small voice saying, "No. Get your hands off me." She came on the phone, said, "Brandon."

"Baby."

"They want money."

"I'll get some."

"You don't have it," Mia said.

"Have they hurt you?"

"No. Not really."

"Are you in Portland?"

A clatter, and the guy back on the phone.

"You know the price."

"I don't have it. I can't get it."

"Your friends have it. That rich dickhead and the Russian bitch."

"They're sailing. They're out at sea someplace. I can't find them."

"Not our problem."

"How long?"

"Forty-eight hours."

"What if I can't find them?"

"You will, if you want to see blondie here again. And no cops. Not a word. If we get so much as—"

He paused, covered the phone. Came back.

"—a whiff of cops, we're gone. And we leave her right here."

"Don't hurt her."

"We don't hurt her. We don't do anything. We just walk out the door. She'll die of thirst. They'll find her 'cause of the smell. Too bad, 'cause she's real pretty. Got a nice little butt, too."

"I'll kill you."

"Get the money, college boy. No cops. Don't mess it up."

He hung up. Brandon stared at the phone, looked up at the parking lot. The last car drove out. The white-haired priest.

Brandon was alone.

Fuller and Kelvin. Forty-eight hours. Lucky might be back. He might not. The storm, the wind. Brandon found himself thinking of the forecast, fifteen to twenty knots, shifting to the southeast. Mia in a room with them, the two of them.

He looked around the empty lot, heard sparrows chirping over his head on the church roof. Punched in a number.

"Nessa," Brandon said.

"Brandon. Where are you?"

"At the church. Listen, Mia can't come get me. Can you drive?"

A long pause.

"I've had a glass of wine."

"How many?"

Another pause.

"Two."

"Two as in two or two as in five? Tell me the truth."

"Really, two. I didn't want to open a new bottle until tonight. I don't want the police officers to think I have a problem."

"Can you come get me?"

"I guess so. Are you okay? You sound funny."

"I'm okay. Just come soon. But go slow."

"I could send Jackie the detective."

"No. Don't do that."

"Brandon, what is it?"

"Just come. Be careful, but come as soon as you can."

It was nineteen minutes but it seemed like an eternity, Brandon's watch standing still, his mind racing. And then there was Nessa, sitting upright behind the wheel of the old Volvo. A hundred yards behind her was another pickup with the two cops from the house.

Nessa turned into the lot, pulled up, stopped, the car still covered in dust. Brandon half ran to the driver's door, opened it. Nessa, in black slacks, a white sweater, brown leather driving moccasins, slid over and turned to look at him.

"What is it?"

"Something happened," Brandon said, wheeling the Volvo around.

"What?"

"They took Mia."

"Who took her? Took her where?"

"Fuller and his buddy. They want twenty thousand."

"Ransom?"

Brandon was out on the road, passed the cops coming in.

"My God," Nessa said. "They can't do that. It's—"

"They did. They have."

She turned in her seat, looked back at the police.

"Stop and tell them."

"No police. They said they'll—"

"Hurt her?"

"Just leave her."

"Leave her where?"

"Wherever they are. Leave her tied up."

"Where will you get the money?"

"I don't know. Lucky, maybe."

"I'll sell the house," Nessa said.

"You can't sell the house in forty-eight hours."

"I'll get a loan on it."

"You've already got loans on it, Nessa. And that takes weeks."

"It's an emergency. They'll understand. I'll go to the bank tomorrow."

"Tomorrow's Sunday."

"I'll go Monday morning."

"And say what? You need money for ransom?"

"Tell them to wait. Tell them not to hurt her."

"There's no time for that."

"There has to be. Oh my God, the poor girl. You don't think they'd—"

"This guy Fuller, it's like he's decided this is his last stand."

"Tell the police."

"They won't be able to find him. They'd be knocking doors down and if Fuller found out—"

They were driving into town, following a slow-moving Mercedes, a white-haired man behind the wheel. Brandon slammed the wheel, barely resisting the urge to put the pedal to the floor, the need to scream.

"Oh, Brandon, I'm sorry."

"It's not your fault."

Nessa paused.

"They know about Lucky?"

"Yeah. I think that's what they're after. They think he has money. A lot."

Another pause, Nessa's eyes welling, her long, thin hand gripping the door handle, houses passing but her eyes unseeing. "It is my fault. That he came back. To Portland, I mean."

"What do you mean, Nessa? You didn't know he was coming."

"But the boat, talking to you. He knew I wouldn't tell anyone."

"Tell them what? That he was alive?"

"Tell them anything."

"What are you talking about, Nessa?"

She swallowed. The tears spilled over, running down her papery cheeks.

"It was about drugs, Brandon. It was. They were taking the boat down south. They were picking up a load of pot."

"You knew that then?"

"Yes."

"And you still let her go? She could have been arrested. She could have ended up in prison. With a little kid? How could you—" Brandon nearly gagged on it, his mother killed on a marijuana smuggling run. Not just a cruise to see the south. Not a jaunt with her friends. A drug run. Her friends all drug smugglers. Her mother in on the secret.

Nessa was crying now, starting to talk, then stopping.

"I couldn't ... I couldn't tell you. I didn't want you to think—"

Brandon had turned off, was wending toward Nessa's house, trying not to speed, trying not to let the cops behind him know something was wrong.

He pulled up to the house, went through the stone gates, pulled in by the garage. The brown pickup drove past on the road. Brandon jumped out of the car, hurried to his truck. Nessa followed, unsteadily.

"Where are you going?"

"The boat."

"I'll call the bank."

"They're closed."

"I'll find out who works there and call them at home," she said.

"Don't let the police know."

"I won't. I'm good at—" Nessa paused. "Hiding things," she said.

"Don't drink, Nessa," Brandon said. "I may need you."

"Okay. I won't. Nothing but coffee."

"How many times had he heard that in his life. Had it ever been true?

"Really. Promise me."

"I do promise, Brandon. I'm here for you."

He'd heard that, too.

CHAPTER 57

On board *Bay Witch*, Brandon at the navigation table. He had a chart out, Portland to Sheepscot Bay, a map of the Atlantic Provinces, a piece of paper with the coordinates from the GPS on *Ocean Swell*. The last trip they'd sailed due east to a point fifty miles west of Yarmouth, Nova Scotia, then turned back, sailing west by northwest back toward the Maine coast. The last leg of the triangle was the run down the coast to Casco Bay. The last coordinate was at the Falmouth house, just offshore.

But the wind that trip had been from the southeast when they'd left, had shifted to the northeast as they'd returned. That made it efficient to make that northwestern swing, then run with the wind for the last leg. This trip it was blowing much harder, seas were higher, and maybe they'd cut things short. The wind was still from the south, making it less likely they'd make that long northwesterly run.

Brandon could see them coming back running due west. That would mean a shorter trip, even if they went the same distance to the east. He had a feeling they'd be back sooner.

He hoped. He prayed. He choked the engine and turned the key. It coughed. Once. Twice. Started and stalled. Started again and sputtered.

"Come on, baby," Brandon said, and the engine settled into a rough idle.

It was almost two o'clock. Brandon stepped out onto the dock, tied the dinghy to the stern davit, started undoing the dock line. He looked up to see a couple, young with a toddler, a four-year-old. They were coming around the dock, headed for him. He thought of Nessa, the drug run, the little boy left behind.

What had they been thinking? Why take the chance?

"Money," Brandon said.

But to make money on something like that, you had to put money down. You had to—

"Hey there," the guy said. He was smiling, the wife, too, the guy saying,

"A woman up by the gate said you're the person to talk to about a slip. We have a twenty-one-foot Grady White."

Brandon gave them the rates, said there were two slips available. He moved back to the bow of *Bay Witch* while he talked. The guy said he'd take the slip for the rest of the season, his checkbook was in the car. Brandon shook his hand, said he could pay after he had the boat in.

A handshake and they headed for the ramp, the kid skipping in front. Brandon felt a wave of déjà vu, skipping along the wharf himself, not realizing that his mother was going alone, that he wasn't going out in the big boat, too. A crushing, suffocating feeling, squeezing the tears out of him.

He shook it off. Money, he thought. How much?

Going to the stern, he pulled the dinghy in close, then lifted, got the bow on board, then braced his feet against the bulkhead and pulled. When the dinghy was most of the way over the gunwale, he turned it, tied it down at both ends. This trip he might want to make some speed, didn't want the dinghy towed behind, slowing him down.

He put the boat in gear, eased out of the slip, and idled. He turned to the outer floats, eased up to the fuel dock, and stepped out. Tied up again, ran to the pump locker and unlocked the padlock. He turned the pump on, trotted back, and pulled the hose up to the stern. Unscrewed the cap and filled the tank. Ninety gallons, topping it off.

Trotted back to the pump locker and locked it back up. As he stepped aboard, he saw another cruiser coming out, the skipper, a guy named Alfred, waving to him.

Alfred wanted diesel. He loved to talk boats. Brandon untied, jumped aboard, hurried to the helm and got underway. *Bay Witch* rumbled away from the dock, and still among the moorings, Brandon hit the throttle.

He didn't look back.

The wind had eased, the rain turned to a soft drizzle. There were a few lobstermen coming in, a late return after a late start in the morning's wind and rain. He passed a big yawl heading out under power, the homeport of Perth showing on the stern, the Australian flag flying off the stern.

Bluewater cruisers on the move. Lucky's kind of sailors. What sort of business had brought Lucky back here? It had to be one with money.

Brandon had the chart folded in front of him at the helm. He'd marked *Ocean Swell*'s route, waypoints off Seguin Island, fifteen miles up the coast, then among the islands, just off Whaleboat Ledge. The last waypoint was just south of Cousins Island, a mile from the Falmouth house.

Would they come back there? They'd have to anchor offshore and take the dinghy in. Would they come back to Portland? If he found them, would they help? What if they decided to anchor off some island, like Lucky had said? For a day? Two?

The forty-eight hours would be up.

Brandon threaded his way through the first band of islands, through the passage between Peaks and Long. The outer island to the east was Cliff, where a few fishing families lived. Beyond it was Jewell, an outcropping of ledge where seals bred.

He figured he'd get out beyond Jewell and start to call.

The seals were there, on the weed-covered rocks, the tide out. Brandon went a half-mile beyond them, shut off the motor, took out binoculars, and scanned the horizon.

There was a sailboat to the northeast, but it was a catamaran. There were lobster boats pulling traps south of Bailey Island. No other sailboat in sight.

Brandon grabbed the mike, started calling. "*Ocean Swell, Ocean Swell,* this is *Bay Witch.*"

Paused. Listened. Heard static. Called again.

The range of the VHF was ten miles, tops. Leaning on his elbows, he scanned the horizon to the east and south. Called again. Called every ten minutes, the boat lifting on the southerly swell, drifting northeast with the current.

He felt the urge to scream, and this time, with only the gulls there to hear him, Brandon did scream. Once. Twice. A harbor seal, trailing the boat, heard the sound and dove. Was this helping Mia? Should he just go to the cops? Had he retreated to the only thing he knew well—boats? Was he making a mistake betting on Lucky and Irina?

Brandon took a deep breath and, putting the microphone to his mouth, called again, "*Ocean Swell, Ocean Swell.*"

Aboard *Ocean Swell* they were fighting a bout of seasickness. Lucky had set a direct course for the Maine coast, no northwest leg. He sailed close to the southeast wind, dropped the sails south of Bailey Island, and proceeded under power. It was dusk when he began threading his way through the islands and ledges, glancing at the depth finder.

Irina came up from below, went to the rail, and emptied a bucket of vomit. As she turned back, weary and drained, she heard Brandon on the radio.

"What does he want?" she said.

"I don't know," Lucky said.

"How long has he been calling?"

"Every ten minutes for the last half-hour at least."

She looked out at the bay, the spruce-bristled rock islands, the open water to the south.

"I wonder where he is."

"If I had to guess, I'd say somewhere to the southwest," Lucky said.

"You don't think he's near the house?"

"Islands would block the radio."

"So we should be okay," Irina said.

"Yeah. We'll unload, give him a call back."

"It sounds urgent."

Lucky shrugged. Looked to the depth finder, eased off to port away from buoys marking ledges that would hang the boat up. That would be disaster.

"Things settling down?" he said.

"Yeah," Irina said, still holding the bucket. "It was the swells."

"Nice to be presentable when we get there."

"I'll do my best," Irina said.

Brandon gave up on the outer bay, turned west, and put the throttle down. Darkness was falling fast. The big V-8 roared and *Bay Witch* hoisted herself up and out of the water, the bow slicing the waves, the boat rising and falling with the swells. He hugged the markers and eased through the gut north of Green Island, where the seals bred, did a slalom through Hussey Sound. North through the islands, he cut close to the channel buoys, leaving them rocking in his wake. And then he hit the shallower waters, with darkness closing in, swung in and along the Falmouth shoreline.

He dodged lobster buoys, peered at the shore, watched for the house.

And there it was, big and grand, a dark presence against a backdrop of trees. There were no lights on and Brandon sagged against the wheel as the boat heaved to a stop.

And then there were lights. Headlights coming down the drive.

They could have put in somewhere else. Cut the trip short because of the weather, slipped into Portland ahead of him. Had mechanical trouble and left the boat up the coast.

Brandon eased to within forty yards of the shore, just south of the house. There were ledges in closer, he couldn't remember where. He leapt from the cockpit, went forward along the deck. Released the anchor and heard the chain rattle out. The line went slack, then taut as the anchor set and the boat swung.

Hurrying back to the cockpit, Brandon went below and took the rifle from the closet, Fuller out there, maybe had found this place. Brandon went to the stern and eased the dinghy over the side. He climbed in, leaned the rifle on the seat. The dinghy drifted off and he turned it quickly, started rowing hard, making for the little pier, grunted as the boat ground into a ledge, nearly threw him off the seat.

He backed off and changed course, making directly for the shore. He'd drag the dinghy up, run over to the house. He didn't want to miss them if they were just pulling in, dropping stuff, going to dinner.

The hull ground again, this time on the stony beach. Brandon stepped to the bow, out onto the rocks, yanked the dinghy six feet up, and dropped it. He picked up the rifle, trotted along the shore toward the house, looking up and over the seawall for the lights.

It was dark again.

"Damn," he said.

He ran another fifty feet, decided to climb the wall, slog through the sodden sea roses and get to the lawn. He slung the rifle over his shoulder, put his hands up on the rough timbers, and swung his legs up. Forced his way through the strip of brambles, and looked again.

Darkness. And then a light. A car door opening and then closing, the light going out. He paused, started to walk slowly to where it had been. Saw the glow of a cigarette, like an orange firefly in the darkness.

Lucky and Irina didn't smoke.

Brandon slowed, veered toward the edge of the trees. Walking, then creeping, he made his way to a point fifty yards from the shadow, turned now so the fire dot of the cigarette didn't show.

He stopped. Eased along so that he was behind the figure. Saw that there were two.

They were standing away from a box truck, the kind that hauls fish or lobster. Brandon stopped. Waited. Listened. Waited some more, hearing a catbird in the dark woods, his own breathing after the catbird was silent.

"Pretty fucking nice, huh?" one man said to the other, an accent like Irina's. "Quiet. Lotsa trees."

"Cold in the winter. I don't do cold anymore," the second man said, the same accent.

"We should move 'em along this time," the first man said. "They can rest on the way. Last time, way too long."

"That was Lucky, the son of a bitch. Hoping to get some."

"Why doesn't he just jump Irina?" the first man said.

"She'd cut it off," the second man said, laughing softly. "Like that lady did, they found it in the road."

"He can pay for it like everybody else," the first man said.

"Here they come," his partner said. "Remember now. Half-hour. No more."

Brandon looked to the water, saw the shape of a boat form like a pale ghost against the darkness, veiled by mist. It came in from the northeast, no lights showing, the low thunk of the diesel barely audible.

And then the motor shut off, the boat gliding slowly. It was *Ocean Swell*—Brandon could tell by the shape of the hull. It drifted, there was a muffled anchor-chain rattle and a splash. One of the smoking men walked to the truck, flicked the parking lights on once, and turned them off.

He stepped to the cab, opened the door, and climbed up and in. Brandon could see his face: white, pale skin, a black goatee, thick black hair.

He climbed into the cab and took something out. Tucked it into the waist of his jeans and dropped his shirttail over it.

A gun.

Brandon heard the sputter of a small outboard and saw a shadow move out from the sailboat, heading toward shore like the head of some black ocean snake.

The inflatable.

It motored in, idled up to the dock. Brandon crouched; the two men started walking toward the water. A flashlight flicked on from the dinghy. Brandon's phone buzzed.

Mia.

He fished it from his jeans, flipped it open. Said in a whisper, "Yes?"

"Hi, is this Brandon?" a young woman said.

"Yes," he said in a softer whisper.

"This is Samantha. From USM?"

"Who?"

"Slavic Studies? I did your translation? It's kinda weird, but I really think I got it pretty much right. You want to get together and talk about it, we could have coffee or whatever."

"Sure," Brandon said. "But what does it say?"

"Okay. It's kinda like a letter. Like somebody writing home. She says— her name is Eugenia. She says—I've got it all written out. We really should get together. It's kinda complicated over the phone."

"Just give me a sense of it," Brandon said. "Please."

"Okay. It starts out like, 'Dear mother. I am afraid, fearful, to tell you— to admit to you, something like that—what I have done. They said I could have an occupation, a position. That means a job, I guess. A job as a dancer, in America. For a year, I could make sufficient money for an apartment, a large apartment where we could all live together, Julia, also.'"

She paused.

"You still there?"

"Yes," Brandon whispered.

"She says, 'I am on a vessel. A ship. I am very scared. The ship is bouncing, or rocking, something like that. It smells like fishes and makes me sick. I think the boat may descend—I guess that means sink—and we are far out in the ocean. It is cold. I would put this note in a jug and put it out the little window, but the woman is watching. She is very mean. I do not think any dancer would start out—embark, maybe—this method.'

"Then it gets kinda messy and smudged. But I think she says, 'I love you. I pray to see you again in the future or in heaven.'"

As Brandon listened, he saw someone climb up onto the dock from the inflatable.

A woman. Irina?

Then another. And another.

Three women, each carrying a small bag. The man with the gun in his pants said something to them in another language, then in English, "Welcome to America." They walked down the dock with him bringing up the rear like he was a guard and they were prisoners.

The outboard motor revved and the inflatable turned back to the sailboat. The women walked up the lawn toward the house.

"Are you there?" Samantha said.

Brandon closed the phone and backed into the trees.

CHAPTER 58

Six trips to the boat, eighteen women. On the last trip, Irina, too.

They were young, teenagers or early twenties, slim, in jeans and sweaters or thin jackets, the kind that came with running suits, their shoulders hunched against the drizzle. As they walked, they spoke to each other in their language. Brief bursts, sounding tired and scared.

When they were inside the house, the second man from the truck came out. He went to the truck, unlocked the cab, and climbed up. He climbed back down with brown bags folded at the top. Four of them, big and heavy, one with dappled grease stains.

Takeout.

He locked the cab and started for the house as the first man came out. They crossed in the drive, didn't speak. The first man went to the truck, again unlocked the cab, and climbed in. He came back out with a backpack, dark-colored and bulging. He slung it over his shoulder, locked the truck again, and started to walk back to the house.

Stopped. Turned to the woods and peered into the gloom.

Brandon remained still. The first man watched. Listened. Put his hand on the gun butt at his waist, but didn't take it out.

Watched for a few seconds more but saw nothing. Heard the ticking, chirping of the woods. Turned away and walked to the house, opened the door by the garage, and went inside.

Brandon let out a long, silent breath.

Fuller was leaning against a tree at the edge of the woods. He smiled. He'd called it. Not exactly—who would have guessed they were smuggling people?—but close enough. He'd seen on TV in the jail how these poor slobs paid thousands of dollars to get into the U.S., work some shit job nobody else would do. They showed them cleaning in some hotel, up to their elbows in toilet water.

Question was, where was the money? His gut said it was right here, the way that guy carried that backpack. And Fuller figured his gut was on a roll.

He smiled again. Heard a crack in the woods on the other side of the drive. Moved back behind the tree and watched.

Listened.

Rested his finger on the trigger of the Ruger.

Illegals, Brandon thought, crouched in the trees. Women from eastern Europe. So that was the deal. Sail out, rendezvous offshore somewhere with a ship, load them into the cabin of *Ocean Swell*. Make the run back, figuring the odds of being stopped and boarded were slim. Land them here and truck them to their next stop.

But why all girls? Why so young? The woman with the note had said the promised job was as a dancer. A strip club? Prostitution?

Brandon watched the house, lights on in the first floor, the dining room, the kitchen, the bathrooms upstairs and down. He had no choice. He still had to make his plea to Lucky and Irina, but alone, not with the hard guys from the truck. A half-hour, the guy had said. Ten minutes gone.

The guy without the goatee stood by the bathroom as the women came and went. The water ran, the toilet flushed. The girls avoided his gaze as they passed by him on their way downstairs, their faces pink from scrubbing, leaving a faint aroma of mint as they went by.

Toothpaste.

And then they were done, the last one taking forever, sick or something. He knocked once, said something in their language. After a minute, the woman emerged, her face pale and her long blonde hair brushed and tied back. Some of them did that, toning their looks down as the trip went on until by the end they were trying to look like nuns.

This one glared at him as she walked by, looked like she wanted to spit. An attitude, the man thought. That was okay. They'd break her soon enough.

Back downstairs some of the women were sitting around the dining room table, eating fried chicken and mashed potatoes. The potatoes were in cardboard cartons. They ate with plastic forks.

The women who had finished eating were admiring the house, the gleaming kitchen appliances, the vast rooms, the furniture like something on television. When they started to explore beyond the kitchen and dining room, the man called them back.

Lucky, Irina, and the guy with the goatee were in the living room, behind the closed French doors. The backpack was open on a glass-topped coffee table, money spread out in banded thousand-dollar packs. Lucky was counting, flipping through the packs.

"All there," the goateed guy said. "Eighteen girls, five grand apiece. Ninety thousand."

"A pleasure, as always, Nikolai," Lucky said, stuffing the money into the backpack. "So we're on for one more?"

"Ship's off Newfoundland," Nikolai said. "Four days?"

Lucky looked at Irina.

"Not a problem," she said.

"You still thinking of South Carolina?" Lucky said.

"October," Nikolai said.

"Oooh, hurricane season," Lucky said. "Lost one of my nine lives down there already."

"You saying no?"

"No, but there may be a weather surcharge. And it may take a little more time to set up the boat. Worked out nicely here because I had a friend in the business."

"You didn't—"

"Tell him? Come on, Nikolai."

"People screw up. Get sloppy," Nikolai said. "Working with friends."

Lucky looked at him, smile gone, eyes cold. "I use the word loosely," he said. "It's business. Just like you and me."

He repacked the money, put the bag in a slant-top desk, and closed the cover. They left the room—Nikolai first, then Irina, Lucky last—and returned to the second man and the women. They had finished eating, one small dark-haired girl still using her finger to wipe the last of the gravy from a carton. She looked up at them and licked her finger, like an animal refusing to give up its kill.

Mosquitoes had found him, whining around his head, lighting on his hands. Fuller calmly wiped them off, told himself this was part of the test. He remembered the time when he was stung by a yellowjacket when he was a kid, his father slapping him, telling him to stop blubbering like a little baby. It was the last time Fuller cried. He'd refused to let bugs bother him ever again.

He leaned against the oak, trying to hear past the mosquitoes, the salty mist dripping in the trees. He thought he'd heard another noise in the woods on the other side of the drive, but then there'd been nothing for the last ten minutes. Probably an animal, Fuller thought, and then he heard the door open. Voices.

They came out the door by the garage, first one of the guys from the truck, then the girls, in a long line like school kids going on a field trip, following by the second guy. The first guy unlocked the truck, climbed in, and started it. Turned on the headlights. The girls milled about, looked warily at the truck. The guy got out, went to the back, undid a lock, and rolled up the cargo bay door.

There was something stacked there, almost to the ceiling. Mesh bags of something dark. Fuller was trying to figure it out when the smell drifted his way on a puff of wind. Fish. Freakin' clams or something. The guy with the goatee climbed up and started unloading them, passing them down to his partner. When he'd passed down twenty bags or so, there was a passage through the wall of shellfish.

The guy in the truck moved in, out of sight. A light went on deep in the back. The guy on the ground said something to the women in another language, and then the hot Russian lady, she repeated it, added some more. Fuller watched as the girls came to the back of the truck. The Russian lady's boyfriend was there now and he held out his hand to help them up.

They ignored him and climbed in themselves, grabbing a handle and hoisting themselves up. One by one, they passed into the passage between the bags. When they were all inside, the light went out. The bags were passed up and restacked. When they were done, it was again a solid wall of shellfish bound for market.

"Sweet," Fuller said to himself, watching from the woods, holding the nine millimeter at his side.

Across the driveway, Brandon still crouched. "So that's it," he said.

The guy with the goatee pulled the door down and snapped a padlock on the hasp. He went around to the passenger side, climbed up and in. The other guy put the truck in gear, a beeping warning sounding as it backed up. The beeping stopped, the truck turned and started out the drive. Fuller eased behind his tree as it passed. Brandon stayed low as it passed.

Irina and Lucky watched the truck go up the drive, red lights under the dark trees, then turned and went inside. Brandon raised himself up, his legs stiff and cramping. He started for the house, the rifle low against his right leg.

Fuller grinned, knowing this meant the money was here, that Brandon would come for the twenty grand to bail his girlfriend out. And where there was twenty, there had to be more.

"Damn," he said, as he eased out from behind the tree. "You are good."

CHAPTER 59

Irina and Lucky were cleaning up, all of the takeout mess going into a black trash bag. Then Irina wiped down the table, the doorknobs, the sides of the chairs, the doorjambs where two of the girls had gone through looking at the house.

Lucky did both bathrooms, first downstairs, spraying all of the surfaces with cleaner, opening the cabinet and wiping down the aspirin bottle inside.

Then he went upstairs to the other bathroom, was there spraying and wiping when Brandon stepped into the dining room, the rifle in the crook of his arm.

Irina was bent over the trash bag, looping a twist tie around the top. She looked up at him, the rifle not in ready position but close.

"Brandon. Are you okay?" she said, leaving the bag and moving toward him.

"No," he said. "Not really."

"What's the matter, dear?" Irina said. "The gun—"

"They have Mia. I need to borrow some money."

"They? Who?"

"Fuller and Kelvin."

"Have her?"

"Yeah. Took her. They want twenty thousand."

"The police?"

"No police, or they leave her where she is, she dies."

Irina was close. She put a hand on his shoulder.

"Don't worry. We'll take care of this. Where I'm from, these things happen all the time. There are ways to deal with these people."

"I'll pay you the money back," Brandon said.

"Oh, don't worry about that. Money's not important. What's important is that we get her home safe. Listen, let me get Lucky. We just got back.

239

Rain and wind, stuck in Kennebunkport Harbor. Miserable. Finally we said uncle. He's upstairs."

"You've been cleaning," Brandon said.

"Left the place a bit of a mess, just picking up."

She went back for the bag, took it through the kitchen to the hall that led to the garage. Lucky had heard the voices, was coming down the back stairs. He was tucking a handgun into the back of his jeans, pulling his shirt down over it.

"It's Brandon," Irina said. "Those two idiots have—"

"I heard."

Softer now.

"He's wet. He's been outside watching. He knows. I could see it in his eyes when I said the part about Kennebunk."

"So now he's in," Lucky said. "Leverage."

"He's a policeman."

"In training. Barely.

"I don't like it."

"We save his girlfriend, he owes us forever. We need somebody local. We need somebody to crew. His grandmother can keep her house. It's perfect."

She looked at him, smiled coldly.

"I know what you like. You like—what is the word?— the ironic. Brandon working for the person who—"

"You think too much," Lucky said. "Let's get it done."

He strode through the kitchen, found Brandon in the dining room, slowed for a split second as he saw the rifle.

"Brandon, buddy," Lucky said, moving to him, touching Brandon's right shoulder, away from the rifle barrel. "Jesus, the gun—what happened?"

Brandon repeated what he'd told Irina, said the rifle was just in case he ran into Fuller, Kelvin.

"Can I borrow the money?"

"Sure, man, but the money's only part of the problem. We gotta get Mia back. We gotta make sure those two morons don't do something really stupid. And Brandon—"

Lucky paused, stared into Brandon's eyes.

"—we gotta be honest with each other."

"Yes," Brandon said.

"You're all wet. How long were you out there?"

"Half-hour. A little more."

"You parked, walked in?"

Irina moved up beside Lucky, something more than sympathy in her expression now.

"So you were there when—"

"When they loaded the women into the truck? Yeah," Brandon said.

"I wanted to tell you," Lucky said. "I told Irina I thought you'd understand."

"Understand what?" Brandon said.

"How we're selling the American dream, man. How these girls, this is their big chance. They've got nothing where they come from. Work some totally shit job, if they're lucky. Live in some crappy two-room apartment with their parents, their grandparents, screaming nieces and nephews. Watch mom and dad drink themselves to death on cheap vodka, parked in front of the one channel on the twelve-inch television. How hopeless is that?"

"Nothing that's good in the future," Irina said. "Just emptiness as far as you can see."

"So they come here," Lucky said.

"They pay you for the passage?" Brandon asked.

"Me, some other people."

"Where do they get the money?"

"Some of them repay part of it with money they make once they get here."

"Doing what?" Brandon said.

"Au pairs, mostly. Domestics. But they meet people, too. We had a girl just get married to a guy, this commodities trader in Chicago. Big house in Lake Forest. Like she died and went to heaven."

"So they're not all dancers," Brandon said, catching the flicker in Irina's expression, a ripple across the screen.

"They have different skills," she said.

Brandon pictured them: all young, attractive, even after the ocean crossing.

"I'm sure," he said.

"What they don't have," Lucky said, "is permission to enter the U.S. I'm being straight with you. It's illegal, what we're doing. But I think of it like the Underground Railroad. It's their passage out of a world of suffering. Ask Irina. She knows."

"Very, very tough where they come from. Bulgaria, Macedonia, Russia, Albania. No hope."

"Are they prostitutes?" Brandon said.

"Oh, God no," Irina said. "They're waitresses. Secretaries. We had a girl who taught yoga. We had one almost has her degree in finance. They come here with many skills."

There was a pause. "So the money?" Brandon said.

Then Lucky said, "How 'bout we don't loan it to you. We pay it to you. You've been really helpful, getting the boat and all. I could really use somebody like you. Last trip got a little hairy, trying to keep her running with the wind, just the storm jib up. Blowing hard and gusty, big seas. Irina, she's below dealing with the girls, making sure they're okay. I could have really used somebody on deck who knew what they were doing."

"The whole twenty?" Brandon said.

"Let's call it ten in advance for the next trip, ten as a signing bonus," Lucky said.

"You have the cash here?"

Suddenly they were all aware of the rifle in Brandon's arms. "Sure," Lucky said. "This is a cash sort of business, as you may have noticed. Money's not a problem."

"Good thing," Fuller said, stepping from the hallway with the Ruger leveled. "'Cause the price, it just went up."

CHAPTER 60

Lucky had his hands up. Irina was to his left and she took a half-step back, ready to go for the gun in Lucky's jeans.

"All your hands showing," Fuller said, moving in and to the right, Brandon watching the open end of the nine-millimeter, dark as a cave. "Blake, hold that popgun by the barrel, put it on the floor."

Brandon did, easing the rifle down.

"Hey, man, take it easy," Lucky said. "We can cut a real nice deal."

"Lotta money in sex slaves?" Fuller said, still moving slowly, a sliding sidestep. "I saw a show on it in jail. Weren't Russkies, though. Freakin' Mexicans. Little girls. There's some sick people out there, dude."

"You got that right," Lucky said, trying to get Fuller talking, get him to ease up, just for a split second. "What they choose to do once they get here, that's their thing. Irina and me, we're in the transport business."

He and Irina were turning with Fuller, their hands still up, keeping him in front.

"We could use somebody like you on the ground," Lucky said. "Brandon here, he's in. You let the girl come home, no hard feelings, we get down to business. This could make all of us very rich, very quick."

"That right?" Fuller said.

"Oh, yeah," Lucky said. "Twenty thousand? That's nothing. You could make ten times that in six months, we work at it. Brandon gets the boats, sails with me. You do logistics on the ground. You're a smart guy."

They continued to turn, but Brandon was slower, could see Irina inching closer to Lucky, saw the bulge at Lucky's waist.

"Could be quite a team," Lucky said. "None of this nickel and dime stuff, man. Big time."

Brandon saw the plan, Irina diving to the right behind Lucky, a roll, Irina getting the shots off.

"Where is she?" he said. "If you touch her—"

"Chill, dude," Fuller said. "She's fine. I left, she was playing Texas Hold 'Em, watching the tube. I get my money. Make a phone call, she's free and clear. After we get a head start of course."

Lucky bent forward, hiked up the back of his shirt so the gun came out. Irina eased a foot closer to him. They were getting ready. They'll kill him, Brandon thought. And Mia—

"He's got a gun behind him. In his pants," Brandon said.

They all froze, the Ruger swinging to point at Lucky's head.

"Well, I can see somebody's thinking here. Blake, you know they don't give a shit about your girl there. Gonna take me out, if they can, let her fucking rot. Dying of thirst, dude. Sucks. Your tongue swells up and turns all black. Not fun."

He motioned with the Ruger to Irina and Lucky.

"On the floor, hands stretched out toward me."

They eased down, kneeling first, then falling forward. The pistol butt was black at Lucky's waist. Fuller eased around, put his gun on Lucky's neck as he bent and yanked the pistol out of Lucky's waistband.

"A Sig, man. Nice little going-away present."

He slipped it into his jeans in front, moved around the front of them, prostrate like pilgrims. Motioned to Brandon.

"Search her."

Brandon dropped his hands, moved to stand over Irina.

"She's the one I don't trust," Fuller said. "Not one fucking bit."

Brandon bent and lifted Irina's shirt at the back of her waist, then the Lycra top she wore under it. He patted her down.

"Nothing."

"The front," Fuller said. "Ice pick in there somewhere. Roll over, Natasha."

She did, her black eyes shining with hatred. Brandon hesitated, then ran his hands along her abdomen. Felt nothing. Did the same with her legs, ankles to crotch.

"Check the bra," Fuller said.

Brandon did, patting through the shirt. Started with the left breast, felt something hard, long.

"Here," he said.

"Take it out, slow. No stupid moves, Natasha baby," Fuller said, "You don't want your boyfriend's brains all over the nice clean floor."

Irina looked at Fuller and said, "You're dead, how do you say it here? Trailer trash?"

Fuller went pale.

"Bitch," he said.

She lifted her shirt, slipped her fingers in. Came out with a four-inch pick with a two-inch wooden handle, pencil thin.

"Nice little shiv," Fuller said. "You've done time, huh? Toss it."

She did and the pick hit the wall under the cabinets, bounced and rolled.

"Okay, now we tell my buddy Blake where the money bag is."

They looked at him with mouths clamped shut.

"Okay," Fuller said. "You want to play games, try this one."

He took three steps to Lucky, put the gun on his forehead. "What should we count to? Maybe a small number 'cause I sucked at math. Let's say eight. I'll start. One, two, three—"

"It's got to be right here somewhere," Brandon said. "They didn't have time to hide it. The women were all here."

"Four, five—" Fuller said.

"No. Don't do that," Brandon said. "I don't know where it is. You kill 'em, we can't find it, we're done. And they can't report it, if you take the money. You kill 'em, you got a big mess. More cops. You got their friends up the line wondering where they are. Give me one minute."

Brandon lunged to the cupboards, started flinging the doors open. He opened the refrigerator, the stove. He yanked a closet door open, pulled jackets from hangers. Pushed through the French doors, heard Fuller say, "Hey," but started yanking drawers. Moved to a desk with a wooden front, yanked it open.

And there it was. A black L.L. Bean backpack.

He unzipped it. Saw the wrapped bills. And sticking out from under the backpack, the barrel of another handgun.

"Six," Fuller called from the kitchen.

Brandon picked up the gun. It was a small revolver. On the left of the butt near the trigger was a safety, no markings. He looked at it, guessed that Irina and Lucky would leave it off. He shoved the gun in the back of his jeans, grabbed the backpack by the top handle.

"Seven," Fuller said.

At the door, Brandon pulled his shirt over the gun butt.

The bag in front of him, Brandon stepped through the doors into the kitchen.

"Got it," he said.

"Eight," Fuller said. "Too late."

Brandon saw the half-smile on his face, the decision already made, money or no money.

"Don't," Brandon shouted. "It's all here." He tossed the backpack at Fuller, pulled the gun out, and fired, all one fluid motion. The shot came just after the thud, the sound of all that money hitting the floor.

CHAPTER 61

The blood had run all over the white tiles, pooling in the grout between them, turning it dark brown.

Fuller was seated, his back against the cupboard in front of the sink. His face was gray like beach sand, and he stared at the blood-soaked towel wrapped around his right thigh. Lucky was wrapping the towel in packing tape. The bleeding seemed to have slowed. Irina watched, crouched on the floor.

Brandon stood against the wall, the little handgun ready, the rifle on the granite countertop beside him, the ice pick, his rifle, the Ruger, Irina's gun, too.

"So you tell me where she is. I bring you into town, pick her up. You and Kelvin get the money. We all go our separate ways."

"Go to hell. I get the money first. Then we let her go."

"Worth dying for?" Brandon said. "I could just leave you with these guys."

"You won't do that," Fuller said. "Remember how I said the tongue swells, it turns black and cracks. Lips, too." He grimaced. "But with a gag in, she'd probably suffocate at some point."

"I'll kill him for you right now," Irina said. "He's scum."

"Tell me about it, you fucking pimp," Fuller said. "Nice friends you got, Blake."

"So here we are," Lucky said. He looked at Brandon. "What do we do?"

"I could just call the police," Brandon said.

"There's a clock ticking, dude," Fuller said, voice weary but still full of resolve. "You won't find her. You can call the National fucking Guard."

"Ten minutes, I have him screaming out where she is," Irina said.

"She will," Lucky said. "She's seen things you wouldn't—"

"Blake, you give her a gun, first person she pops is you," Fuller said.

"You give her that shiv, she'll stick it in your neck."

"No," Irina said. "I want Mia back, too."

Fuller laughed, but it turned into a cough. He winced, but still said, "Who you kidding? You want to tie things up here, take your money, and get the hell out."

"Shut up, you piece of shit."

"She'll get it out of him," Lucky said. "She will."

"He'll beg to tell you," Irina said.

"Interesting business you're in," Brandon said.

He paused. Felt all their eyes on him. Thought of Griffin. What would he do?

The gun still in his hand, he went to the closet, took out extension cords he'd flung aside when he was looking for the bag. Tossed one to Irina.

"Hog-tie him," he said.

She smiled.

"Now you're talking sense, Brandon," Irina said.

"No," Brandon said. "I mean Lucky."

Fuller gave a snort. "You lose, Natasha," he said.

"Such a bad decision, Brandon," Lucky said. "Still time to reconsider."

"I'll live with it," Brandon said.

"You were always at risk," Irina said. "Now it's your little girlfriend, too."

She tied expertly, not the first time. Brandon took the other cord, told her to lie on her belly, and she did. He put the gun in his waistband, quickly knelt on her back, and tied her wrists, then lifted her ankles, tied them, too.

"Your knots are better," Brandon said.

"Dead," Irina said. "You're all dead."

Fuller started to try to lift himself up, fell back to the floor. "Blake. I can't do it," he said.

"I'll get the car," Brandon said. "Where is it?"

"Two driveways up, toward Portland. Fifty feet in there's a little tractor path, goes to a shed. I pulled it in."

"Keys."

"Here."

Fuller winced as he stretched to fish the keys from the pocket of his jeans. They were wet with blood. Brandon took them and picked up the backpack and the rifle and walked out of the room, out the door. Paused to tighten the trigger with the thumbscrew and started to run.

Out of the house and down the driveway, the woods dark and deep. Onto the road, turning right, keeping to the grass by the stone walls. A car passed and Brandon slowed to a walk, his rifle pressed to his leg. Breaking into a run again, he loped past the first driveway, lanterns on stone posts. Reached the second driveway, no lights at the entrance. Turned and ran down the drive, almost missed the path.

It was two ruts in the lawn, receding into the darkness. Brandon trotted, saw the shape of the car, small and white. He opened the door, slung the backpack in. Put the key in and started the motor, easing out of the path with lights out, turned them on when he was coming out of the drive.

It was a VW, stickers on the dash. University of Maine. Dave Matthews Band. Brandon pulled over, turned on the interior light. Reached between the seats and pulled out papers. A parking ticket, Portland. Receipt from a Burger King. A gas receipt, twenty-two dollars. A name on the receipt. Timothy Gould. Another card: hotel parking. He looked at it. No name, no address. Brandon squinted to see the date.

June 2. 4:09 p.m.

That afternoon.

He dialed his phone. Waited, lights out now, sitting in the dark, wind rustling the trees.

"Nessa."

"Brandon. Where are you? I've been so worried. I thought—"

"Listen, Nessa. I need you to do something for me. Are you okay?"

"No. I was frantic."

"Have you been—"

"No. I promised."

"Good. Take the phonebook, call all the motels and hotels in South Portland, then Portland. Ask for Timothy Gould. Say he checked in today."

"Timothy Gould. Who is he?"

"It doesn't matter, Nessa. Just call me if you find him."

"I will. Have you heard from—"

Brandon hung up. Sped up the road, took a left and floored it down the drive. Pulled over and stopped.

Opened the passenger door and dropped the money bag out, then drove on.

As he slid around the circle in front of the house, the headlights flashed over the shore, *Ocean Swell*, still riding at anchor. He pulled up to the door by the garage, left the car running. Before getting out, he slid Fuller's Ruger under the driver's seat. He trotted to the door, opened it, and listened.

All quiet.

Walked down the hall, rifle out. Pushed the door open. Saw Fuller, still leaning against the cupboards, eyes closed. Irina on her side on the floor, still tied. Where was—

Lucky hit him from behind, sent him sprawling. He landed face-first on the floor, rolled sideways, and Lucky landed on him, but only on his arm, grabbed for the rifle. Brandon scrabbled backward onto Irina, who screamed to Lucky, "Shoot him, shoot him." He rolled over Fuller, who shouted, "My leg."

Lucky raised the rifle and smiled.

"The money," he said. "I'll take it back now."

"It's not here," Brandon said.

"Untie me, Lucky," Irina said. "I helped you."

"Let's go get it, Brandon," Lucky said. "You can take your twenty, be on your way."

"Untie me, you idiot," Irina shouted.

Lucky motioned with the gun.

"Let's go."

"You son of a bitch," Irina said.

"I'll be back, baby," Lucky said.

"He's going to kill you, Brandon," Irina said. "He's going to kill all of us. Just like he—"

The gun swung, pointed at Irina.

"No," Lucky said.

"Doesn't matter now if he knows," Irina said.

"Knows what?" Brandon said.

"She's crazy. Crazy Russian bitch."

Irina smiled.

"He's going to kill all of us, just like he killed your mother. He killed all of them. He was on that boat. Shot them, sunk the boat with them in it."

"She wasn't there," Lucky said. "She doesn't know."

"He told me. He was very drunk. Stoli, I remember. So drunk somehow some little bit of guilt shook loose. The next day he remembers nothing. But I don't forget."

Brandon felt the room go still. No one in it but he and Lucky. The rest of them gone, disappeared.

"Why?"

"I wasn't there. I was late. She's just trying to save her pretty ass."

"Why?" Brandon asked again.

"Probably a freighter. Somebody asleep on the bridge."

"Why? What did my mother do to you?"

"Never would've known what hit them, one guy at the helm, everybody else asleep below."

"She liked you guys. I remember when you all left. How happy she was. Nessa took me down to say goodbye. And you killed them? You're crazy. You're a psycho. You are, aren't you?"

Lucky stared at him, finally shook his head. Smiled.

"No, not a psycho, Brandon. A businessman. I was supposed to get my cut. Thirty thousand, after we moved the dope. Then Ketch says it's gonna be ten. Like the whole conversation never happened. I get pissed, he says, 'Okay. Five.' I say, 'Hey, man. What's going on?' He says, 'Two and a half." I say, 'No way.' Money was right there, on board. I said to myself, 'That's just not fair. You want to break the rules, I'll break the rules.' And I popped him. Took all of it. A hundred and twenty thousand, forty of it from Nessa, by the way."

So that was it, Brandon thought, her life flashing before his eyes. Pain that all the wine in the world couldn't ease, guilt that greeted her every morning, bid her goodnight at the end of the day.

"I did Nikki first. She was asleep," Lucky said. "I can tell you, she never felt a thing."

"Victor'll find you, you bastard," Irina said from the floor. "They'll hunt you down."

"What's there to hunt?" Lucky said, "if we all go down with the ship?"

CHAPTER 62

Out the door to the car, lights on, still running, starting to overheat, maybe what Timothy Gould had brought it to the garage for. Lucky motioned Brandon to the driver's seat, climbed in the back behind him.

Brandon put the car in gear, started around the circle.

"Why Nessa? Who talked her into that?"

"Didn't need talking," Lucky said. "It was pot. A victimless crime. A lot of money to be made."

"And she needed money," Brandon said.

"What was it? Husband blew their savings on some bimbo, then up and died? I forget the story. But no more talk. Let's get the money."

"You don't care about Mia. You didn't care about Nikki."

"Caring was irrelevant," Lucky said. "It was business."

The car was passing the money bag, invisible in the dark—except for a band of reflective tape. The backpack.

"Stop," Lucky said, jabbing the rifle barrel into the back of Brandon's head. He braked, the car skidding on the wet gravel drive.

"Back up," Lucky barked.

Brandon did, watching as the backpack showed in the mirror.

"Stop here," Lucky said.

As Lucky got out, Brandon reached for the gun under the seat. Lucky lifted the bag, felt its heft. The rifle still trained on Brandon in the car, he squatted, unzipped the bag, felt the money.

He grinned. "Get out, my friend," he said.

Brandon opened the door, stood there, his right hand behind his back.

"Let's take a little walk," Lucky said.

"Okay," Brandon said, and brought the gun around, pointed it at Lucky's face. Lucky pulled the trigger on the rifle. It didn't move, screwed down tight.

He tried again, his finger flexing.

Nothing.

"Drop it," Brandon said.

A moment passed. Another.

And then Lucky lowered the rifle, dropped it to the soft ground. Brandon pointed the pistol at Lucky's chest. "Now let's go for that walk."

They started into the darkness, toward the trees, Lucky five feet in front. The ground was spongy and wet, the trees rustling with the wind gusts, the air heavy with the scent of sea and fir. When they reached the treeline Brandon said, "Stop." Lucky did.

"Kneel down," Brandon said.

Lucky did, but as he lowered himself, he turned and smiled.

"You shouldn't do this," he said.

"Justice," Brandon said.

"You're not like us, me and Irina," Lucky said, turning away. "It'll eat you up. You'll be like your grandmother, drinking herself into a haze. And you know what? Every morning when you wake up, it'll still be there."

"You did that to her."

"Hey, she bought in, and when she did, she sold a piece of herself. Nikki, she was a very attractive young woman running in some fairly risky circles. Could've been a lot of things happened to her."

"But it was you."

"You can kill me, but if you get Mia back it won't be the same. You won't deserve her and you'll know it."

Brandon held the pistol out, saw it wavering, still pointing at Lucky's head.

He swallowed. Tightened his finger slowly.

Aimed the gun at the back of Lucky's head.

Relaxed, and let his finger fall away.

He slipped his phone from his pocket. Started to dial. Heard a car start at the house, followed by a splintering crash. The Jeep, coming through the garage door.

The motor roared. Gears ground. Brandon stepped back toward he drive. Saw taillights, then headlights, the Jeep lurching as it started up the drive.

Lucky turned, still on his knees.

"Stay there," Brandon said, and the Jeep approached, no top, just a roll bar, swerving onto the lawn, back onto the drive. It was doing forty when it passed, just missing the VW, Fuller hunched over the wheel like a wounded man on horseback.

"He knows you got the money," Lucky said. "Probably going to grab your girl, take off again. Next time it'll be a lot more than twenty grand." He paused. "Or maybe he's just gonna kill her."

Brandon turned back to him, the gun still pointed. Lowered it and fired. Lucky bellowed. Clutched at his ankle and writhed on the ground. Brandon ran to the car, scooping up the bag of money on the way.

CHAPTER 63

Brandon turned left, saw taillights in the distance, headed for the city. The lights disappeared over a rise and he floored the VW, felt it shudder and cough.

Red lights came on in the dash and it slowed. The lights went off and the engine revved again.

"Damn it," Brandon said.

Fuller was out of sight, headed for the Route 1 bridge, the city. Brandon reached for the phone, pressed the nine, the one.

Stopped.

Would Fuller talk? Would he say he knew nothing, let Mia die where she was? What if they shot him, shot the cop killer, shot him for Officer Griffin? What if he drove into an abutment, better that than to do forty years?

Mia dying would be Fuller's last revenge.

Brandon pressed the gas pedal to the floor. The engine sputtered but then smoothed out and the little car whined, the steering wheel shaking. He hit sixty, slammed on the brakes as a car pulled out from a side street, hit the gas again and passed it. In the distance, on the bridge, he saw the single taillights.

The Jeep. Fuller caught in traffic.

Brandon was on the bridge, the black, glittering bay to his left. Fuller was going off the other side, the Jeep waggling as he looked for room to get around a slower truck, suddenly swerving right and passing.

Following, Brandon saw the Jeep turn onto the Interstate ramp, southbound into the city. It disappeared and the car in front of Brandon braked for the turn, sat and waited for oncoming traffic. Turned slowly.

Brandon followed.

Onto the highway, traffic heavy. Four lanes headed into the city. No Jeep in sight, and then flashing blue lights in the passing lane ahead.

"No," Brandon said, and he floored the little car, moved left to follow. The city skyline on the left, the bank saying it was fifty-nine degrees. The VW doing eighty, in pursuit. Brandon creeping up on the police car, which suddenly swerved right as a car in front moved into the breakdown lane. Slowed.

The Jeep. Fuller.

The gun in his pocket? The cop walking into it? If Fuller missed, he'd be shot dead right there.

Brandon slowed, drew alongside the cruiser, its spotlights on, facing forward. Brandon beeped the horn, saw the cop look over, a young woman, startled.

He held up the gun, made sure she saw it, her eyes widening, head jerking back, hand going to the radio mic. Brandon floored the VW and pulled away. The cop had to wait for a break in traffic, then pulled out, five cars back, the blue lights flashing.

And the phone rang.

"Yeah."

"It's me."

"Nessa."

The engine was whining, an oily, sweet smell filling the car.

"I called all over," Nessa said.

"What did you find?"

"Well, the Sheraton. He wasn't there. The Hilton by the mall? He wasn't there, either. It was a different Gould. You know they don't want to tell you anything, these hotel people?"

"Nessa, did you find him?"

The blue lights still back there, the cop caught in traffic.

"I'm getting to that."

"Get to it now. Please."

"Well, yes. I did. Timothy Gould. He's staying at the Royal Arms. Right in town. At first they didn't want to tell me, said they would give him a message, if he were staying there. If. I said, I need to reach my son and I need to know if he's gotten this message. I said it was an emergency."

"It is," Brandon said. "Thanks."

He closed the phone and tossed it beside the gun. Turned the lights out, and swerved off the next exit, downshifting, no brakes, hanging onto the steering wheel as the car lifted, tires squealed. He came off the highway, cut across two lanes, and rolled into an Arby's parking lot.

He sat. Waited. No blue lights came off the highway. He counted to twenty, hit the headlights and pulled out again, past the post office, up the hill, driving slowly with the traffic now, his heart racing.

Through downtown, Brandon watched the mirrors. Held his breath.

Eased right past slower cars, down darkened Congress Street past street kids, two African women waiting for a late bus.

Down the hill to the Old Port, always people there, everybody young and hip, the VW fitting right in. He parked in front of a fire hydrant, fished in his wallet. Got out and crossed a courtyard to the hotel entrance, brassy and grand. A doorman opened the door for him, said, "Good evening, sir."

"Good evening," Brandon said, not slowing. He strode to the registration desk, stepped up beside a couple with suitcases, a little girl. Brandon flashed his police-intern I.D., looking intent and undeterrable, because he was.

"Police business," he said. "I need to talk to a guest here. Tim Gould. It's very important."

The guy behind the counter blinked once, hesitated. Looked too late as the I.D. went back in Brandon's jeans. The guy looked around—for a superior?—then bent to a computer screen.

"Four twenty-three," he said, pointing to the hall. "The elevator is around the corner to the right. But listen, could you tell me your name so I can—"

Brandon was already moving, down the hall to the elevator. He punched the button. Heard the clerk say, "Oh, hi, Mr. Gould? Is everything okay?"

Brandon slipped the gun out, pressed against the wall. A moment passed. Another. Fuller didn't appear. He moved to the corner of the hallway, saw the desk guy out from behind the desk, short and slight, like a crab out of its shell.

He saw Brandon and said, in a stage whisper, "Back stairs."

Brandon turned, saw a stairwell beyond the elevators. He started for them, was blocked by three men stepping from the elevator. Dodged them, slammed the doors open, bounded up the stairs.

Second.

Third.

Fourth.

Room number 405 was facing him and he turned, gun out now, went to the next door. It was 403.

Brandon turned back, followed the corridor, some sort of loop, numbers going up as it turned. He hurried, making no sound on the carpet, the corridor silent except for TV from a room. Heard a knocking ahead as he approached the next corner, peeked around it to see Fuller, a glimpse as he stood, one hand on the wall, waiting for the door to open.

When it did, Fuller stepped inside.

The door clicked shut.

CHAPTER 64

She was in the chair by the bed, hands tied in front of her with a computer cable, gagged with a blue bandanna. There was a large black suitcase against the wall, half open.

Inside was the pink bath towel they'd used to cushion Mia's head.

The television was on. Kelvin watching a show about people in a contest to lose weight. He'd turned the screen so she could see a big guy struggling up a long staircase.

When there was a knock.

"It's me," Fuller said.

Kelvin got up, opened the door. Fuller stepped in and Kelvin said, "What happened? You're all bloody."

"No shit," Fuller said. "I got shot. Her fucking boyfriend shoots me in the leg."

He reached for the handgun on top of the television. Griffin's Glock.

"So you get the money?" Kelvin said.

"Not yet. We gotta go."

"How come?"

"He's got the car. He'll find the name. Cops'll figure it out."

"Where we gonna go?"

"I got a Jeep. We drive right the fuck out into the country, dump it in the woods. Hit some houses until we find another car. Then we drive west, New Hampshire. New York. The hell outta here."

"That's what I said we should do—"

"Shut up," Fuller said. "Get her up."

"We're taking her?"

"You bet your ass we are. There's a backpack full of fucking cash out there now and Blake's got it."

People were cheering on the TV as the heavy guy made it to top of the stairs, all sweaty.

"Maybe he won't even call the cops," Fuller said, wincing. "Maybe we can still work him."

"But what if—"

"If he won't deal, we dump her in the woods," Fuller said. "Let's go."

He went to the TV, slammed it off. Kelvin went to Mia, helped her up.

"We're gonna go again," he said gently, as if her ears had been gagged, too.

"And you listen to me, blondie," Fuller said, stepping up to Mia, putting the barrel of the gun on her forehead. "I oughta kill you just to get even. But I'm not gonna. But let me tell you something. You make one peep, I'll shoot you right in your pretty little head."

He pressed the gun against her, forcing her head back.

"I'm telling you right now, bitch. I got nothing to lose."

Leaning against the wall, Brandon punched in the number.

Nine. One. One.

He told the dispatcher who he was. He told her where he was. He told her there was a possible hostage in a room on the east end of the hotel. She told him to stay on the line. He hung up, turned the ringer off, and put the phone in his pocket.

Held the gun against his side as he started down the covered walkway. As he approached the door, he slowed.

Heard voices.

Fuller.

Angry.

Brandon stepped across the door, leaned against the wall. The door opened and there was a rattle, Fuller saying, "Take the goddamn chain off for God's sake."

Brandon started to slide the gun up his leg. The door closed again and there was more rattling. Then the sound of a siren, distant. Closing.

The door opened and Kelvin stepped out. He looked away from Brandon, in the direction of the sound of the siren. Kelvin paused, listened to the tone, the cadence. He took a step into the hallway and listened as the siren got close, then turned off.

"Cops," he said.

A suitcase appeared, big and black, on wheels. As Brandon watched, he saw something inside it move.

Mia.

"Stay still, bitch," Fuller said. Then Brandon saw a gun in Fuller's hand, a big handgun. Griffin's. Then the bandaged leg. The face twisted in pain.

He heard another siren approaching.

"We're toast," Kelvin said.

"I ain't going to jail," Fuller said. "And I'm taking her with me."

He glanced to his right as he started to pull the suitcase backward. Saw Brandon, the gun pointed.

Fuller smiled.

"Hey, Blake," he said.

"Don't shoot," Kelvin said, his hands going up.

Fuller started to raise his gun, then reconsidered.

"Easy there, Blake," he said, and he lowered the gun slowly.

"Throw it down," Brandon barked. Then again, "Throw it down."

Fuller grinned, the gun still held low, the other hand on the suitcase handle.

"Brandon, dude. Just chill. We gotta talk. You know, you and me, we're a lot alike. Your mother went down with the ship, dude, left you standing on the fucking dock. My old man, he hated my guts. Ma, she could take or leave me. Doesn't it suck? I mean, I get this judge who screws me over. You got these fucking criminals coming, taking advantage of you. Isn't it a fucking mess? I mean—"

"Throw it," Brandon shouted.

Fuller smiled. Shook his head.

"Can't do it, Blake," he said.

He let the gun barrel rest on the top of the suitcase, muzzle down. It touched the fabric, scraped over the handle, stopped on top of a round lump.

The lump moved.

Mia.

Brandon fired. Once, twice, three times. A second, maybe two. Fuller let go of the suitcase and it fell with the gun as he staggered backward, cried out as he put a hand on the wall and slid slowly to the floor.

Seated on the carpet, bandaged leg in front of him, a hand on his side, he looked down. Blood ran between his fingers. His face contorted and he cried out. A child's low wail.

CHAPTER 65

Dozens of cops. Uniformed outside the hotel, detectives in the corridor, gawkers standing around the cars outside by the cruisers, the fire trucks, and ambulances.

It was a white-washed room with a Formica-topped table and plastic chairs. Brandon sat on one side of the table, four detectives sat on the other. O'Farrell was there, along with two detectives from Falmouth P.D., and Jackie, too, but she left.

Brandon told them everything that had happened. The detectives listened, the digital recorder measuring the story in minutes and seconds. After Brandon had finished, the detectives looked at each other. Jackie came back in.

"So we need that truck," O'Farrell said.

"Just stopped it," Jackie said. "New Hampshire tollbooth."

"Full of women?" he said.

She nodded.

"Right now they're both saying they're victims of a home invasion," O'Farrell said. "Holding them on a firearms charge, sawed-off shotgun. I guess we got more to talk about."

"She'll turn on him if she has to," Brandon said.

"She's been on the phone with some New York City lawyer. Speaking Russian or some goddamn thing."

"And Lucky?" Brandon said.

"Maine Med. Surgery. Came around long enough to ask for his New York lawyer, too."

A pause, and then Brandon said, "So did he make the hospital?"

"Joel Fuller? D.O.A.," O'Farrell said, like it was a good thing, the cop killer getting what he deserved. "But Kelvin is spilling his guts."

Brandon closed his eyes, took a long, deep breath. "I wouldn't have shot him if there'd been a choice," he said.

"I know," O'Farrell said.

"There just wasn't any."

"Right."

"He would have killed her. He was going to."

"Very likely," the detective said. "Did Grif, no big deal to kill her, too."

"Still," Brandon said.

Another deep breath. Felt tears welling up and fought them back. Not now, not ever. The detectives watched him closely.

"There's counseling," O'Farrell said. "Helps sort things out. We can put you in touch with somebody."

"Maybe for Mia," Brandon said. "I'm okay."

"Sure you are," the detective said. "And when you're a little more okay, we'll talk more."

"I'm fine now. Talk about what?"

O'Farrell hesitated. "About how you screwed up. Should've called us right in."

"Fuller said they'd kill her if there was even a hint of cops. That's what he said. Leave her to die of thirst."

A long pause. Jackie cleared her throat.

"You got lucky, Blake," O'Farrell said.

Brandon didn't answer.

"Yeah, well. We all need at little luck on this job. Speaking of which, when you're ready, when this is all cleared up, we'll talk about the academy."

"Back on the horse?"

"If you want it."

"Sign me up," Brandon said.

The cops looked at him.

"You doing this for Griffin?" O'Farrell said.

"What if I am?" Brandon said.

O'Farrell paused, looked at him.

"For a kid," he said, "you're one tough son of a bitch."

CHAPTER 66

It was a good sailing day, clouds clearing early, becoming sunny with a northwest wind, fifteen knots. Boats were streaming out of the harbor at eleven, sails going up, heeling with the first pull of the breeze.

Nessa was on the porch, the Portland newspaper on the table in front of her, a bottle of Chardonnay, too. A single glass.

Brandon sat in the chair, looked out at the bay, but for once didn't see the sails, the lobster boats, the black-hulled draggers chugging in from the fishing grounds.

They both watched, were silent. A gull landed on the lawn, snatched something from the grass, and flew off.

Finally it was Brandon who spoke.

"You had no way of knowing," he said.

Nessa didn't answer, just shook her head.

"You wouldn't have hurt her, Nessa. Not for anything," he said. "You were her best friend."

Nessa sighed.

"I shouldn't have been her best friend," she said, her voice quivery and weary. "I should have been her mother. I should have been the one to say, 'No, honey, this is a bad thing. Don't do this.' Instead I … I joined right in."

"But there was no way to know what was going to happen," Brandon said.

"There was a way to know right from wrong," Nessa said.

"Nessa," Brandon said. "What would you have done if you had known someone was going to hurt Nikki?"

"I'd stop them."

"And they didn't see it coming. Nobody did."

Another shake of the head. Nessa reached for the bottle, uncorked it, and began to refill the glass.

"I couldn't bear to tell you," she said. "All these years."

"It was crushing you, wasn't it."

"Yes."

"Well, now you're even," Brandon said. "We're even. Both of us. We'll shake it off together."

He moved over and took a seat beside her on the couch and put his arm around her shoulder. Nessa, tears running down her pale cheeks, put the glass down and took his hand.

CHAPTER 67

The counselor was a woman in her fifties, with short salt-and-pepper hair, a soothing voice, and an attentive, unblinking stare. Mia went once and Brandon went once and then they asked if they could go together.

"Of course you can," the counselor said. "This is all about you."

Mia talked about how she kept having dreams, and no matter how they began, they ended with her in a box, or a tunnel, or a big plastic bag. She couldn't sleep with blankets over her, couldn't wear her favorite sweatpants to bed because they made her feel like her legs were trapped. She couldn't be in the dark.

That led to talk about Mia's father, her feeling that she couldn't shake loose from his expectations.

"It's your life," the counselor said. "You have the control. Not your father. Just you. And when you were locked in that case, it was the ultimate loss of control. You've got to take it back."

Brandon had dreams, too. Fuller came to him every night, shot full of holes, blood streaming out. But Fuller was smiling, standing by Brandon, and saying over and over, "Dude, we were just bullshitting. You didn't have to kill me."

Brandon said, "I didn't know there were bullets in the gun."

Fuller took Brandon's hand, like Jesus with Doubting Thomas, stuck Brandon's finger in the holes.

The counselor nodded, like it all made sense. "A tremendously traumatic thing, to take a life," she said, "no matter what the circumstances. And you have unresolved issues about loss, about separation, all stemming from your mother, early responsibility for your own caregiver. Internalized grief, a very strong propensity to shoulder everything alone."

"But I'm not alone now," Brandon said. Mia, sitting beside him on the couch, took his hand.

"No," she said. "We've got each other."

Brandon and Mia were stretched out atop the covers on the cabin berth, rain drumming on the deck above their heads, a single light left on. They were quiet, staring at their intertwined hands held above them.

"You okay?" Mia said.

"Yes," Brandon said. You?"

"Yes," she said.

A wake rocked the boat and then it was still, or at least as still as a boat ever can be.

Mia smiled, turned to him. "You know, I don't want you to think I'm one of those people, you save their life and then you can't get rid of them."

Brandon kissed her hand.

"Oh, baby," he said. "Don't you know it's the other way around?"

THE END